He picked up the telephone.

"Hello?"

"George? George? Is that you?"

George took a deep breath. "Yes, Dad. What the hell are you ringing . . ."

"Don't give me any bloody excuses." Tony Kyriakides' normally faint Greek accent was pronounced by his anger. "You've got to get out of that place right now, do you hear? Right now!"

"Don't be ridiculous. I'm in the middle of dinner, and I've been invited to stay for the weekend. I'll be back on Sunday evening."

"George!" his father screamed. "You don't know what you're doing. That woman is a dangerous scheming bitch. I've been fighting her for three years. You don't want to believe a thing she says. You get out of there now, or I tell you, you lose everything, every bloody thing I ever gave you. And your mother is very upset. She's right here beside me, crying her eyes out."

"I can't, Dad, d'you hear? I'm in the middle of dinner, and I came in my chopper. I've drunk too much to bring it back."

"I don't care about your bloody dinner. And if you're too pissed to drive *my* helicopter, that's your bloody problem." Tony Kyriakides' tone became conciliatory for a moment. "It's not just for me, it's for your mother. I know you don't want to hurt her, even if you don't care about me." But the anger crept back. "You just get out of that place now, or, by God, you'll regret it."

Bearing Gifts

Peter Burden

CORONET BOOKS
Hodder and Stoughton

First published in Great Britain in 1994
by Hodder and Stoughton Limited,
a division of Hodder Headline PLC

Coronet edition 1994

British Library Cataloguing in Publication Data

Burden, Peter
Bearing Gifts.
I. Title
823.914 [F]

ISBN 0 340 60956 7

Typeset by Hewer Text Composition Services, Edinburgh
Printed and bound in Great Britain by
Cox and Wyman Ltd, Reading

Hodder and Stoughton Ltd,
A division of Hodder Headline PLC
338 Euston Road
London NW1 3BH

To all my friends from Cyprus

Contents

Author's Note

Bearing Gifts is a novel. All the characters are invented and none is intended to portray a real person. Certain names of well-known places or individuals or institutions are used to give a realistic background to the story but none of the firms or hotels or restaurants described corresponds to an existing real-life organisation.

PROLOGUE

Hampshire, May 1991

George Kyriakides mouthed a mild curse and banked steeply. He shouldn't have come in the helicopter. He could tell from the layout of the house and grounds below him that the owner would think it offensively flashy.

He considered flying back to Andover and renting a car. But the people in the house would already have heard the Jet Ranger, and Anna would have told them to expect him in the chopper. He would look a real fool if he then turned up in an Avis Ford.

He circled the house a couple of times, looking for a suitable place to land. It was a grand, patrician sort of a place; early Georgian in weathered, russet brick; white-framed windows of strict, elegant proportions. Down the full length of the south-west front was a broad stone-flagged terrace on which stood a cluster of solid, old-fashioned timber benches around a well-covered lily pond.

The gardens of the house stretched a hundred yards down to the chalk-bedded river, where the trout still ran. Behind the house was a courtyard surrounded by lower, redundant domestic buildings – dairy, laundry, coach-house, grooms' rooms. George wondered if they had ever been fully de-commissioned. The only hint of twentieth-century occupation of the house was the collection of cars scattered in the courtyard; subdued, utilitarian vehicles for the most part, except, of course, for Anna's deep maroon Aston Martin – a convertible.

How on earth, he wondered, did the pushy, entrepreneurial Anna feel comfortable in these understated surroundings?

For there was nothing understated about her. Anna believed in maintaining as high a profile as any gossip column, business page or television appearance could provide. She didn't actually telephone the papers when she started a new affair, but nor did she shrink from giving them the details when they asked. She was always popular and friendly with journalists, who usually treated her well.

George smiled. She was so voluptuously forthright. It was this, as much as her manifest physical attractions, that fascinated him. He had no need to be concerned about the Montagu-Hamiltons' reaction to him with Anna as his sponsor. But he was still unsure for which of several possible reasons she had asked him to come.

It was a Friday evening, a beautiful May evening, when the reasons for the original siting of Bishops Lowton House were most obvious. From the main rooms Anna could see the grounds which swept down to the river, lit obliquely by a lowering sun which gave a softness of colour, an impressionist's texture to the landscape. The blackbirds and thrushes and a distant cuckoo provided the soundtrack to this perfect scene, until the distant shuddering drone of a helicopter intruded, approached, and drowned the birdsong.

Anna Montagu-Hamilton glanced with a smile at her stepfather. "That'll be my Greek."

"Can you think how intolerable life would be if everyone were to drive around in those things," Sir James Montagu-Hamilton observed. He was a long-legged man, of the type that Osbert Lancaster used to draw. Forty years in the diplomatic corps had left him with an impressive, restrained dignity which contrasted sharply with the dynamic enthusiasm of his wife's daughter.

"You'll have to make some allowances for George. He uses a chopper because he's impatient, not because he's flashy."

"Those two failings frequently occur together."

"Don't prejudge him, Father. I think you'll like him. He's perfectly presentable and intelligent, and quite English-looking; at least his clothes are."

"I'm not sure about Greeks in tweed jackets, though of course I'll keep an open mind. But I'd like to know if you've asked him here for the weekend simply as a ploy in your skirmish with his father."

"Skirmish? 'Out and Out War', this morning's papers called it. And they think I'm winning. But I've asked George because I like him. He's clever, witty and seems to know anyone in Europe worth knowing."

"And good-looking too, I dare say, knowing your vulgar tastes," said Sir James.

"Horribly," Anna agreed. "And he can get wonderfully shirty when he's annoyed – wearing Savile Row suits hasn't subdued his Cypriot instincts."

"If you're attempting to recruit him to your camp, you're not being very subtle about it."

"I'm not. His attitude towards his father is too complicated for that. Tony Kyriakides treats him like a moron and a playboy, and he's neither. But I do see a role for him as a semi-willing fifth columnist." Anna's white teeth flashed with a confident smile. "And I thought it would be useful if he and I were friends when we've got control."

"We?" Her stepfather raised an eyebrow.

"Maggie's 'we'," Anna grinned.

She and Sir James were sitting in his high-ceilinged library with the remains of an old-fashioned tea on a table between them. A pair of French windows, wide open to admit the breeze and sounds of the spring evening, gave on to the terrace. As the noise of the helicopter came overhead, they stood and walked outside to see the aircraft disappear towards the back of the house before coming round again and hovering down between two oak trees. It landed fifty yards from where they stood.

Neither of them moved forward to greet Anna's guest. They watched as the engine was turned off, and the rotors slowly spun to a rest. The door nearest to them was opened. A tall man clad in a buff flying-suit jumped down clutching a leather Gladstone bag and strode across the lawn towards them. He did not speak until he was fifteen feet away when he produced a dazzling smile.

"Good evening. I see I've come to the right place."

His English was standard public-school with a hint of Mediterranean olive oil in the throat. His dark eyes shone with good humour and his untidy, black wavy hair gave him a disarming jauntiness.

"Hello, George. We've heard you coming for about half an hour," Anna said.

He was standing in front of them now. "But I only left Battersea twenty minutes ago."

"This is my stepfather, Sir James Montagu-Hamilton; George Kyriakides."

The two men shook hands briefly. To their slight surprise, they were inclined to like each other.

"Good evening. I'm delighted you could come," Sir James said in his diplomat's voice. "I expect you'd like to change out of your boiler suit. Anna will show you your room. When you come down, we'll be having drinks out here."

George nodded. "Thank you. I'll look forward to that," he said easily and followed Anna through the French windows.

They walked through the library into a tall, gloomy central hall. George sniffed the cool air; it had the curious aroma of another age, as if the air was as old as the house itself.

Humourless, kilted ancestors gazed out from heavy gilt

4

frames twelve feet above, between vast, stormy landscapes of heathered hills and the stuffed heads of stags which had once roamed them. Anna gave George a smile and a gesture which dissociated her from all this sombre baronial Scottishness.

"Aren't you proud of them?" he asked as he followed her up a broad flight of polished oak stairs. "Don't you go in for good old British ancestor worship?"

"They aren't my ancestors to worship," she replied with a shrug.

"But I always thought you were Scottish." George had attributed her dark colouring to a Celtic ancestry.

"My mother is, but her forebears were humble Lowland engineers who didn't have their portraits painted until they'd made their packet out in Sicily. They're still hanging on the walls out there. It fascinates the guests."

George remembered those portraits. He had visited the Villa Ypolitta several years before, long before Anna had announced she was going to bid against his father for Scottish and Lakeland Hotels.

He had not been long then on the board of his father's company, Theodore Hotels. His brief – issued reluctantly by his father – had been to study every aspect of Anna's business, which owned hotels in five European countries, two in the Indian Ocean and one in the Caribbean.

"Yes," George said, "I've seen them. I imagine they do."

He saw her falter a fraction of a second between steps.

"No one ever told me you'd been there," she said lightly. "You must have booked in under a false name."

They reached the top of the stairs and he was ready when she turned and gave him a sharp, speculative look.

He smiled blandly at her. "Yes, I did."

He saw a quick flash in her eyes, but she relaxed as she said, "What did you think of it?"

5

"Sensational," George said, "I wish we had an hotel like that in our group."

She laughed, "I bet you do." She strode on down a broad corridor and stopped in front of a tall, panelled mahogany door. She flung it open. "Here's your room, with all the inconveniences of an English country house. There's a bathroom next door, and no room service."

George walked in. The room had a high ceiling and a perfect view of the grounds and river. It had been tastefully decorated but not for twenty or thirty years. The furniture had probably been there for two hundred. He smiled his appreciation of the rightness of it.

He tossed his bag on to a high, broad single bed and watched it bounce.

He turned to Anna. "It's odd, isn't it? However hard we try, or however much we spend, we can never quite reproduce this in any of our hotels."

Anna shrugged. "Most of the punters who like this kind of thing haven't got the money anyway."

"You're right. But look, we mustn't lower the tone with commercial talk."

"Suits me. I didn't ask you here to talk business." Anna was standing with one hand on the doorpost and the other on her hip. She was just a few inches shorter than George, though her legs – brown, smooth and bare beneath a short, flame-red dress – were at least as long as his. Her short-cropped, jet-black hair made a soft, spiky frame for her tanned face. Her well-shaped jaw was balanced by a mouth that avoided being too big by a millimetre. Her high-set cheeks dimpled very slightly when she smiled, as she did now. The message in her eyes was clear. "It's a pity you've got to change out of those oily overalls," she said thoughtfully. "You're not by any chance wearing a sweat-stained singlet underneath?"

George started slowly to unzip his flying suit. Anna gave

him a quick grin, spun round and left the room, thumping the door behind her.

George carried on unzipping his overalls and allowed the banausic garment to crumple slowly round his feet. He kicked off his docksiders and, clad only in a T-shirt, shorts and socks, surveyed himself in a long glass. He was in good enough shape to tolerate a lot of teasing from Ms Montagu-Hamilton. She hadn't disguised her interest on the three previous occasions they had met.

Of course, she had forgotten, until he reminded her, that they had met at Oxford when he was a freshman and she was in the full glory of her final triumphant year.

The hottest female property at the university, with eyes for no one but the celebrities she managed to entice down to enliven the Oxford Union debates, he had philosophically written her off then as being impossibly out of reach. After she had gone down he heard and read about her with increasing frequency. She did not follow the expected trail to the bar and Tory politics. Instead she surprised everyone by diving head-first into commerce.

The Villa Ypolitta, her first venture, quickly captured the public imagination. Anna had transformed her mother's old family mansion on the East Sicilian coast into a home from home for some of the world's richest fun-seekers.

She had, it was reported, modelled her approach on that of Anouska Hempel at Blake's in London. She succeeded spectacularly and compounded her success by repeating the formula, in a less exclusive way, first in mainland Italy, then in France and Greece.

As her fame grew, so did her reputation for efficiency and attention to detail. She had gone on to create tropical fun-paradises in Mauritius and the Virgin Islands. She had also grown more beautiful.

Yet, even now, the English didn't really like such outspoken ambition and independence in a woman and, despite Anna's cooperativeness, the gossip columns tended to pander to their readers' tastes. As her empire and influence had burgeoned she felt, at the age of thirty-eight, as desirable as she ever had, and her soft, tanned skin did not display its ability to withstand most of the innuendo or insult that was sporadically hurled at her.

George understood the English well enough to appreciate the paradox of Anna's background and her blatant enjoyment of commercial success. It puzzled and intrigued him. And now Theodore Hotels, the £70 million public company controlled by his father, was locked in a bare-knuckle fight for survival with Anna's Mediterranean and Tropical Hotels.

Although Anna's completely unexpected invitation for the weekend had arrived smelling of Rochas and skulduggery, George accepted it without hesitation. But he did not tell his father. Tony Kyriakides would have become apoplectic if he knew that his son, his boy lamb, was walking right into the lion's den. Though he would admit it to no one, Tony Kyriakides was scared of Anna in a way he would never have been of a male opponent.

George, though, understood Anna; he was sure, from a look of knowing complicity he had seen in her eyes at their previous meetings. And that gave him an edge which he couldn't ignore. Besides that, she was the most exciting woman he had ever met. One way or another, when this weekend was over he would not be leaving without a prize.

Anna went back to the library, where she found her mother helping the housekeeper, Dolly, gather up the tea things.

Susan Montagu-Hamilton was sixty-five, small and soft. But she had had few physical pressures to try her. Her first, hearty oaf of a husband had drowned when his yacht sank off the Needles, thirty-five years before.

Sir James Montagu-Hamilton had snapped her up as an ideal wife for an ambassador. And he had been right. She had never hurt or insulted anyone in her life, and the embassy staffs adored her. James' intellectual and sexual demands on her were not great, and now, in his retirement, she was generally content to run their quiet household. The only element in her life which seriously disturbed her was Anna.

Sir James had accepted his role as Anna's father without reservation, though his idea of fatherhood had not gone much beyond choosing schools, paying the fees, and giving her his name. He and Anna were as different in temperament as it was possible to be, so they understood one another, and viewed each other with benign tolerance.

But to Susan, Anna was an enigma.

How Anna had achieved the academic results she had, while apparently leading a life of debauchery that would have finished off most people, Susan could not understand. How she now ran a chain of hotels, scattered all over the world, while she seemed to be at parties or concerts or clubs every night of the week, was completely beyond her. And why did she show no signs of wanting marriage or, even more oddly, children? Anna's blunt answer was that she was perfectly happy the way she was, yet she was fond of her mother in the way some people are fond of an old childhood teddy-bear, though she often wondered if the man with the affable, vacuous smile in the photographs of her mother's first wedding could really have been her father. If he was, she felt, the rules of genetic inheritance must have been circumvented. That was a more likely explanation than that of her mother having had an affair. But she had never wanted to upset her mother by asking her.

When Anna came to stay at Bishops Lowton, three or four times a year, she usually made an effort to dispel

Susan's worries about her. But as she now walked into the library Susan gushed in a way which was usually a prelude to a gentle prod towards marriage. "Oh, hello, darling, I hope you don't mind, but I've asked Harry Brighton for dinner."

"Not tonight?" Anna asked, exasperated.

"Well, yes. I thought you might like to see him again. After all, you've known each other since you were both three, and it's so nice these days to be able to find a genuine bachelor who isn't queer."

"He may not be a poof, but he's not much else either, and it'll mess up the numbers."

"No, it won't. The Fakenhams are bringing Charles's sister."

Anna's closed lips widened in annoyance, but she had asked the Fakenhams herself. Charles was a banker and her principal adviser in the Theodore take-over bid. His wife was beginning to suspect – quite wrongly, as it happened – that something was going on between him and Anna. Anna was proposing to allay her suspicions by making use of the far more obviously desirable and much younger George.

"Hm." Anna was resigned. "At least Janey's thick enough for Harry. If she hasn't already had a crack at him she'll certainly try this evening."

"I thought she might be suitable for this Greek business-man you've asked down. By the way, I presume that's his helicopter on the lawn?"

"Yes, it is, but I don't think Janey'll do much for him. And I haven't asked him here to talk business."

"Haven't you, dear? But James said you had."

"You know he doesn't like to worry you, Mum."

Susan looked distraught. "But what's he like? I always used to find the Greek diplomats too smooth for words. One could never take them seriously, however charming they were."

Anna laughed. "For God's sake, Mum, I'm not marrying him or anything; his father controls Theodore Hotels."

Susan was aghast. "But surely that's the firm you're buying out, isn't it? Doesn't that make it all rather tricky?"

"Don't you remember, when I was little, the obstacle race was always my favourite?"

"Well, you'll never have a go at the mothers' race if you don't do something about it soon." Susan beamed at the wittiness of her retort.

Anna indulged her with a smile, glad to be able to end the conversation lightly.

"Have the Franconis confirmed that they're coming?" Giulio Franconi was Anna's pet architect.

"Yes," Susan said with a smile. "He said nothing could keep him away from seeing us again."

"Great! We should have a good party, in spite of Harry Brighton."

"Do try and be nice to him, Anna. After all, he's the only guest I've invited."

Anna put her hand on her mother's shoulder and leaned down to give her a quick kiss on the cheek.

"Of course I will. He's booked twenty people into the Coconut Cove for a week, and I'm always nice to the punters." She grinned and pretended not to notice Susan's grimace before she turned and swung out of the room.

George Kyriakides had bathed and dressed for dinner. Now he was sitting with his legs stretched out on a faded eiderdown and his back propped against the high mahogany headboard of his bed. He was reading from one of the bound volumes of 1890s *Punch* which were all that the bookshelves in the room had to offer.

Although Sir James Montagu-Hamilton seemed affable enough, George decided that he would rather deal with him diluted by a few more guests. Now, through the open window, he could hear people approaching the front door, engaged in an indistinct, hissing argument. He gave them time to be ushered through to the terrace before he slid off the bed to make his way down the great oak staircase.

Charles Fakenham was in his mid-fifties, smooth-skinned with a head of perfectly groomed, glossy black hair. On the face of it, he was the archetypal old-fashioned aristocratic English banker. The reason he had survived in the harsh banking world of the late 1980s was that, beneath his patrician charm and traditionally-cut suits, he was a man of single-minded, steely self-interest. He and Anna understood each other well, though even she was sometimes alarmed by his ruthlessness when it came to recovering an unsatisfactory investment.

Not that Anna had anything to fear on that front. The growth of her business was not due to highly geared borrowings and overpriced acquisitions. Charles Fakenham's b..nk, Berkley Berrington, had recently handled the public flotation of Mediterranean and Tropical. They were now preparing to launch a rights issue which was confidently expected to be fully subscribed, such was the reputation – and underlying profitability – of Anna's company, even at a time when most of the world travel market was weak from a dearth of clients and a glut of debt.

Now Fakenham, in correctly understated evening dress, shepherded his wife and sister before him on to Sir James Montagu-Hamilton's terrace. The slight tetchiness on his face disappeared without trace as soon as he saw his host.

The old diplomat was not fooled by the banker's charm, and pointedly turned his attention to Monica, Fakenham's wife, and Janey, his sister – two women who, in his view, deserved better.

"Jane, how lovely to see you." Sir James bent gracefully to kiss her chubby cheek. "How are all your mares? Pleasingly fecund, I hope?"

"Not exactly," Jane answered heartily. "I sent Stella Maris to be covered by Pit Pan. She's been rogered rotten for the last three months since she foaled, and all she's done is lose weight." She glanced down at her own rotund body. "Maybe I should send myself to him?"

"That would be a little drastic. Anyway, there's nothing wrong with your figure. It's all these matchstick women who are nature's freaks."

James turned to Monica who was still standing beside him. Monica had been a star model of the early sixties and the features which had made her then had not suffered from the trials and stresses of motherhood, or anything else. As unfaded as her looks was the acerbic manner which had so riled the photographers of the time. James always enjoyed seeing her and was keen to bring her into the conversation.

A Portuguese servant intruded for a moment to hand round large, lead-glass goblets of Pimms. James glanced across the terrace at his wife and Charles Fakenham.

The banker was looking around with barely disguised boredom, but his eyes lit up when he saw Anna step through the French windows from the library.

Anna gave Charles Fakenham a quick smile, but came over to join James' group, taking a glass of Pimms on the way. She had just reached them, when her greetings were drowned by a loud crash at the centre of the small circle. Simultaneously, her ankles were splashed with sticky drops from the glass which Monica had dropped.

Anna caught the fleeting remains of a look of horror on Monica's face. Monica had been staring over Anna's shoulder at the French windows, from which George Kyriakides had just emerged.

George saw the look too, but tried to hide his puzzlement. Despite his vanity, he thought it unlikely that the woman had dropped her glass because she found him too devastatingly attractive. She had obviously recognised him, but he had no idea who she was.

Monica used the confusion of the breakage to hide her shock. She gushed apologies at everyone and helped the servant by bending down to pick up one or two shards of glass. James, Jane and Anna stood back to make room, and Monica straightened herself, and walked quickly into the house, muttering that she must clean herself up.

"I don't know what she's complaining about," Anna said. "She didn't get a drop of this sticky muck on her. Why on earth are we drinking it, by the way, Father?"

"Your mother found an ancient bottle or two in the cellars and thought it might never be used otherwise."

"Perhaps she should have left it there. I suppose I'd better go and wash it off my feet before it rots them," Anna laughed, and she walked back into the house, lifting an eyebrow at George on the way.

She was crossing the hall, on her way to a back cloakroom, when she heard a female voice in her father's study. Curious, she stopped to listen for a moment. She heard Monica's voice, with a note of panic, saying, "I just thought you'd want to know, that's all. And . . . Oh, shit!" Evidently the other end of the conversation had disconnected.

Anna took a few silent paces further down the corridor, and turned to watch Monica scurry out of the room to rejoin the party.

On her way back from rinsing the drink from her ankles, Anna found three more guests being shown in by Dolly, her mother's mouse-like housekeeper. She flashed her eyes and a broad smile at Harry, seventh Earl of Brighton, and watched him redden with pleasure. Giulio Franconi took her hand and kissed her lightly on the cheek.

"Good evening, most beautiful client."

"*Buona sera*, most expensive architect," Anna returned with a laugh. She turned to Claudia, Giulio's wife. "Hello,

Claudia. I'm very glad you could both come. Have you met Harry Brighton?"

She introduced them formally to one another, and they all walked through the library to join the others outside.

Susan Montagu-Hamilton's ancient rum-based Pimms was working well as a tension breaker. The oddly mixed party was beginning to relax as defences were lowered. James, out of long professional habit, identified and introduced common ground between the most unlikely pairs. He didn't particularly enjoy parties of this sort, ill-informed and trivial as the conversation tended to be, but Susan liked to arrange these things for Anna's visits, and he was content to cooperate for her sake.

Half an hour later George was talking to Harry Brighton while Janey Fakenham's round rufescent face gleamed up at him. When he caught Anna's eye, he excused himself and joined her.

"You said this wasn't a business gathering, but so far I've met your banker and your architect. When I told them who I was I could see a nasty, knowing glint in their eyes. So what are you up to?"

"Believe me, it's entirely social. They're friends as well as people I do business with," Anna shrugged.

"Charles Fakenham? A friend? It seems to me that Charles Fakenham's only friend is Charles Fakenham, though he obviously fancies you like hell. But I can't understand his wife. She can hardly look me in the eye."

"Yes, I noticed that. Have you never met her before?" Anna seemed surprised.

"Not as far as I can remember."

"It's that oily Greek charm of yours, I dare say. Anyway, relax, I'm not about to spring any traps on you. I just thought it would be nice if we got to know each other better."

"You mean, 'Know thine enemy'?"

Anna reached up and gently tucked a black curl behind George's ear.

"We're not enemies, George. You know that."

Sir James and Lady Montagu-Hamilton sat at each end of the large mahogany table in their Georgian dining-room. Evening light still showed through the tall windows that gave on to the park.

The eight guests were seated appropriately down each side. Anna was between Harry Brighton and Giulio Franconi, and George was opposite Franconi, next to Janey Fakenham.

George and Anna occupied themselves with their neighbours, but every few minutes their eyes met in tacit acknowledgement of a bond growing between them. Anna felt a hot tingle of anticipation and radiated her sexuality to the men beside her. Harry thought he was making progress, but Franconi shook his head at her, and said quietly, "Be careful, Anna. George is not a fool."

They had finished their soup and their grilled trout and were about to be served with lamb *en croute*, when the housekeeper scuttled in apologetically and whispered to Susan.

Irritated, Susan glanced down the table at George.

"George, there's someone on the telephone for you. Apparently it's very urgent, so I expect you'd like to take it. Dolly can show you to James' study."

Susan glanced at Anna as if to say, "What can you expect from a Greek?"

George didn't respond at once.

There was only one person who would phone him now, in these circumstances, and he really didn't want to take the call. But past experience told him that if he didn't he would have to face a tedious barrage of abuse when he got home.

Quite drunk now, after what must have been several

16

glasses of Pimms and too much Chablis, he pushed his chair back and lurched to his feet.

"I'm terribly sorry," he remembered to say to his hostess. "I'm sure it won't take long."

He was damn sure it wouldn't take long, he thought as he followed the housekeeper to the study. How the hell did his father know where he was? Perhaps the old bastard had phoned the heliport?

He picked up the telephone.

"Hello?"

"George? George? Is that you?"

George took a deep breath. "Yes, Dad. What the hell are you ringing . . ."

"Don't give me any bloody excuses." Tony Kyriakides' normally faint Greek accent was pronounced by his anger. "You've got to get out of that place right now, do you hear? Right now!"

"Don't be ridiculous. I'm in the middle of dinner, and I've been invited to stay for the weekend. I'll be back on Sunday evening."

"George!" his father screamed. "You don't know what you're doing. That woman is a dangerous scheming bitch. I've been fighting her for three years. You don't want to believe a thing she says. You get out of there now, or I tell you, you lose everything, every bloody thing I ever gave you. And your mother is very upset. She's right here beside me, crying her eyes out."

"I can't, Dad, d'you hear? I'm in the middle of dinner, and I came in my chopper. I've drunk too much to bring it back."

"I don't care about your bloody dinner. And if you're too pissed to drive *my* helicopter, that's your bloody problem." Tony Kyriakides' tone became conciliatory for a moment. "It's not just for me, it's for your mother. I know you don't want to hurt her, even if you don't care about me." But the anger crept back. "You just get out of that place now, or, by God, you'll regret it."

The line went dead. George stared at the telephone in frustrated fury. He would have to go. Whatever else, his father would not have invoked his mother's name lightly. God help him if he had, George swore. But he would finish his dinner first, as if nothing had happened, and excuse himself afterwards. He would be back in London by midnight, just when he should have been making his first bodily contact with the lovely Anna.

George apologised again to Susan Montagu-Hamilton, slipped back into his place, and rejoined the conversation. As dinner went on he was tempted once or twice to change his mind, but convinced himself that, by going, he would be doing nothing worse than delaying the inevitable between himself and Anna. And maybe it would be a good thing to establish control of this relationship. So far, his contribution had been very passive.

Charles Fakenham was already looking at his watch as they all walked through to drink brandy and coffee in the drawing-room, but he saw with approval that his sister Jane had at last attached herself to the jovially drunk Harry Brighton. He also noted that Anna and George had slipped into the library. He trusted Anna to know what she was doing, but George Kyriakides was just a little too good-looking for his peace of mind.

"What do you mean, you're leaving?" Anna's eyes flashed with anger, and a disappointment that she could not hide.

George took strength from this.

"I can't tell you why," George said calmly. "But you've got to realise it's important. Of course, I'd much rather stay here and make love to you."

"But you're too pissed to fly!"

"No I'm not. I can do it in my sleep."

Anna tried another approach. She put her arm around the back of George's neck and pulled his face towards hers. He could not resist. Their lips met for the first time in soft deliquescence and a twining of tongues.

She drew his body to hers and felt a hardness beneath his loose-fitting trousers.

"Soon," she whispered, "You won't know whether you're coming or going."

He put a hand on her buttocks, which tightened under his touch, and lifted her mound towards his groin.

Then, abruptly, he released her and looked at her, holding her at arm's length.

"Oh, I know what I'm missing," he said, "But it won't be for long. I'm going now, but when I come, you'll know about it."

He laughed and let her go, and walked from the room. Over his shoulder he said, "Please give your mother my apologies."

George knew he would not resist another attempt by Anna to make him stay. Earlier, with the excuse of going to the lavatory, he had been to his room, packed his bag and brought it down before the end of dinner. He grabbed the bag from where he had left it beside the front door, and let himself out. He walked round to the side of the house and across the velvet turf to the helicopter.

Anna, frustrated and unusually hurt by his rejection, lingered in the library for a while to compose herself, before going back to the drawing-room and owning up to George's departure.

The starter whined and kicked the rotors into life. Quickly, George tried to check all his instruments, but he wanted to be away before Anna or anyone else came out of the house to stop him. Light suddenly spilled from the library window as someone drew back the curtains to open the French windows. He increased the revs, and felt his machine lurch unevenly from the ground. He went straight up for two hundred feet, because he could not remember where or how tall the trees were.

He hovered there for a moment to get his bearings, and looked down at the dark bulk of the house in the new moonlight, and cursed his father again.

As he checked his heading and swung the helicopter towards the east, already the whole episode with Anna was seeming like a dream, and the swelling in his groin had diminished.

He soon picked out the lights of Andover, then Basingstoke. From there the M3 would act as an easy guide. He settled down at a steady 250 mph and an altitude of 500 feet.

Now he was airborne, flying his machine almost instinctively, his thoughts returned briefly to Anna and he smiled to himself. It can't have been all that often that she didn't get her own way in her love affairs or her business.

But when he thought of his father, waiting for him in London, his smile died.

This was the last time he would let this happen; the last time he would let his father assume he would come running as soon as he was called.

It was Tony Kyriakides, not he, who had brought their famous, once spectacularly successful company, to the brink of ruin, and he had done it out of sheer vanity. It was he, George, who was taking the initiatives now, and his father hated that.

"I've had enough of this shit!" George muttered to himself. "Anna and Fakenham have got us by the balls and he just won't admit it! I'll split with the old bastard now, before it's too late."

But he knew he wouldn't.

He knew that through his own idle acceptance of the

indulgence his father had lavished on him he had forfeited the right to go his own way.

He knew, too, that when it came to a confrontation he didn't have the courage or the strength to fight a man like Tony Kyriakides.

PART ONE

Antonios Kyriakides

1

Cyprus 1938

On the western slopes of the Troodos mountains the spring night was clear and cold at two thousand feet. A small boy crouched behind a chunk of white rock. On the far side of the rock a narrow track, barely wide enough for a donkey cart, zigzagged down the valley-side.

When the boy had set out from his home that day the sun had been strong, but he had wandered across the flowering hillsides, absorbed in dreams where time was forgotten.

He shivered; he was wearing a tunic and knee-length, coarse cotton trousers; his feet were clad in crude leather sandals; and he was terrified. He backed himself in among a clump of prickling gorse as footsteps and clear, angry voices came closer down the track.

Four men passed by, a few feet away. If they had glanced back, behind the outcropping limestone where the boy crouched, they would have seen his large brown eyes peering from the wind-stirred bushes, reflected in the light of the lanterns they carried. But their minds and eyes were focused on a white stone farmhouse in the valley floor, easy to see in the high, blue moonlight.

"Theo Kyriakides will be surprised to see us," one of them muttered with a hoarse laugh, and spat.

The boy glanced down at his father's house, where feeble oil lamps cast a glimmer through one small unshuttered window. He was eight years old, small for his age, but sharp. He knew who these men were and why they spat at his father's name.

He knew also that his father despised him for being slight, and clever; sons who could read and write did not help the vines to grow, and they were bored tending the goats and olive groves. But here was a chance for him to earn his father's respect and thanks.

The footsteps and low voices passed on down the track, three hairpins away from the valley bottom. When they were out of earshot, Antonios Kyriakides took a line straight down the hill towards his home. With frantic, numbing urgency, he slid and tumbled down the hillside, catching his scanty clothing on thorns and rocks, grazing his skinny legs and hands as he gasped for breath.

He reached the track below before the men. He paused for a moment to listen. He could hear them above him, to his right, coming down the easy way. He crossed the path and carried on, half running, half sliding on his back towards the glowing square of the window below. He crossed the track again, and the ground became less steep as he ducked beneath an old olive tree and ran between the rows of low vines that dressed this side of the valley.

The vines gave way to a field where his father grew potatoes and aubergines. Antonios sprinted down a track rutted by the donkey cart which each autumn carried in the grape harvest.

He reached the long, low house, burst through a blue-painted plank door and collapsed, exhausted, on a settle beside an iron range.

"Tony, where the hell have you been?" His father glanced up angrily from where he sat at a table in the centre of the room, bent over a bowl of steaming moussaka and an earthenware mug of wine.

Tony gasped to get more air into his small lungs. "The Andreous are coming, now. They're half-way down the hill. They're coming to fight you."

"What are you talking about?" Kyriakides snarled at

the idea of anyone daring to fight him. "If the Andreous wanted to fight, they would send someone else."

Kyriakides' wife came through from the bedroom at the sound of her third and youngest son's breathless shouting. "What is it, Tony?" She sat beside him and wrapped her arms around him. She glanced fearfully at her husband. Her clever little boy seldom made mistakes.

With a sympathetic listener and his breath coming more easily, Tony said again, "The Andreous are coming. Four of them, I heard them talking as they passed. It's because you've agreed to sell the grapes to the Paphiote."

"Theo, it must be true," Tony's mother said. "They've threatened so many times; they have to do something. Now other people are talking of selling their grapes away, because you've done it. The Andreous can't let you; people have to know they are strong."

Theo Kyriakides gargled a mouthful of thick red wine in the back of his throat. "Those bastards can't do anything to me. They can try and hurt me, but it won't stop me selling what I want to who I want. Let them come, and if I have to, I'll go to the bloody British."

"The British! They won't support you over the Andreous! The Andreous have been to fancy schools; to London! They go to weddings at Government House." She wanted to go on. She was not a big woman, but she was brave. She probably didn't care any more whether Theo was beaten or killed. He had tried to crush the spirit out of her for all the twenty years of their marriage; now she had two big healthy sons to run the farm – and run it so that they need not live in a constant state of siege.

But when she heard the hammering on the door her mouth snapped shut and her throat was suddenly dry. She did not want Tony to see. She turned his head into her bosom and wrapped her shawl around him. "Oh, my God," she muttered. "They've come now because they know Stelios and Nicos aren't here. What can we do?"

Theo shot a scornful glance at her and growled at the door. "Who is it?"

They didn't answer. They let themselves in. First, three of them, small, wiry mountain men, stone-faced with the seriousness of their task. Then, last, ducking to pass under the stone lintel, smiling beneath chilly grey eyes, Panos Andreou.

Panos was the eldest son, where the investment had been made. He knew how to make good use of that investment. A perfectly cut camel-hair coat was draped over his shoulders. Gold rings glittered on the slender fingers of his left hand; in his right, he absently clicked his amber beads. He was confident and in complete control as his two younger brothers and cousin stepped aside to let him pass into the room.

"Theo, my friend," Andreou said quietly, with a warmth his eyes did not match, "I am so sorry to interrupt your dinner."

"Sit down; have some wine," Kyriakides grunted. He picked up his carafe and, without looking at her, beckoned his wife to bring more mugs.

Andreou shook his head. "We don't want your wine. We want your grapes."

Kyriakides glanced up at him, then back down at his moussaka. He concentrated on spooning a pile of oily aubergine beneath his thick spreading moustache to his mouth. He ate noisily, and slurped a gulp of wine. He waited for Andreou to continue.

Andreou shrugged. "Savva from Paphos was here, they tell me. He is a sophisticated fellow. I don't think he came just to hear your filthy jokes or discuss affairs of the world."

Kyriakides belched loudly to underline Andreou's point.

The tall young man went on, "You know my family look after the interests of all the other families in this valley. For two generations we have freely given our time to our people. All we ask in return is a little loyalty. You have hurt my father's feelings."

"Your people?!" Kyriakides shouted angrily and glared up at Panos Andreou's bland smile. "Who the hell do you think you are? You're not kings. Your grandfather was a brigand; and a murderer. Your father doesn't have feelings; he can't, he doesn't have a soul. You don't look after 'your people'; you just scare the hell out of them if they don't do what you want. Well, you don't scare me, turning up here in your city clothes with your monkey brothers. You don't want my wine; you can't have my grapes; so, you can go." He shrugged, dropped his eyes to his food and carried on eating.

Tony, in his mother's arms, had slowly turned his head and was staring at Panos Andreou. The cold eyes, the shiny black, slicked-down hair; the crisp collar and tie, the calf-length coat of soft, sand-coloured cloth, the gleaming English brown leather brogues, with barely a scuff mark from the half-mile walk down the track from the road. As far as Tony was concerned, he was from another planet.

What chance had his father against someone like this? Why should he be so mulish? Everyone else sold their harvest to the Andreous; why did his father have to be different?

He looked at his father, stubbornly munching.

Andreou took a step towards the crude pine table at which Kyriakides sat, and spoke again, still quietly. "All right, Theo, do you want to come outside where the woman and child won't see? Or shall we teach you your lesson in here? Then maybe they will learn at the same time."

For reply, Kyriakides picked up his bowl, still half full, and hurled the rest of his meal at Panos Andreou.

Andreou's suave features were abruptly disfigured with dripping oil and melted cheese which dribbled off his chin.

Small pieces of ground mutton and tomato dropped from his neatly clipped sideboards on to his shoulders.

He did not flinch; he still smiled, and delicately spat a strand of cheese from his lips. But his voice was huskier when he spoke. "Deal with him, Stavros."

His cousin, the stockiest of the other three, stepped forward, leaned across the table and grabbed Kyriakides by his grimy leather jerkin. Before Kyriakides had time to think, he had been tugged forward over the table with the help of the two younger Andreous. His head crashed on the worn stone flags of the floor beyond.

Christina screamed and clasped her son tighter, pulling his face back towards her chest.

Tony heard the thud of thick-soled boots on yielding flesh; and his father's screams of pain. It seemed to last a long time; at each cry Tony winced with anger and shame. Then he heard Panos say, "That's enough. We'll give him a chance to tell Savva he won't be getting his harvest."

Tony wriggled free of his mother's arms and turned to look at his father.

Theo Kyriakides lay face-down where he had fallen, heaving slightly, sucking in breath in big gulps. Blood trickled from a torn ear. One eye, bruised, reddened and unmoving, gazed across the floor.

Panos Andreou turned to Christina. "I'm sorry he didn't want to come outside."

Tony looked at Panos.

Panos had not joined in the punishment; he had stayed in the same spot since issuing the order. He had wiped most of the moussaka from his face. Now he stared without emotion at the beaten body on the ground in front of him. Abruptly, he spun round. His metal-capped heels clicked on the stone floor as he walked towards the door and strode out into the night. Silently his three companions picked up their lanterns and followed him.

They left the door swinging. The sounds of their passage

back up the track and their laughter floated into the quiet house. Theo Kyriakides' panting subsided; his eye was closed now. He seemed to be asleep. Tony looked down at him from his mother's lap with dismay, and disgust.

Stelios and Nicos Kyriakides arrived back towards noon the following day. Tony watched his elder brothers traversing the hillside down into the valley, driving a hundred scrawny ewes in front of them. They had been on the road for two days, but they bounded down the hill with noisy energy. They were already hard young men, nineteen and sixteen, childhood well behind them; they had little in common with their mother's late-born favourite – 'the last bunch on the vine' they called him. Tony often felt he was part of another family, but he was overjoyed to see them now.

"Mum," he called back into the house, "Nick and Stelios are back. I'm going up to meet them."

He ran up the track until he reached Nicos, the younger of the two.

Nicos greeted him with a smile and ruffled his hair. "Hello, Tony. Have you been keeping out of trouble?"

"Yes, yes. But Dad hasn't! The Andreous came last night."

Stelios had caught up. "So?" he asked. "What did they want?"

"The grape harvest, of course," Tony said, "but Dad has promised it to Savva from Paphos."

"The bloody old fool. Did the Andreous change his mind?" Stelios said lightly.

"No, no! They beat him till he couldn't move. He's alive, but he hasn't spoken since last night. Mum and I had to carry him to bed. He was so heavy!"

Nicos was more shocked than his elder brother. "My God! Poor dad. Is he going to be all right?"

"Mum says it's only bruises; I don't know."

"He's a fool," Stelios growled. "Savva's just as big a crook as the Andreous, and he doesn't live on our doorstep."

"He said he would get twice the money from Savva." Tony wondered why he was trying to justify his father's stand.

"Twice the rate for half the crop, by the time Savva's men have unloaded it. Poor Mamma. Maybe it'll teach the old clown it's time we took a few decisions."

"Stelios! How can you say that?" Nicos was always appalled by his brother's callousness. "He may be badly hurt."

"Then he won't be able to interfere, will he?"

Tony joined them driving the sheep down into the fold by the house to sort and brand them before taking them up to the mountains for the summer. He did not speak while his brothers argued. He could not decide whose side he was on.

Theo Kyriakides recovered from the beating. His wife tended him dutifully, and persuaded him to sell the next autumn's harvest to the Andreous.

But while the physical effects of Theo's beating abated, the damage to his pride did not. He seemed tacitly to agree to leave more of the decisions – and the work – to his elder sons. He filled his new leisure-time with extended, self-pitying drinking sessions. Sometimes he did this at home, when the atmosphere in the cramped house became unbearable. At other times there was a respite, particularly for Christina, when Theo set off on one of the donkeys to the village. There he would spend the day in the taverna and return home slumped on the donkey's back, relying on the beast's sense of direction and sureness of foot.

Sometimes taking his youngest son to school provided an excuse, and Tony would be left for hours at the end of the day curled up in a corner of the bar while he watched his father slop brandy down his front and listened to him rant about the Andreous to anyone within earshot.

Any sympathy Tony might have felt for his father was soon eroded. As far as he could see the Andreous had won the day easily, as they always did. He could not imagine the suave, immaculate Panos Andreou slurping drunkenly for hours on end in a smelly bar. He had only seen Panos that once, when Panos stood by and watched the beating, but since then Tony had woven a fantasy about this powerful being from another world.

It was absurd for his father to defy a man like that. Of course Theo had a few admirers in the village; old men who had longed to tell Panos Andreou, or his father or grandfather, to go to hell but had never had the courage. But the opinion of those wrinkled, whiskered old men meant nothing to Tony.

To his father's disgust the early signs of Tony's academic ability were proving accurate. His teacher, fiercely proud of his progress, did everything he could to encourage him. The boy became a voracious reader, especially about foreign people and places. His mother told him that Panos Andreou had been to London, so he read all he could find about Britain and the British, the foreigners who governed his country and who were even more powerful than the Andreous.

Whenever possible he read the newspapers that were left lying around the taverna, and learned how the British were threatening to stop Adolf Hitler trying to govern Poland. He thought: if the British run Cyprus, why shouldn't the Germans run Poland?

Sometimes the old men talked of the Great War, and the armies and navies that had briefly passed through the small ports down on the coast, and of the British soldiers garrisoned in Nicosia.

His teacher gave him books to help him learn English

and Tony began to realise that there were horizons far wider than the mountain-crests that surrounded his home; that beyond those crests was the sea, which he had never seen, and beyond the sea a vast world where his valley – the whole island of Cyprus, even – was of no account.

In 1940 the British were at war with Germany and Italy. The activity in the military camps and ports had become intense. Some of the village boys talked of brothers who had joined the newly formed Cyprus Regiment, down in Polemidia near Limassol, to fight for the British.

Reports came back to the villages that an Indian cavalry regiment, fresh from routing the Italians in Ethiopia, was patrolling the island in motorcars; and a transit base for British and Australian soldiers wounded in the North African desert had been set up. The lack of a good deep-water harbour meant that the island was not a prime target for the Germans and their allies, but that did not stop the women generating rumours of imminent invasion, and magnifying them as they passed them on.

Life changed little up in the mountain valleys. Flocks and vines still had to be tended. The market for produce was stronger and there was money to be made. Stelios and Nicos listened to the priests and bishops; they had no intention of leaving the land to fight for people who had no business being in their country anyway.

As far as the selling and distribution of their produce was concerned, the Andreous still ruled, though not quite so securely; the quartermasters who bought for their troops were not bound by old loyalties, past arrangements or fear. Then, in the spring of 1941, old Spyros Andreou, Panos' father, who was eighty, died.

Theo insisted he was going to make the twenty-mile trip to the funeral in Paphos.

"I should like to see the old bastard one more time, just to remind myself what an ugly pig he was."

"But Theo, you can't!" Christina pleaded. "They won't let you in the church."

"They can't stop me; it's my church too."

In the end Christina and her sons agreed that they would all go, to prevent any nasty scene occurring.

The grape cart was cleaned off and an extra bench was fixed to it. It was manoeuvred up the track to the rutted highway at the top by four unruly donkeys, and the family set off, all for their separate reasons, in festive mood.

Tony was ten years old, but he had never been so far from home. The four-hour journey would have seemed interminable to him but for the excitement of seeing new places, new villages, cars, buses and lorries on the dusty highway.

The Andreous' original source of strength had been their lands on the valley floor of the Ezuza river, which drained the western Troodos mountains into a wide, fertile plain. But their influence had spread far beyond their native village. Spyros Andreou had inherited his father's reputation and even more of his ruthlessness. It was he who had established their family as the leading merchants in Paphos. They had become the biggest makers of wine and brandy in the western half of the island. So it was in the grand old basilica in Ktima – upper Paphos – that the funeral was to be held.

As the Kyriakides drove into the town on their donkey cart, they were passed by large black cars which still gleamed through their coating of dust from the dirt roads. Inside Tony could see impressive, important-looking men and women. Tony glanced at his father's back, lurching on the bench in front of him. There would be no shiny black cars coming to his funeral, he thought.

Theo's earlier glee at the prospect of seeing a dead Andreou had soured. He sat beside Stelios and stared silently at the great, red-tiled dome of the ancient basilica.

They drove into the square in front of the church. It was full of cars and horse-drawn vehicles more elegant than their own. Stelios prepared to turn off into a side street, to leave the cart on the edge of town. His father grabbed his arm with a gnarled fist.

"We stop here. It's a public place. We have the right."

"But there's no room, Dad."

"Make room then, you spineless worm. You don't have to worry about what anyone says to us. I am my own man, remember?"

A long procession of people, dressed in their best, most sombre mourning clothes, were already filing under the elaborately carved stone entrance of the church. A chanted dirge from within mingled with sounds of the muted excitement of the crowds still arriving. Reluctantly Stelios drew up the cart and managed to back into a space between two cars.

Nicos and Stelios leaped down before their father and firmly placed themselves on either side of him when he climbed down.

Tony, enthralled by the sight of all the people who had come, took his mother's hand, and they followed behind Theo and the older boys. He listened to the voices all around them, not mountain accents, some speaking English. Merchants, important politicians from Paphos, from Nicosia even; and British, from the colonial government and the garrisons in Nicosia and Polemidia; all relaxed and greeting each other.

As they neared the great oak doors of the church, both wide open to allow in the hundreds of mourners that were expected, Tony felt his mother stiffen. They walked inside, out of the bright sunshine. Despite the hundred or more candles burning in a dozen elaborate chandeliers, the corners and side-aisles were dark and musty. Tony followed his brothers. They were now just inside the door, a little to one side, crowded up close to his father, arguing in angry whispers with two hard-looking men. There was some pushing and grabbing of arms. A scuffle was about to erupt when Panos Andreou appeared from the front of the church.

He wore a black suit and tie, and a shirt of brilliant whiteness. With no raising of his voice or eyebrows, he spoke sharply, authoritatively. The two doormen instantly let go of the fistfuls of clothing they were clutching, dropped their hands and stood aside to let Theo and the family through. Without speaking, Panos nodded Stelios towards a place at the back of the church, standing among the local peasantry who had come in their drab, rumpled suits and collarless shirts. Several of Christina's relations were there too. After some token resistance, Theo let himself be persuaded in, and he stood with a defiant scowl, rocking on his heels beside his wife's tubby Uncle Neo. Neo had come all the way from Larnaca; a good funeral was a great chance to gloat and celebrate.

Tony sat beside his mother on a bench from where he could look at the magnificent gilt icons, statues and crucifixes that decorated the distant screen in front of the altar in the apse. And high up on a pillar of carved stone perched a pulpit encrusted in gold even more ornate than the monastery of Khrysoroyiattis on the hill above their valley.

And there, propped almost upright in front of the screen and a shrine containing a holy human relic, was Spyros Andreou in his coffin.

The corpse was dressed and scrubbed, combed and manicured as if he were to be presented to the King of England, nestling in the snowy-white silk of his coffin lining.

The chant came to an end and five deep-bearded, high-hatted clerics – the bishop and his assistants – processed from the back of the church to the altar behind the screen.

For the most part invisible to the packed mass of mourners, they began to chant for the repose of the soul of Spyros Andreou; the people joined in some of the prayers in an expressionless mumble and the priests intoned again until the high point of the ceremony was reached.

Starting with his family, the mourners were to approach and pay their last tribute to the dead man. As Spyros' widow left her seat and walked with slow, arthritic dignity towards her dead husband Tony watched with horrified fascination. When she reached the open coffin, she leaned forward and planted a kiss on one lifeless cheek. Panos, who was close behind her, did the same, followed by a boy, about the same age as Tony, and a younger girl. The children bent and kissed one exposed hand, bowed and returned to their place.

The priests struck up another dirge as, row by row, the people filed out and shuffled up to the altar. Tony and his mother stood aside to let Stelios, Theo and Nicos go first, but Tony was not thinking of his father as he followed him. The thought of kissing the cold, wrinkled white hand appalled him. But Panos Andreou's children had, so he must too.

They were almost at the altar. Stelios went first, then Nicos. They each followed the example of those before them, and kissed the dead man's hand, bowed and moved aside.

Theo, unbending, walked up to the corpse and confronted it. He stared at the pasty face and vein-flecked eyelids as if he could see into the eyes beneath them. Abruptly, he leaned forward and with all the force he could muster, spat a large gobbet of frothy, stained saliva on to the dead man's face.

There was a loud, horrified gasp from the crowded nave. The dirge faltered and died away. An anguished wail arose from the lips of Spyros Andreou's widow.

From the back of the church a rush of family retainers and strong-arm men arrived to uphold the honour of their deceased master.

But Panos Andreou left his place with quiet dignity. He walked over to his father's corpse and, taking a fluffy white handkerchief from his breast pocket, he wiped every drop of dribbling spittle from the white mask.

When he was sure it was all gone, he handed the handkerchief to a man who hovered behind him and confronted Theo, who was being roughly restrained by the two brothers who had helped to beat him up two years before.

"Let the animal go," Panos said quietly. "Kyriakides, you and your family are not welcome in our valleys. You have insulted the honour of one of the finest men of these parts. You will be shunned by every man in the district of Paphos. Never, ever let me see your face again."

He turned away and calmly resumed his place at the front of the church.

Theo stared at him, then for a moment at the corpse before turning round and walking solemnly back down the middle of the church and out of the doors into the sunlight, watched by everyone in the church except Panos Andreou.

Tony had felt his mother become rigid with shock the moment her husband committed the outrage. Now she seemed to collapse at the colossal indignity of her position. She gazed at the floor, unwilling to move or draw attention to herself or her relations. Tony looked up, and could see Panos' children staring at him. He felt himself blush and looked away. Then – he could not stop himself – he looked back at the girl, whose eyes seemed to understand his embarrassment and not to blame him for his father's gross, unholy coarseness.

Stelios and Nicos came and took their mother's arm. Gently, they turned her and led her away, as if in a trance, to follow her husband out of the church.

* * *

As weeks, then months passed at home Theo became tranquil, happy to have repaid the insult of the Andreous' beating. When Christina and Stelios berated him for his outrageous, idiotic behaviour he simply shrugged and bade them get on with the work.

"The Andreous can't touch us any more, I tell you. Panos wants to be a politician; he wants to get in with the British; he knows that running a feud with us will go against him. Don't worry about them."

It began to look as if his complacency was justified. Though every week they expected a visit from the Andreous or at least to have their goods refused or purchases embargoed, they continued much as before supplying the buoyant market that the Allied forces had created. The threat of some kind of revenge from the Andreous receded.

Panos Andreou, Tony read in the papers, had become more involved in trading with the British forces, and in the internal government in Nicosia. Maybe he had forgotten to issue instructions for the promised boycott of the Kyriakides family. Maybe – and Tony thought this more likely – the fate of the Kyriakides family was just too unimportant to waste time on.

In some ways things even improved for them, for the family all agreed that there was now no question of selling their grapes to the Andreous. So Stelios contacted a respectable old wine-maker in the next district who paid a good deal more than the Andreous would have done for what turned out to be a bumper harvest. They congratulated themselves on their shrewdness, and joked about the Andreous' show of strength.

At the time of the incident Tony couldn't believe that his family would survive. No one, least of all the Andreous, could overlook such an insult. But the Andreous were seldom seen now up in the mountain valleys, and Tony's fears too began to fade. The threat was always there but, as months passed, it was no longer the oppressive black cloud it had been at first. Tony began once again to concentrate on his school books and roamed the hillsides as he always had.

Two years later Tony read in a newspaper which his father had brought back from the taverna that Panos Andreou had bought an old cannery in Limassol from where he was shipping thousands of tons to the Allied troops in North Africa. He must be making millions now, Tony thought, no wonder he hadn't bothered with a little peasant family up in the mountains.

Pruning the vines that evening with Nicos, he said: "Do you think the Andreous will ever come here again – for what Dad did?"

Nicos, stooped over a row of foot-high vines, straightened up to look at Tony with a hint of fear in his eyes. "I shouldn't say so to you, but there still isn't a day goes by that I don't think they're going to turn up."

"Do you really think that, Nico? You never show it."

Nicos shrugged. "What's the point? If they come, they come. And there's a lot of work to get on with. We can sell everything we grow while this war's on, and at a good price. The Andreous are making a packet down in Limassol, and that's keeping them busy, thank God. In the meantime we may as well make the most of things, especially if you're going to stay on at school. Maybe you'll go to the college one day, become the educated member of the family and make all the money." He grinned. Nicos, unlike Stelios and Theo, was as proud as Christina that Tony had just passed his first batch of secondary exams, with the hope of a place at the academy in Paphos. He always took his young brother's side when it was mooted that Tony should leave to start working on the land. "Even if you came to help us full time, we'd still never be more than peasant farmers, and these good prices won't last forever."

"Why does Stelios want me to come and work with you? He's always saying how useless I am."

"That's just sour grapes. Don't worry about it. You concentrate on becoming a lawyer or something. They make a pile up in Nicosia. Then you'd be able to get out of this place." Nicos waved a hand across their family's patch of rocky, sloping ground.

"But I wouldn't want to go away from here," Tony said.

"You will, when you've seen other places, places where the Andreous can't reach you."

For a while the black cloud of the Andreous' threat darkened Tony's life again. But he never talked to anyone about it now that he realised the rest of his family probably felt the same.

The war was coming to an end, they said, and Tony wondered what change it would make to their lives; nothing beneficial as far as he could see, but he tried to put a brave face on his misgivings. He was fourteen now, and though his schooling and reading were still the most important things in his life, he found that he couldn't ignore the strange, exciting feelings that now troubled him. He had become more interested in girls and, specifically, more interested in what was underneath their blouses and skirts. He had heard his parents and sometimes his brothers talk about things men and women did, and how the boys must be sure to marry a girl who had been well brought up, away from other boys. He did not know what it was that boys and girls did when they were together, but from the way his brothers sniggered and his mother disapproved he guessed it must be fun.

He had been taught that Greek girls, if they were worth anything, were not available for exploration or experimentation, but he had frequently heard the Turkish girls referred to in disparaging terms – especially the beautiful ones. Of course, Greek boys did not marry Turkish girls, but there was one he found particularly fascinating, from the small village of Vrecha, in the next valley.

Vrecha was an entirely Turkish village with its own mosque, shops and school. Tony sometimes passed through it to reach the bridge across the river upstream. He had been taught to respect the religious peculiarities of the Turks; he knew that he must not ride on a donkey through the village, to avoid offending the inhabitants by looking through the small high windows and seeing the women unveiled in their houses. The village, like any Greek village, was surrounded by olive and lemon groves, small fields of maize and vegetables. The villagers grazed their goats up on the hills adjoining the Kyriakides' traditional grazing lands.

Tony first saw the girl when, like himself, she was tending the family herd.

It was a hot, burning day. A few crickets chirruped quietly and the sound of a single lark echoed across the valley beneath. She was asleep, half sitting against a thick old almond tree. Tony tip-toed towards her and crouched behind a gorse bush to peer through its branches at her, a few feet away.

She had a small brown face and long black eyelashes which rested and flickered on her cheeks. Her hair was shining, raven black. She had discarded a cardigan and her slender arms were exposed, as well as her fragile-looking ankles and feet. The shape of small breasts showed through her blouse though she could have been no more than eleven or twelve. He watched her for ten minutes before she stirred, and her eyes blinked open. Tony raised his head above the gorse bush and smiled. She was startled for a moment, but his smile reassured her. She fumbled uncertainly for a garment to cover her shoulders, but slowly smiled in return.

Tony could speak some Turkish, and knew that she would know no Greek, so he used her language.

"Hello. My name's Antonios. What's yours?"

"Fatima." Her voice was high but husky. It thrilled Tony.

"Can I sit down with you?" he asked.

"My father would kill me, to sit with a boy – especially a Greek boy," she said.

But she had not said no, so Tony sat with his back to the tree, almost touching her. It was a magical new experience to him.

They talked as best they could with Tony's scanty vocabulary, about the things they liked to do, and the countryside that they shared. She had seen Tony before, from her house when he had walked through her village. Her father had done some business with his father, bought or sold each other goats or fodder. And they knew that was the extent to which both their families would countenance contact. To these two young people, glowing in their proximity to each other, it seemed absurd.

When she said she had to go, Tony was not disappointed; he understood, and watched her zigzag down the mountainside to the dusty lane that led back to Vrecha. There was a contentment in him that made his head light and made him want to sing the whole way home.

That summer he met her at the almond tree half a dozen times. Each time repaid hours of waiting and watching, for he knew that making arrangements was out of the question, but she admitted that she too made a point of always trying to come to the spot where they had first met. He brought grapes and oranges for them to eat. Once he touched her hand as he gave them to her, and an inexplicable, delirious tremor rippled through him.

For Tony those months passed in an innocent, blissful

flash. He worked hard at his books, made his Turkish fluent, and relegated the horror of the Andreou funeral to historical memories at the back of his mind. But as summer turned to autumn he discovered with alarming grief that he would not be seeing Fatima again; she was to be betrothed to a Turkish boy and assume the life of a young Muslim woman. He felt this was bitterly unfair, but he did not dare tell his mother the reason for his sadness, and suffered the cruel injustice alone.

Tony was sitting in the cool, resin-scented shade of a stand of Aleppo pines five hundred feet above his home. The goats he was tending for his brothers ranged among the rocks and shrubs that grew on the thin, sandy soil or sat lazily in the shade of the gorse bushes whose spiky leaves they chewed. Crickets chirruped and buzzed loudly in the late afternoon sun while the rocks gave off the day's accumulated heat. A crested lark, spiralling up the valley, was trilling its lonely song. Below it, a kestrel hovered over the last living moments of a scavenging shrew.

The sound of a car crunching up the track on the far side of the valley was faint, but enough to catch Tony's attention. The car drew up at the top of the track which led down to the Kyriakides' house. Tony's heart thumped; anyone visiting them in a car must be trouble.

He was too far away to see their faces, but he knew who they were. There was an inevitability about the steady progress of the four dark-suited men as they descended the track to the solitary house. Before his eyes, the scene he had been dreading, and had pushed to the back of his mind, was about to take place.

He scrambled to his feet and started off down the steep, rocky hillside. He didn't give a thought to the goats he had been tending as he leaped, almost flew towards the valley bottom. He stumbled and fell often but the cuts and bruises didn't hurt. Memories of the last time, five years before, when he had fled down to warn his father of the Andreous' coming flashed through his mind. On that occasion too his brothers had been away. A dozen terrifying images clammered for attention in his head as he ran with his eyes on the low white house. But he was only half-way down the valley-side when the men reached the house, and he glanced heavenwards to gasp a panting prayer.

As he reached the last few terraces of vines before the valley floor, the four men left the house and, more quickly than they had descended, walked back up the track towards their car.

He was still a quarter of a mile from the house, but he sprinted up the track between the vines, yelling at the departing visitors. They stopped and turned to look at him, just for a moment, before they got back into the car and drove off in a cloud of dust.

Tony flung himself through the door into the gloom of the house. It was a few seconds before he could see his mother, crouching on the floor in the middle of the room, but he heard her desperate moaning. He flung himself down beside her and saw his father's still staring eyes; then his mouth, slightly open and dribbling blood. On his chest, a little below his heart, a dark bloodstain, the size of an orange, spread around a small gash in the coarse grey fabric of his tunic.

It was a long time before Christina spoke or moved from her husband's body. Then Tony helped her to her feet and sat her on a chair.

"Twenty-five years I gave him. Twenty-five good years of my life, for this to happen," Christina muttered, tenderly, then bitterly.

"They will pay," Tony said, with a bravado he did not feel.

"No! No! There must be no feud. Or they will kill all my sons too."

"We must tell the police now," Tony said.

Christina wailed, "We can do nothing. We must tell no one. If we tell the police they will kill you, they said so; and they meant it. You would never be safe."

Tony gazed at her with his grave, brown eyes, and understood why the men had left so casually, so unconcerned at his witnessing their leaving. His mother was in no doubt about the validity of their threat.

"Which of them came? Which of them did it?" he asked.

"I don't know who killed him." Christina glanced at her dead husband and shook her head. "Does it matter? Not Panyiotis, of course, he didn't come. He is too big now to commit his own crimes, but you can be sure he agreed to it. But why did they come now," she began to weep again, "just when we thought we were safe?"

"That was the reason. You know Father was right about the Andreous."

"But who are we to die for telling that truth? What good has it done?"

All the village came to witness Theo Kyriakides' interment in the village burial ground. The family had announced that Theo died from an accident with his ancient, muzzle-loading shot-gun. The old men in *vraka* and *podines* – baggy breeches and boots – and knitted hats, stroked their long moustaches and told each other later, after a few drinks in the taverna, what a fool he had been to make such a stand against the Andreous.

Stelios, the eldest son, did not go back to the taverna that evening. He found it hard to demonstrate a satisfactory grief. It was clear to everyone that he wanted to get back to the land over which he now assumed control, at least until his brothers challenged him for a share.

But Nicos was too gentle, too affably submissive to advance his claim, and Tony knew that his own future lay in his learning, not through tending their uncooperative land.

The two elder boys settled down to the running of the farm in comparative harmony, and the next few years proved them to be proficient farmers. Tony helped out at weekends and during school holidays. Christina approved, encouraged their labours, and discouraged their interest in girls. She did not want any additional, probably disruptive claims on their time or income. She knew that, soon enough, Stelios and Nicos would have to battle over their scrubby patch of mountain land; and that her youngest son could never expect a living from it.

But Christina did all she could to encourage Tony's other gifts. She entered into a conspiracy with the schoolteacher and the little money she made herself from rug-making was willingly ploughed into books for the boy. She did not divulge to Tony her dreams of his going off to Paphos one day, or even Nicosia, to become a doctor or a lawyer, but he was aware she expected exceptional things of him.

Stelios was less sympathetic, less ambitious for his youngest brother. When the time came and Christina floated the idea that the farm should pay for Tony to go on to school in Paphos, Stelios angrily argued how unjust that was.

Besides, with the end of the war in Europe their produce was not so easy to sell. Tony would have to leave school and pull his weight on the farm. He was, after all, fifteen now and school work was not going to teach him anything of use to them. Tony listened, guilty and frustrated, as Christina vainly pleaded the long-term benefits of investing in an educated member of the family. Nicos could see Tony's disappointment but Stelios easily persuaded his amiable but dimwitted brother to his point of view.

Tony had to accept the inevitable and took his place at the bottom of the pecking order on the farm. He did, though, persuade his brothers to make use of his fluent English and mathematics to sell their produce to markets further afield; to places where the village people didn't go.

He started with the merchants in Paphos, then the wineries that had been set up by competitors of the Andreous in Limassol. He made his journeys by donkey-cart, or on the buses which were now beginning to ply up the foothills of the mountains, and stayed with his mother's relations in the coastal towns; they were amused by his young energy and optimism. It took a year or so for his efforts to have a significant impact on the prices the Kyriakides could get for their grapes and olives, but then even Stelios had to admit that Tony had helped. But he still grumbled that Tony would be more use dealing with the goats than spending days at a time down at the coast.

Tony, growing confident, argued his case without raising his voice, and his family deferred to him. It may not have been the future he and his mother had dreamed of, but at least it gave him the chance to spend time in Paphos and Limassol and experience vicarious contact with a greater world.

Tony's physique developed in quite a different way to his elder brothers'. He was taller now than they were, though still slimly built. The childhood curliness of his hair had settled into an orderly waviness. And his dark, steady eyes made him appear older than he was. There was a knowingness about him, which the people he approached in the towns admired him for. They liked and trusted him too; he talked less than his competitors, and meant what he said. It was not long before he was given his first important introduction to the quartermaster's stores at the British garrison in Polemidia.

Once there, a mix of open-faced charm and barefaced cheek brought him to the attention of the procurement officers and he found himself taking orders for quantities and even produce – potatoes and oranges – that their farm could not supply. Tony grabbed at this chance to be a merchant, not just a salesman for his brothers.

When he arrived home with the orders his brothers laughed, but he scoured the valleys for farmers who were willing to supply him with a few days' credit. The margin between the prices he paid, and the prices at which he had sold was not great, but the quantities were substantial and he knew that the British would not try to beat him down on the price they had agreed. His neighbours wished him well and helped him load the superannuated army truck which he arranged to come up from Paphos to carry his order fifty miles along the pitted, dirt coast road to Limassol.

When he returned in triumph he immediately paid the six farmers who had supplied him and talked them into returning a contribution towards his transport costs.

He passed on the whole proceeds of the deal to Stelios, who gaped at a sum that represented a good month's farming profits. But his eldest brother was still sceptical.

"What happens when the Andreous find out you've been dealing with the British? Do you think they'll let us get away with it?"

"They won't find out," Tony said confidently. "I told the captain that if they did, they would try and stop us to keep the business for themselves, at much higher prices. Captain Roberts is a good man. The man before him used to get cases of brandy and wine from the Andreous and didn't care too much about the prices. Anyway," Tony went on, "the Andreous aren't interested in us now."

That was the family's considered opinion; the slate had been wiped clean; Theo's insult to Spyros Andreou had been openly avenged and, provided the Kyriakides did not choose to escalate a feud, the matter was closed. Besides, the deal Tony had just done with the army would have been very small beer to the Andreous.

The Andreou family had been so successful, trading, building wineries and canneries, finding political influence under the wings of the bishops and the British, that they moved the centre of their operations to Limassol where the ships called. They were seldom to be seen in Paphos District now. Nonetheless Tony could never forget the shame and horror of his three encounters with them. Sooner or later, he knew, Panos Andreou would come between him and his ambitions.

During the months that followed, Tony worked hard on the trade he was doing at the Polemidia garrison, until it became the main source of income for his family. On one of his regular trips there, as he was unloading three tons of small new potatoes into a warehouse at the edge of the camp, he saw an Englishwoman walking through the barrack gates to a salute from the sentry. Beside her was a Greek girl in her teens, like him, and to him unbelievably beautiful. He was sure he had seen her face before but he couldn't place where. He asked one of the Cypriot warehousemen.

"She's called Thalia Andreou."

Tony was stunned. He remembered at once the glimpse of the girl's eyes in the church at old Andreou's funeral.

Tony jumped down off the truck. He hid behind it to watch her covertly as she passed, quite near, laughing and smiling with the other woman.

"Who's she with?" he asked.

"Major Cuthbertson's wife. Since the war ended quite a lot of the officers have brought their wives here. The girl's dad is Panos Andreou – a big cheese in Limassol. He's made a packet out of the army and now he's built the big new winery by the port, you know?"

Tony nodded. Of course he knew. "But what's the girl doing here?"

51

The storeman shrugged. "How the hell should I know?"

Another, younger man, who, like Tony, had been dazzled by Thalia, was better informed.

"She teaches Greek to some of the Englishwomen."

"But she doesn't look old enough," Tony said.

"Maybe not but, like he said, Andreou's a big man round here. He's well in with the commanding officer."

Tony froze.

Even with the captain's promise, Panos Andreou might yet learn that the Kyriakides were supplying the base. If he did, he only had to give the word and Tony would lose the business.

Much worse, he would never allow a Kyriakides to see his daughter.

2

Tony was alarmed by the depth of his feelings for this girl he had never met.

Up to the moment he saw Thalia Andreou walk through the Polemidia camp gate he had come to terms with his function in the family. The only way he was going to pull himself – and the family with him – a few rungs up the ladder from mere peasanthood was by being smarter than his neighbours. He was driven not just by the thought of his father's humiliation and death, but by the cool authority of the man who had caused them.

Now he was feeling the inexplicable surge of love within him and he saw that same man as an inevitable obstacle to his own happiness. To succeed with Thalia, he had not only to match her father, he had to surpass him.

Takis, the affable rogue who delivered Tony's produce in his ancient, untrustworthy truck, was surprised by his young client's silence on the way home from Limassol. He was used to Tony brimming over with schemes and gossip. The boy seemed to have an uncanny skill in attracting knowledge to himself, absorbing it and filing it away for later use.

But Takis guessed the reason. "You've fallen for that girl, haven't you?" he said.

Tony didn't answer.

"You must be crazy," the driver went on. "You know whose daughter she is?"

"Yes. So what?"

"For God's sake! Everyone says he had your father killed for spitting at old Spyros' corpse."

"Of course he didn't."

"But he must have agreed to it; he's the boss of the family."

"My father had an accident." Tony shrugged. "I'm not frightened of the Andreous; I wouldn't be selling to the British if I were. They're not going to cause me any trouble."

"They will if you go near that girl."

Tony turned to him calmly. "No they won't; as long as no bastard tells Andreou until I'm ready."

Takis laughed. "Who the hell do you think you are?"

"It's not what I am. It's what I will be," Tony snapped. He turned back to stare at the dusty road ahead and refused to speak until Takis dropped him a two-mile walk from his home.

With every step he took towards the isolated farmhouse he became more determined that one day he would not have to trudge this journey. He was going to own a car, a place in Paphos, well away from the constraints of these valley-sides. He was going to be somebody – somebody who could look Panos Andreou in the eye.

Tony had no reason to go to Polemidia or Limassol for another three weeks – weeks which seemed to drag for an eternity as he plagued his brothers and his neighbours to hurry with their crop. He was fortified only by the thought that, on his next visit to the garrison, he would see Thalia again.

When the day came and Takis arrived with the truck at the top of the path, Tony's stomach was tight with excitement. His mother noticed. As she waved goodbye, she wondered who was the cause.

Tony and Takis arrived at the quartermaster's stores and unloaded. When the truck was almost empty Tony sat for a moment, limp with disappointment that there had been no sign of the girl or the Englishwoman she had been with last time. He lingered in a way Takis had not seen before.

"Did you think that girl would be here then?" Takis laughed. "You've got it bad! You'll have to go into Limassol and try and find her, but don't let her old man catch you."

Tony considered this. "Okay," he said. "You take me now."

"It'll cost you a few drinks."

Takis was ten years older than Tony, married with a clutch of small children, but he was game for trawling Limassol to track down Panos Andreou's daughter. He wanted to see what Tony would do if he found her.

They got off to a good start. A few enquiries led them to Panos Andreou's grand old house, one street back from the seafront. It was surrounded by a high wall and a lush garden – the home of a rich, important man.

"Well, are you going to go in?"

"No. You were right about my family and the Andreous. Let's wait and see if she comes out."

"But we could be here for hours."

"That's okay, we can wait in that bar; we can see the gate from there. I'll get you the drinks I owe you."

Takis raised his eyes and forehead, but good-naturedly, and the two settled down to a session of black grainy coffee and brandy. They listened to some gossip in the bar, played a few games of *tavli* – backgammon – while the old men looked on and clicked their worry-beads through their fingers.

Every few seconds Tony's eyes flickered up to watch the gates on the other side of the road. A few tradesmen went in and out and once a middle-aged woman Tony guessed was Thalia's mother, she was so well-dressed and so elegantly unlike any of the peasant women around his home.

But that was it. After two hours Takis' good nature was running out.

"Come on, Tony. Where's your courage? Just walk across there and ask where she is. You don't have to say who you are."

"I can't. Look at me! They'll know I'm just a village boy. Did you see that woman who went in? How beautifully dressed she was?"

"Maybe the girl won't look at your clothes, and it's her you want to impress – not her mother. You're a good-looking boy, and one with all the chat."

"No. I'm sorry I've wasted your time, Takis; you were good to come with me." Tony tried to disguise his disappointment as he stood up. "Come on, we'd better go before you're too drunk to keep the truck on the road."

"Don't worry about that," Takis struggled to his feet, "That truck knows its own way home."

After that journey Tony was more certain than ever that he had to get his own transport.

With some misgivings he persuaded Takis to drive right to the top of their track. The last few miles along rutted mountain road had been a nerve-shredding experience, but Takis' instinct for survival prevailed. As Tony started off down the hill, Takis called after him, "There, what did I tell you? No trouble at all!"

Tony smiled with relief at being on his own feet; he may not have found Thalia, but at least he was alive; and at least he knew where she lived, and what he had to do to see her again.

Although he made several more trips to Limassol, it was three months before Tony tried to meet Thalia again.

In the meantime he acquired a truck, bought with his brothers' agreement from Tony's profits over the previous year. The three brothers all learned to drive and widened their track so that they could bring the vehicle right down to the house.

With greater difficulty Tony also persuaded his family to plant some of their best flat land with orange trees. He had heard talk among the sharper merchants in Limassol of a growing demand for oranges, not from within Cyprus but for export to Northern Europe, where the orange juice habit had been established by the departing American troops.

Stelios was scathing. "Why should we tie up land which won't bring in money for three or four years? Don't be crazy!"

"One day, every valley in the region will be covered with orange trees," Tony said, "And whoever plants them first will make the first big money."

"From who? Who's going to buy all these oranges? Everyone has enough already."

Nervously, Nicos broke into the discussion. "Tony already said, it's to go abroad."

Abroad was somewhere that didn't enter Stelios' consideration, but Nick, Tony and his mother out-voted him and it was agreed to sacrifice ten precious acres to future prosperity.

In the same way that Tony was prepared to think ahead in business, so he hadn't wanted to spoil his chances with Thalia by rushing her before he was ready. He wasn't deterred by the fact that he had never met the girl, that she had no idea who he was, and that, when she found out, all her family's prejudices would be against him.

Nevertheless, aware that other people might think he was being absurdly ambitious, he told his family nothing about Thalia. They noticed the new clothes he bought, the neatly trimmed hair, the polished shoes and, with a laugh, put it down to his aspiration to be a businessman, from which, after all, the whole family was benefiting. Only his mother guessed the reason for his new spruceness but, try as she did, she could not find out who it was all for.

When Tony was ready to launch his quest for Thalia, he and Nick drove into Limassol in their truck with a load of potatoes for a shipment to Israel. They arrived after lunch and Tony persuaded Nick to go on alone to the docks with the truck. "Just make sure you get someone to sign for the load and watch them taking it off," he instructed, "Then pick me up by the castle in two hours."

Nicos agreed. He was used to Tony giving the orders and, unlike Stelios, he didn't resent it.

"Okay. What are you going to do?" he asked.

"I've got to meet someone."

"A girl?" Nicos asked with a wink.

"Maybe."

"Good luck. I'll see you later."

His brother drove off and Tony looked at his watch. He had plenty of time, but on this occasion, he had no intention of hanging around. He had done his research on previous trips.

One of the maids from the Andreou household, subtly approached and questioned, had told him that Thalia usually went to collect her twelve-year-old brother Ari from school on this one day of the week and they would walk back through the municipal gardens on Vironos Street at the far end of town.

Tony walked briskly along the seafront to the park. There were a few children's swings and see-saws there among the colourful beds of flowers and stately old trees. He stationed himself on a bench beneath a large eucalyptus from which he nervously picked off the bark and breathed in the aromatic scent. He composed, then rejected a dozen different ways of opening a conversation with Thalia Andreou.

The June sun was high and even in the shade of the great tree its heat penetrated the curtain of leaves and baked the

58

still air. Insects droned and shrilled among the shrubs and brilliant flowerbeds. Tony had at least an hour to wait. He leaned back and closed his eyes.

He awoke with a start. Something had hit him. He sat forward and looked around in the dappled sunlight, trying to remember where he was. A leather football rolled away from him and came to rest among the knobbly protruding roots of the old tree.

"I'm sorry. My brother always kicks his ball too hard."

Tony blinked at the girl's face in the sunlight.

His heart raced. He gulped. Everything he had thought of saying to her fled his mind. He stared at her and tried to speak.

"Are you all right?" she asked. "Did it hit you hard?"

With an effort, Tony regained control of himself.

"No, no," he muttered, rising to his feet, "Of course not. It doesn't matter at all. I must have fallen asleep."

He had carried around a picture of her face in his head since his glimpse of her at the British base three months ago. Up until a moment before, that vision had been to him the apotheosis of beauty. Now the real thing put the vision to shame.

She smiled and her deep, coffee-brown eyes seemed to light up like beacons and flood him with a warmth that challenged the baking sun.

"It's easy to do in this heat." She fanned her face with her hand and stepped into the shade of the eucalyptus tree. A boy ran up from behind her, picked up the ball and took it out into the open to dribble it across the coarse brown grass.

"Is that your brother?" Tony asked, though he knew.

"Yes. I've just picked him up from school. Usually my father's driver does, but Ari likes a walk through the town with me."

Tony smiled. "What a thoughtful sister you are." He waved a hand at the bench as if it were a throne. "Why don't you sit for a while and watch him kicking his ball around. He doesn't expect you to play football with him, does he?"

The girl shook her head and grinned. "No. He used to, but I was so hopeless, he gave up."

For an agonising moment, Tony did not know whether or not she had declined his invitation. When she gathered the full skirt of her fashionably waisted white cotton frock and turned to sit, his knees almost gave beneath him. He recovered enough to say, "Do you mind if I join you?"

"Please do," she said.

Tony sat beside her, a decorous distance away. He took a deep breath, "What's your name?"

"Thalia Andreou." The words sounded magical to Tony; words which he had repeated to himself a thousand times, maybe more, since he had last seen her. "I've seen you somewhere before," she went on, "but I don't know your name."

Tony knew that if he lied now, he could pay a terrible price later. He gritted his teeth. "Antonios Kyriakides. My family call me Tony."

Thalia had been watching her brother; now her gaze turned back sharply to the neat, handsome features and earnest black eyes of the young man beside her. She looked at him. There was no malice in her gaze.

"I saw you in church, didn't I, at my grandfather's funeral – years ago?"

Tony did not move for a moment. Then he nodded, slowly. "I saw you too."

She was looking at him with more interest now. He didn't seem at all like a village boy, especially not from the lowly peasant family which had so infuriated her father. He was well-dressed and obviously educated. In his eyes there was an intelligent, thoughtful candour she had seldom, if ever, seen in any of the Greek boys she knew, and none of the blustering braggadocio.

And she had never heard about old Theo Kyriakides' 'accident'.

"What are you doing in Limassol?"

"I had people to see," Tony replied vaguely, "I'm a merchant – produce, mostly."

"You look more like a lawyer or something."

Tony shrugged. "There's no particular advantage in looking like a peasant."

After a moment's silence, Thalia said, "I can still remember how forlorn you looked, standing in the church after your father had disgraced himself." She laughed. "Didn't you mind what he had done to your grandfather?"

"Not particularly. He was a horrible old man. He never listened to anyone, not even my father, and just shouted all the time until he got his way."

Tony looked hard at the girl. It seemed incredible that she should come from the family which had for so long been an inescapable, dark presence in the life of his own family. There was a torrent of words inside him waiting to gush out; he had longed to tell an outsider how their life had been tainted by the ill-matched, unresolved feud.

But he held it back now. There would be plenty of time for that later. Instead he asked her about herself.

When she was sure he was interested, she gave herself a free rein. She told Tony about her ambitions to travel, to teach, to help poor children. She told him about the Englishwomen she knew at the British garrison, how she had got to know them by offering to teach them Greek, and what friends she had made there. She talked about her elder brother, whom she did not care for, and her younger brother, on whom she doted, "Though I dare say he'll end up bullying and boasting, like the rest of the men in my family – like most of the men in Cyprus, as far as I can tell."

Tony did not press her on this. He wanted only to listen and soak up every piece of knowledge she offered.

But when she asked Tony about himself he was reticent. He didn't want to discuss his past and talked only of his future plans, and then he was sketchy about the details. He didn't want her to let slip anything to her father that might jeopardise his growing business.

Then they talked about other things, other places – Athens, London, America, their ideas for the uncertain future of Cyprus. They both found it hard to believe, and it exceeded all Tony's most optimistic hopes, that they should find themselves so much in harmony. Time raced by until Ari, bored with kicking his ball around and swinging on his own, demanded to be taken home for supper.

Tony walked in a dream along the seafront to the old castle by the port, an hour late for his rendezvous with Nicos.

His brother was astonished. "What happened? You're never late. Who did you see? She must have been something special."

With an effort Tony forced himself down to earth. "I'm sorry. How did the delivery go?"

"No problems. I even got the money." He proudly handed a wad of notes to his younger brother. "But they really wanted to see you."

"Okay. I'll go next time."

"Now tell me about the girl," Nicos asked with a leer.

Tony sighed and shook his head.

The following Thursday, without any spoken arrangement, Tony met Thalia again at the park; only this time Ari wasn't with her. Tony was encouraged. He asked her if she would like to have a cup of coffee with him.

"I can't; if anyone who knows my family sees me I'll be in trouble. But I'd like to," she added.

Tony had overlooked this practical difficulty, but he knew she was right.

"Well, we don't need coffee anyway," he said. "But if . . . when we meet next time, I could drive you in my truck to Pissouri, or somewhere where no one knows you, or we could go for a picnic in the hills – whatever you like, as long as we can meet without getting you into trouble."

"It will have to be during the day," Thalia said, "when I can say I'm shopping or going to give a lesson to one of the Englishwomen."

"Don't worry," Tony said, "I'll think of a hundred places."

Thalia didn't doubt him, and smiled at the thought of their conspiracy.

During the months that followed Tony and Thalia arranged to meet almost every week. They would walk along the beaches and talk, sometimes sit and drink coffee in a small bar in Pissouri. There were public places in Limassol where they thought it was safe. The gardens by the medieval castle was one of their favourites, below the ancient walls of the Great Hall, where, it was said, Richard the Lionheart, the first English occupier of Cyprus, had wed his queen, Berengaria of Navarre, on his way to the Crusades. Here they sat on a bench beneath a vast, spreading olive tree, where they happily spent hours until the days grew colder in autumn.

They were magical months for Tony. Sometimes he could hardly believe his luck, but he could not bring himself to risk touching Thalia. Although he thought day and night of almost nothing else but holding her and kissing her and touching parts of her body which he had not yet seen, he didn't want to do anything that might scare her away.

But Thalia was becoming impatient.

She decided to talk to her one close friend in the household. Teresa was the maid who had first told Tony about

Thalia's movements. She guessed that the handsome, serious boy was right for her.

She didn't pretend to be surprised when Thalia told her that she had been seeing the boy for three months.

"Are you happy with that?" she asked.

"Oh yes. He's wonderful to talk to; he always knows what I'm trying to say, and he listens. He's got much more to him than all those arrogant brats my parents try to push at me. I do believe I love him. The only trouble is, he hasn't touched me yet; he hasn't even tried!"

"That's strange," Teresa said. "With those eyes, you'd have thought that was what he wanted most. But maybe he doesn't want to scare you. He's from the country; maybe he's a bit old-fashioned."

"No, he's not old-fashioned."

"Then probably he doesn't want to scare you. Perhaps you should give him a little encouragement."

"How? I can't just invite him to kiss me."

"No, but you can put him in the mood, in the right place. When the family go up to Paphos next week, why don't you stay behind, then you could invite him for a meal. I'll still be here; I'll help."

"What am I going to tell my father? He won't even let me go out in the evenings when he's here, unless I'm with him or Mamma."

"Well, you're not going to go out. Say you'll have to stay behind because one of the English ladies from the base wants you to give a lesson to some important man's wife, or something. You know how he likes you to mix with the English."

"That's not why I do it, but it's a good idea."

"Of course it is! You could give your Tony a wonderful dinner with some of your father's best wine, it'll be really romantic, and then afterwards, when you're alone in the house with no one to see, let him know with your eyes that

64

you want him and if he's any kind of a man he'll want to touch you."

Thalia's eyes lit up at the scene Teresa painted.

"Teresa, you're brilliant!"

"Me? Brilliant? I can't even read," the maid laughed.

Two days later, as usual, Thalia and Tony were walking through the town, though a bitter wind blew from the north.

"It's freezing," Tony said. "Let's sit in the cab of my truck."

Thalia agreed and, when they were sitting close to one another on the battered old bench seat, she told him, "You're invited to dinner next week."

Tony looked at her sharply, even a little angrily. "Where?"

"At my house, of course."

"Do your family know who I am?" he asked in panic.

"Of course not. We agreed I wouldn't tell them. Anyway, they won't be there. They're all going up to Paphos. I'm staying because Mrs Cuthbertson has asked me to give some lessons to the new colonel's wife."

"When?"

"Next week, Wednesday, when you're in town."

Tony relaxed and smiled. He felt he had reached the end of a long journey.

Tony's mother watched him give his hair a final brush and his shoes an unnecessary last polish before jumping into the freshly painted, prewar truck. She wasn't surprised when he called to her, almost in passing, "I may be late tonight, in fact I may have to stay in town, so don't worry if I'm not back."

Stelios arrived. He lived in the village now, with his new wife. "He's got some fancy girl in Limassol, I'm sure of it. Why should he always be dressing up to deliver vegetables?"

"Maybe he has. He deserves it. He's worked hard," his mother said, breaking one of her cardinal rules to show Tony no favour in front of his brothers.

"What has he done to deserve it?" Stelios growled, "Nick and I do all the work round here, and I've got a family to support."

Christina looked at him sadly, but said nothing and turned back into the house.

Tony set off on the Paphos road. After a few miles, the rain began to fall, then to cascade. Tony was bursting with impatience to get to Limassol. He found it hard to concentrate on the slippery dirt highway and the rain drummed so hard on the windscreen that the wipers couldn't keep it clear.

Just before Paphos a donkey-cart, driven by a man wrapped from head to foot in a sheet of rubber, shot out in front of him. The truck didn't hit the cart hard, but it nudged it, donkey and all, up the soggy track while the astonished driver yelled abuse and hung on to his bench. The truck's front tyres at last found some purchase and it swerved violently to the left, across the road, into a ditch where the front axle buckled and lodged fast on a rock.

With a groan, Tony clambered out into the driving rain. The cart had pulled up a few yards further down the road. Tony walked up to it and remonstrated with the peasant for driving straight out in front of him. The old man was having none of this, so Tony changed his approach, became more conciliatory, and persuaded the driver to wait while he had a look at the damage to his truck.

The vehicle was certainly not going to move under its own power that day, so he begged a ride into Paphos on the donkey- cart, shivering in the drenching rain and in his soaking best clothes.

In Paphos Tony went to see everyone he knew with a truck. After an hour he found his old friend Takis, who agreed to come back with him and transfer the load to his lorry. Two hours later they were on their way, with Tony praying hard as Takis slithered into every bend on the coast road to Limassol.

They arrived at Tony's customer and unloaded. Tony saw Takis off with instructions to salvage the Kyriakides' truck from the ditch.

Gloomily he trudged towards the Andreous' house in the old town, with squelching shoes, his clothes sodden and muddy, and two hours late for dinner.

At first sight of him, Thalia was so relieved he had finally turned up that she broke into uncontrolled laughter. Tony shuffled his feet and scowled until Thalia said breathlessly, "For heaven's sake, come in. You're soaked; I'll find you some other clothes. It's wonderful to see you, though. I was thinking you'd changed your mind and weren't coming."

For the first time Tony stepped over the threshold of the Andreou house into a cavernous hallway. Even in his embarrassment he noticed the quiet opulence of the place. Thalia briskly ushered him up a broad curving flight of stairs to her elder brother Michael's room. Here she flung open a large oak wardrobe and fished inside for some clean clothes.

"There you are," she said, laying them on the bed. "And here's a towel. I'll run a bath for you next door; that'll warm you up. Then come down when you're ready. Dinner can wait."

She left Tony bemused by this unaccustomed treatment. He stood and gaped round the room and in its quiet privacy began to discard his soaking clothes. He wrapped the luxuriously soft towel around himself and padded along the thick corridor carpets to the bathroom. He sank into the deep, steaming tub and realised more than ever the difference between the rich and the poor. He could even appreciate the irony that this first taste of comfort should have been provided by the man who had ordered his father's death.

With his confidence restored by the bath and fresh clothes, Tony sauntered down the grand stairs, knowing that, however dreamlike this experience was, it was real; he was in Panos Andreou's house, wearing his son's clothes, and about to be entertained by his daughter, who undoubtedly loved him.

They sat facing each other across a highly-polished oak table in the large dining-room. A fire burned in the grate and fresh candles in the candelabra. Teresa served an extravagant *mezé*, before leaving them discreetly to themselves.

"I thought as this was the first time you've been a guest in this house you would like to eat in here," Thalia said, "I hope it's all right?"

"It's magnificent," Tony said truthfully. "I've never been anywhere like it. It's a pity your parents can never know."

"Maybe they will, one day, when you are a big business man."

"Maybe," Tony said, "But I would never come unless they invited me as an equal and I don't think that's very likely, do you?"

Thalia shook her head sadly. "I don't want to talk about it now."

"All right, but there's something I must ask you. I haven't before, but you can guess what it is."

Thalia didn't answer; she knew what was coming.

"How much do you know about what went on between your family and ours?"

"I knew a bit, before I met you. There was a lot of talk, after that scene at the funeral – I was only eight or nine then – talk between my father and his brothers. They don't like the women to hear about these things, but Teresa told me what she'd heard. I do know my uncles wanted to go to your farm and . . ." she faltered, "and burn it. My father persuaded them not to. He said that the Andreous were just becoming a family respected throughout the island, and by the government; that there were millions of pounds to be made in trading – he said – provided the family was seen to be respectable. They had to shake off the reputation of their father and grandfather. He cursed your father's name, but said that one day, maybe, there would be a suitable opportunity to avenge the insult he had paid our family, without anyone knowing who was responsible."

Thalia's eyes showed her remorse at being connected in any way, however blamelessly, with the conspiracy. "But then," she went on, "they did nothing, and your father died. After that, I never heard him mentioned again. I'm so sorry; it must have been terrible, having that hanging over you all for so long. In a way it must have been a relief when your father died."

"It was," Tony said quietly. "Do you suppose it brought things to an end, though – as far as your father is concerned?"

"I don't really know," Thalia admitted.

"So, he could still decide to do something?"

"He might, though God knows I hope not and I think he's forgotten about it now. It would need something to remind him." She looked at Tony with tender sadness. "Isn't life horrible! Trust me to want the most unsuitable man in Cyprus!"

"Why *do* you want a peasant like me? Any man in Cyprus would have you, any man in Greece or England."

Thalia reached her hand across the table and stroked his with her fingertips. She looked at him with wide, welcoming eyes. "All I know is, I've wanted you since I first found you asleep in the gardens. You must realise that. Does it matter why?"

3

"Would you like some brandy?" Thalia asked when they had finished eating, "We could go and sit in the drawing-room and listen to some new records my father brought back from London."

Tony nodded, though now that he had seen the invitation in her eyes he was not sure what to do. He let his instincts guide him.

They settled side by side on a sofa, their shoulders and thighs touching, while a wind-up record-player squawked out Victor Silvester's dance music.

Slowly but firmly, Tony lifted his arm and placed it around Thalia's shoulders. She nestled closer and turned her face towards him. Their cheeks touched for the first time and Tony felt as if someone had put a flaming torch to him. Every nerve on the surface of his body tingled. His pulse thumped wildly.

But he couldn't let her know that all this was new to him. His mouth found hers. He pressed his lips to hers; he wondered why she tried to part them but he let her, and unlocked a door to a feast of sensations he had never even imagined.

The record, unheard, hissed and clicked monotonously on its final groove while they lost themselves in each other. Their hands searched blindly and caressed through hot, rumpled clothing. Their breath came faster until their faces were bathed in sweat and the dampness of their mouths.

Tony drew back. He looked at her cheeks, red with heat and his evening stubble. Her eyes were black with excitement. He pulled her towards him and began to kiss her again, while his hand slipped for the first time beneath her cotton skirt and up her stockinged leg. He found the suspender clips; with spontaneous adroitness he flicked them undone. His hand crept up between her thighs until they touched warm silk.

Thalia abruptly pulled away from him.

"Tony, don't. I want you to, but you can't, not now, not yet."

Tony saw her desperation. Fighting against the bidding of every hormone in his body and a throbbing erection in his trousers, he smiled and slowly withdrew his tickling fingers.

"I understand," he said. "But you do love me, don't you?"

"Of course I do!" she answered with passion. "But no one's ever touched me there before and I feel so confused and out of control."

He kissed her again, with gentleness. "So do I," he whispered.

"Maybe you'd better go, before anything happens," Thalia said.

Tony pulled himself back with an effort and a crooked smile. "I don't want to scare you," he said, truthfully.

He took his hand from where it rested on her leg and stood up. "But I'll have to go now, before I lose complete control."

Thalia sat up and looked at him with wide, wistful eyes. "I'm sorry."

"Me too, but I'll see you soon. We'd better put your brother's clothes back."

Thalia stood and slid her stocking back up to its clips. Tony saw the bare flesh of her thigh and longed to pick her up and lay her on the sofa beneath him. Instead, he went to the gramophone, turned the handle, and replaced the needle on Victor Silvester.

Now that it was decided, Thalia said briskly, "Come

on, I'll get your clothes from the kitchen, they'll be dry by now and Teresa will have ironed them. I'll bring them up to Michael's room."

They held hands leaving the room and parted as if for ever at the bottom of the stairs. Tony slowly climbed the grand staircase, sure that the sacrifice he was making would be worth it.

In the bedroom he stripped off Michael's clothes, and wrapped the towel he had used earlier around himself.

The door opened and Thalia put her head round it shyly. She was carrying Tony's own clothes, dry, pressed and warm.

He smiled as he took them and dropped them on the bed. Then he took one of her hands in his, drew her to him and put an arm around her shoulder. She lifted her chin. Their mouths and tongues met hungrily.

He slipped his forearm below her bottom and lifted her from the ground. In one flowing movement, he swung her on to the bed and lay down beside her. Their lips had barely parted in a passion that was now beyond control.

For the second time, Tony unclipped one stocking top, then the other. Thalia kicked off her shoes and he slid the silk mesh down her legs and off her toes. She arched her back while he unbuttoned her skirt and suspender belt. He felt for her breasts. She laughed and whispered, "I'll have to do this."

They let go of one another while she sat up and discarded her blouse and bra. When she lay back, she slid her skirt from beneath her buttocks until she lay naked except for her pants.

Tony put a hand beneath the frilly top of the pink silk garment and caressed her flat stomach, until his fingers reached the curls of her pubis and the warm waiting entrance they guarded. The towel he had wrapped loosely round his waist had fallen open. Thalia needed no guidance; her small, fine hands found his tightly clustered

73

testicles and the rigid shaft above them. She massaged them fondly while his fingers began to play a gentle rapid rhythm across the tender button in her vagina until she felt her body melt and her head explode. Without thinking, not caring about the pain she had once dreaded, she whispered, "Tony, I want you in me, please."

She lifted her back again to let him slip her knickers from under her small bottom and down her legs. He rolled over on top of her, and her legs parted.

He was amazed at the intense pleasure he found as he slowly entered the clinging, moist warmth of her body. She tensed for a moment, gave a gasp of pain, and relaxed as he probed far into her small body.

He drew back to enter her again. This time she was ready to have him. Her hands gripped his buttocks and her tongue licked the sweat from his chest as he withdrew and thrust again and again until she lost all control and gasped with the blissful frenzy of it.

When he came, Tony felt as if the world had ended. His head swam in a sea of triumphant ecstasy where he would have been happy to stay for the rest of his life. He left his flaccid penis inside her and rolled her over on top of him to hug her in gratitude for the pleasure she had given.

She returned his kisses between short deep breaths. Her hips still moved in slow contented gyrations. Quite soon, he was hard and they began to make love again.

She was already dressed when she brought him coffee in bed next morning. He found it hard to believe that this serene, gentle woman had such a voracious passion in her. And he was proud that it was his secret.

Only in the early dawn had he finally fallen asleep. The times they had made love had merged in his memory into one extraordinary, unbroken sensation. He could still scarcely believe just how good it had been. He was bursting with gratitude and – he guessed – love for Thalia.

He sat up to drink his coffee, feeling as alive as if he had slept the night through. And he asked the question he had been wanting to ask since he had woken to find her gone from the bed. "When can we meet again?"

She smiled and touched his cheek. "Soon, I hope. But it's not often I get the house to myself. Thank goodness Teresa is a friend; the others would tell my parents."

"We don't have to meet here," Tony said, "I've thought of other places. And why are you dressed already?"

"I told you, the reason I stayed here on my own was because I was giving a lesson to the Colonel's wife. Mrs Cuthbertson will soon be here to pick me up and she mustn't see you here. You'll have to go so that Teresa can sort out Michael's clothes and change the bed."

"Haven't we got time to make love once more?"

Thalia laughed, "What? Eight hours? Don't be so greedy. Anyway, I don't want you to lose your appetite. Now, get out of bed. You've got to hurry."

Winter came. Thick snow lay on top of the Troodos Mountains and rain fell on the coast. A cold north wind weakened the winter sun when it appeared, while Tony and Thalia met and made love on empty sacks in the back of the truck. It would have made no difference where they were; and, each time, the pleasure they gave each other was even more intense than on the first, virginal occasion.

Thalia knew the risks of becoming pregnant; she was careful and subtle about timing their meetings. Teresa had told her when it was safest, though sometimes she didn't care anyway. If Tony thought about the possibility of pregnancy he didn't mention it to her. He reckoned she knew more about the risks than he.

As important as their love-making was the friendship that grew between them. They could talk with trust and openness to one another. Tony liked to tell her all his great plans and dreams. They talked about books they read, the future of Cyprus and the growing strength of the movement for unification with mainland Greece, ENOSIS, which neither wanted. But mostly, it was Tony's plans for their future that filled their conversation.

The passion which they brought to their meetings and their love-making was heightened and spiced by the danger of discovery.

"What would your father do?" Tony asked Thalia on one occasion.

"I don't even want to think about it," she answered. "He wouldn't give a thought to my happiness, I know. There are terrible things he's done which I'm utterly ashamed of; it's so hypocritical. Now that he's a big, respectable businessman he seems to have wiped all of them from his memory. Of course, he's never told me, but Teresa has overheard a lot over the years, when she's been serving dinner or bringing more wine. My uncles Chris and Spiros still don't understand why they can't behave the way they used to; at least my father keeps them under control most of the time. But really they're all as bad as each other."

"What does your mother think?"

Thalia shrugged. "She doesn't care, as long as the money comes rolling in. I guess she knows what a pig my father is, but she wouldn't fight him; she knows it would be a waste of time."

"What did *you* think when my father spat at your grandfather?"

"I told you, he was a horrible old man, so I felt nothing, but I remember so well turning to look and seeing you, behind your father, white with shame. I remember thinking then what sweet eyes you had."

"Thank God you're not like your parents," he said with a laugh as he reached across to stroke her cheek.

* * *

Thalia had become a good friend of Mrs Cuthbertson and spent a lot of time at the British base.

Mrs Cuthbertson's husband was second-in-command and, in Tony's estimation, an important man. He was surprised when Thalia told him how quiet and ordinary the major was, compared with his vivacious and good-looking wife.

Mrs Cuthbertson herself, having talked her husband into letting her join him on this posting, was making the most of getting to know the island.

"I'd love to take you up to meet them some time," Thalia told Tony, "but I daren't yet. I'm sure my father would find out."

Tony nodded. "Your father mustn't know about us until I'm ready; but business is good, and it's getting better, so it may not be too long."

In the spring, flowers began to blossom in the mountain valleys, and for a short while the coast became brilliant green and bright with orange blossom.

Tony drove down to Limassol in his truck, feeling bullish about the orders he would take from the traders and canners in town for his early small potatoes. He had been working hard over the past few months to persuade more farmers to sell to him. His persistence and the good name he was making for himself had brought him suppliers from all over the Paphos District. Now he was able to deal in quantities that interested the most important merchants in Limassol.

His confidence was rewarded. He took the biggest order he had ever received and, when the deal was concluded, he set off to meet Thalia.

They had arranged to meet by Limassol Castle and drive into the hills with a picnic. Tony arrived a few minutes early. He parked his truck within view of the coffee-shop that was their rendezvous and stretched his legs across the passenger seat. He had been up since dawn and, before he had time to stop himself, he fell asleep.

He woke with a lowered sun shining in his eyes, and looked at his watch in panic. It was two hours past the time they had arranged. He jumped down from the cab and looked around. Usually she sat at one of the outside tables of the small café opposite the castle, but there was no sign of her. He ran across and asked a waiter if she had been there or left word for him. The waiter shook his head and made a face which, for him, summed up the unreliability of women.

But Tony knew that no feminine whim would have prevented Thalia being there or leaving a message at the bar. In an instant his optimism turned to black dejection.

He ran back to his truck, gunned it into life and hurtled wildly round the square and off into the narrow streets hooting frantically at donkey-carts and slow-moving, black-clad women. But by the time he reached the Andreous' house he had regained his reason and rejected his plan to go in and confront Panos Andreou.

He drove a few yards past the house and parked. He would have to be patient. Only Panos Andreou could have stopped Thalia coming or sending a message, but Tony desperately wanted to talk to Teresa.

He clambered down from his lorry and crossed the street to the taverna opposite, where he and Takis had first watched the house. He tucked himself into a corner where he could still see the back entrance and waited.

Two hours later no one had come or gone from the house. Tony mentioned this to the jovial little proprietor of the bar.

"Sure," the proprietor said, "They've all gone away, this morning."

"The maid, Teresa, too?" Tony asked.

"I don't know. But if she's stayed, she will have gone to see her mother. She won't be back till later."

"I'll wait, then, to see."

"Are you her boyfriend?" the bar-keeper asked, doubt-fully.

"No. Just a friend."

Tony moved to a table outside and waited while the sky turned from gold to pink above the dome of the great basilica. Swallows and house-martins swooped and twittered back and forth from their small mud homes, clustered in a colony under the eaves of the Andreous' house. In the street below, a dusty, emaciated cat stalked a sparrow between piles of empty crates and rusty bicycles. Then, to pass the time, he played some games of *tavli* with one of the old men, but his heart wasn't in it and he didn't play with the flamboyant rapidity of his opponent. Nevertheless he took his time and had won most of the games until, abruptly and to the chagrin of the old man, who felt he was owed a chance to win his money back, he leaped to his feet and ran across the road. He had seen Teresa walking down the street. He caught her as she was about to let herself into the back gate.

She was startled for a moment. Her eyes flickered nervously at the dark-windowed house, and up and down the street.

"They mustn't see you," she said, almost in a whisper.

"But I thought they'd gone away."

"Yes," she nodded, "They have, but other people tell them things. They don't know it's you."

"What do you mean?" Tony asked urgently.

"They don't know it's you who has been seeing Thalia. It's a miracle, after six months, but she was very careful. They know she's been seeing someone, and they've taken her away."

"Where? Where have they taken her?" Tony demanded, unable to keep the anger from his voice.

"Don't shout at me. It's not my fault, and I don't know. They didn't tell me – I'm just the maid, and I didn't even have a chance to speak to Thalia. Poor little thing, she looked so miserable; her father was very angry."

"The bastard! I don't suppose you know when they'll be back, then?"

Teresa shook her head.

"Will you let me know if you hear anything?"

She nodded. "I'll send a message to you in your village. But you must keep out of sight. If Mr Andreou finds out his daughter has been seeing a Kyriakides, he'll go mad!"

Tony flushed hot and cold with frustration and fury. "How dare he look down on me! I promise you, whatever he does, I will have his daughter, sooner or later," he hissed. More softly he added, "I love her."

"I hope so," the maid said, "But be careful. You may have to be very patient."

Tony nodded. "I'll be patient."

And he was. He kept a lid on his desperate, angry passion like a pressure cooker.

His determination to make money and succeed was fired by his hatred for Thalia's father. He was prepared to chase every deal and work all night to deliver if he had to. He had a virtual contract to supply the garrison now as well as one of the factories that had been set up to process oranges into juice for export. This plant was in direct competition with one of Andreou's new factories, which gave him particular satisfaction. Though his brothers were not yet producing oranges, he had scoured the country around Paphos and found several willing suppliers who had promised not to tell Andreou's men who their buyer was.

The money was rolling in, at least in comparison to the living the family farm had previously provided, and Tony was now tacitly if not willingly accepted as the decision-maker in the family. He had his mother's full support, but only she would listen to his idea to set up a factory of their own one day.

She also sensed that, underlying her son's determination, something else was motivating him, and troubling him.

By now Nicos, like Stelios, was married and he had moved into a house in the village provided as a dowry by his new in-laws. Nicos tried to persuade Christina to move in with his family, so that Stelios with his family could move into the old farmhouse, but she had insisted on staying there, even though it was so isolated.

When Tony was not down in Paphos or Limassol, he was often alone with his mother in the evenings.

"Tony, you've got a girl down in Limassol, haven't you?" she said one evening after he returned from a three-day trip.

Tony didn't answer.

"You can tell me," she persisted, "I'm your mother. I understand, There's nothing to be ashamed of . . . Or is there? Who is she?"

"There was a girl," Tony said, "But she went away, three months ago."

"Went away? Where?"

"I don't know."

"So, it's finished with that girl, then?"

"It certainly isn't. Her father made her go, but I'll get her back."

Christina was alarmed by her son's vehemence.

"Why should her father make her go away? What did you do? Who is her father?"

Tony looked at her for a few moments, making up his mind before speaking. "Panyiotis Andreou."

Christina gasped, and stared at her son, not wanting to believe it.

"My God!" she whispered. "Are you mad? He'll never let you get away with it. He would sooner see you dead!" She leaned across the table and clutched his arm. "My Tony, why have you done this? Please don't let the Andreous take one of my sons as well as my husband."

Tony stood up. "They won't, but they won't keep their daughter from me either. Why do you think I work as hard as I do? To keep my brothers in comfort? I have to beat Andreou at his own game; and I will."

"You can't, Tony, ever. It can only end in misery."

A few days later Tony took a truckload of lemons into Limassol. He had Takis with him, as he often did these days. When he had finished supervising the unloading into the shipper's cavernous corrugated-iron warehouse, Takis tapped him on the shoulder.

"There's someone over there doesn't seem too pleased to see you." He nodded towards the office, where Pavlos, the shipper, and two other men with their backs to him were in deep conversation.

"Who is it?"

"I don't know," Takis shrugged, "but he was pointing you out to old Pavlos. You'll see in a minute."

At that moment, Panos Andreou turned around with his brother Christos.

Tony had not set eyes on Panos Andreou since old Spyros' funeral, but Andreou seemed hardly to have changed at all as he strode purposefully towards Tony's lorry.

Christos, who wore a badly cut brown suit, stayed where he was, reluctantly it seemed, because there was a scowl on his face. By contrast, Panos was crisply dressed in a lightweight, dark-blue suit, white shirt and maroon silk tie. The highly-polished toecaps of his black shoes flashed in the sun. His dark eyes were fixed on Tony's face as he reached him and stopped.

"What's your name?"

Tony caught a whiff of some expensive male scent and tried not to clear his throat before answering evenly, "Antonios Kyriakides."

Andreou winced, very slightly, as if he had been hoping he had been misinformed.

"That is a terrible pity," he said quietly.

Tony stared back at him, but didn't speak; he didn't want the other man to know that he could not.

"I hear you've been busy." Andreou's tone was conversational, "Trading with the garrison, selling oranges to my competitors." His voice was hardening. "Seeing my daughter!" He spat the last words out.

Tony blinked, and cursed himself.

"A Kyriakides! Of all people! And I was told that she had been seen with a good-looking, prosperous young fellow! Not a snivelling peasant whose chances of prosperity have just been killed." Without thinking, he drew a finger across his throat in the age-old gesture. "You won't be seeing my daughter again – ever!" he hissed.

Tony felt as if a vast pit had been dug beneath his feet and desperate, burning anger flared inside him. He wanted to lash out at the sneering face; he wanted to kill Panos Andreou for taking away everything he yearned for.

But he knew what he must not do.

He raised an eyebrow, with a slight lift of his shoulders and turned to Takis, grinning behind him.

"Get that tarpaulin into the back of the truck, Takis; we've got to get out of here; it smells worse than usual today."

Takis happily joined in the charade and, without looking back, he and Tony climbed into the cab, and drove slowly out of the warehouse yard.

Tony didn't speak for a few minutes as Takis headed for the Paphos road until Takis asked, "Did Pavlos give you the money?"

"Sure," Tony said. "While you were unloading. I wouldn't have gone without it."

"He wouldn't have given it to you, with Andreou there."

"Pavlos is a straight man."

"But you won't do any more business with him now, not with the Andreous leaning on him."

Tony knew he was right, and in fatalistic mood he said, "Drive to Polemidia. I want to see if he's tried to cut me out there."

Andreou's large black Humber passed them on the way out of Limassol, heading – Tony was sure – for the garrison.

When they arrived fifteen minutes later Captain Roberts was genuinely apologetic.

"I'm sorry," he said, "I've had word from the colonel that your profits go towards funding the Enotists."

"But . . ." Tony started to protest.

"I know it's not true," the captain interrupted. "But I have to obey orders. Andreou is a friend of the colonel's and powerful. I really am sorry; I've enjoyed doing business with you, and if circumstances ever change . . ." He shrugged his shoulders.

Tony didn't answer. He turned away to hide the despair he felt.

"*Endaxi*, it's okay, Captain Roberts. I understand," he said as clearly as he could, and walked back to his truck.

"Drive back into town," he ordered Takis.

At every customer he visited it was the same. Andreou's people had been there before him.

Stelios crowed. He seemed indifferent to the sudden reversal in their fortunes, but Christina was distraught. Nicos and Stelios didn't know about Thalia; Christina didn't refer to her until they had gone.

"I told you, Tony. Why did you let it happen? You were doing so well, working so hard and now you've thrown it all away."

"I had no choice," Tony said. "I wasn't going to stop seeing Thalia because I was frightened of her father, was I?"

"But maybe you only loved her because she was Andreou's daughter."

"Maybe, but I fell for her before I knew who she was. She's very beautiful, very kind." Tony thought of their love-making, and the unbelievable excitement of it. "I'm going back to Limassol to find her," he announced.

He went the next morning, despite his mother's pleading. "Tell Stelios to move in here with you, if you're worried," he told her as he left, feeling guilty.

In Limassol Tony made contact with Teresa. He believed her when she told him she still had no idea where Thalia was.

Word had got round many of Tony's regular haunts that he had fallen out with Andreou, and several other doors were closed to him. He pitied the spinelessness of those who, he knew, liked him but feared Andreou more.

To eke out the money he had brought with him Tony moved into a small guest-house. He had no source of income now, but he had no intention of asking anyone for a job, even if they had been prepared to take him on. He made a sort of living playing *tavli* with foreign seamen in the Sailors' Club by the port. He was careful not to win too much but had the advantage of knowing that few of his victims ever stayed for long.

During the day he hung around, sometimes near the Andreou house, in the vain hope that he might be there when Thalia eventually returned. He began to drink more and to get a reputation for being something of a wide boy. Respectable people, who previously had welcomed him, now avoided him.

He had left Stelios and Nicos to do the best they could with what they produced although they had neither the skills nor the knowledge to make the kind of deals he had done. He could have searched for new business further afield, in Larnaca or Famagusta or Nicosia. But Andreou would be on the look-out if he were to make any major contacts; and he couldn't motivate himself into trying until he had seen Thalia again.

He despised himself for his weakness and cursed his father who had put him in this position. He never lost hope of regaining Thalia or of eventually reviving his snuffed-out business career; but when that time came he knew he would have to look beyond the shores of Cyprus.

Occasionally he went back to his village where his neighbours were sympathetic. Stelios tried to lecture him for what he called his selfish foolishness. His mother, sensing Tony's state of mind, had more constructive ideas.

"You know my Uncle Neo from Larnaca? Maybe you don't remember him; he married my mother's youngest sister. He went to England after the war, when he left the Cyprus Regiment. He has started a business there, a restaurant, in London. He sends money back to his brothers every month to repay the loans they made when he left. He has made a great success. I could ask him if you could join him there. I'd miss you, but at least you'd be safe."

"For God's sake, Mamma, I'm safe here. Andreou's hidden his daughter from me; he's destroyed my business. He won't do more; he thinks he doesn't need to."

"But you are beaten, Tony. Don't you realise? You can never beat him. Please, go to England; start again. With your energy, your ideas, you can do well there, far better than you ever could do in Cyprus. You mustn't let these people destroy your life. And there will be other girls."

But Tony couldn't accept what she said. He went back to the coast and carried on his drinking and gambling, waiting and hoping. In his darkest moments he dreamed it was Thalia who had rejected him, that she had chosen not to see him again, and he searched and searched his memory for any signs she might ever have given to show she was rejecting him. He reinterpreted a hundred small gestures or remarks, and tore them apart to find signs of weakening interest. Sometimes, if he tried hard enough, he even found those signs and relapsed into misery without hope.

One night, four months after Andreou had confronted him, Tony had been playing *tavli* for five hours with an English sailor. The sailor knew what he was doing and had remained sober.

Unusually for Tony, the sailor was well ahead at the end of the session. "D'you want to go on, mate?" he asked.

Tony had lost his previous three weeks' winnings, and it showed in his gloomy face.

Tony shook his head. He knew he could not win again that night.

"I'll tell you what then, as I've cleaned you out, I'll pay for the women."

Tony's head jerked up. He was drunk; he had not touched a woman since he had last seen Thalia, but just then, he felt he would never see her again. With little reluctance, he let himself be led outside, past the harbour to the run-down part of town where the prostitutes waited above bars so seedy that, even in his current condition, he would usually avoid them.

The girl was a sad-looking Turk, driven by circumstances Tony did not want even to guess at to jettison the strict rules of Islam. Tony thought briefly of Fatima tending her goats on the hills above Vrecha, then pushed the image aside and made love to the girl bursting with lust and anguish. But the morning and sobriety brought him a shock of guilt. In disgust at himself he left the musty little room, with its stinking mattress and discarded condoms under the bed. He could not even look at the miserable girl to whom he had patently given no joy. He left the room in silence and fled down the stairs. His opponent of the previous night, and provider of the woman, was already sitting in the bar and called to Tony as he walked through.

"How was it, mate? She's a lovely little shag, that one."

Tony carried on to the door without answering. He wanted to be sick.

Outside, in the fresh morning air, he walked back to the centre of the town. He realised he had to bring his drifting to an end.

He wanted to find a friend of his who owned a prewar rattle-trap of a taxi. He tracked him down at his usual haunt behind the Continental Hotel. A quarter of an hour later he was at the gates of the army camp in Polemidia.

He asked a doubtful sentry for Captain Roberts.

The captain looked up as Tony was shown in to his office. "Good heavens, Tony, what have you been up to?"

"Andreou stopped me from dealing with everyone in Limassol, not just you."

"I heard," the captain said with genuine regret. "I am sorry. I must say, I thought you had gone back to the mountains."

"I came back," Tony replied. "There's someone I have to find. One of the officers' wives here may be able to help me. I wonder if you can tell me where I could find her – Mrs Cuthbertson?"

"Mrs Cuthbertson? Yes. She and Major Cuthbertson have one of the nasty little sheds that pass for married quarters on this camp." He stood up and came from behind his desk. "I'll take you to it."

The captain's friendly assistance came as a surprise to Tony, who had become accustomed to being shunned by most of his previous customers. It did a lot to restore his confidence.

Tony walked up the path to the front door. It was an

ugly, grey prefab, heavily disguised with flower-boxes and surrounded by a small patch of lovingly tended garden, bright with flowers and shrubs that could never have existed in the English garden it emulated.

He knocked on the door. It was opened by a woman in her late twenties, pretty in an uncontrived, unenhanced way. Her eyes and her whole manner showed an open kindliness.

"Hello?"

"Hello, Mrs Cuthbertson?"

"Mm," she nodded.

"I wanted to talk to you . . . about Thalia."

Her grey-blue eyes showed sudden comprehension and a moment's panic. She took a small, defensive step back before composing herself.

"You're a friend of Thalia's, then?"

"Yes. But I haven't seen her for some time. My name's Tony Kyriakides."

The woman tried to look as though this was new to her. "Oh. Well I haven't seen much of Thalia either. She's been away."

"Please," Tony was not ashamed to plead to this woman, "May I come in and talk to you? No one will tell me anything."

She weakened before the appeal in the young man's deep brown eyes, and opened the door wider while she threw an anxious glance over her shoulder. She showed Tony into a small sitting-room furnished in a way that was strange to him. It was cluttered with vases of roses, framed photographs of uniformed men in tidy ranks, a small gold carriage clock, chintz-covered chairs and sofas.

"Do sit down."

Tony sat in one of the chairs and she perched on the edge of the sofa opposite him. He wondered if she would offer him anything, but she didn't.

"You are the young man that Thalia . . . knew, a few months ago?" It was not really a question.

Tony nodded.

"What exactly did you want to know?" Mrs Cuthbertson asked.

"What's happened to her," Tony replied simply.

"Well, er, she was ill, not very seriously, but I think her parents thought she needed a rest, so she went to stay in Kyrenia with her mother's family for a bit. After that, my husband was due some home leave; we asked Mr Andreou if Thalia would like to come with us to England – she had been teaching me Greek, you know, and became quite a friend. She wanted to come, and her father agreed, so she spent three months in London with us. You must have guessed, her father wasn't any too keen on her seeing you. I don't know why," she went on hurriedly. "From what Thalia told me you were very kind to her, but her father has become an important man in Cyprus now and . . ." Her voice tailed off as she could not think of a suitable way to phrase her thoughts.

"He didn't want his daughter having anything to do with a peasant from the hills," Tony said for her.

"Well, yes, and I think there was something else as well."

"There was. It was something my father did; not me. I was ten years old at the time. That's when I first saw Thalia."

The woman shook her head. "You speak marvellous English; you're obviously educated. I don't know why Panos – Mr Andreou – should object to you so strongly, but there it is. You know what Greek fathers can be like." She gave a small laugh.

"Yes. I've suffered from my own," he replied with bitterness creeping into his voice. "Sometimes the attitude of my own people disgusts me. I am going to leave Cyprus and go to England. My mother has relations in London."

This news seemed to cause Mrs Cuthbertson some relief. "That might be a good idea."

She was on the point of expanding, perhaps enthusing on the plan, when a child cried in another room. It was a short, single bleat of a baby waking for a moment, but Mrs Cuthbertson leaped to her feet.

"Oh dear. You'll have to excuse me, the baby wants feeding."

Tony stood up with her. "If you see Thalia, could you tell her that I am desperate to see her?" he asked simply.

"I'll try," the woman said, truthfully, Tony thought. He controlled his urge to press her further; he realised he would achieve nothing more.

"Thank you very much," he said. "Tell her she can leave a message for me at the taxi office behind the Continental."

The message came two days later. Tony was to come to the Cuthbertsons' house the following morning.

The sentry on the gate let Tony through. Major Cuthbertson's wife had left instructions.

Tony's knees weakened as he approached the house for the second time. He straightened himself and knocked on the door.

Thalia saw Tony just as she had last seen him: clean-shaven, hair neatly cut, clothes freshly pressed and laundered. The only outward changes in him were a hint of doubt in his dark eyes and the slight bags under them.

She wanted to leap out and throw her arms around him, but she took a step back and shyly gestured him in.

When she had shut the door, she turned and raised a tentative hand to his cheek.

"Oh, Tony. I've missed you so much."

He could not speak at first. He put his arms around her and squeezed her, felt her stiffen, and relax.

"I'm sorry it had to be here," she whispered, "but this is the only place my father will let me come on my own. Mrs Cuthbertson has taken the baby for a walk. I'm afraid we only have one hour."

4

The tickets to London cost £28 each, but that was not enough to protect Tony and Thalia from the Melteme – the northerly wind that whipped down the Aegean and across the ship's open deck where they huddled.

Tony prayed that this first leg of their voyage would be the worst – five days and nights on the deck of a 10,000-ton, rusting carrier of oranges to Marseilles. Thalia, conscious of the new life inside her and with some misgivings, prayed she had made the right decision.

In the blackest, coldest moments, with two thick, expensive coats wrapped around her and a blanket over her legs where she lay beside Tony with a damp coiled rope for a pillow, she felt for his hand. Surely he was brave and clever enough to make a success of his life wherever they went, provided only that it was a long way from the vicious influence of her own family.

Tony understood the courage and the rashness of her decision to come with him.

He put his mouth close to her.

"In the morning the wind will be gone and the sun will shine. I promise this is the worst you'll ever have to endure."

She nodded; she wanted to believe him; to believe, certainly, that he believed it. He put his arms around her and she relaxed her shivering body into them.

She thought of her mother's puzzled eyes and her father's anger in the morning when they realised she had gone, and she shivered again. She would not miss his anger. Soon, despite the wind howling around her, she slept.

When she opened her eyes, the sun was creeping over a silver horizon, giving a sparkle to the sluggish wake of the shuddering ship. She stirred and stretched, and looked up into Tony's dark, steady eyes.

"You were right."

The wind had dropped; the seagulls that kept them company cruised effortlessly now, with no violent cross-wind to fight.

Thalia wriggled out of Tony' arms and the blanket. She stood and looked forward at the stars that still hung in the dark western sky. She took a deep breath. Yes, Tony had been right.

They breakfasted on bread, *fetta* cheese and oranges which Thalia had packed into a large basket with Teresa's help. The food would last only a day, then Tony would have to see what he could buy from the profiteering crew. But for now they ate sublimely in the crisp air of a September dawn.

Marseilles was like nothing Tony could have expected. He had read about it, and a dozen other bigger cities. But as the battered tub that had been their home for five days crept into the old port between the ancient lighthouse and centuries-old fortifications, he was intensely excited by the vast, vigorous metropolis which stretched up the coastal hills as far as he could see.

"Just look at this place! It's incredible – the size of it! And London must be twice as impressive."

"Don't get too excited about London," Thalia warned. "There's a strange, damp climate there – nothing like the Mediterranean."

"I don't care about that," Tony declared, "It's all the people and action – being at the centre of things that I'm looking forward to. Didn't you find that when you were there with the Cuthbertsons?"

"To tell the truth I spent most of my time in their apartment, and a week or so at a small house in the country. It was very nice, but I didn't have long enough to get used to it or see much."

"Well, you'll see plenty of it with me, I can tell you. I won't be sitting around inside all the time." He breathed in gulps of maritime air, tainted with the smells of oily ships and rotting fish, and watched the world spread out before him.

They had to spend a day in the busy markets between the port and the Gare St Charles. Beside this place Limassol was a village. Tony found it hard to believe the variety of goods on sale and the buccaneering panache with which they were offered. This, at last, was the real world. He was almost sad when their train chugged out of the city and rattled up the Rhône valley to Paris.

They scarcely noticed this most glamorous of capitals, so quickly did they race across it to catch the next train, over the featureless flat lands of northern France to the English ferry, and, at last – in depressing contrast to Marseilles – Victoria Station in the heart of London.

It was late afternoon when they arrived. London had not seen the sun all day, and cloud sat heavily over the city, trapping the fumes from a hundred thousand cars and a million coal fires in the tall, narrow streets.

Tony had known freezing nights in the Troodos mountains, but the damp air here seemed to seep right through his skin. The stern faces of the people, wrapped up and hurrying to get indoors, away from the fog, gave him no welcome.

He and Thalia stood outside the station with her handsome leather suitcase and his canvas sack, and peered through the swirling smog, hoping that Tony's Uncle Neo would see them and know who they were.

"This is a terrible place. Maybe we should have stayed in Marseilles."

Thalia smiled at him. "Well, I warned you and we're here now. Maybe it'll be sunny in the morning."

A few minutes later, the sun seemed to come out with Uncle Neo's smile. He saw them, glanced at the photograph he clutched, and held out his arms in greeting.

Tony had seen Neo at Spyros Andreou's funeral and once or twice after that but it was seven years since they met last. Then Neo had taken the chance to go to London with the returning troops; the British dared not refuse entry to the subjects of Crown Colonies who had stood by them so loyally.

Neo Michaelides wore a double-breasted blue serge suit, cut in the English way, but over-generously, making him look as wide as he was tall. A dark-red shirt set off a garishly Gauguinesque tie. But everything about the stout little man reassured Tony.

"Welcome to London, my handsome young nephew." He took both Tony's hands in his and squeezed them warmly. Tony returned the warmth, and introduced Thalia. Neo looked her over with obvious appreciation. After nine days of arduous travel she was still beautiful, and Neo knew all about the Andreous.

"You will find life very different here from Limassol," he said to her. "But we will try and make you as comfortable as we can." Gallantly, he leaned down to take her case and beckoned them to follow.

Parked in a street beside the station was a gleaming new Humber. Neo proudly ushered Thalia into the rear and Tony into the front passenger seat. He climbed in the driver's side and, with his headlights full on in the fog, pulled out to join the creeping traffic.

"This is what they call a pea-souper," he turned to tell his protégés. "They often come in autumn and winter, but," he shrugged, "you get used to them."

Tony thought he would never get used to them. He didn't want to get used to them.

"Uncle Neo, how can you stand it after Cyprus?"

"Listen, Tony. I can stand it because here I can make a living. D'you think I wanted to stay in Larnaca and take over my father-in-law's camels? No one will be needing them any more, now there are trucks and roads. How could we live off a small patch of salty land?" He beamed encouragingly at Tony. "It's not always this bad, and the English are quite good to us. There are so many of them, you can always find something to sell them."

"I was doing pretty well back home, selling vegetables to the British garrison and to the new canneries," Tony said, but he settled back in the leather seat of the Humber and acknowledged that this beat the old family truck which had been his pride and joy. "Did you buy this car out of profits from the restaurant?"

"I did," said Neo, "And that's after I have sent back money every month to my family."

After what seemed an impossibly long journey through miles of fog-choked streets and a city that never ended, Neo drew up outside a tidy, detached house in the North London suburb of Wood Green.

"This is my home," he announced. "You both stay here for a few days with me, then Tony can move into the flat over the restaurant. Thalia can live here until you are married."

He did not seek their approval for these arrangements. There was no question of any other.

Thalia glanced at Tony. Neo will get a shock when the baby arrives, her eyes said.

Neo clambered out of his seat and bustled through a small wrought-iron front gate, shouting as he went, "Paul! Fanis! Your cousin Tony is here. Come and help with the luggage." He turned to Thalia and Tony who had climbed out of the car behind him. "Welcome to my house. Don't worry about your cases; my boys will look after them." He pulled a bunch of two dozen keys from his trouser pockets and inserted one in the front door. He ushered them through with ceremony, leaving the door open for the fog to creep in, while he shouted again.

"Maria, Maria. Come here to welcome Tony and Miss Andreou."

A woman who matched Neo contour for contour, though shorter, came through a door from the back of the house, wiping her chubby hands on her apron. She held them out to greet Tony and then almost bowed to Thalia.

"Did you have a terrible journey? Neo, close the door."

"No. The boys are coming out to get the luggage."

"Isn't this fog terrible? The boys aren't here, Neo."

"Where the hell are they?"

"I'll shut the door," Maria said with a lift of her eyebrows, "They are still at school, to take the exams for the law. They told you," she said to her husband. Then to her guests, "My boys, Paul and Fanis, are to be lawyers. They got very good exams from the grammar school, and now they will go to the solicitor's office to learn the law."

Neo was less impressed. "That's all very well, but they are never here when we need them."

"Don't be silly, Neo. You get the cases in. Now, you two must eat. We'll have a little something now, then we all go down to the restaurant for dinner."

Tony and Thalia had not tried to join in the conversation. Now they smiled their gratitude. They were ravenous. Maria led them into the front parlour where plates of cakes and *baklava* covered a small table. Neo went out to collect Thalia's case and Tony's sack and returned, red-faced and gasping for breath from the effort. Maria carried in a tray of coffee cups and a small pan of the thick black coffee which Thalia and Tony were used to.

They sat around a low table. Maria drank in the beautiful young woman opposite her, glancing more than once at her as yet unrevealing stomach.

Dinner at the restaurant was wonderful. The *klephtiko* was a leg of lamb of a tenderness and flavour seldom found in Cyprus. This was served after a vast *mezé* of all the foods which Tony loved best. Neo, clad in an old dinner-jacket and a small, slightly greasy bow-tie, constantly refilled their glasses from a large carafe of good quality Retsina.

The restaurant, the Olympus, was lit with dozens of candles, guttering down empty wine bottles. The walls were hung with prints of the Acropolis and scenes from classical Greek history. The place was busy with English people, laughing and shouting in a way Tony had never heard them in Cyprus. For most of the time Maria was in the kitchen with two young Turkish helpers. A wild-eyed young Cypriot called Costas backed up Neo as a waiter.

Neo's boys, Paul and Fanis, were eighteen and nineteen. They sat at the table with Tony and Thalia, speaking for the most part in fast, vernacular English. Because they arrived in England at the same time they had, despite the year between them, entered the education system at the same level and learned side by side ever since. When Neo was at the table, giving Tony and Thalia advice about life in England, they disagreed with most of what he said. Neo tried to dismiss their interruptions, while his eyes ceaselessly darted about the restaurant to check that all the customers were being looked after. Every few minutes he leaped up and scuttled over to a table, usually to be greeted with friendly familiarity by his regular clients. From time to time a gale of laughter would erupt from a table he was attending, as he told a joke or a story in his idiosyncratic broken English.

Tony talked to his cousins, but found that they considered the views of a mountain peasant of little importance. Though a few years younger, they preached patronisingly at him, while they shyly ogled Thalia. They talked to one another in English, but pointedly reverted to Greek with Tony and Thalia.

"Dad says that you're going to help here," Paul, the elder of the two said to Tony.

"Yes, until we've settled down."

"What are you going to do then?" Fanis asked.

"Trading. I was trading in Cyprus."

Neo's sons were not impressed. "I think you'll find it harder here, especially if you don't speak English. Dad can't even speak it properly after all this time."

Tony and Thalia looked at each other.

"I expect we'll learn," Tony said quietly.

"Anyway, Dad can do with the help. Costas is robbing him, I'm sure. At least you're a relation."

But whereas the boys were discouraging, almost hostile, Neo and Maria were delighted to see the two young refugees. When Neo rejoined them at the table, Tony asked him all about the restaurant, where he got his supplies of Greek foods, and his wines and where his customers came from.

"All types I have at my restaurant – mostly English," Neo said proudly. "Some lords and judges, businessmen and students. They love Maria's cooking, and it's cheap. People in England don't have so much money now. Sometimes we have a bazuki player here and they sing and dance. We are always busy. You will love it, working here."

"What about Costas?" Tony asked.

Neo shrugged. "We'll see. He is not a good boy, but his

father is an old friend from Larnaca. I promise him work for one year more."

"You should get rid of him now, Dad," said Paul, "I bet he's stealing from you."

Neo's dark eyes blazed above his podgy cheeks. "Listen, son, you may think you are so clever, with all your exams, but don't you ever tell me how to run my business. When it's yours, you can do what you like with it, but not till then."

"What makes you think I want this place?" his son retorted.

"You may be smart, but you are an ungrateful little dog. How the hell do you think we paid for our home, and all the good clothes you need for your grammar school, and all the extra lessons you had when were younger? Not because I have passed any exams; no, because I work hard and I look after my customers. I suppose you think you are too grand for that."

Cowed for the moment, Paul relapsed into surly silence, but Fanis answered for them.

"I can tell you this, Dad, I won't have my wife slaving away in a stinking hot kitchen night after night."

Tony glanced at Neo and saw tiny tears of rage and frustration seep from the corners of his eyes.

Thalia had been given the guest room at the Michaelides' house, while Paul and Fanis had to share to give up a room for Tony until the rooms above the restaurant were ready.

Tony sank gratefully into a bed made with fresh white cotton sheets. He had been in London barely eight hours, but already he felt he was beginning to know something of it, thanks mainly to Neo and Maria. He had never felt such gratitude as he did now for the delight with which they welcomed him and Thalia. Paul and Fanis he had marked as rivals, but unassailable for the moment; he was not going to lose any sleep or patience over them.

He did not see Thalia until after breakfast. She had slept solidly for ten hours, and looked sensational in a simple dress that was no less fashionable in London than it might have been in Nicosia. Tony left her with Maria, and drove down to the restaurant with Neo.

The fog had lifted in the night. The transformation was extraordinary. The sun shone at an angle which was strange to Tony at this time of day, and the blue of the sky was pale and insipid compared with Cyprus, but it was a clear September day and the leaves were still on the trees that lined the streets and filled the parks. Tony saw Neo's bow-fronted, tile-hung 1920s villa in a quite different light from the day before.

As they drove through the busy streets he felt more at home for seeing a few Cypriot names on the shop fronts. As they left Wood Green and headed down broad roads towards the centre, Neo gave a continuous commentary: Lord's cricket ground, Regent's Park, the Zoo, London University, the British Museum, until they reached the Olympus, a hundred yards from the Museum in Coptic Street.

It was in a terrace of late eighteenth-century buildings, with two or three storeys above each shop. In the terrace opposite was a large gap, as if a tooth had been removed ten years before by the Luftwaffe. On both sides of the street the buildings were dusty and unpainted, but there was a raffish colourfulness to the displays in the bookshops and picture galleries which dominated the street. Over the Olympus was a crudely painted sign, depicting a conical mountain surrounded by bunches of grapes. The name was written in a stylised Hellenic script. Beneath the large window which overlooked the street was a long box of tired geraniums and vigorous weeds.

Inside, the front part of the ground floor was the

eating area. Along one wall ran a bench seat with a back upholstered in well-worn brown oil-cloth. Otherwise the seating at the dozen or so tables was provided by a miscellaneous collection of bent-wood chairs. At the most the restaurant could seat fifty people.

"Sometimes we are full at lunch," Neo said, "But in the evenings some people come early, and we might do two or three sittings, maybe a hundred and twenty dinners, at ten or fifteen shillings each. That makes eighty or ninety pounds."

Tony was amazed. "That's five hundred pounds a week!"

Neo smiled, "And with lunches too, sometimes we take six or seven hundred."

"No wonder you have a new car and a big house." Tony was more impressed than he had wanted to show. He was beginning to understand why so many people had left Cyprus for this cold, foggy land of plenty.

Neo showed Tony all over the building, starting with the musty cellars, where the wines and tinned foods were stored.

"This street is built over an underground river and when I first came here the rats used to run through, all the time, thousands of them. The council rat-catcher came dozens of times, but the rats still came back. So I stopped every single hole myself," Neo said with pride, "And I still check every week. I haven't seen or heard one now for six years but I still daren't put the kitchen down here in case they found a way in. If I did, I could get thirty more customers in the restaurant."

He led Tony back up to the ground floor and the kitchens at the back. They were equipped with an old but spotless gas range of a dozen rings. Gleaming pots and pans were stacked on the shelves and hung from the ceiling. The floor was covered in white tiles. "Maria insisted on white," Neo said, "So that she could always be sure it is clean. Some restaurants around here are so filthy that even the rats won't eat in them; and the customers know that. I can invite mine in here."

This meant very little to Tony, but he absorbed and stored away in his mind everything his uncle was saying.

Neo showed Tony the lavatories, one for men and one for women, each with wash-basin, fresh towels and soap. "The English like clean lavatories," he said.

On the first floor were two rooms full of ingredients with a long shelf-life – rice, jars of olives, flour, tinned tomatoes, bottled chillis and aubergines – everything neatly stacked on shelves labelled in a coarse Greek hand.

"Now, I show you your rooms." Neo led Tony up the narrow, bare stairs to the second floor. There were two more rooms, like the store rooms, on either side of a small, windowless landing. The front room, which overlooked Coptic Street, was large – thirty feet by twenty – and light, with a pair of deep sash windows and a big open fireplace. The dampness of non-occupation had partly peeled the wallpaper which had been applied thirty years before. The elaborate cornice that had once decorated the tops of the walls was crumbling and parts of the ceiling were falling away to reveal rotting lathes. "You will have to do a bit of work, but this is a nice room, maybe for your living-room. You can put a small kitchen in the corner, but mostly you eat in the restaurant."

They crossed the landing to the back room. This was not as large, but a good size even so. Its one window looked down into a dark gully of back-yards and outhouses of the adjoining buildings and the street that backed on to them. It was in a worse state than the front room. Neo waved his hands apologetically. "It's not too good, but you can make a bedroom here, no?"

Tony nodded. "I'll make something of it." For himself, it was no worse than he was used to, and he still had a vivid picture in his mind of the elegantly decorated room where he and Thalia had first made love. "But I don't want Thalia to see these rooms until I've done them."

"You're right. She is a beautiful young woman; she must have a beautiful home," Neo said, a little doubtfully.

An hour later, the two Turkish helpers arrived, followed shortly by Maria and Thalia. Maria and the Turks began preparing for lunch, while Tony tried to pass on to Thalia something of what he had already learned from Neo. He also told her that she couldn't see their new home until he had made it ready for them.

"But please, don't take too long," she whispered when they were alone for a few minutes.

5

The Greek Orthodox Church of St Ambrose sat incongruously between an early Georgian terrace and a Victorian red-brick block of flats.

Inside, though, it was not very different from the basilica in Paphos where Tony's father had desecrated the corpse of Spyros Andreou.

The chandeliers, the dull-red glow of the sanctuary lamps, the gleaming icons and statues, even the smell of the place took him back to that terrible moment. But now a tall, bearded priest was listening to his request, nodding patiently, agreeing that Tony and Thalia could be wed in his church two weeks from then.

Tony would rather have waited, but Thalia, despite the distance and the silence from her family, didn't want the gap between their marriage and the birth of their child to be any shorter than necessary.

They had been in England for two months. Tony was working ten hours a day in the restaurant, and another three or four in the two rooms which were to be their home. He still refused, though, to allow Thalia into the flat until it was ready and they were married.

Neo had helped by calling in two builders to do some of the major repairs, with the cost being deducted from Tony's weekly wage of £4 10s. From the money Tony was earning in tips he bought a bath and had it installed in an extra room he created from part of the landing.

A regular customer Tony had come to know well owned a small firm of electrical contractors. He arranged for the flat to be re-wired on friendly, deferred terms.

Tony chose the decorations and installed them himself. It was a job which, to begin with, was new to him, but he went to the trouble of going into the big furniture stores in Tottenham Court Road and looking at the displays and designs that they suggested.

He would spend a few evenings each week with Thalia – sometimes, on his evening off, seeing her in the Michaelides' house when Neo and Maria were working and his cousins were out. Occasionally, as a treat, they went to the cinema in Wood Green and for a drink afterwards in a busy, barn-like pub. Despite the traumas of the preceding months, Thalia felt well in her pregnancy and they both longed for the fleeting chances to make love.

When Tony announced that the flat was ready, she was overwhelmed, and relieved at how happy she felt now they could get married.

Maria asked two Greek seamstresses to make an elaborate traditional Cypriot wedding dress, which she gave to Thalia as a present. Tony bought a new dark suit from a Cypriot tailor, his first since arriving in England.

The wedding ceremony itself was a small, solemn affair, with no one besides the Michaelides and a few new friends to attend it. By the time the priest gave his final blessing, though, Tony and Thalia felt happily, irrevocably married. But the real celebration came afterwards.

On the day of the wedding Neo shut the restaurant. He gave a wedding supper for Tony and Thalia to which he invited every Greek he knew with the most tenuous connection to their family or business. Tony invited some of the restaurant's English customers whom he knew and liked; nearly all accepted.

Neo had booked three musicians to play and sing for as long as anyone was sober enough to listen; and Thalia made no objection to the old peasant tradition of guests pinning money to her wedding dress as she and Tony danced around the floor of the restaurant to the music of pipe and bazukis.

Neo beamed benevolently and kept sending Costas running for more and more wine as the wedding party turned into a full-scale revel. Even Paul and Fanis were warm in their enthusiasm. Each pinned a bundle of pound notes on to the dancing bride.

At midnight, the wedding-guests cheered as Tony lifted Thalia from her feet in her wedding dress, now covered from neck to hem in British currency, and carried her out of the restaurant, up the two flights of narrow stairs to their new home.

Tony had remained firm in not allowing Thalia to see the flat until that night, so she had little idea of the tremendous effort it had cost him. But as he carried her into the front room, he had the satisfaction of seeing that it was a lot finer than she had expected.

He had contrived to build a small kitchen into the corner of the room without it intruding on the air of quiet elegance he had achieved with Georgian-striped wallpaper and brocade curtains. He had also acquired a good mahogany dining-table, as well as a sofa and chairs, reclaimed and re-upholstered at bargain prices by helpful friends.

Maria had filled both rooms with flowers, and on the table were a bottle of champagne and glasses, presents from the two Turkish cooks.

Tony carried Thalia to the sofa. Smiling proudly, he opened the champagne and poured two glasses for them. He sat down beside her and kissed her.

"It's not a palace; it's not as good as you're used to, but I promise you, one day we will have a palace." He placed a hand on her slightly bulging stomach. "We'll need a lot more room for all our children."

Thalia touched his face with light fingers. "It's beautiful,

and it's ours, Tony." She laughed. "When you think of the
way we got here, this *is* a palace."

"You're still not regretting that you walked out on your
family?"

"I miss my mother a little, and Ari, and Teresa sometimes, but otherwise I don't regret it at all. Maria and Neo
have been so kind, and all the people I meet."

"That's because you're a beautiful woman."

Thalia smiled. She felt very beautiful that night.

"Look what they've all given us," she gestured at the
coating of notes on her dress. "They've been so generous.
How much do you think there is?"

Tony laughed, "What a dress! Let me take you out of it;
we can count the money in the morning. We've got more
important things to do now."

By now Tony had become indispensable to his Uncle
Neo. At the end of his second month there was nothing
in the running of the restaurant that he could not handle,
apart from the cooking which Maria oversaw. Using the
bargaining skills he had learned when he first started to buy
his neighbours' produce in the mountain valleys, he was
able to improve on the prices and terms of payment from
some of their main suppliers. This gave him confidence
to persuade Neo that there were dishes on their menu
which could carry a higher price with no risk of losing
business. The profitability of the place began noticeably
to increase.

At the same time, Neo's weight was beginning to tell,
and his stertorous breathing to become more pronounced.
The fact that he could now take days and evenings
off without worrying about what was happening at the
Olympus tended to encourage these ailments.

Tony threw himself into his job wholeheartedly and Neo
rewarded him fairly. In the new year of 1953 his wages
were doubled and, as he spent more time than his uncle

on the floor of the restaurant, his share of the tips almost doubled again.

He paid no rent for his flat and he and Thalia ate free. He had easily shed the drinking and gambling habits he had acquired in Limassol in the grey days when he thought he had lost Thalia; now he was content to live frugally, and to save every penny he could.

But he made a point of taking Thalia out once a week to a film, or even occasionally to a play, and then to the restaurant of some friendly rival – Greek, Italian, French or English; more often than not they would be treated to their dinner.

When Thalia had asked him if she could enrol on an inexpensive course to perfect her English, he gladly agreed. In return, despite her pregnancy, she was willing to spend most evenings in the restaurant with him. She became known and liked by their regular customers. Sometimes she would help out in the kitchens, particularly if Maria and Neo were having an evening off together.

Tony, though well aware of his own skills and qualities, was continually grateful for his luck in having a wife from a rich and powerful family who was prepared to tolerate this existence. He took it as a sign of her faith in his ability, and this strengthened his already healthy ambition to rise to better things. For her part Thalia was happy simply to be in a warm home with the man she adored and with his baby in her womb.

George Kyriakides was born above the restaurant on the day after Queen Elizabeth II was crowned.

Tony liked to joke that all the bunting in the streets and windows was to celebrate their event and added a Greek flag to the display in the window of the Olympus.

George was a big, strong baby. Tony was impatient to show him off to the others in the Olympus, but his initial joy was short-lived. Thalia had suffered great pain and

111

loss of blood. The large baby in her small frame had caused havoc inside her. Tony wept after the doctor had been the next day when she was carried, pale-faced and wet-eyed, on a stretcher to an ambulance below and then to the Middlesex Hospital.

After an emotional discussion, it was decided that the baby George would go to the Michaelides' house in Wood Green, to be looked after by Maria until Thalia could return.

Tony carried on working relentlessly, dashing when he could between the hospital to see his wife, and to North London to see his son, with his mind in a storm of anxiety and indignation that fate should treat them like this.

Neo was sympathetic. He told Tony not to work, but Tony insisted; it was the only way to stop himself going mad with worry. Also, with Maria at home looking after George, Neo needed Tony's help. For a month the doctors in the hospital could not tell when Thalia would recover. Only the joy of seeing George grow a little each day kept Tony from despair.

At last Thalia was out of danger but she was still weak and her fight for full recovery seemed to have barely perceptible results. But one day Tony arrived after lunch with a bouquet of spring flowers to find Thalia sitting up in bed with a smile on her face for the first time since she had been carried there. He ran down the ward and flung his arms around her.

"Can you leave? Are you better? Thank God!"

"Don't be so hasty, Tony. They say I might be home in a week."

"That's wonderful!" Tony crowed with excitement.

"But," Thalia put a hand on his arm, "I won't ever be able to have a baby again."

Tony stared at her as the words sank in. Then he forced a smile. "It doesn't matter; it doesn't matter at all. I'll have you back, and we have George."

"How is little George? I can't wait to see him!"

"Thalia, he is beautiful. You have produced the most handsome boy in England *and* Cyprus."

Thalia's homecoming was almost as much of a celebration as the wedding had been six months before. The restaurant was crowded that night with well-wishers, but when they had all gone the small family went upstairs exhausted to their rooms.

George's cot had been prepared by Maria and was now in their bedroom. Once again the flat was full of flowers. When Thalia had changed the baby and settled him to sleep, she and Tony were together in peace and privacy for the first time in five weeks.

But Thalia was still weak. Tony did everything to make her comfortable; and he had vowed to himself, despite his bitter disappointment, never to mention her inability to give birth again.

When Thalia was certain that Tony wouldn't be angry, she told him something else she had been dreading to mention. "My mother is coming to visit us. She wants to see George, and me."

Tony was silent for a moment. He struggled with his raw sensitivity and short temper. When they first arrived in London he made Thalia promise not to contact her family, not until they could go back to Cyprus in triumph and look the Andreous straight in the eye. He knew that Thalia was not being disloyal to him in wanting to see her mother, but he couldn't stop himself feeling that she was.

"How does she know about it? Or where you are?"

"Because I wrote to her, of course. You were wonderful to me in the hospital, you couldn't have done more. But I had to tell my mother; surely you can see that? It truly doesn't mean she's more important to me than you are, but she means something else to me. I asked her never to tell my father where we are; and I know she won't. She'll tell him she's coming to

England to visit old friends and to do some shopping. He'll believe that."

"I bet he will," Tony said with a smile. They had often laughed about her mother's extravagance which was so alien to Tony's upbringing. "But she won't think much of her daughter living over a restaurant, married to a waiter."

"Tony, my angel, I have nothing to be ashamed of in you. She'll see for herself how much you've done for me."

Tony brooded for a moment, but accepted Thalia's wish to show her baby to her mother.

"I wrote to my mother too," he admitted. "Of course, she can't afford to come but she did send a little gift for George." He went and rummaged in a cupboard, then pulled out a brown paper parcel and unwrapped a tiny cardigan, hand-knitted in the natural colours of Cyprus sheep. "Unfortunately, it's too small for him."

"Oh, Tony. It's very beautiful. What a shame; it must have taken her weeks to make."

Tony nodded. "I guess it did, but I wrote back to thank her, and I didn't say it didn't fit."

"Did she sound pleased in her letter?" Thalia asked.

"What do you think? She's thrilled; you'd think she was used by now to being a grandmother. Stelios has three and Nicos two."

Thalia's eyes clouded. "How are they?"

"Struggling, I think, but when the orange trees start to yield things should improve, provided that oaf Stelios doesn't plough them up."

"You must miss them, Tony? Won't you want to go back and see them some time?"

"No," he answered firmly. "I miss my mother and Nico, but I won't go to Cyprus until I'm a bigger man than your father; and that's a promise."

* * *

114

Mrs Andreou had already indulged herself in one shopping expedition to Bond Street before she turned up at the Olympus the following week. She swept into the small restaurant, failing to hide her disdain. Good-looking, and still voluptuous even in her mid-forties, she looked as though she had chosen her clothes from the pages of that month's *Vogue*. Her scent preceded her and subtly put the lingering lunchtime smells to flight. Tony greeted her with awkward, ill-received politeness. He showed her up to the flat while Thalia was still in the bedroom with George waiting noisily to be fed.

Mrs Andreou sat and looked around their comfortable and tidy living-room with some approval. "I must say," she said candidly, "you don't look at all like the peasant boy that my husband described. What exactly are you doing in the restaurant?"

"I'm managing it for my Uncle Neo," Tony said, almost truthfully.

"Is it a success? It doesn't seem to be in a good part of London."

"It's quite a popular restaurant now. The Museum and the University are near by. They bring a lot of customers, and many come back to us from other parts of London."

"And what do you stand to gain by working here, in the end?"

"I plan to open restaurants of my own, dozens of them, all over London, all over England."

Mrs Andreou did not express her doubts. It was – she thought – just possible that this good-looking young man, with his serious eyes but charming smile had what it took. There was nothing to be gained by discouraging him. "My daughter was brought up to very high standards. I would hate her to lose them for ever."

Tony glared at her fierily. "Mrs Andreou, I promise you your daughter will become used to far higher standards here than she ever knew in Cyprus."

"Well, that would be nice. Now, you must tell her I'm here, and let me see my grandson."

Tony crossed the landing to the bedroom and went in to be met by a wail of frustration as Thalia removed an empty bottle from the baby's mouth.

"Your mother's here," he said.

"Where?" Thalia asked with excitement.

"In the living-room."

"That's wonderful. Here, you take George and give him this other bottle." She thrust the baby at his father and rushed out of the room.

Tony calmed himself. He sat down on the bed and thrust the fresh teat into his son's mouth. The little boy sucked with single-minded greed while Tony listened to snatches of the conversation between his wife and mother-in-law through the half-open doors. A smile spread across his face as he heard Thalia indignantly defend him as her mother castigated her for eloping with him.

"Tony will do very well, you'll see," Thalia said. "And anyway, wasn't it obvious I was pregnant when I left? And I couldn't . . ." She began to cry. Tony didn't hear what she mumbled, and the door was closed. Tony put George down to sleep and went down to the restaurant.

Mrs Andreou left after an hour without seeing her son-in-law again. He heard Thalia show her to the top of the stairs and say goodbye with no great display of affection. He ducked into the first-floor store-room until his mother-in-law had gone down, then ran up to find Thalia in the bedroom.

"I wish she hadn't come," Thalia burst out as she flopped down on the bed. Tony stroked her long black hair.

"It was better you see her as she really is, and not as the fantasy mother you remember. You always used to say she was a cold and selfish woman."

"She had to be, to stay married to someone like my father. But no one I know has a mother like that, not in

116

Cyprus. She was just trying to criticise me, and put you down."

"She's had to listen to your father for years. After all, he thinks he has a lot of reasons for loathing me – or at least my family."

"One day, Tony, one day, you must *show* them. My mother said that my uncles Spiros and Christos went mad when they realised I'd gone off with you. They wanted to come after us, but my father stopped them. I made Mamma promise she wouldn't ever tell anyone where we were, though."

"I hope she keeps her promise," Tony growled. His dark eyes peered steadily at her. "And don't you worry, I will show them. Never doubt it."

Over the next few months Tony lived in private dread that Mrs Andreou would tell her husband where he and Thalia were living. But as time passed he began to believe she may have kept her word. He also knew, although Thalia apparently did not, that Mrs Andreou had by no means completely disapproved of him. But he did not tell her that. Now she was his, and his alone.

Britain was at last pulling itself out of the long post-war gloom of rationing and hardship. Young businesses were budding, and old businesses beginning to find that there were profits to be made once more. The City of London was still the centre of the financial world, and the rump of Empire continued to provide markets and raw materials to which British ingenuity could add value. There was money around in a way there had not been for twenty-five years, and it was more widely spread. Going out to eat became less of a special event and over the next two years the Olympus benefited from this as much as any restaurant in the West End.

Tony had become *de facto* manager of the restaurant, in all but name. His cousins Paul and Fanis were aware of this. From time to time they would come in, ostensibly to have dinner with young English friends from the legal practices to which they were articled, but really to make sure that Tony was not getting above himself. Tony simply treated them like any good customer. But not far from his thoughts was what would happen if Neo's health failed completely. He had judged it unwise to ask Neo; but he trusted his uncle's judgement.

In the meantime Tony was making most of the decisions in the Olympus. With Neo's reluctant agreement he sacked Costas when he found him clumsily making out his own bills for customers and pocketing the money. He replaced him with the son of the man who supplied Greek cheese to the restaurant; and this helped to keep down the cost of some of the most popular dishes on their menu.

To allow Maria more time at home with Neo, Tony took on a hard-working young chef, fresh from Nicosia. The increase in profits and turnover easily absorbed the extra expense. Thalia was glad to oversee the chef and occasionally make suggestions. In recognition of the effort he was putting in, and the increasing profit he generated, Neo offered Tony a percentage of the turnover as his salary. Tony declined. Turnover was not what mattered, he said. Quoting a customer from one of the nearby ready-to-wear fashion houses, he remarked, "Turnover is vanity; profit is sanity." Neo agreed to give him a percentage of the profits.

Now, after being in England two and a half years, at the age of twenty-five, he was earning nearly £1000 a year; and he began to discuss with Thalia buying another flat, one large enough for them and their growing son.

It was George's second birthday. Thalia and Tony planned a small tea-party at the restaurant in the afternoon. They said goodbye to the last customer after a busy lunch-time session, and sat down to a quick cup of coffee before getting things ready.

"I got details of flats from the estate agents this morning," Thalia said. "There's a beautiful one in Russell Square. It sounds just what we want."

"They always sound better than they look," Tony warned.

"Do you really think we can afford to move out and buy a bigger place now?"

"Yes. I've saved quite a bit; Neo's been very fair about my share of the profits and," he smiled, "we seem to get busier every week."

"Why is it that the English like coming here so much?"

"They haven't got much choice if they don't want to spend a lot of money. There's no such thing as a good, cheap English restaurant, only workmen's cafés. The French places are expensive. Now that people are going out more, there's a gap in the market for us and the Italians."

"It's a shame we don't see so many of the Cypriot families here now. I feel guilty that we don't make enough effort to keep in touch with them."

"We see Neo and Maria and the boys. That's enough for me. I didn't come to England to pretend I was still in Cyprus. Anyway, all they do is gossip about each other's businesses. Don't tell me you want to move into the Greek ghetto?"

"No, not at all. I like the English, and you're right, we've decided to make our home here, so we should enter into English life. Actually Mrs Sherwood has asked me if I'd like to help her with fund-raising for a new charity for the homeless, and I said I would. It makes me so sad to see those old men and women wandering the streets, living under the bridges and on bomb-sites. Sometimes you even see young mothers with children too. It's terrible. We never saw anything like that in Cyprus."

"How are you going to find time to do that, with all that we have to do here?" Tony asked testily.

"Don't worry. Mrs Sherwood said it wouldn't take up a lot of time. I'll make sure it won't interfere. We've been very lucky since we came to England and I just feel I should give something back."

"Lucky! It isn't a question of luck; it's been my bloody hard work. But do your charity work if you must." Privately Tony liked the idea of his wife mixing with the wives of English professional men, especially if they were good customers. And Edward Sherwood was a successful young lawyer who ate at the Olympus at least once a week with his wife and their friends.

"Thank you Tony, but I don't need your permission."

Tony noted his wife's uncharacteristic display of independence, but he didn't remark on it. "Right now, you'd better go and check on George. I'll get things ready for the tea-party."

Thalia went up to their flat and Tony started to arrange a table in the middle of the room, when there was a knock on the locked door of the restaurant. Impatiently he went to see who it was.

Two men stood outside. Tony didn't know them. They both wore narrow-brimmed grey trilbies and fawn macintoshes, despite the mildness of the spring day.

"Good afternoon, sir," one of them said, "We are LCC health inspectors." Both men produced identification cards. "We have the right, under the Public Health Act, to inspect your restaurant and its kitchens without notice. So, if you wouldn't mind letting us in and showing us over your premises?"

Tony didn't answer. He shrugged and opened the door wider to let them in; he was becoming accustomed to British bureaucracy. Inside he waved his arm around the room. "Help yourself. Mr Michaelides, the proprietor, is very fussy about hygiene; you won't find anything wrong here."

"And who are you?"

"My name is Kyriakides. I'm Mr Michaelides' nephew and the manager of the restaurant."

"You seem very young to be a manager," said the younger of the two, as if this were cause for suspicion.

"Maybe, but I have things to do, so don't let me stop you doing your job," Tony offered with exaggerated politeness, before turning pointedly back to the job of moving the tables.

The two men headed for the kitchens and, with an easy conscience, Tony listened to them clattering about. After a couple of minutes they emerged from the kitchen in what they contrived to make a solemn procession.

The leader held his hand forward, palm up with a piece of brown paper on it. He walked towards Tony with the expression of an outraged schoolmaster.

"I'm sorry to have to tell you we've found these," he said and thrust his hand at Tony.

On the paper were two small, black, oval objects. Tony took a moment to register what they were, then he froze; the blood drained from his face.

He was looking at rat droppings.

"Were you aware that you had an infestation of rats here, sir?" the inspector asked sarcastically.

Tony took a hold on himself. "No, I was not aware," he answered quickly. "We've always been very careful about it. There hasn't been a rat in those kitchens for ten years. I can't understand how they have appeared now without us noticing."

"They aren't hard to notice, sir. The brown rats in London are very large," the second man said cynically.

Tony wanted to hit the smug little man.

"I don't think those droppings came from our kitchens," he said.

121

"Are you suggesting that we go around the place planting rat droppings in premises just for the fun of it?" the senior of the two asked incredulously.

"I'm saying that we check almost every day and this is the first sign I've ever seen. It's strange that it should be on the very day you come here."

"Yes, I agree, it's very strange, but you'd be amazed how often we find it happens. If you'd like to come with me, I can show you the egress holes in the skirting behind the cooker."

Tony followed the men into the kitchen where the gas range had been pulled out to reveal the unmistakable, freshly gnawed opening in the rotten wood.

Tony shook his head in amazement and tried not to think what Neo would say.

"I'm afraid we'll have to close you down, forthwith, until you can satisfy us the problem has been dealt with," the older man said, with no regret in his voice. "The council rodent officer will attend as soon as possible. In the meantime you'd better post a notice on your door to the effect that you'll be closed until further notice."

When the inspectors left, Tony tremblingly picked up the phone to tell Neo at home what had happened.

Neo rushed into the restaurant half an hour later, sweating and panting.

"Tony, what have you done to me? What the fuck is goin' on?" he tried to yell in English, then reverted to Greek. "We haven't had rats in the kitchen for ten years; not since I blocked up all the holes."

"They've found a way in again." Tony showed where the ancient skirting board had been gnawed through. "It was just terrible luck that the inspectors had to come today, before any of us had even seen them."

"It wouldn't have happened if I had been here," Neo yelled. "It's the most important thing for a restaurant.

I always used to check. I've told you dozens of times. What's wrong with you? You know so much you don't have to listen to an old man?"

Tony choked back an angry reply. Calmly, he said, "Uncle Neo, I always check too. It was just bad luck. Now, please don't panic. I'll deal with it."

"How are you going to deal with it? We can't even open the restaurant. We'll have to sack all the staff. What am I going to do?" The little Cypriot was panicking beyond all reason and as he grew more excited, his face grew redder.

"For God's sake, Uncle Neo, it's not the end of the world. I've told you, I will deal with it."

"You'll deal with it all right. You can sack the staff, and look for somewhere to live. I'll see you here tomorrow for the keys." Then, abruptly, with tears in his eyes, he said in English, "You ruin me, you bastard!" He stormed out of the Olympus, slamming the glass door behind him so that it rattled.

Tony stood for a moment rooted to the spot. He could not believe what he had heard.

He had expected Neo to be annoyed but not like this, hysterically. The man was ill, overwrought. He would realise what he had said before he got home. The inspectors had only asked Tony to have the rodent officer round to deal with the rats and to declare them gone before the restaurant could open again – a matter of a week, no more.

Tony raced out into the street; he had to tell Neo now. He looked for Neo's car – a brand-new, bright red Jaguar – but he couldn't see it.

Sometimes Neo parked in the adjacent street; Tony ran down towards the next junction. He reached the corner to see his uncle pull out and speed off to the next crossroads.

Hopelessly, Tony ran after him, waving and yelling until the car had turned out of sight.

Fuming with frustration now, he walked back to the restaurant. It was crazy; he could hardly believe it, but Neo had asked him to go; to leave his flat, and the Olympus – the whole secure world he had made for Thalia, George and himself since escaping from Cyprus and Panos Andreou's malign influence.

6

Tony Kyriakides' head was drumming. He didn't know how to explain it to Thalia.

Thalia was still upstairs, making a list of flats to look at and getting George ready for his party. Tony couldn't bring himself to tell her what had just happened.

For the first time since arriving in England, even since Panos Andreou had destroyed his business in Limassol, he felt the humiliation of losing control over his own affairs; and that scared him. There was nothing he could do to correct Neo's crazy conclusions until he had a chance to see his uncle in a calmer state. To drive out to Wood Green now and confront him would almost certainly inflame things. Somehow he would have to hold his frustration in check and hope that Neo would realise how absurd he had been when Tony was able to tell him how relatively small the problem was, and how simple the solution.

But Neo had always taken such great pride in his restaurant's reputation for cleanliness. Where others paid lip service to the fairly lax health regulations, he was scrupulous in his observance of them. In the face of this closing down of the Olympus, there had been an appalling finality in Neo's manner towards Tony, the culprit.

Tony flopped down at the table he had been about to lay for George's tea-party. He folded his arms, rested his head on them and tried to decide on the best approach to take with Neo. After a while, to help him concentrate his mind, he began, mechanically, to lay the table. Half an hour later, he was jerked out of his thoughts by Thalia's voice calling from the top of the stairs.

"Tony, come up. Maria's on the phone. Something's happened to Neo." She sounded worried – about Neo, not about Tony.

Tony ran upstairs. Thalia had the phone in her hand. She passed it to Tony.

"Maria?" Tony panted.

"Oh, Tony," his aunt wailed, "You must help me. I can't find either of the boys. Neo has had a crash. They've taken him to the hospital in Finchley. There's a taxi coming to take me, but will you meet me there, please?"

"Of course. Is he badly hurt?"

There was a quiet whimper and a snuffle. "I think so. They don't say exactly."

"He may not be, Maria. Don't worry too much. I'll see you there as soon as I can. I'm leaving now. Goodbye."

"Goodbye, Tony. Thank you."

Tony handed the phone back to Thalia. "I'm sorry," he said, "Neo's had an accident. It sounds serious. I'll have to go. And I'm afraid something else came up downstairs and I haven't got everything ready for the party. You'll have to look after it on your own."

"Okay," Thalia said, resigned. "I'll manage. Let me know if Maria wants me round later."

Tony ran down the stairs and into the street again. He hailed a cab outside the Museum.

As the taxi rattled north, visions of Neo passed through Tony's mind: the warm, welcoming smile on the chubby face when Tony and Thalia first arrived in London; the kindness and trust he had shown them; his happy enthusiasm at their wedding, and at Thalia's return from hospital; his quiet understanding of Tony's problems with the Andreous; his wholehearted appreciation of Thalia. And today, his extraordinary, violent reaction to the rats.

The cabby dropped Tony at the hospital with a sympathetic nod. Inside, the smell reminded Tony of his daily visits to Thalia at the Middlesex and increased his apprehension. He asked for Neo Michaelides. A nurse at reception spoke on a telephone, glancing awkwardly at Tony as she spoke. She put the phone down.

"A doctor will be out to see you in just a moment. Please take a seat," she said.

As Tony turned around to look for a place to sit he saw Maria being escorted through the main door of the hospital. Her normally neat grey hair straggled from her bun. Tears dribbled down her face. Tony went quickly up to her and took one of her pudgy little hands.

"Come and sit down, Maria. The doctor's coming out to talk to us."

He led her to a seat, helped her into it, thanked and paid her taxi-driver. He remained standing, with Maria's hand still in his.

A young houseman in a white coat walked into the lobby. "Mr Michaelides?" he asked Tony.

"No. Kyriakides. I'm Mr Michaelides' nephew. This is his wife."

"Come with me, please," the doctor said quietly.

Tony helped Maria up. She was still in a tearful daze. They followed the doctor down a broad, lino-floored corridor along which nurses bustled and porters wheeled blank-eyed patients in their iron beds.

They arrived at the door of a room. The doctor turned to them before opening it.

"I have to tell you, I'm afraid, the chances of his surviving are slim. Not only did he have a massive heart-attack, but he sustained serious damage to his chest in the crash. It's unlikely he will be conscious or know who you are." He opened the door to a room containing a single bed.

Neo was barely recognisable. His head was heavily

bandaged. His bright black eyes were closed and his face was pale grey.

Tony let Maria go in first. She walked slowly towards her husband, picked up a limp, white hand and gazed down at him. She gave a cry of anguish. Her body heaved as she silently sobbed.

Tony looked at the doctor, who answered with a resigned shake of his head. Then Maria tried to speak. Even as she said her husband's name, it was plain she did not expect a reply.

"Neo, my precious Neo," she whispered in Greek, "What have you done to yourself? Please tell me. Please hear me."

Tony beckoned the doctor out of the room. They left and closed the door.

"Will it be all right if she spends a few minutes with him on her own?"

"It won't do any harm."

"My aunt and uncle were a very devoted couple and the kindest people you could meet. She knows he's going, but she would just like to be with him."

"That's all right. We'll give her a few minutes."

"How . . ." Tony started to ask, and faltered. "How long will he take to die?"

The doctor shrugged. "Ten minutes, ten hours?"

"Can she stay with him until the end?"

"I suppose there's no reason why not. I'll arrange for a nurse to look in every few minutes, just in case anything happens."

"Thank you very much, Doctor. I would like to tell the other members of his family."

Tony spent an hour on a public phone, tracking down Paul and Fanis. He told them candidly about their father's condition and suggested they came straight to the hospital.

By the time they arrived their father was dead.

*   *   *

Tony announced to Neo's family that he was going to close the Olympus for two weeks as a mark of respect on its founder's passing.

They agreed. None of them had heard anything about the rats.

After they had buried Neo in the Greek cemetery a week later Maria was able to talk lucidly.

"He went off in a great hurry after you phoned him that afternoon," she said. "You had some problem, he said."

"Yes, but it was nothing – a problem with a cooker; I dealt with it. I'm afraid there was no need for him to come."

"How I wish he hadn't. He always drove that new Jaguar much too fast. He was like a small boy with it," Maria said with affectionate memory.

"I don't think it was the crash that killed him, Maria. He could have had that heart attack any time."

"I know, I know," she agreed, "it could have happened any time. It wasn't your fault." She took her nephew's hand. "He was very fond of you, and so pleased with all you've done. He would never blame you for anything."

The next day, Tony's cousin, Paul, phoned him.

"Can Fanis and I come and see you this evening?"

"Things are in a bit of a mess here," Tony answered. "I thought, as we were closed I would take the opportunity to move the kitchens up to the first floor; it's something we had in mind for a long time."

"Well," Paul replied, "We'd like to see that. After all, the restaurant's ours now."

"But surely, it's your mother's?" Tony burst out, with alarm.

"No. My father left a very specific will. My mother is very well provided for by several insurance policies he had. He's left half the Olympus to Fanis and me," Paul paused before going on with a hint of bitterness, "and half to you."

A few hours later Tony and Thalia welcomed his cousins into the flat. Paul and Fanis Michaelides, in almost identical navy-blue pinstripe suits, arrived from their respective solicitor's offices in the West End. Paul was articled to a Jewish practice in Soho which specialised in entertainment, and Fanis was with a firm in Mayfair.

Fanis, whose nickname had always been Fanny, had announced recently that he was now to be known as Peter Michaels.

"Hello, Paul. Hello, Fanny – sorry, I mean Peter." Tony opened a bottle of Dom Pérignon. "Let's drink to the memory of your father, and the future of the Olympus."

The brothers took the champagne and made the toast with a solemn lifting of their glasses.

"We aren't sure what the future of the Olympus should be," said Paul.

"What do you mean?" asked Tony sharply.

"Well, neither of us is much interested in being in the catering business; our careers lie elsewhere. I don't think we want the capital tied up."

Tony had expected something like this.

"Capital? What capital?"

"The value of this place, obviously."

Tony shrugged. "There isn't much value. There's a lease which might be assigned for a few thousand pounds, some very second-hand equipment, and some very old furniture."

"But if the business was sold as a going concern, it would attract a good price," said Peter, who after two years in his firm, thought he had the London property market at his fingertips.

"Who would buy a Greek restaurant?" Tony asked.

"Another Greek, of course."

Tony shook his head. "You haven't been to Cyprus for so long, you've forgotten what they're like, if you ever knew. They wouldn't pay a premium for an existing business if they thought they could go out and start their own from scratch, much cheaper. No, if we decide to sell the place, all we'll get will be a couple of thousand each. If that's what you want, I won't try and stop you."

"You really think as little as that?" Paul asked.

"Don't take my word for it. Try putting it on the market. See what happens." He said it as if he were completely indifferent.

"But what would you do?" Peter asked.

"I'd start another from scratch. I've saved a bit. I have a good track record. My suppliers would help me, and I would own all of it."

"How much is this place making now?" Paul asked cautiously.

"Don't you know?"

"No. I never talked to my father about that sort of thing."

"After paying everything, including the percentage your father paid me, I suppose it clears two hundred pounds a week."

"What! Ten thousand a year?" Peter said with his eyes gleaming.

"I should think so. But your father had a special way of keeping his accounts for the tax man, so I can't show you precisely."

"I had no idea it was making as much as that," Paul said.

"It wasn't when I came here two years ago, but I improved a few things, and now it does. But I can do the same somewhere else. So, let's put it on the market."

Tony drained his glass of champagne.

"Maybe that would be a bit hasty," Paul said in his idiomatic English, "don't you think, Fanny?"

"Yes. We should run it on for a while, and see just how much it makes."

"Fine," said Tony, "Who are you going to get to run it? Because if you two want to get involved, and mess around with it, you can buy my half, and I'll be off."

The brothers heard the edge in his voice.

"Look Tony, we understand your position. After all, you arrived here penniless . . ."

"And speaking no English, remember?" Tony interrupted.

"We were wrong about that, sorry, but most of them coming from Cyprus are totally ignorant when they arrive. What I was saying was: we appreciate what you've done here and obviously, if we decide to keep the place on, it would be with you running it."

"Only if I have absolute control," Tony said. "I won't cheat you out of a penny. I would continue on the same terms your father gave me, and after that, we split the profits, half for you two, half for me. But, I mean it, absolutely no interference from you. Come and eat here, of course, but you must pay when you come, and tell all your English friends that it's your restaurant, if you're not ashamed to. As long as you leave me and Thalia to get on with it."

"What about Mum?" Paul asked.

"If she wants to come and work here, of course she can. That's up to her. I'm very fond of your mother."

"Okay," Peter said, making up his mind. "Let's open another bottle of champagne, and drink to that."

Paul nodded. "Sure, but maybe not such an expensive one this time?"

Although Thalia was in the room throughout the discussion she didn't say a word. Women, whatever valid contribution they might have been able to make, were not expected to join in. Only after the Michaelides had left did she speak to Tony.

"That was some performance. But you don't think they'll change their minds, do you?"

"No. They won't change their minds. They're children, those two. Once they had it fixed in their minds that the place might be worth two and half thousand a year each to them, they lost interest in arguing."

"But you were lucky they didn't call your bluff."

"I knew they wouldn't. Anyway, if it had come to it, it wasn't a bluff. It's good that half this place is mine now, but I'd rather have all of my own business."

"But does the business really make ten thousand a year?"

"More," Tony said with an excited grin, "and when I've added another thirty seats, it will double. And where the old kitchens were we can make into an area that can be closed off for private parties. We often get asked for that, but as we are we can't do it. And I'll rent brand-new cookers for the new kitchen, re-equip it so it's cleaner and faster."

"You can't say that the old kitchens weren't clean. Old Neo was fanatical about it."

"Sure," Tony said quickly, "But not very efficient."

"But what about getting the food up and down the stairs; they're very narrow," Thalia observed.

"That's simple, we'll have a small food lift put in. Not so far for us to walk. Food down, dirty plates and orders up."

"Are you going to tell Paul and Fanis about all this?"

"They could see for themselves that I was having the kitchens moved, but I won't tell them about the other things until they're done. I want them to know that when I said no interference, I meant no interference."

* * *

133

The notice in the window of the Olympus had told their customers that it was closed for a fortnight out of respect for Neo Michaelides. The regulars understood. So did the LCC health inspectors. By the end of the second week after Neo had died the new kitchen had been installed upstairs and the rest of the building thoroughly de-infested. Even the cellar was entirely rat-free for the first time in two hundred years.

The inspectors gave the restaurant a clean bill of health. A sign went up to announce the reopening and the customers came flocking back, wanting to offer their sympathy for the death of the popular little Cypriot.

The extension of the restaurant into what had been the kitchens was a great success. From a sale-room in North London Tony had bought two dozen solid, rush-seated chairs, more comfortable than the bent-wood. The lighting in this back part was provided only by subdued wall-lights and candles; the whole effect was more intimate than the front.

Tony had also allocated a small space for a musician; now there was to be live music four or five nights a week. This helped to give an authentic Greek atmosphere which the customers liked, but it didn't cost Tony anything; he had employed an additional waitress to cope with the extra seating – a pretty, twenty-year-old Yugoslav girl who took two collections a night from the customers for the musician. All Tony gave him was his supper.

From one of his customers who was a commercial artist, Tony sought ideas for a new fascia board. Within a month a more sophisticated, less folksy sign appeared above the front window along with two reproductions of classical Greek sculpture just inside it.

Thalia suggested they should change their butcher. There was an element of disloyalty to the memory of Neo in this, for the Olympus had always been supplied with meat by an old friend of his, a jovial but erratic Cypriot who made up for the variability of his meat with friendly prices. Tony agreed at once and demanded from the Cypriot butcher's replacement – an Englishman – a higher standard of lamb for the *klephtiko* and lamb kebabs. As Thalia had predicted, the customers were quick to notice the improvement.

Tony's two cousins were not in the least ashamed to bring their friends as the Olympus' standards rose and it grew in popularity with a richer clientele, despite its unfashionable position outside Soho.

Business boomed that summer. Tony took a long lease on the large six-roomed flat in nearby Russell Square which Thalia had found; he and Thalia had decided not to settle in one of those parts of London where other Cypriot immigrants had made their own ghettos. They tended to make their friends now among the English. They both spoke fluent, idiomatic English and regularly used it to each other. Thalia had become an active fund-raiser and administrator in Anthea Sherwood's new charity for the homeless, and she had also enrolled on several courses run by the British Museum. As a result she was making a wide circle of friends. And though she and Tony didn't exactly feel British, they no longer felt entirely Cypriot. As neither wanted to return to Cyprus at that point in their lives, this did not worry them; they wanted to forget the differences that had existed between them there, and the violent animosity between their families. Tacitly they agreed that George would be brought up an Englishman. So, while in Cyprus Colonel George Grivas and his militia agitated for union with mainland Greece, and Archbishop Makarios exhorted his followers towards complete independence, Tony and Thalia Kyriakides remained indifferent to Cyprus' politics, and prospered in London.

* * *

When Panyiotis Mina asked Tony Kyriakides round to the Aphrodite restaurant to put a proposition to him, Tony was privately doubtful, but ready to listen. Panyiotis Mina came from the Paphos district of Cyprus. Although some fifteen years younger, he had been a good friend of Neo Michaelides since they had both arrived in England. Like Neo, he had opened his own restaurant shortly after the war. The Aphrodite was in Charlotte Street, a busier area for restaurants, and it had survived despite offering only the most basic Greek cuisine and wine.

Panyiotis' father was dying and his brothers were arguing. He was the eldest son and his mother had summoned him back to Cyprus. He was taking his wife and three children; but he had no one he could leave in charge of the Aphrodite. Would Tony like to lease it for that year?

Tony asked how much rent Panyiotis wanted for the year. When he was told, he shook his head.

"No. I could hardly make anything if I had to give you that. You can't expect to be able to leave the place and earn the same," Tony said.

"But Tony, I have to have some income. We have nothing in Cyprus," Panyiotis said.

"Don't tell me you haven't saved plenty. And if I run it for a year, it will be making a lot more when you come back."

Panyiotis knew this could be true; that was why he had asked Tony. He lowered the amount he was asking for rent, but Tony still declined, and left the Aphrodite with a friendly wish that Panyiotis could find someone else to take the place on. As he left, he considered all the changes he could make to the place without tying up too much money in such a short lease.

Mina phoned two days later.

"Tony, what will you offer me for the year?"

"Ten per cent of the turnover," Tony answered.

"But how will I know what the turnover is?"

"Because I'll tell you every month, of course, when I send you your share."

"But how will I know that you're telling me the truth?"

"My friend, you won't know. You'll just have to trust me."

Panyiotis was silent for several seconds, then, with a sigh, he said, "Okay. Your Uncle Neo always spoke well of you; on his opinion, I'll trust you. We'll sign an agreement."

The following evening Tony went back to his flat where Edward Sherwood, now his solicitor as well as a friend, was waiting for him with the agreement and a bottle of champagne.

"Well done, Tony. I had to change a couple of things, but Mina was sensible. He knows you can transform the place for him, and I don't think he even considered doing a deal with anyone else."

"I'm sure he didn't," said Tony. "The other Cypriots may complain behind my back that I'm not loyal to Cyprus and don't spend much of my time with them. But they know Thalia and I understand the English."

"Thalia knows more about English history than I do," Edward said.

"Thalia's always been an Anglophile. I first saw her at the British base at Polemidia."

Edward returned to the contract. "Anyway, you're confident you can make this one work for a year and still give Mina his ten per cent?"

"Sure. I'll run it as I do the Olympus. I don't have to spend too much, and that's mostly on furniture which I'll take with me for another restaurant when I have to move out."

"Well, don't spend too much. We had to leave in a clause that he could give you a month's notice at any time, in case he decides to come back sooner."

"He won't. He's got plenty to keep him busy in Cyprus, and he's homesick."

"Just bear it in mind, though. If he does come back early, I won't be able to do anything."

The first month at the Aphrodite proved harder than Tony expected. A large number of the regular customers were students who, while they preferred the cleaner presentation and the better food, didn't like the higher prices. So Tony redecorated simply and inexpensively. He replaced the plastic-topped tables and tubular steel chairs with wooden ones; and discouraged the plate-throwing, which had been such a feature of the restaurant. Slowly less price-conscious customers appeared.

After four months, because of its position on the fringe of Soho, it was doing better than the Olympus. And Tony was looking for a third, more permanent site.

He took to dividing his time now between his two restaurants. Thalia still helped at the Olympus and Maria willingly took charge of the kitchen in Charlotte Street where she wasn't constantly reminded of Neo.

Paul and Peter – as Fanis was now known – showed signs of resentment that they were not involved in the Aphrodite, but they couldn't complain about the performance of the Olympus. They were both, anyway, preparing to sit their law exams. Tony treated them fairly and kept his promise not to cheat them out of their share of the profits. Neither of them turned out to be profligate in the way Tony had first suspected when their father died. They had sensibly, and cheaply, carried on living with their mother at home. Like Tony, they were determined to make the most of living in England and to put their peasant origins behind them. They recognised that they had this in common with Tony and were astute enough to realise he could be useful to them with his instinct for trading and appetite for work. Tony, for his part, didn't want to antagonise them; he knew he would need their cooperation if he was to open the kind of restaurant that he had in mind for his third. So the truce between the cousins developed into a mutual respect.

One evening early in 1957, while London shivered through a cold grey winter, Tony was overseeing the Aphrodite. As was to be expected on a Monday night at this time of year, the restaurant was only half full.

Tony knew most of the customers by sight, but there was a man sitting alone in a dark corner whom he didn't recognise, though he seemed familiar in profile. He hadn't noticed him come in.

"Who's that on table nine?" he asked Telis in the kitchen.

The waiter shrugged. "I don't know. I've never seen him before. He's a Cypriot, though, and rich, by the look of him."

Tony was intrigued. He approached the table.

"*Kali spera*. It's a pleasure to welcome a new face to my restaurant."

The customer, still wearing his coat and scarf against the unaccustomed cold, did not look up at first. He continued to pick at a *mezé* he had ordered, and took a sip from his glass – one of the few expensive French wines on the list.

When the man answered, Tony froze at the sound of his quiet voice.

"It is not your restaurant. It is Panyiotis Mina's. And he is taking it back."

The man turned his head towards Tony.

As he moved, the light from the candle on the table gleamed on his oil-black hair, lit his smooth, chestnut-brown features and bounced a flickering reflection from his motionless eyes. In the fraction of a second before he saw the face Tony had prepared himself, but he had no control over the sudden violent tremor which shuddered through him.

Panos Andreou had changed little since Tony had last seen those arrogant features, stretched tight with furious frustration, five years before in Limassol.

Tony took a hold on himself.

"Mr Andreou, you are mistaken. Mina doesn't want this restaurant back. He wrote to me last month; he is having a lot of trouble sorting out his affairs in Cyprus. He offered me another year here."

"It's you who are mistaken, *Mister* Kyriakides." Andreou's voice was quiet but with a sharp edge. "He asked me, as I was coming to England, to arrange to terminate your lease. I have his authority. I have seen his lawyer. You are entitled to a month's notice. Today is 31 January; you must be out by the end of February." Andreou put a hand inside the jacket beneath his coat and pulled out a long cream envelope. He offered it to Tony.

"Here is your notice to leave."

Tony ignored the envelope. Andreou dropped it on the table with a shrug. "How is my daughter? Is she happy being married to a waiter?"

"If that was what I were, I'm sure she would be. She is certainly happy not to be living under the same roof as a pig-headed, grasping bastard," Tony said, cursing himself for rising to the bait. With an effort he went on more calmly, "Don't pay for what you have eaten, Mr Andreou, and leave now." Tony drew back to make way for Andreou to pass, and watched with satisfaction as his father-in-law weighed up the position, and decided to do as he had been told.

As Andreou left the restaurant without a backward glance, Tony felt a surge of elation. From the way Andreou had spoken, it seemed possible that Mina hadn't told him about the Olympus. Losing the Aphrodite would not be the blow Andreou evidently thought. To lose a few months' profits would be something, of course, but at least he would be able now to concentrate his energy on setting up his newest restaurant. Just three days before, Paul, Peter and he had exchanged contracts on the freehold of a run-down Chelsea café.

But the sight of this man, who had so blighted his family's life, left a very bitter taste.

7

"Which do you want to hear first?" Tony said grimly to Thalia as he walked into their bedroom later that evening. "The bad news, or the not-so-bad news?"

"You may as well start with the bad," Thalia said sleepily.

"We had a customer we haven't had before." He paused. "A certain Mr Panos Andreou."

Thalia sat bolt upright. "Good God! What's he doing in London?"

"He came to give us notice to quit the Aphrodite – that's the not-so-bad news."

"My father? But why? What has it got to do with him? I suppose he heard about it from someone and terrorised Mina into it. But surely, it *is* bad news?"

"It's not the end of the world. I only reckoned on having it for a year. We've lost a few months, but we'll have the King's Road place open in a month. Now I can use my furniture from Charlotte Street for it." Tony laughed. "He thinks he was really shitting on us."

"But why should he do it? I'm his daughter, for God's sake! If he thought he was harming you, he must have thought he was harming me too. My God!" she said as a thought struck her. "You don't think my mother told him where to find you?"

"To give her her due," Tony said grudgingly, "I don't think she can have told him everything. He didn't mention the Olympus and he hasn't come here. She might have said something just to annoy him, but my guess is he heard something from Mina's family."

"But what would he achieve by coming here, trying to damage your business? What did he think I would do?"

Tony shrugged. "I don't know. I suppose he thought you would leave me in despair and go back to Cyprus."

"Men like him never learn."

Over the next three days they neither saw nor heard from Andreou, and they assumed he must have gone back to Cyprus. A few enquiries among London Cypriots confirmed that Panyiotis Mina had been heavily pressured into forcing Tony from the Aphrodite. Mina's family depended on the Andreous to export their small citrus crop, and the Andreous had not lost their taste for using commercial muscle in a personal vendetta.

Tony showed his cousins the document which gave him notice to leave the Aphrodite. They were both qualified solicitors now. They confirmed that the notice complied with the terms of the licence to occupy which Mina had originally issued. They were a lot more agitated by this nasty, unexpected event than Tony. They blamed Tony, or at least his late father, for this reminder of their peasant roots. But Tony shrugged it off. He knew what a success could be made of the new restaurant, whereas they could only guess with conservative pessimism; the difference between the entrepreneur and the professional. But Paul and Peter had learned to take Tony seriously.

Against his first inclination, Tony had invited them to participate in the short lease of the Aphrodite. They had declined, fearful it would affect business at the Olympus, and tried to talk Tony out of the idea. Since then the Olympus had shown a steady increase in turnover and profits and they realised they could have been making an extra three or four hundred pounds a month from the Aphrodite if they had followed Tony's lead. When he proposed the buying of a Chelsea freehold, they had been quite prepared to help – after all, if it didn't work as a restaurant once it had been tidied up a little, they could almost certainly resell the premises at a profit.

George Kyriakides, now a robust four-year-old, liked to climb trees as much as any other small boy. When his mother told him to go and find his ball among the shrubs that grew beside the Regent's Park lake, he had happily crept in under a spreading rhododendron. In this musty cave, the search for the ball was immediately forgotten. A long gnarled trunk bent parallel to the ground a few feet up. It demanded investigation. George scrambled up on to it and gleefully worked his way along the swaying bough. He reached the end of the trunk, and considered which branch to take next.

He quickly lost himself in a distant child's world beneath the canopy of waxy leaves but the fantasy he was working out was abruptly interrupted by a parting of the leaves in front of him. An unknown adult face peered at him in the gloom. It was the face of an older man, clean-shaven and sunburnt, with fierce black eyes.

He faced the intruder defiantly for a moment, then doubtfully. He looked back over his shoulder. "Mum," he called.

"It's all right," the face said in Greek. "I am your grandfather. Let me help you out."

Two arms appeared behind the hands, and reached forward to grasp him beneath his shoulders, and swung him out through the curtain of leaves into the real world outside.

George was taken by surprise, but he protested loudly with another yell for his mother.

This time he was answered.

"George!" Thalia came running round from the far side of the shrubbery, there stopped, horrified. "Father! My God! Leave him alone. You're scaring him."

The strange man held on to George's shoulder with an

iron grip. George struggled and winced, and puzzled over his mother's reaction.

She was staring at the man. "Let him go!" she said again, and the grip on George's shoulders relaxed enough to let him slip out and run the few paces to his mother's side. He turned and looked at the man from the safety of the full folds of his mother's skirt.

So, he realised, this was the dreaded father of whom he had sometimes heard his parents talk. The man did not look anything like as horrific as he had imagined. He wore a fine long coat, bright polished shoes. His dark, slightly greying hair was tidy and his features no more frightening than any of his father's friends who would come and see him in the restaurant or the flat. But his mother was obviously frightened.

"What do you want?" she almost whispered this time. "Have you come to make my life a misery again? You won't succeed. You can't hurt Tony here. Losing Mina's restaurant means nothing."

The man held up a hand at her torrent of words,.

"Have you forgotten," he asked in a low, quiet voice, "that Antonios Kyriakides is the son of a man who violated the memory of my father? Have you forgotten that he tried to defy me by interfering with my business, and then, as an act of spite, by stealing my daughter?" His voice had risen slightly.

"He didn't steal me!" Thalia gasped. "He loves me, and I love him. I went with him willingly, and I've never regretted it, not once. I never wanted to see you again. I know what you can do. I know what happened to Tony's father. You're a murdering thief. You don't give a damn about me, or you wouldn't be trying to ruin my life here."

"I just want you to come back to Cyprus where you belong, not among these émigrés; I want to see you with a man who is your equal, not this peasant. You have a fine son, I can see our family in him; he should have a proper upbringing, among people of his own kind."

"What? Your villainous brothers and cousins? Your grandfather was no better than the Kyriakides."

"Your mother misses you too, you know."

"She's almost as bad as you. She came to see me. Did you know that? She tried to get me to leave, and I despise her for it. I feel nothing for her now, even though she is my mother. And you I detest, for all the things you did to me and made me do. I'll never let my son near you."

She spun round, with George's hand in hers and swept across the tired winter sward of the park towards the gate. She didn't look back, but her whole body shook with fear and anger. George could feel it in her hand, and wanted to comfort her. Never had he seen her so angry or full of hate.

But Andreou's words echoed in Thalia's head – his implication that Tony had taken her only to spite her father. It wasn't true. It wasn't true, she told herself, and prayed that it was not.

Thalia and George took a taxi straight to the Olympus, where she knew Tony was meeting his cousins. Still shaking from the event, she told him what had happened.

Tony's eyes blazed. "The bastard just won't accept that he's lost you. Why can't he leave you alone? Of course, it's me he wants to hurt."

"He said that was why you had taken me – to hurt him," Thalia said, crying now.

Tony didn't answer for a moment. Then he gave a short, bitter laugh. "He's smarter than I thought. He's trying to make you think I'm like him."

"But, Tony, in some ways you are."

"No, I'm not – only in that I want to succeed. Do I go round beating up my rivals? Do I sabotage their businesses? No. I can win by being better, smarter than the others. That's not something your father would even consider."

Thalia conceded this. "But suppose he tries again?"

"He won't. He won't want to hang around and be humiliated by achieving nothing. Don't worry, he's out of his depth here. He'll give up and go back to Cyprus."

Thalia was less sure of her father's lack of tenacity and for the next few weeks she couldn't stop herself expecting to see him any moment. When she didn't she acknowledged, with relief, that Tony had been right.

But Panos Andreou's visit had succeeded in one respect. He had planted a doubt in his daughter's mind about Tony's motive in originally wanting her. She was aware that she was becoming excluded from much of his daily life. She worked less in the restaurant now, and devoted most of her time to bringing up her son and involving herself in Anthea Sherwood's Society for the Provision of Shelter to the Homeless.

The Society, staffed mainly by non-working, upper middle-class women of a liberal bent, had been effective in finding empty or abandoned buildings where temporary shelter could be offered to the army of tramps and vagrants who habitually crowded the arches of the river bridges and the hot-air vents of the hotels around Covent Garden. This provided an outlet for Thalia's naturally compassionate nature and she threw herself into it. The pragmatic commercial disciplines she had learned by being married to Tony, and by being her father's daughter, were proving especially useful among the other well-meaning but more woolly-minded women on the committee.

The task suited her well. She sometimes didn't see Tony from seven in the morning until one o'clock at night. The Aphrodite had been handed back to Panyiotis Mina, who had to return to England to run it, and Tony now threw himself into preparing the King's Road restaurant.

By the end of 1957 the New Acropolis opened, and soon earned a following among the cosmopolitan Chelsea-ites. Now that he owned the freehold, albeit jointly with Paul and Peter Michaelides, Tony was obsessed with it. But he had his finger right on the pulse of the times, and made sure that he responded to it. Both restaurants were busy and very profitable. Tony felt at last that he was becoming a man of substance.

Thalia seldom went to the New Acropolis, she felt in a way that she was intruding. But two years after it opened Tony held a dinner there for her twenty-eighth birthday.

It was a fine dinner; the musicians made a festive occasion of it, and Thalia's friends were enchanted to have been asked to such a pleasingly Greek event. Tony behaved with charm towards the women and their husbands, whom he had never met. Thalia certainly couldn't complain that he had not made an effort for her.

After the guests had gone, she and Tony left the staff to lock up and drove home in Tony's new Rover. There was an uncomfortable distance between them.

"Did you enjoy your party?" Tony asked.

"Yes, of course, very much. Thank you for organising it."

"It was a good opportunity to bring a different sort of crowd to the restaurant, at least."

"Is that all you think about? Would you have minded if they hadn't been potential customers – some of the poor old tramps that we try to look after?"

"Why would I want a lot of old tramps in the place?" Tony asked, genuinely surprised by the question.

"You don't understand, do you? All you think about is your bloody restaurants and making money. You don't have any time for me or George now. We never go out together."

Tony turned to her angrily. "What are you talking about? I've just given a party to be proud of, all for you. I lost an evening's trade from it, for God's sake! What are you saying?"

"I'm saying that I hardly see you now. I'm not some little peasant woman who's happy to sit around while her husband's out hunting or carousing. I'm an individual in my own right. I have ambitions too, you know."

"You? Ambitions? Why do you want ambitions? I'm making plenty of money; I've got great plans for the New Acropolis. Next year I'm going to change its name to something more English, more in the mood of the times. I don't just sit back and expect the customers always to come rolling in. People are fickle; they want new places, new surroundings."

He would have gone on, now that he had started, to expand all his plans and ideas, deaf to Thalia's agitation. But she stopped him.

"Shut up, Tony. I don't want to hear about that now. I'm talking about me for once. I hardly have anything to do with the restaurants now, so I'm going to take a full-time job with the Society."

"You're what?"

"I've been asked to take on the job of full-time secretary to the Society, and I'm going to do it."

"You can't. What about George? You're his mother; he needs looking after."

"You may not have noticed but George is at school. My hours will fit in, and I won't work so much during his holidays."

Tony was amazed. He knew his wife spent an inexplicable amount of time worrying about tramps and homeless women, but – a full-time job!

"Why haven't you asked me about it before? If you wanted to work, there's plenty you could do for me."

"I'm an individual, Tony. I know that's hard for a Greek man to understand, but I want to be an independent person in my own right, with my own aims, not just an accessory to my husband. So I'm taking this job. I'm committed to it, and there's nothing you can do to stop me."

Tony struggled with his ego and the slight to his virility but, pragmatically, accepted the inevitable. He chose to put a positive face on his wife's decision and salvage some satisfaction by encouraging her and her friends to use the two restaurants more. He ignored the palpable rift that had appeared between him and Thalia, or rather he buried his awareness of it by working and, to an increasing extent, finding his amusement among new friends, without his wife. Now, when he had finished at the restaurants, he no longer went straight home. He would drop in on one of the West End clubs to play backgammon and drink for a few more hours, though not enough to cause damage either to his health or his wealth.

Tony celebrated his own birthday – his thirtieth – with the opening of the re-vamped King's Road restaurant.

Now he called it the Vine and Pine – a reference to the gallons of Retsina that Tony expected to sell there. In doing the place up again Tony had eschewed the decorative clichés that afflicted most Greek restaurants; he knew, in a way that most immigrant caterers did not, that he was dealing now with a more sophisticated diner, especially in this part of London. The atmosphere was relaxed and cosmopolitan, but he instructed his new head waiter always to wear a dinner-jacket and black bow-tie, which somehow helped to achieve the slightly raffish mood he wanted of the place. He was also careful to chose a man for the job who possessed the facility of remembering people's names and greeting clients with affable decorousness.

On the day of the opening Tony had been in the restaurant since dawn, making sure no detail was over-looked. The long, low-ceilinged room was floored with large terracotta tiles, and the walls were whitewashed.

Between the simple wooden tables, with pale green cloths and rush-seated chairs, was a profusion of green plants – yucca, palms, rubber plants and ferns – lit by simple spotlights.

For the party the tables had been moved to the edge of the room, and carried *mezedes* of great variety, prepared mainly by the excited and tireless Maria. Ice-buckets containing the best Greek wines were lined up to slake the thirst of the two hundred guests Tony expected.

Four Greek musicians arrived and set their chairs on a small dais at the back of the room. Tony told them, as they cheerfully unpacked their pipes and bazukis, that they might have to play for five hours.

Tony had encouraged Paul and Peter Michaelides to ask a lot of their English friends and clients; he didn't want a get-together just of expatriate Cypriots. He invited his own English friends, and friends of friends, as well as old customers who, he felt, would support and add something to the Vine and Pine.

By eight o'clock the place was packed. There were three hundred people – models, lawyers, students, actors, and people who appeared from time to time in the gossip columns. Tony had little idea who half of them were or where they had come from. But he looked around at the good-looking men and beautiful women enjoying themselves, and he relished the sounds of animated talk and laughter over the Greek music. Dressed in a white tuxedo, he drifted among his guests and impressed them with his charm and dry wit.

Thalia arrived in a simple, elegant dress of pale silk, with George neatly dressed and bow-tied. She made an effort to enter into the spirit of the evening and chatted happily to the people she already knew. Though quieter and less confident, she looked as good as any woman there, and Tony allowed himself a moment to glance at her and acknowledge that.

By midnight thirty cases of wine had been drunk, and the *mezedes* had been demolished to the last olive. The musicians, well lubricated now, played with increasing verve, and the party showed no signs of breaking up.

Tony, though he didn't let it show too much, was glowing with excitement. This was his first venture outside strictly Greek restaurants and he knew he had launched a winner. Despite some opposition from his two cousins, who had made a significant investment in the place, he was creating a restaurant that offered a new sort of mood. The new decade, he told Paul and Peter, was going to see a new kind of casualness in England, a taste for originality, and an explosion in spending. The Vine and Pine looked as if it would appeal, at least as much as Tony had anticipated, to the rich, arty and sophisticated who made up a large part of the local Chelsea population.

Tony felt a tap on his shoulder, and turned to find Edward Sherwood standing beside him. Scruffily handsome, a few inches taller and about five years older than Tony, Sherwood, though essentially English, had the wit and imagination to enjoy unusual foreigners like Tony Kyriakides. Of all the people Tony had met since his first days at the Olympus with Uncle Neo, Edward had come closest to knowing and understanding the young Greek's fierce ambition and his intelligent perception of his market.

"Congratulations," he said, only slightly drunk. "I would say you've got a definite success on your hands. I hope you don't fall out with your cousins over it."

"Why should I? They accepted the option clause; it's perfectly fair."

"But when they signed it they hadn't had a real taste of success. In my experience, that changes people's idea of fairness; greed is not a rational vice."

"There's not much to be greedy about yet, Edward,"

Tony said with a pessimism he did not feel. "The Vine and Pine hasn't taken a penny so far."

A few weeks after the reopening Tony received a letter from his mother. It was a Saturday and he was breakfasting at home. He had promised Thalia he would take George to the Zoo.

"What does she say?" Thalia asked.

"She says she wants me to come back to Cyprus."

"Why? Why now? She hasn't written for months."

"Don't worry. I'm not going. She's fussing about nothing. She's getting old, that's all. She says Stelios and Nico are arguing – probably because they are making a bit of money now. And she's worried about Independence. For God's sake, Makarios comes from the next village, he'll look after the people in those valleys. He never wanted union with Greece like Grivas did. And at least the British soldiers aren't chasing the bloody Enotists all over the island any more."

"But will Independence work?"

"I don't know. As long as the Turks feel they're getting a fair deal, I guess it will."

"But the Turks won't get a fair deal. They're only twenty per cent of the population."

Tony shrugged. "There'll probably be trouble. But what can I do by going out there to see her? Maybe only cause her more trouble if your family decides to throw their weight around. I'll tell her to come and see us here."

"You know she won't come."

"At least I'll have asked her, though." He dismissed the subject as unimportant. "Right, if I'm taking George to the bloody Zoo, I'd better get on with it."

When he left, with George a little nervous at going out alone with his father, Thalia reflected on Tony's apparent indifference to his mother's state of mind. She and Tony had been growing apart, developing different priorities, for years. She had no complaints about their standard of living – and since her birthday party a couple of years before, he had shown an uncharacteristic tolerance towards her activities, but his increasing heartlessness alarmed her.

And it hurt her when he seemed to take so little interest in George. It was almost as if he didn't dare to get too close to a boy who would be the only son they could ever share. On her own, in the big flat that she had made so elegant and comfortable, she allowed herself some bitter tears at the unfairness of it.

8

A woman stood, tapping an impatient, white-booted foot on the steps of a stucco-fronted house in Queen's Gate, a wide Kensington street of large Victorian houses which were now mostly consulates, embassies and hotels. She was a young woman, twenty-three, with the confidence of old-fashioned English beauty. Five feet nine with manifestly female proportions, she was dressed in Mary Quant black and white. From patent-leather boots, her white-stockinged legs stretched up to a tiny strip of white leather that barely did service as a skirt. A skimpy, sleeveless polo-neck in black-and-white geometric cotton jersey displayed a pair of self-supporting, well-shaped breasts. White-rimmed dark glasses rested on the tip of her nose, not quite obscuring eyelashes of implausible length. Rich, dark-brown hair fell straight from a central parting to frame her face from fringe to chin.

Monica Fakenham didn't like to be kept waiting, but then, that was part of Tony Kyriakides' appeal. He simply wouldn't know or care if he was late.

She had first seen him at the opening of the Vine and Pine, five years before. A photographer working with her that day had said, "Some bubble's giving away free Retsina and barbecued goat to attract the punters to his new eatery. D'you want to come?"

She had come, and had noticed the slim, dark, handsome man in the white tuxedo as soon as she walked through the door. She was an eighteen-year-old model, at the top of the tree at the time and seldom off the covers of fashion magazines. Tony barely gave her a second glance as he greeted them with a quiet sophistication which put the photographer's nose out of joint. And she had a strong feeling that, sooner or later, she and Tony would become lovers.

Before that happened, though, she met and married Charles Fakenham, a dashing, opulent, hard-headed City banker. She soon discovered that Charles Fakenham's idea of a wife's function was part ornament, part social secretary as well as receptacle for his harsh love-making.

Charles' money, the mind-numbing boredom of the job, and her now unfashionable contours had encouraged her to give up modelling. Now she and Charles lived in an historic house in an acre of ground off Aubrey Walk, Holland Park. He loathed all her friends and refused to entertain them in the house; so Monica was more likely to be found in one of the fashionable new clubs and restaurants that were sprouting everywhere. One of her favourite lunching places was the Vine and Pine.

Standing in Queen's Gate, Monica glanced at the large, blank-faced watch on her wrist and sighed. Carefully she lowered her scantily covered bottom on to the stone balustrade at the top of the steps outside the door where she was waiting and assumed an expression of impatient boredom. Having never before had to make an effort with a man, she was now forced to do favours and pull strings for the Bubble to keep him interested.

Or so she thought.

Tony Kyriakides saw her sit down. She had her back to him as he walked beneath the shadows of the plane trees that lined the street. He looked at the boarded up windows of the building behind Monica. His first thought was that there might be somewhere inside where they could make love. His pulse quickened. Sometimes he felt that he could spend all day in bed exploring Monica's warm, luscious body. There seemed no end to the pleasure they gave each other. How long could it last, he wondered? So far it had been a month.

He had seen her at once, of course, the moment she walked into his opening party with the unshaven, uncouth cockney photographer. And he had seen her quick look of interest when the photographer said, by way of introduction, "This is Tony, the Bubble whose dump this is; this dopey tart's called Monica; you'll see her boat-race on *Vogue* next month."

She didn't guess that he would go out and buy the magazine to refresh his clear memory of the beautiful, wicked face.

He had felt a pang of disappointment two years later when he saw pictures in the papers of her wedding to 'old-Etonian banker' Charles Fakenham. Since then she had been back to the restaurant often, sometimes when he was there and sometimes not. He always acknowledged her but they never held any kind of conversation. He did not trust himself.

For despite Thalia's suspicions, Tony was still committed to her and respected without reservation her courage in dealing with her family, and the consistent loyalty she had shown him since they had left Cyprus. But after George's birth she no longer derived much pleasure from an act whose fundamental purpose was now irrelevant to her.

Tony wanted still to make love with the passion and abandonment of their early days together, when the sensations they aroused in each other transcended everything else in their lives. Thalia did not. But he had not sought this passion elsewhere; he knew the dangers that presented.

But a month before their assignation in South Kensington, on a hot June day, Monica had come to his restaurant on her own. She was meeting a girlfriend – a sometime modelling colleague – for lunch. Mr Luca, the manager, placed her in the centre of the room at a table he usually allocated to the day's best-looking customers. She sat, and fished a magazine from a capacious shoulder-bag. She flipped through it while she waited. After half an hour she was becoming impatient and glanced up, with a stab of excitement, to see Tony Kyriakides walk in.

He nodded at her with a smile, as well as at several other lunchers, and carried on to his office at the back of the restaurant. A few minutes later he reappeared, and came across to her table.

"Mrs Fakenham, we've just had a phone message for you. The lady you were meeting for lunch can't come. She's sorry, but her session's overrun."

"For God's sake, please don't call me Mrs Fakenham. How long have I been coming here? And the girl I was supposed to be meeting for lunch is no lady; she's probably gone to bed with the photographer. Well, I'm not going to sit here and eat alone," she went on, with a challenge in her wicked eyes, "so you'd better join me."

His hesitation was so brief that she didn't see it.

"No," he said. "You join me."

He sat opposite her and called to Luca for a bottle of Dom Pérignon. "After all, as you say, you are an old customer."

"Do you invite all your old customers to lunch?"

"Very seldom, and then they get Retsina," he laughed.

They talked lightly over lunch, about people, restaurants, nothing serious, nothing that would allow the other too close. But all the time a tacit understanding was growing between them that they would become close, until at the end of the meal she said, "You must let me do the liqueurs. I've got a studio in Old Church Street with a fabulous roof garden. It was let to a friend of mine, but she's gone to Italy for the summer. I've got the keys on me. I'm sure there's a bottle of Sambucca or something there."

There weren't any bottles of anything in the studio flat. Monica's friend evidently didn't believe in waste. But there was a bed.

"We'll have to skip the drink," Monica shrugged, gazing into an empty, bright orange tin trunk which served as a drinks cabinet.

"I don't really want a drink." Tony's voice didn't betray the nervousness he felt, now that the consummation of two hours mental fore-play was so near. They were standing in the middle of the large studio room, facing each other, inches apart. Behind Monica, the large bed was covered with a patchwork of goatskin. Tony reached out a hand, and placed it behind her neck, and gently drew her towards him. Their mouths met, and locked together.

At first there was a feeling of desperation about their love-making. For both it was the first encounter for a long time with a new partner. Both had lost confidence through the lack of mutual enjoyment in their marriages. They were two people with big libidos, looking for an outlet.

They both knew what they were looking for and, after a while, they found it.

There was nothing that they didn't want to do for each other; no part of each other's bodies that they left unexplored. There was no need for explanation or guidance; their bodies locked together – made to fit – until they were floating in a turbulent pool of physical euphoria.

For both it was an utterly fulfilling experience, an unlocking of the pent-up tensions of several years. And Tony could not believe his luck when he realised he felt no guilt.

As Tony now approached the building in Queen's Gate and his lover waiting on its steps, his thoughts returned for a moment to Thalia whom he had just left. They were good, proud thoughts. She was taking their son to see his new school, St Paul's, where he would start the following term. Because he felt no guilt about Thalia, he felt no resentment either. After all, what Monica gave him was not on offer from his wife.

He bounded up the steps, two at a time, and feasted his eyes on the long white legs.

She turned to him, and looked sternly over the top of her dark glasses.

"You're late, Tony Bubble."

"And hasn't it increased your appetite?" He gave her a quick, indiscreet kiss.

"It doesn't need increasing." She picked up the white shoulder-bag on the balustrade beside her and fumbled inside for a large bunch of keys. "Come on, let's get inside." She handed Tony the keys, and he found the right three for the locks which secured the front door.

Inside, she gazed at the peeling walls and dusty, half-pulled up floor boards of the hall. Mahogany doors eight feet high hung half off their hinges in the doorways of the rooms off the hall. Piles of broken glass had been swept up in the corridor beside the broad, shallow staircase.

"Shit," Monica said, "We won't find anywhere to fuck in here; and I'm feeling so randy in this heat."

Tony grinned at the sound of her beautifully enunciated obscenities. He pulled her to him and reached a hand beneath the skimpy skirt, over the top of her tights and knickers to the mat of curls around her warm slit. She pulled his head and mouth towards hers as he played his fingers in her.

She pulled her tongue from his mouth. "Oh," she gasped, "If I come now, I'll collapse."

He slowly withdrew his hand. "We'll find somewhere; but I want to look at this ruin first."

She laughed weakly. "You bastard. Why do you turn me on so much?"

He released her with a smile. "I'm not immune either."

"Yah," she said, "I felt Excalibur stirring." She grabbed

his bulge and squeezed. "Mm. My goodness, I do believe he's growing."

"You can find out later." Tony jangled the bunch of keys. "Let's get the work done first."

"It may be work for you."

"You'll earn something out of it, if I buy it."

"The trouble with being married to someone very rich is that earning becomes rather pointless."

"Wouldn't you like to make some money of your own? Haven't you any pride?"

"Of course not. Pride's a vice."

"Anyway, what's the story on this place?"

"The five houses belong to one of Charles' clients who's overstretched himself and is going bust. I overheard a discussion which I wasn't supposed to. They're planning to auction them, but they'd sell now, for a quick deal. There isn't permission to convert to anything yet; that's a risk you'd have to take."

"Okay, let's have a look."

The property consisted of five large, six-storey houses within a long terrace on the east side of the road. They had belonged to a family of big landowners since the 1920s. After being crudely converted into flats, they had been let. But the conversion had not entirely destroyed the solidly pleasing mid-Victorian proportions and fittings of the houses. The rooms on the ground floor, large and light, could probably be knocked through into each other to make substantial public areas. On the top four floors of the five houses there was a surprising number of rooms – over ninety. Allowing for staff rooms, Tony reckoned he could convert them to thirty-five bedrooms with bathrooms. He had learned quite a lot about building since he arrived in London. He had converted their first flat; then the Olympus restaurant, and, most recently, The Vine and Pine.

They found the keys which let them out on to the roof

of the building and scrambled across it in the hot sunshine. Considering the neglect of the previous forty years the roof appeared to be in good order.

They clambered back from the roof, and as Tony gazed around the derelict rooms, he could see how they would be transformed. The thought gave him as much excitement as Monica had in the hall below.

Tony wanted to look through each of the buildings in turn, until Monica became impatient.

"Come on, Tony, it's too hot to hang around in this filthy dump. Let's get back to the flat."

He agreed. He had made up his mind anyway. "As long as you tell me who to get in touch with over this place."

"As long as you don't talk about it for the next two hours."

Tony nodded with a grin, and led the way back down to the street.

He kept his promise. He didn't want to talk about his plans until they lay side by side on the goatskin rug, exhausted and elated while the afternoon sun shafted in through half-drawn curtains.

"I'm glad you suggested that place," Tony said. "I could do a lot with it."

"It looked like a complete dump to me, but you said that's what you were looking for."

"And I thought you might hear of something."

"If you buy it, whatever happens, Charles mustn't know I had anything to do with it."

"Why not? Does he know about us?"

Monica shrugged. "I don't know. I don't think so, and if it wasn't shoved in his face, I don't think he'd do anything about it, so long as I come home at nights, but I'd rather not take the chance. Mind you, I know he's got a little tart of his own who's prepared to give him a good thrashing with his old hunting whip in the way he likes." She gave a small grimace. Tony suppressed an urge to feel sorry for her. On balance, he guessed, she was not dissatisfied with the deal she got from her marriage to Charles.

"Charles won't know anything about your connection. I'll get my solicitors to make enquiries on behalf of a nominee. I just need to know who's handling the deal."

"I'll do a deal with you; let's make love some more, then I'll write it down for you."

"That's a terrible deal, but . . ." Tony raised an eyebrow at her and ran a tongue around her nipple while his hands crept towards the warm dampness between her thighs.

By acting fast Tony Kyriakides bought the run-down property at a bargain price because the agent acting for Charles Fakenham privately held the view – erroneously, as it transpired – that planning permission for change of use to an hotel would be hard to obtain, and that, because demolition was not allowed, the cost of repairing the place would be too high for residential use.

Buying it was a major gamble for Tony; but he had never been afraid of a big bet – not since his days of playing *tavli* with the sailors in Limassol. Besides this, before he had completed a contract to buy, he had a contract to sell, if he chose, to an associate of Peter Rachman's who reckoned he could let the flats profitably with minimal repairs. There were, this landlord maintained, always punters for cheap, dirty flats.

But Tony did not need that escape route. Though the building and safety conditions were stringent, the planning committee of the Royal Borough of Kensington and Chelsea was sympathetic to the proposals of the convincing young Cypriot.

But these building conditions almost doubled Tony's original estimate of costs. His clearing bank had, they said, done all they were prepared to do by financing the purchase – because even they recognised that it was a bargain. But they questioned Tony's lack of experience in running hotels. With a sense of frustration and humiliation he was forced to go begging around half a dozen fringe banks – loan sharks in over-decorated Mayfair offices – to raise the funds needed to finish the reconstruction. His cousins were horrified at the interest rates he had to pay. They were, they said, content with their share of the two restaurants. This time, they were not prepared to be persuaded. Even Edward Sherwood, still a staunch admirer and supporter of Tony's, advised against it.

Thalia watched with alarm as Tony, on his own this time, became completely absorbed by the project. She knew that any expression of doubt on her part would be counter-productive; she gritted her teeth as she saw everything he had accumulated over a dozen years of hard work and cautious investment mortgaged to the project.

Tony had no intention of lowering the standards he had set himself in order to save any of this expensive money.

He employed the most innovative hotel designers of the time to produce a completely original mood of laid-back chic. He wanted to appeal to the rich young musicians and movie people who expected to pay a lot for the gratification of their whims and no hassle, and who represented the biggest untapped market of the time.

One of the designers discovered that Oscar Wilde had once spent a few weeks living in the building, and suggested the name. This also suggested a theme of subtly updated art nouveau.

Tony studied the plans and schemes minutely, made some small practical alterations, and accepted them enthusiastically.

The Oscar Hotel opened in the autumn of 1966, and it was an instant hit.

By Christmas the Oscar was *de rigueur* for any visiting rock star. The Beatles took over the whole hotel for a party; Bob Dylan stayed there while he was on a European tour. Most days film stars and starlets could be seen in the bars and restaurants of the hotel. The standards of the place were universally acclaimed by the travel writers. The trade press heralded the Oscar as a whole new concept of an hotel. This was all achieved with a ratio of two staff to each customer, and no stinting on any aspect of a guest's comfort. Even so, as long as the hotel was eighty per cent full, it was making a trading profit.

Tony, Thalia and George moved into a splendid apartment on the top floor. It was an entirely independent dwelling, which Thalia could call her own and cook in if she wished. With its view across the top of the plane trees in the avenue outside and the roofs of South Kensington and Chelsea, it possessed a calmness that set it apart from the hotel below.

Thalia, although she was less involved in Tony's business by choice now, knew the hotel was doing well. Both the restaurants were running smoothly and profitably. But she was worried about Tony himself. He had become restless, short and snappy with her in a way which was new.

Tony was thirty-six, as handsome as he had ever been, with a firmly grafted veneer of London chic. This chic expressed itself in an aloofness of manner that he combined with sporadic displays of charm and dry wit. He was popular at functions and parties but was never asked to those of the old rich English, whom he aspired to join.

One night, after the hotel had been open for nine months and full for the last six, Tony and Thalia were sitting in their drawing-room of white marble and Charles Eames black leather furniture. Tony had drunk most of the bottle of Dom Pérignon on the glass table between them.

He was brooding on the banks who wanted their money back, and on Monica. Neither subject relaxed him. He poured himself another glass of champagne.

"Tony, why are you drinking so much?" Thalia asked. She had been wanting to ask the question for several weeks.

He glanced up, half glad that she had noticed, but forced a smile and gave a dismissive laugh. "It's nothing important. Anyone who wants to be a businessman has to deal with problems. If there weren't problems, everyone would be having a go."

The telephone rang beside Thalia and, with an apologetic glance at Tony, she picked it up.

It was a call for her in her capacity of Secretary of the Society for the Homeless. As she listened, with occasional excited questions, a smile spread across her face, and when she finally put the phone back, she wore a look of triumph.

Tony was glad to forget his problems for a moment.

"Sounds like good news. What is it?"

"It's only to do with the Society. It wouldn't interest you."

"But it would. Just because I'm always busy doesn't mean I'm not interested. It's good if you've had some success."

"As it happens, we have. We raised a lot of money over the last few years, with all those sales and dances I organised, and I proposed we should buy a big building, somewhere central, which we could convert into a hostel. Not a permanent place for people on the streets, but somewhere they could come for a few days at a time if they were ill or trying to get themselves together. I found a big run-down house off Notting Hill Gate, and I've just heard that we've bought it, with permission to convert to a hostel. It'll be the first of its kind, besides the Salvation Army places."

"And it was all your idea?" Tony asked, pleased with her.

"Well, yes," she said modestly. "And I saw the planning people too. I didn't think they'd allow it."

"Well done. I'm glad one of us is getting things right."

"Oh, Tony, you're depressed, aren't you? I've never known you so gloomy. Please tell me what's wrong."

Tony sighed. He resented his weakness in wanting to tell her. "You've done well since you've been in England. Because of your charity work, you're accepted here while I'm still a bloody foreigner. Even though I've come here and worked my arse off, given employment to hundreds of English people, taken a lead in the way I run my restaurants and hotel, the English in their pinstripe suits still think I'm just another 'Bubble'."

"What Englishmen in pinstripe suits?" Thalia asked. "We don't get many in the hotel."

"The City bankers. I had to borrow over £1 million to buy this place and refurbish it; it's costing me £220,000 a year in interest, and that's more than the place makes when every room is full. None of the big banks will re-finance me at a proper rate. They acknowledge that my first few months' trading figures are fantastic for this type of business, but still they smile while they shake their heads – the bastards. If I was an upper-class Englishman they'd be falling over themselves to do business with me. Edward Sherwood's been great; he's aimed me at every possible banker he can find, but – like I say – to them I'm just another Cypriot wide-boy because I started from nothing and made it quick." He paused. "I just hope George doesn't find the same."

"He won't. He's getting on very well with the other boys at his school. He gets asked back to friends' houses almost every weekend. He even sounds like a little Englishman now," she added with a hint of sadness.

"Better than sounding like a bloody immigrant."

Now that, for once, Thalia had Tony talking about his problems, she wanted to make the most of the chance.

"But if the big banks won't lend you the money, and the interest from the others is so high, what are you going to do?"

"I don't know," Tony admitted bleakly. "Of course, I could sell this place – that's what the bankers want. I could repay the loans and come out of it with a very big profit. But I started this place; it's been the most successful new hotel to open in London in the last ten years. I won't give it up."

"The restaurants are still making money, aren't they?"

"Sure, thank God."

"And they didn't cost so much to set up. Why not open more?"

"Borrow more money to open restaurants to pay off the interest on this place? That would be crazy."

"Tony, you're too close to the problem. What are you best at? Setting up operations, conceiving them, giving them originality. No accountant wanted you to do this deal; everyone advised you not to borrow at the rates you did. They were right, in one way, but then, so were you. You've made your mark, and you're known for it. You know what the public wants. Now you should use those skills to start a chain of restaurants but, this time, don't finance them yourself."

Tony leaned forward in his chair, prepared to listen. "How?" he asked.

"Do what that man has done with Pizza Express. Start a franchise operation. That way, you start getting your money from the moment they sign up. And if they have to buy supplies through you as well as giving you a percentage of their turnover for the use of the name and idea, you'll have money coming in with none of the risk."

Tony looked up at her with an appreciative grin. "Why haven't I asked you before?" He shook his head in self-criticism. "I suppose I never really thought you had a business head on you. I should have known that having a bunch of crooked wheeler-dealers like yours for ancestors must have left its mark." He stood a little unsteadily and walked over to kiss her forehead. "Of course, with a franchise, half the operators would try to rob me, but even so, with the right presentation, you're right; I could sell dozens of franchises, and no bloody risk at all. I don't know why I haven't thought of it before."

She smiled up at him. "Come to bed, Tony. You need a good night's sleep; I'll see to that." Her eyes shone in a way he had not seen since George's birth.

In the sober morning light Thalia's franchise idea still looked good to Tony. He set about studying every other restaurant franchise operation he could find. He visited dozens of towns, and hundreds of sites. He had detailed fitting-out specifications drawn up.

With Edward Sherwood, he produced a franchise agreement similar to existing ones, with an additional clause requiring a defaulting or breaching franchisee to offer his premises and business back to Tony's company at valuation.

"I don't think many will let that go through," Edward commented.

"They won't have a choice. I'm not setting this operation up so that people can use my ideas until they're established, then change the name and sell out to a brother-in-law."

Edward shrugged. "I don't see how you can monitor their purchasing, either."

Tony planned to set up a wholesale merchant's, importing and supplying all Greek foods, as well as English lamb, pork and beef.

"Our agreement entitles us to inspect their books; that's standard with most franchise operations. Of course, they'll fiddle them for the tax man as well as me. But they'll have to show *some* trade. I'll settle for that." They had, anyway, set a low percentage on turnover and a high franchise entry fee, though payable over two years. It was these entry fees that Tony was most interested in. He showed his plans to his lenders and they agreed to defer their demands for the repayment of capital until he had launched the scheme.

* * *

The Pitta and the Wolf franchise was launched with great razzmatazz at a reception at the Oscar. Antonios Kyriakides was something of a hero among the still growing Greek Cypriot community in England, and especially among the younger, second generation.

At the launch Tony was, for a change, unashamedly Greek, though less than half the turnout was. The Oscar was a place which most of his audience had only read about in gossip columns. The fact that Tony was its creator and sole owner gave undeniable weight to his presentation. The trade press reviewed it enthusiastically, while finding fault with some of the more stringent conditions of the franchise agreement, but they praised it as an exciting formula for the sixties – fast food with a hint of ethnicity about it, presented and sanitised in a way that the broad mass of young English would accept. There was no reason, the reviewers said, why a well-cooked kebab, of good quality meat in fresh, unleavened pitta bread should not have as much appeal as the ubiquitous, mighty hamburger. It was all a matter of the right presentation and image: and this was what Tony Kyriakides was offering.

The Greeks in the audience listened with interest, and left inspired to copy Tony Kyriakides; few of them felt they needed his franchise. But large numbers of the English who had come liked the potential profitability with the promised advertising back-up. Before the end of the day over forty prospective franchisees had shown an interest. Within a month twenty were actually signed up, and after six months over fifty were in operation. It looked like the franchise success of the decade.

But from an early stage it became clear that the theory of the operation was not going to be matched by the practice.

One by one the franchisees were coming back to Tony and explaining that things had not quite taken off, and the next tranche of the franchise payment would not be paid for a little longer.

The external, visible evidence of performance – the number of customers walking through the doors – in almost every case didn't bear out the operator's excuse of slow trading. But it was a cash business; there was no practical way of stopping the operators buying their meat and pitta bread, or anything else, from wherever they felt like, and they could write up the books to suit themselves. Had the cases of non-payment been isolated, Tony could have called their bluff, and sued for breach of contract, but, as it was, that would have meant closing down half of them within the first year. Somehow they all seemed to know this, spread though they were from Aberdeen to Plymouth, and from Norwich to Swansea.

The first flush of first tranches had a considerable impact on Tony's borrowings. But now the cost of administering the franchise, and – more onerous – the cost of running the contracted advertising were barely covered by the trickle of subsequent tranches and turnover payments.

A year after the launch, Tony had to look himself, and his creditors in the face, and admit that he was no better off now than before the launch of Pitta and the Wolf.

This time, though, he could not face going to his wife for sympathy; this time he went to his mistress.

9

Tony Kyriakides squeezed his Daimler Sovereign through the lunchtime traffic in Beauchamp Place. He stabbed his brakes angrily as an old woman pulled out abruptly from where she had illegally parked outside a hat shop. His impatience grew as he drove on and tried to find a space in Hans Crescent, behind Harrods. He always looked forward to seeing Monica, but this time there was more urgency about his need.

Usually he saw her once or twice a week, but she had been away for a month with her husband and Tony wanted to restake his claim. After five frustrating minutes he found a parking place and walked quickly to the red-brick building where he had bought an anonymous flat in which he and Monica met and made love.

They saw each other for a few hours at a time but the relative infrequency of their meetings had sustained their ardour. They still made love with as much intensity as the first time in Monica's old studio. But now they talked as well. Monica understood Tony as much as anyone did; and she thought she understood his frenetic, instinctive drive and the sexual energy that powered it, better than his wife.

Tony nodded at the porter as he walked through the polished front doors of the building and up the broad mahogany staircase to the first-floor flat.

He flung the door open and went in to find that he had arrived first. Feeling suddenly uncertain of himself, he tried to remember what arrangement he had made with her, but then he thought of the traffic outside and relaxed.

The drawing-room, furnished by Monica, had the impersonal air of an hotel room. There were no books or magazines and the pictures looked as though they had been bought from a catalogue.

Tony took his jacket off in the stuffy heat of the place and walked through to the kitchen. He and Monica never ate in the flat. The fridge contained nothing but bottles; the cupboards only glasses and the equipment and ingredients for making fresh Greek coffee.

Tony took a bottle of champagne from the fridge and carried it with two glasses to the drawing-room.

He poured himself a glass and picked up the telephone to call to his office. He was putting the receiver back when Monica arrived.

"Good Lord, you're here before me; you must be in trouble," she said calmly. "And everyone's been saying how the kebab franchise is going to make your fortune – the first kebab millionaire. Or is it a marital problem? Has the good, sweet Thalia been complaining that you don't fuck her enough?"

"If she did, I wouldn't tell you," Tony snapped. "How many times have I told you not to discuss her with me?" His eyes blazed and Monica quailed.

"Okay, okay," she said quickly. "What did you want to talk about?"

"I'm going to sell the Oscar." He felt a wave of relief at saying aloud to someone else what he had been repeating to himself with dread for the past few weeks.

Monica didn't say anything. He picked up the bottle and filled a glass for her.

"Let's drink to the start of a new stage in the affairs of Antonios Kyriakides," he said. "D'you know, until I just told you that, I hadn't made up my mind. I'd been trying to convince myself I didn't need to sell; something would turn up." He gave a triumphant smile. "The best decisions are always the hardest."

Monica understood the emotional processes he had been through. "Sanity has triumphed over vanity," she responded. "I'll drink to that."

They made love with a new tenderness that the sharing of Tony's decision gave. Up to this point their relationship was sustained by a simply understood mutual need for uncomplicated, emotionally undemanding sex. This was the first time Tony had let his lover glimpse the sensitivity and self-doubt which his father's disgrace and death had bequeathed him.

But if this greater understanding, added to Monica's knowledge of her lover, provided a basis for their affair to develop into something deeper and more dangerous, they both summoned up their practical, selfish reasons for not allowing it to do so. It would be a long time before Tony would admit any other uncertainties or weaknesses to Monica.

The next Friday evening, two days later, Tony was called to the telephone in his office at the Oscar.

"Mr Kyriakides? This is John Sullivan." There was a pause to allow Tony to recognise and react to the name.

Tony gave no sign that he recognised it.

"Of Scottish and Lakeland Hotels," John Sullivan continued. His voice was that of the self-made cockney whose business was service.

"Of course," Tony said. "I was told you had rung this morning."

Scottish and Lakeland Hotels was a mixed bag of thirty-five hotels, a dozen of which had been bought ten years before from British Rail. They were all in Northern England and Scotland. Recently a great deal of funding, and John Sullivan, had been introduced to the group by a consortium of disgruntled bankers. Sullivan's brief was to give the group some stock-market gloss, and a higher public profile by acquiring well-known hotels in the south-east of England, including a London flag-ship.

The Oscar was not in the primest part of London, but its reputation for glamour and high standards made it eminently suitable for Sullivan's purpose; so did the fact that it belonged to an individual, who was far more likely to take a profit on it than an established chain would be.

"I understand the Oscar is on the market," Sullivan announced bluntly.

The only person besides Tony who should have known that was Monica. Tony hadn't been going to announce it until he had decided on the price he was going to ask. Nor had he yet told his accountants of his intentions although he had asked them for some projections which he was expecting the next day.

"I understand that all your hotels are on the market," Tony replied.

Sullivan laughed. "Everything has a price."

"As a matter of curiosity, what do you think the Oscar's is?"

"What are you asking?"

"You're asking; I'm not, and frankly, I don't know how you got the idea that I was."

"Berkley Berrington Bank are one of our principal shareholders. I was having dinner at Charles Fakenham's last night."

"Charles Fakenham doesn't know anything about my business."

"I arrived a little early. Mrs Fakenham was kind enough to entertain me for ten minutes before her husband came in."

Tony smiled to himself. Monica had led him to the Oscar; now she was trying to lead him from it.

"If you want to make an offer for my hotel, I'll listen, of course. But you come here, and you make the offer."

Sullivan was experienced enough to know when it was, or was not, worth arguing a minor point.

"All right," he said, "I'll let you know if I want to take it further."

It was Friday; Tony judged that Sullivan would ring him again the following Tuesday.

Sullivan telephoned on Sunday night.

George answered the phone in their flat. Tony took his time going to speak; even the most hardened of operators was susceptible to these unsubtle stratagems.

"Good evening," he said, without enthusiasm.

"Hello, Mr Kyriakides. I'd like to make you an offer for the Oscar."

"All right. When do you want to come and see me?"

"I've already had a good look at the place. There's no need for me to come round. Your lawyers can send mine all the documentation and figures I want to see."

"They won't be doing that until you've been round here and made your offer – the right offer – in person."

"Are you sure you're in a position to dictate petty terms, Mr Kyriakides?"

"I'm in a position to do whatever I like, Mr Sullivan. If you want to, ring my secretary in the morning and make an appointment. Now, if you'll excuse me, I am playing a game of chess with my son, and he's waiting for me to make my move, so I must go. Thanks for calling. Good night."

He replaced the receiver slowly, with a smile.

He had won that move, and this was a game where each winning move could be worth £100,000.

John Sullivan was stocky, about five foot nine, well-groomed in bad taste.

As Tony observed this, he admonished himself for picking up bad English habits, but he enjoyed seeing Sullivan perched awkwardly on the edge of the Barcelona chair opposite him. Sullivan had made the appointment, and they were in Tony's office at midday on Monday.

"I'll want to see an interim audit of these sales figures," Sullivan was saying, as he leafed through a folder Tony had given him.

"We are not due to start our audit for a few weeks yet," Tony said with a shake of the head. "You can have one, by all means, but you'll have to pay."

"For God's sake, that's a matter of a few thousand quid."

"You want to buy, you pay the costs. Of course, if I had publicly announced any intention to sell, I would expect to prepare prospectuses and figures and so on; but you approached me, remember?"

Sullivan remembered all right. And he could think of half a dozen operators who would love to get their hands on the Oscar if they had known it was possible.

So could Tony, who reckoned that the thought of buying the Oscar from under the opposition's noses would make Sullivan act more hastily, less cautiously, than in an open race.

Even as they were speaking, a sympathetic – or at least subornable – and respectable firm of commercial property agents was composing a flattering valuation that would stand up well enough to cursory scrutiny.

The interest charges which Tony was paying were the liability of a separate, arm's-length company he had formed which, in turn, had made an interest-free loan to the company which actually operated the Oscar. The auditors knew nothing about the finance costs of the business, and their interim audit would give no indication of Tony's personal straits.

Nevertheless he thought he should make his point more strongly.

"Frankly, I think Mrs Fakenham may have been acting out of . . . well, I don't want to malign her, but you are obviously a man of the world, and we had a short affair, shorter than she wanted, and . . ." Tony shrugged and felt he need say no more.

He watched Sullivan trying to decide how much to believe him.

Sullivan thought there might be some truth in what the Greek was saying. Though Kyriakides had no particular reputation for womanising, he was good-looking, very much in control; and Monica was manifestly too young and zappy for a stuffed-shirt like Fakenham. And she was certainly the sort of woman who might get her own back by a bit of selective bad-mouthing. On the other hand she wasn't beyond setting up the whole thing with Kyriakides.

But he would never forgive himself if he missed an opportunity to get at the Oscar by the back door. Kyriakides may have been playing it cool but Sullivan judged that he would certainly sell, at the right price.

He didn't underestimate Kyriakides' achievements in conceiving the place – the man was a natural – but with the benefit of Scottish and Lakeland's marketing experience, booking organisation and buying power, they could certainly make more of the place.

While these thoughts raced through Sullivan's mind Tony was thinking of life without the Oscar, life without blood-sucking, confidence-destroying debt.

"Okay, Mr Kyriakides, obviously I'm interested in buying the Oscar, or I wouldn't be here. Subject to property searches and valuation, and the interim audit, I'll be making you an offer by the end of the week. Can I have your word that you won't seek other offers until I get back to you?"

"I've already told you, I'm not seeking your offer."

"So you say," Sullivan said impatiently, then, in a last, unhopeful attempt, he asked, "Now, so that we don't waste each other's time, will you give me an indication of what you would accept?"

Tony looked back at Sullivan, slowly shaking his head with a slight smile.

To himself he said three million might do it.

To Sullivan he said, "It's up to you. After all, I won't know what the place is worth until you've made your offer."

Sullivan stood up from the stainless steel and leather chair with some relief and thrust a short-fingered hand across Tony's large, black desk.

"Okay, Mr Kyriakides . . . Tony. As soon as I've seen the figures, you'll be hearing from me."

Tony watched Sullivan leave the room. He wondered how he would contain himself until then.

The chief executive of Scottish and Lakeland Hotels rang Tony Kyriakides on the following Thursday.

"Good morning, Tony," John Sullivan boomed, to give weight to the proposition he was about to make. "I've been authorised by my board to offer you three million pounds for the Oscar."

Tony kept his response unenthusiastic. "I thought you were keen to buy it."

"For God's sake, that's more than ten times its earnings."

"But it's not even two years old. When did you last open a new hotel and see it profitable within the first three years?"

"And we've had to make some allowances for your valuation," Sullivan went on.

"Frankly, Mr Sullivan, I don't care how you've arrived at your figure; it's not enough."

"I've given you my offer, now you can tell me your price."

"Four million," Tony said.

"We won't go to that," Sullivan said immediately, and Tony believed him. "I'll ring you back in ten minutes with our final offer."

The phone line died with a click.

Tony did not move from his seat as he waited for the instrument to sound again.

When it did, he resisted the urge to pick it up at once. Then his secretary said, "I've got Mr Sullivan for you again."

"Tell him you can't find me, and to hang on."

"Yes, Mr Kyriakides."

Tony waited another minute before taking the call.

"Hello, Mr Sullivan."

"We are prepared to increase our offer to three million, three hundred thousand pounds."

Tony smiled to himself. Sullivan had gauged it close.

"Three and a half, and that's my last price," Tony said quietly.

There was no response from the other end for a moment or two, then an audible sigh. "Okay. We'll deal at three and a half million, conditional on our having a contract of sale within forty-eight hours, and that our offer is not made public until that contract has been signed. Otherwise, it's withdrawn."

"That's fine," Tony said, "I'll instruct my solicitors right away. May I invite you to lunch here to shake hands on the deal formally?"

"Why not? I might as well get used to the Oscar's chef. I'm planning to move into your office."

Leaving the Oscar had strong, contrasting effects on Tony. Though he considered them a sign of regrettable weakness, he couldn't ignore the elation and relief he felt in emerging from beneath a three-year cloud of debt.

But the elation was far outweighed by a profound sense of loss – like the loss of a child spawned as it was, entirely through his vision and his relentless work. When, as its owner, he left by the front doors of the Oscar for the last time a deep shameful sadness entered his soul –

a sadness which he knew would never be expunged or diminished until, one day, he could win the Oscar back. He consigned this ambition to the most private corner of his mind, determined to offer no outward sign of regret to Thalia, to Monica, or to anyone.

After inevitable haggling over the finer points of the sale, and disagreements about the furnishings of the flat, he had come away with a clear cash profit of just under two million, and both the restaurant accounts had substantial cash balances.

His first move on completing the sale was to buy an elegant house in Argyll Street, Kensington, where he pondered his next move, and enjoyed watching his wife make a classic English home of the place from the antique shops of Bond Street and Chelsea.

It was costing a lot of money, especially compared with the doing up and furnishing of their first flat in Coptic Street, but he wanted to indulge Thalia.

Since Monica had helped him find his willing buyer for the Oscar a greater intimacy had grown between them. But Tony found, to his irritation, that for the first time a sense of guilt now interfered with his feelings for his mistress.

Despite this, the physical excitement of their relationship had not waned. Yet the greater intimacy did not trick Tony into ignoring the probability that Monica was only tolerable in small helpings.

He knew he had escaped lightly from the Oscar. Privately he gave himself little credit for the deal, which was due to Monica's initiative and John Sullivan's rashness. But he was determined he would never again allow himself to become a captive of debt. Though he had profited hugely from this last debt-supported venture, he knew he had been lucky. The chances of creating such an outstanding success again from a cheap shell of a building were very slight.

In future, when he needed funding, it would be supplied

by the public in the form of shareholders' funds which were controllable and, generally, cheap. He set about developing a strategy for re-entering the hotel market in a way which would allow a public flotation of his company's shares as quickly as possible. Very few people had been aware of his real circumstances when he did his deal with Scottish and Lakeland, and the deal itself had done a lot to embellish his reputation.

For the first time since arriving in England sixteen years before. Tony Kyriakides felt he could face going back to Cyprus to see his family. But he refused to consider Thalia making contact with hers.

They had heard very little from the Andreous. Stories reached them of Panos' increasing wealth and influence under the shaky regime of Archbishop Makarios, and his volatile Greek – Turkish government. But Panos had not achieved the international style of trading that other, more broad-minded Cypriots had. In many ways, it occurred to Tony, and despite the English suits and cosmopolitan air he had affected, Panos was still a small-time trader.

Certainly he seemed a distant, irrelevant threat now; especially since his only attempt to disrupt Tony's life in England over the Aphrodite had failed so dismally. Nor had Thalia's parents made any further contact with her since her encounter with Panos Andreou in Regent's Park. Tony believed Thalia when she claimed, with some bitterness, that she could live without seeing her own family. She had a number of close friends in England now and she was still close to Maria Michaelides, who doted on her and her son.

George himself had become a source of unrestrained pride to Tony. He excelled in most things at school. Like most of his friends, he was a day boy at St Paul's, but the school had taken over his life.

He was a good cricketer and soccer player. Academically he was well above average. Although he had only just started his first year in the sixth form, his headmaster spoke enthusiastically of his chances of getting into Oxford.

It sometimes amazed Tony that this tall, good-looking boy, so confident, so English-sounding, had been born to a Cypriot mountain peasant boy. He admired his son for these qualities and yet he was aware that George would never benefit, as Tony himself had, from the need to struggle, to climb from the grinding penury of a thin-soiled, unyielding hill farm, and an ignorant, illiterate father.

Tony felt it was time that George saw where his roots lay.

10

In April 1969 Tony Kyriakides set foot on the island of Cyprus for the first time since he left on the cargo ship bound for Marseilles in 1952. His wife and son came with him.

When their BEA Trident touched down in Nicosia Tony felt as if he had come back in a time machine. He had travelled little in Europe – one or two visits to France and Spain – but these places seemed a great deal less foreign to him than his own country did now.

George was fascinated in a detached sort of way to be seeing his parents' birthplace. Tony had encouraged him to practise Greek with his mother, and George had built up a mental picture of his grandmother, his farming uncles and their simple existence. He looked forward to seeing it, so bizarre would be the contrast with his own.

At the airport Tony hired a driver and the biggest car available, a Ford Zodiac. From there they headed for the south coast without going into Nicosia itself.

The metalled road was less patchy and pot-holed than it had been the last time Tony had driven it, and there were a great many more vehicles on it. But old men in *vraka* were still driving or straddling donkeys as they ambled from field to village.

The fields were full of flowers and fresh in their spring green. Bulbous clouds hung above the tops of the mountains to the west and the rivers had yet to sink beneath their cracked dry summer beds. At the sight of the mountains Tony felt almost nauseous at the violent and tender memories they evoked.

But they were not going straight to the mountains. Tony wanted first to acclimatise himself in Limassol for a night.

The outskirts of the busy port showed more signs of change than the country around it. The town had sprouted suburbs of box-shaped villas, and a few resort hotels on the coast to the east.

But as they drove along the seafront of the old town, memories of his courtship flooded back to Tony, and he turned to look at Thalia.

She had been brave – he knew that now more than he had at the time – but, thank God, her trust was beginning to be repaid. For though he was already a millionaire and one of the most successful of Cypriots to have emigrated to London, he had achieved only a few of the targets he had set himself.

That was the reason he had told Thalia they could not visit her parents. And he didn't want her to see them alone. Even after all the time that had elapsed since she had last been taken from him by her father, still, though aware of the absurdity, he thought it could happen again.

Thalia had anyway told Tony that if she came with him, she didn't want to see her father. But now, driving through the streets which were the background to his early triumphs and miseries, he felt more than big enough to confront a tin-pot local fruit merchant and wine-maker.

Tony had cabled a booking to the Continental, one of the older hotels not far from the port where he had whiled away so many evenings, gambling with passing seamen.

The proprietor greeted the Kyriakides family with open arms and considerable awe. The legend of Antonios Kyriakides had reached Cyprus loud and clear.

Despite his vanity, Tony was surprised. His only contact with the island had been through a few of the London Cypriots, whom he seldom saw these days, and letters from his mother, who had probably only gone to Limassol once or twice in the past seventeen years.

It hadn't occurred to him that news of his career as a prominent London restaurateur and hotelier had come back to Cyprus. But it had, and Tony found it hard not to bask in the adulation that the exaggerated tales of his success had spawned. And it made him feel bigger than any of the people he had left behind in this small-time port.

"Let's call on your family this evening," he suggested to Thalia, only half joking.

But she shook her head vigorously. "There's no point. If my father sees you've been successful and proved him wrong, he'll hate you for it. He'll forgive you less than if you had failed. I told him I never wanted to see him again, and I don't. But my mother – even though she tried to set me against you – I would like to see her. And my brothers. I haven't seen them since the night I left. But I won't."

"Why not?" Tony said lightly.

"I won't risk you coming into contact with my father and his brothers."

George was intrigued by this conversation. Over the years his parents had let slip odd remarks about the relationship between their families. But neither had ever told him the full story.

"I'd like to see your father," he said. "He really gave me the creeps that time he appeared when I was climbing in the bushes in the park. I bet he wouldn't recognise me."

"Please, George," his mother asked, "Don't see him. You've no idea what it could start."

Thoughtfully, George went to his own room down the corridor. There, he lit an illicit cigarette and looked out of the window to the sea and down on to the busy road, where donkey-carts, dilapidated trucks and old women shambling along in widow's weeds jostled each other for leeway.

Young, vigorous and curious, George was not put off

by his mother's pleadings. He half understood his father's reluctance to see Panos Andreou and the retreat of that reluctance in the face of the obvious esteem in which Antonios Kyriakides was held on this backward island. He knew that there had been conflict between his father and his mother's family, but the details had been brushed over, as if Cyprus were no longer a part of their history – so much so that he had been amazed when Tony had announced this visit. But now he was here, he wanted to find out the truth.

He unpacked and had a shower, noticing with disparagement the shabbiness of the hotel compared to the Oscar. Afterwards he went and knocked on the door of his parents' room.

"What is it?" his father growled without coming to the door.

"It's George, Dad."

He heard his father cross the room. A moment later the door opened and Tony looked at him impatiently.

"What is it, George? Your mother's tired. She's having a sleep."

"I just wanted to tell you that I'm going out for a walk around."

"What for?" Tony asked suspiciously.

"Just to have a look at the place, and see what the girls look like."

Tony laughed. "You won't see any worth looking at. But go ahead, just be back in an hour for dinner. And don't do anything stupid."

George was sure his father knew what he planned and didn't entirely disapprove.

"I won't, Dad. See you later."

George went down to the lobby and out into the street. For a few hundred yards he walked past the noisy, strong-smelling bars on the seafront. When he thought he was far enough from the hotel he hailed a taxi and climbed in. He asked the driver of the old Austin Cambridge if he knew where Panos Andreou lived. The driver nodded, as if it were a silly question and drove George a few hundred yards through a maze of back streets before drawing up and saying, "This Andreou house," and waving at a long, blank wall, with a single door set in it.

The fine house in the old town had recently been painted dark cream with white mullions and door surrounds. The garden behind the high walls was tended in a way that would have been considered excessive twenty years before. There was an obvious air of opulence about the house which reflected, as it was intended to, the respect with which the Andreous were regarded.

Panos Andreou's elder son, Michael, still lived there. He had eschewed commerce, to his father's disgust, and had become an archaeologist, quiet, private and unmarried. The younger son, Ari, had married and lived in an ugly new villa on the road to Paphos. Ari already ran one of the factories for his father, and usually owned the fastest car on the island.

The Andreous' family business, led indisputably by Panos, had expanded as the economy of the independent republic had expanded, but no more. The family were as wealthy as any in Limassol, and this satisfied Panos and his wife.

Thalia's departure, seventeen years before, had severely dented his pride; her marrying the son of Theo Kyriakides in London had embittered him. But now he was resigned to it. No one ever referred to Thalia and the rest of the Kyriakides family in Cyprus had stayed in the obscurity of the Troodos Mountains. Panos no longer wasted energy resenting Antonios. He knew that his son-in-law was beyond his sphere of effective influence. Although he had been to London every few years, he had resisted the temptation to make a fool of himself again by trying to see his daughter and grandson. But he had, from a distance, seen what Tony had achieved and, if he was honest with himself, he admired and envied him for it.

His brothers, Spiros and Christos, did not.

They had never forgiven Tony Kyriakides for compounding Theo's insult to their father by running off with Panos' daughter. These two brothers, so different in manner and appearance to Panos, were still mountain men who would tolerate no compromise. But as long as Panos controlled the business and the purse-strings, they wouldn't risk pursuing any vendetta themselves.

That afternoon, though, they had come to see Panos in a mood of defiance.

They were in Panos' house, in his formal drawing-room with the English furniture and fussy chintzes they despised.

"Panos," Christos said as soon as he was shown in, "Antonios Kyriakides is here."

"Here in Limassol?" Panos was astounded, if this were true, that he hadn't already heard it himself.

"Yes. And your daughter is with him. If she hasn't told you she is coming, she doesn't mean to see you. They are prepared to insult you again, by ignoring you. Everyone knows they're here. You can't allow them to do this."

"They'll come. They wouldn't have come to Cyprus if they weren't ready to, I'm sure of it," said Panos, unconvinced but undecided how to deal with this event. "We can't lower ourselves to indulge in peasant vendettas. I've told you, I've done what I can in England."

"That was nothing, though, was it?" Spiros said. "Everyone knows how successful he's been. You can't curl up like a dog waiting to have its belly scratched now that he's deigned to come back here. You must protect the honour of our family and our father's name."

"I'll decide what happens. I'll deal with it," Panos said icily. "Thalia is my daughter, and don't forget that if it wasn't for me, you'd still be running around bullying a few mountain villages with nothing to offer. What standing and money you have, you owe to me. You know that, so leave it to me. If you take the matter into your own hands, I won't forgive you and you can go back to the mountains or to the devil!" His eyes blazed with a finality they recognised well.

They looked back at him with sullen but impotent defiance.

There was a knock on the door.

When George arrived outside the gate of the elegant old house, he climbed out of the taxi and asked the driver to wait. He wasn't sure what he was going to do. He looked at the gate, then at the taxi driver who gazed at him indifferently, wondering why the Greek-looking English boy didn't just tug the bell handle in the stone gate-post. George turned back, took a deep breath, tugged and waited. He couldn't hear a bell ringing inside and half hoped now that it didn't work.

A moment later, the gate was opened a crack by what he took to be some kind of maid, about his mother's age, with the faded, martyred look of a woman whom life had passed by.

The woman looked at him, thinking she recognised him. "Yes?" she asked in Greek.

George answered in English.

"Is this the house of the Andreous?" he asked.

The woman nodded.

"Is Mr Panos Andreou in?"

The maid looked hard at him.

"Where are you from? You look like a Cypriot."

"I am, but I'm from London."

"You're Thalia's boy!" the woman almost shouted with excitement. It was with an effort – or so it seemed to George — that she did not leap from the gateway and throw her arms around him. "I am Teresa," she explained, then looked hurt as it was clear this meant nothing to the tall, handsome boy. "I helped your mother when she ran away from here to go to England."

"She hasn't told me about that," George said inadequately. "She's told me nearly nothing about her family; that's why I'm here."

"Does she know? Does your father know?"

George shook his head. Teresa looked worried.

"But I want to meet my grandfather," George said. "Is he here?"

"He is here," Teresa said slowly, "And so are your uncles." She opened the gate wider to let him through. He followed her up the short path and the few steps to the open front door. In the gloomy hall, she turned to him.

"You are called George, aren't you?" she whispered.

George nodded. Teresa gestured him to wait while she knocked on a large door that opened off the hall. As she opened the door, the sound of husky Greek voices reached him, then stopped as Teresa went in and announced that George Kyriakides wanted to see Mr Andreou.

Teresa came back and beckoned George into the room.

It was the main drawing-room of the house, large and impressive. George noticed the inappropriate English furnishings. There were three men in the room; two of them seemed uncomfortably out of place in these surroundings. The third George had no difficulty in recognising as Panos Andreou.

Panos, in his mid-sixties now, still had a head of dark, immaculately groomed hair. He wore a traditional English suit that made no concessions to the changes in fashion of the last few years. The intensity of his dark eyes had not diminished since George had gazed into them in Regent's Park twelve years before.

George was sixteen now and full of the self-confidence that an English public school can give, but his step faltered as he was hit by the glare of three hostile pairs of eyes.

"You are Antonios' son," Panos said. "Why have you come here?"

George gulped. "I'm your grandson too. I wanted to meet you and my grandmother."

"You had another grandfather. You must know he insulted my family. I cannot welcome a Kyriakides here – even my own grandson."

The other two men, shorter, coarser versions of their elder brother, nodded with surly aggression. The youngest, Christos, growled, "What are you doing in Cyprus? You are not a Cypriot. Your father turned his back on his own country."

"Maybe he felt his country had let him down. Anyway, he's here now."

"We know that, of course. Nothing happens here that we don't know," Christos said.

"Are your father and mother also planning to visit me while they are here?" Panos asked less menacingly.

"I don't know. I don't think so. That's why I came."

"Kyriakides must be mad to come here, to Cyprus," Spiros, the second brother, hissed. There was savage anger in his eyes. "Does he think he can come back after what he has done to Panos? After what his father did to ours?"

Panos rounded on him. "Spiros, I told you, I want no more of your craziness."

"You *want* him here – thinking he is someone? He has only come to insult you."

"I've told you; I will deal with it, Spiros," Panos said with quiet anger. "You two go. I want to speak to my grandson alone." There was a hard, incontestable edge to his voice.

Spiros and Christos glared at him resentfully. Christos opened his mouth to speak, changed his mind and left the room without a word. Spiros followed.

"Don't forget what I say," Panos said as they went.

George couldn't help being impressed, as his father had

once been, by the strength of Panos' authority. He heard the other two leave the house, with Christos' furious eyes etched on his memory. Panos didn't speak until the gate had clanged shut behind his brothers.

"Your mother's uncles are not civilised men," he remarked, almost apologetically. "Does your father know you are here?"

"No."

"Your mother is in Cyprus too?"

George hesitated. He knew Thalia's dread of seeing her father again. But Panos was hard to lie to. He nodded.

"Where are they staying?"

"I can't tell you that," George croaked nervously.

Panos did not press him. George guessed he already knew.

"I would like to see my daughter. I am not interested in ancient feuds, unless they are thrust under my nose. I have no argument with you." There was a softening in his manner, a hint of rueful sadness. "You weren't part of what went on before, and you are my grandson. You look a fine boy to me. How old are you now?"

"Sixteen."

"Do you remember when I saw you last?"

George nodded.

"Did I scare you? I'm sorry. I wanted my daughter to come back. Even though she disobeyed me and brought disgrace to her family. But you are a credit to her. You are brave to come here on your own."

"Why should I have anything to fear from my grand-father?"

Panos shook his head slowly. "They haven't told you all that happened, have they? Neither will I. I will say only this. Your father should leave, immediately. That would be best." His hard, black eyes allowed for no compromise. "But I would like to see my daughter. Will you tell them that for me?"

"I think my father will do what he wants," George ventured.

Panos' eyes blazed. "Not here in Cyprus he won't, not while my family is here. Do you understand?"

The brief moment of softness was passed. George didn't answer.

"You go now," Panos said, "And tell your parents what I have said. My brothers are simple men, but they have long memories."

George left the house limp with guilt at the thought of the trouble he might have caused. The taxi had gone without waiting to be paid, and his heart sank. He wasn't feeling brave now.

He tried to remember the way the taxi had brought him and turned into a narrow alley that he guessed led to the sea-front. He had walked a few yards when he felt a hand tap his shoulder. Fear churned his guts as he turned. He was quickly reassured by the expression on the face of the person who had accosted him. The man was in his late thirties, quite tall with a handsome, open face. He gave a quick smile.

"Sorry to frighten you," he said in heavily accented English. "I am Michael Andreou."

It took George a moment to register that this must be his mother's brother. He recognised his mother's eyes and his grandfather's mouth.

"I didn't want to speak to you in sight of the house."

George judged that Michael had no malicious intent and relaxed. "You're my uncle?"

Michael nodded. "Yes. I would like to see Thalia, but that could make a lot of trouble. I know what my uncles are. Tell her you saw me, and that I send my warm wishes to her. But you should all leave Cyprus at once, my friend, believe me."

"That's what your father just told me, but my father won't listen, I know."

"He is a proud man, I have heard, but his pride will be dangerous for him," Michael insisted earnestly. "At least, tell your mother to go, and you." He put a hand on George's shoulder and squeezed it, before turning on his heels and walking quickly back up the lane.

George stared after him. He wanted to call after him and ask him more questions but, as he opened his mouth to shout, a small three-wheeled truck hurtled round the corner into the lane and drowned his call with its unbaffled two-stroke engine. George hopped into a doorway to let the vehicle pass. When he stepped down his uncle had disappeared.

He shrugged his shoulders – Michael had told him no more than Panos Andreou. He turned and walked down the street in the direction of the sea-front, glancing over his shoulder every few yards to see if he was followed.

He found the sea-front and walked back to the Continental. His parents were waiting for him in their suite. His mother greeted him with more relief than he had ever seen in her.

"For God's sake, George, where have you been?"

"I just went for a walk through the town," George answered as casually as he could. "Why shouldn't I?"

His mother believed him because she wanted to. Tony did not, but he didn't say so in front of Thalia.

"You shouldn't have taken so long," Tony admonished mildly.

"I've only been away an hour, like you said."

"Did you know he had gone out, Tony? For God's sake, why did you let him?"

"He's back, isn't he? Nothing happened; stop fussing."

Later, in the bar, Tony and George waited for Thalia to join them for dinner.

"You went to see your grandfather, didn't you?" Tony asked while they were still alone

"No."

"George, don't lie to me. What did he say?"

"He said you should leave – at once. But Dad, what can he do about it?"

Tony laughed. "He's a big cheese here. He forced me to leave once, years ago. He thinks he can do it again. Things have changed more than he knows."

"But his brothers were there. They're real peasants, they'll cause trouble, I'm sure. God, I'm so sorry. When Mum said it would be dangerous to see her father I couldn't see why, but the other two . . ."

"You shouldn't have gone," Tony shook his head, but he understood the boy's curiosity, and admired his boldness.

"Maybe I wouldn't have done if you and Mum hadn't always been so cagey about what happened. Why not tell me, now we're here? Your father did something to Mum's grandfather, didn't he? It must have been something terrible, though; the other two brothers still seem to want revenge; it was really grim, Dad."

"They won't do anything. It's old history, and they took their revenge over twenty years ago. They're still annoyed because they didn't want your mother to marry me."

"Annoyed! They were hopping mad, if you ask me. But Mum's father told them to get out and not do anything."

"Sure," said Tony. "There'd be no point in him getting involved in old feuds. Don't worry about it. Just don't tell your mother you saw them, d'you promise me?"

George nodded as Thalia walked into the bar.

Next morning they left after breakfast to be driven up the coast to Paphos. The road had changed little since Tony had travelled it so often in his old Bedford truck. The first few miles out of Limassol had been metalled as far as Episkopi, where, since Independence and the treaties with the British, a sprawling new garrison had sprung up on both sides of the road. The neat villas of the British officers sat incongruously among lush gardens of Cyprus flowers.

Tony turned to Thalia.

"Do you remember the Cuthbertsons' prefab at Polemidia?" He spoke in English so that George would understand and the driver of the car would not. "I've never forgotten how strange and English it looked, but I've never been in a room quite like it since I lived in England. They're a strange breed, those old-fashioned army types."

Thalia was remembering it too, and tears had seeped into the corners of her eyes.

"I wish we hadn't come, Tony. I didn't want to. It brings back too many bad memories. I'd like to have seen my brothers, especially Ari, but I think it might upset me too much." She turned to him with large eyes pleading in a way she seldom allowed herself.

"Thalia, we're here now. I'm not just going to go back, as if the place had defeated me."

"What's there to be so proud about? You defeated your background years ago. And we both always knew that meant denying it. We don't belong here. I don't see how my family won't get to hear that we're in Cyprus, and if they do, you know what it will be like."

George kept a guilty silence, but turned round in the passenger seat to catch his father's eye.

"They won't do anything," Tony said quickly. "We won't be here long. My mother is expecting us; I can't let her down now."

They drove on, only breaking their silence when landmarks, still familiar, prompted some memory.

There was a dusty track that led down to the beach where they had swum and made love in the moonlight.

There was the place where the tyre of Tony's truck had burst and his cargo of oranges had spilled down the cliff; and the corner by Petra tou Romiou where Takis had nearly driven off the road in the rain.

These sights were like glimpses of another life. They had no connection at all with the sophisticated, rich people talking English in the back of the big, quiet car.

When they reached Ktima – Upper Paphos – they could see the dome of the basilica where old Spyros Andreou's funeral had been held; where Tony had first caught sight of the warm, understanding eyes of the little girl who was Spyros' granddaughter.

Tony leaned forward and abruptly told the driver to carry on through the town and head out on the road to Polis, away from the memory.

The road was worse here, not much improved in twenty years. The traffic became scarcer as they turned off and headed towards Pano Panayia and the mountains.

The greenness of the country here took Tony by surprise. He had forgotten these few months of the year, after the rains, and before the sun began to burn in May. The roadsides were crowded with flowers of a dozen colours. Poppies speckled the fields, and the sharp-edged hills looked as though they had been draped in rich green velvet. Beyond, the 6,000-foot snowy peak of Mount Olympus glittered in the bright sun. As they rose, past Panayia, the mountainsides became more wooded and Tony wound his window right down. The scent of the pines jerked him back to his boyhood on the hillsides where he had sat for hours at a time, dozing with the family goats, and suffering pangs of love in his heart as he waited for Fatima.

Six years ago, Nicos Kyriakides had persuaded his mother to move from the isolated family house to the village. Nicos had built a crude extension to his own block-built dwelling. He and Stelios still farmed the family land, but the old farmhouse was fast deteriorating now and housed only animals and their feed. These days the Kyriakides family all lived in the village.

The triumphant return of Christina's youngest son was

expected around midday. The whole village knew about it. All the men, except Stelios, lingered on their close fields or didn't work at all, so they would be there when Tony arrived.

Excited children in the playground of the village school spotted the black Ford, dusty and spattered from its journey, two miles before it arrived. Any private car was still a rare sight this far up the mountains. Christina and Nicos ran out to greet it as it bumped down the deeply rutted track into the village.

His first sight of his mother since he had left for England abruptly reminded Tony that he really did come from this distant, backward place; that it wasn't all a half-remembered dream. He saw the school, and the taverna where his father used to lounge about, boasting and getting drunk. He told the driver to pull up. He leaped from the car and ran towards his mother. When he reached her, he wrapped her in his arms and she buried her tearful face in the folds of his expensive suit.

Nicos, behind her, beamed in pride and wonder at this sophisticated, alien man who was his brother. Nicos, now in his late forties, was clad in breeches and boots, much as his father had been, with a thick, curling grey moustache.

Tony returned Nicos' smile of greeting, released his mother and held her at arm's length to look at her. The strong, wary eyes hadn't changed, but her face was wrinkled and hirsute. Light grey wisps of hair showed from beneath her black shawl.

"You haven't changed at all," Tony said.

"Of course I have, Tony, I'm nearly dead," she laughed. "I've waited so long for this moment. It's wonderful to see you. You look so handsome, so rich, I can hardly believe it's my son arriving in a big car. And look at my handsome grandson." Her eyes looked past him to where George and Thalia had got out of the car and were walking towards them. Tony turned.

"George, come and say hello to your grandmother."

George felt awkward. He found it difficult to reconcile himself to relationship with these primitive people. But he came and shook his grandmother's hand, and let her hold on to his while she looked at him. She wanted to kiss him, but was afraid.

Thalia stood by and looked at Tony's face and realised how right they were to have come, despite the risks. She walked up to Christina and, needing no words, no introductions, wrapped her arms around the old woman and hugged her tightly.

The driver of the car, who lived in a block of flats in the middle of Nicosia, clambered out of his seat and looked around disparagingly at the mean little houses, chickens, goats and garbage in the street, as he unloaded the suitcases and heaved them into Nicos' ugly, flat-roofed dwelling.

But Tony was too pleased to notice these signs of poverty as he led his wife and son into his brother's home. The main room had been decked out in welcome and Christina fussed around with cakes and brandy. Nicos' shy wife, unable to cope with this invasion of her house, hung back while her three sons, grown up and in their twenties, sidled in to introduce their own families.

Tony beamed as he shook their hands and patted the heads of the tiny children. "Now, I've brought wine and presents for you all." He turned to look for the driver and shouted at him to bring in the boxes that were crammed in the boot of the car. He unwrapped bottles of the best Cyprus wines which he had bought in Limassol, and dispensed presents of clothing, jewellery, radios, watches and English toys for his brothers and their families. Stelios had not appeared, but his four children arrived, two of them with a clutch of children who dived into the piles of toys with glee.

Thalia shook hands warmly with them all and George

tried to understand and answer all the questions that came in a barrage once his relations had relaxed with some wine inside them and lost their awe of Tony who was, after all, one of them.

Tony, delighted by their pleasure, laughed as they all tried to talk to him at once and the children shrieked and squabbled over the toys. The noise was deafening with the small house filled to bursting. Tony held up his hands to quieten them all.

"There are too many of you to fit in here, and I want to see some of my other old friends, so we'll all go over to the taverna."

The celebrations continued in the bar and spilled out into the street until the whole village was involved, except Stelios.

Stelios appeared two hours after Tony had arrived. He walked into the taverna and pointedly paid for his own glass of wine. He stood in a corner scowling at the jovial gathering. Tony went across to him and held out a hand which Stelios ignored.

"Do you think you can make up for running out on us by turning up out of the blue with a few presents?" Stelios growled. He was a well-ravaged fifty now, doggedly wearing the clothes and attitudes of a prewar farmer. For answer Tony shook his head and turned away. But as he turned, Stelios' eldest son, Andi, a good-looking young man of twenty-one, grabbed his arm.

"I'm sorry about my father," he said.

"So am I, but it's not your fault," Tony said.

"I'm not the same as he is," Andi went on in a confidential tone. "I want to do what you've done – get away from this place and make something of myself."

They were beyond Stelios' hearing now.

"How are you going to do that?" Tony asked.

"Will you give me a job in England?"

Tony looked into the young man's eager, forthright eyes

and smiled. He hoped his own son would show as much initiative. "Of course," he said, "But your father will try and stop you."

"He can try," Andi said dismissively. "He's always grumbled about you, because the only thing that really brings in money now are the orange-trees you planted. We've put in lots more since then. But I don't want to end up like him. I've got enough brothers and cousins – too many – to carry on the farm."

"Well, think about it for a bit and if you still want to come in a month or so, let me know."

"I will!" Andi's eyes gleamed. He wanted to go on talking to this magnificent relation, but others were clamouring for Tony's attention, so he looked for his father to taunt him with his news.

Thalia slipped out of the taverna, and went back to the house with Christina to help Nicos' wife prepare an evening meal.

"Tony may be rich," Christina said, as they prepared vegetables in the simple kitchen, "But he has worries."

"Of course," Thalia said, "Wealth always brings worries but he thrives on them. It will do him a lot of good, though, to stay here for a while, and remember that life needn't be so complicated. I'm so glad he's come."

"You are a good woman, Thalia, too good for him in a way. I can hardly believe that you are your father's daughter." Suddenly, another thought struck her. "Does he know – your father, does he know you are here in Cyprus?"

"Maybe; I hope not. I can't see him, not with Tony here."

Christina stopped what she was doing, shut her eyes and shook her head. "Who would have thought one stubborn old man would cause trouble so long after he had died." Christina opened her eyes. "Do you ever see your mother?"

"Not for sixteen years."

"That's terrible, and it's all Theo's fault."

"It isn't, Mrs Kyriakides. She could see me if she wanted to. And your husband only tried to stand up to my father's bullying. He must have been a brave man."

"He was brave, but he was a fool. Tony is brave, but he's not a fool; it's a big difference. I hope your son George will be like that."

"Who can tell?" Thalia started to say, but she was interrupted by Stelios bursting in.

"Your husband –" he said angrily, "my brother, is trying to set my son against me. What does he think he's doing, coming back here to break up families?"

"Shut up, Stelios," Christina's voice was strong and firm. "You've always sat on the boy. What do you expect? And do you know what a fool you look, sulking at Tony's homecoming? Everyone in the village is pleased to see him except you, and everyone knows it's because you are jealous. Now go back and behave."

Stelios stared at her, but said nothing and left. Thalia was impressed by the old woman's authority – a trait she had passed on to her youngest son in large measure.

Despite Stelios' outburst, the celebrations at Tony's homecoming carried on with unstinted merriment. The consensus among the revellers was that success had not spoiled old Theo Kyriakides' boy; he was an example to all young men of what could be achieved.

After everyone had eaten there was music provided by an old gramophone, and dancing until late into the night. But at last Thalia and Tony retired to Christina's bedroom which she had vacated for them. They lay in a swaying old iron bedstead between clean white sheets. Thalia fell asleep almost at once, while Tony lay and listened to her steady breathing in the mountain silence.

11

Thalia and Tony were woken by a cockerel outside their window. A bright, spring sun was already piercing the flimsy curtains.

"What would my father say if he knew I had spent the night here with your family?" Thalia speculated. "Your mother has been kinder to me than my own would have been."

Tony nodded and kissed her, before springing out of bed to dress.

"Where are you going?" his wife asked.

"For a walk. I want to go down to the old house, to see it before Stelios and Nicos get there."

A few old men were already up and heading for the fields with their donkeys. Tony fell into step beside one who was heading in the direction of the old Kyriakides' house.

"I'm glad you haven't forgotten your village," the man said. "Your brother Stelios said you would never come back. But we knew what the Andreous did to you. Of course, your brothers never went out and traded like you did, so we all suffered a bit. But things aren't so bad, with Independence."

"What about this squabbling with the Turks?" Tony asked. "Will that ever end?"

The old man shook his head. "No. We can live side by side, but always with suspicion and tension. The Turks always feel they are getting the worst deals. Mostly, they are, but that's natural, there are fewer of them. Maybe the Enotists were right, and Makarios wrong. Maybe we should have become part of Greece."

Tony thought again of Fatima, probably still in the next village, leading the harder life of the Muslim. His companion left him at a fork in the road, and Tony carried on up the valley to the zigzag track that led to his old home.

He stopped at the top of the track and looked down. From here the place looked unchanged since the last time he had seen it. But when he reached it, he found the house sadly dilapidated. The roof had caved in at one end; bales of hay filled the old bedroom, and the kitchen floor, where his father had lain after his beating, was covered with sheep droppings. There were pigs in a pen outside the front door which hung half off its hinges. Pigeons and martins had colonised all the roof that remained. Mud nests lined the rafters and the deserted house echoed to the cheeping of hungry young birds.

Tony sat on a hay bale and lit a Davidoff cigar. The rich smell helped to rid him of the intense depression caused by the squalid remains of his childhood home.

After a while he stood up, stretched and set off back towards the village. As he walked, surrounded by other reminders of his youth, things which had changed or crumbled, he found it easier to let go of the memories and to convince himself of their irrelevance to his life now.

He considered his position. He had made his way towards the top in an entirely different world, but what had happened with the Oscar had shaken him, made him pause to reflect on what he intended to do with the rest of his life.

He had no illusions about himself. He knew his weaknesses and his strengths, and how to deploy them. On the foundations of the small fortune he had already made he could build as big an empire as anyone, so long as he was prudent and patient. He didn't care about Panos Andreou any more; he remembered how the man had mystified and impressed him as a child, but Tony had little in common with that child now. Panos Andreou was a small cheese with a talent for acting big – that was all. Tony had realised this when Andreou thought he had scored such a victory by forcing him from the Aphrodite. But it was only now, seeing the scale of the theatre in which he operated, that Panos Andreou's relative insignificance came home to him. Where once Tony had been motivated, at least in part, by a yearning to impress Panos Andreou, now he was driven by a need to create a giant and successful business for its own sake, for the satisfaction of doing it better than anyone else, as much as for the material rewards.

Abruptly, as he strolled through the quiet spring morning, he found that he had decided how he was going to go about the building of his empire. He threw down his half-smoked cigar and ground it into the chalky soil with his heel. With the single-mindedness of a man in a desert needing water, he wanted above all else to get back to London and throw all his energy and skills back into the task. He quickened his stride, impatient that he had walked so far from the village.

Half an hour later he strode into his brother's house, where Thalia and George sat with Christina drinking coffee and eating bread and cheese. He greeted them brusquely and fidgeted while they finished. He declined his mother's offer of food.

"Come with me, Thalia," he asked, before she had finished.

"What's the hurry, Tony? We've got all day," she said, but she followed him out of the house and walked beside him up the village street.

"Thalia, I'm sorry, I have to go back to London right away and I can't leave you and George here on your own."

Thalia was annoyed by this sudden change of their plans, and disappointed.

"Why on earth must we go back? We've only just got here," she protested.

"I have to. It's hard to explain, but ever since I sold the Oscar I've been thinking about how I should go on from there, and walking down in the valley this morning, I realised what I must do and I've got to get on with it. You'll just have to accept that I can't hang around here."

"But Tony, I was looking forward to this trip – spending some time with your mother and your family. And everyone here has made an incredible effort to welcome you back. You can't just leave after a day; it's too unkind."

"I can't help that. You know what I'm like," he half apologised. "When I've made a decision, nothing else matters."

"What about your poor mother? She's been so pleased and she's such a strong, brave old woman. I'd hate to see you hurt her."

"She'll understand; she'll have to. I'll tell her that I'll come again soon, and I will, once I've got things moving back in England. And," he added, almost as an afterthought, "there may well be trouble with one of your uncles, if not your father. It was a mistake our coming without knowing their attitude."

"That's not what you said yesterday. You said you wanted to go and see them yourself."

"I was joking. I didn't want you and George to worry. Anyway, we have to leave, so you'd better get ready. I'll go and tell Mamma."

He turned and strode back towards Nicos' house, leaving Thalia looking at his back, shaking her head with disbelief and frustration.

He walked into the house and called to his mother. She came through from the kitchen with a smile on her face.

"Did you have a good walk, Tony? Did you go and see the house?"

"Yes, I did."

"I'm glad. It's good to see the place where you were born. I have been worried these last few years that you had forgotten about your childhood here, that maybe you were even trying to forget us."

"Of course I haven't forgotten where I came from. That's why I came back," Tony said brusquely. "And I'm pleased I did, but I'm afraid I have to go."

Christina gaped at him with forlorn disappointment. "You have to go . . .?" Tears crept into her eyes. "But Tony, you only came yesterday. Why go so soon? Are you uncomfortable? Are you too grand now to stay in your family's house?"

"No, I'm not. I can't explain to you why I have to go; it's to do with my business. I had decisions to make. Being here has helped me make them. I would like to stay longer, of course, but I can't and I can't leave George and Thalia."

His mother remembered the futility of arguing with her youngest son once he had made up his mind. Over Tony's shoulder, she saw Thalia come in. Thalia noticed the plea for help in her eyes, but she shrugged her shoulders and shook her head; she, too, knew what Tony was like when the impulse took him. He would be irrational and obsessed until it was obeyed.

"You are very cruel, Tony," Christina said, "to come and stay for one night. It would be better if you hadn't come at all!"

Tony was not to be emotionally blackmailed. He gave a rich, warm laugh. "Of course it wouldn't. It's been wonderful to see you all, and I'll be back soon. And you can come and see me any time you want. You just have to ask and I'll send you a ticket."

"You know I wouldn't go in one of those aeroplanes. If God had wanted us to fly he would have given us wings."

"So, I'll send you a boat ticket. Anyway," he went on

to stem any more objections, "we've got to go." He turned to Thalia. "You and George get your things ready. I'll find the driver."

As he walked through the peeling, pale blue front door, his brother Nicos almost bumped into him.

"Tony! Good morning. You went for a walk?"

"Yes, but unfortunately, we have to leave now."

Nicos looked at his younger brother's eyes, and his face fell. Then he brightened. "You won't be able to go right away, that driver of yours is still in bed above the taverna; he says he's ill."

"What does he mean, ill? Stupid bastard just drank too much village wine," Tony said. "It doesn't matter, I'll drive. He'll have to go home by bus. I want to catch the next plane to London."

Thalia was behind him now. She made one last attempt to dissuade him. "But why must we go so suddenly, Tony? What has changed since yesterday?"

"I told you; I've changed," Tony said. "I wanted to have a look at myself, and now I have, I want to get back to London. It's as simple as that."

The bags were packed in silence. Stelios arrived and greeted the news of Tony's departure with some satisfaction. But this turned sour when his son Andi arrived.

Andi rushed into the house to find Tony.

"Uncle Tony, they say you're leaving today," he said breathlessly.

Tony nodded.

"But you haven't said yet when I can come and work for you in London."

"Think about it for a month, then, if you still want to, write to me and tell me. Then I'll arrange it."

Stelios glowered at his son. "Don't you have any loyalty to your father?" he hissed.

"Maybe if you had shown some trust in me – sometimes let me take a few decisions and praised me when I'd done well – I would have done. Anyway, the farm will never support all of us, so," he expanded his hands in a gesture of generosity, "I give up all my claims to it."

Stelios spun on his heel and stormed out of the house.

"Do you think that was wise?" Tony asked Andi.

"What am I giving up? Not much, not with all of us cousins. And what do I gain? Liberty and the chance to really make something, like you've done."

"Let me know in a month," Tony said again and turned back to the business of getting his family's luggage out to the car.

The Ford Zodiac pulled out of the village amidst tearfulness and warm farewells. Tony drove away too fast over the bumpy track. He hated goodbyes.

The first four miles of the route back to Paphos was by a mountain road of earth and broken rock, shaded for the most part by thick pine and cedar woods. There were great clefts between the mountains – valleys four or five hundred feet deep, falling sheer away from the side of the earth track.

Normally, all that passed along this road were the daily village bus to Ktima, a few trucks and fewer private cars. Even now, twenty years after Tony left, not many farmers or villagers could afford them.

There were occasional places where the road was wide enough for two vehicles to pass, usually on the inside corners of the hairpin bends which succeeded one another along the mountainside.

Tony was pleased how well he remembered the road which he had driven so many times as a young man. He pushed the big car as fast as he could where the mud was dry and flat, leaving a trail of dust and broad cornering marks behind them.

Thalia protested, but he laughed.

"I remember these roads and how to drive them. I used to take some terrible old trucks up and down here, and I never left the road once." He glanced across at his wife, sitting beside him. Her face was rigid with fright.

With a light hand on the wheel, Tony steered down a straight stretch of road towards a gentle left-hand inner turn at a cleft in the rocks where a stream gushed down and under the road. It was a wide corner. A level passing place had been made there, deep in the fissure, behind a jutting rock. Tony reached out a hand and squeezed Thalia's knee.

"Would I do anything stupid with you in the car?" he asked, sensitive for once to her fear. His eyes were off the road for an instant.

It was George, in the back of the car, savouring the danger and peering at the road in front, who first saw the truck nose out from behind the rocky cliff ten yards before the Ford reached the bend.

"Look out, Dad!" he yelled in sudden panic.

Tony jerked his eyes back to the road in front.

A three-ton pick-up was now broadside across the road, leaving a space just wide enough for the Ford to pass in front of it along the unguarded edge of the gully.

There was no stopping; they were travelling at sixty miles an hour on a crumbling surface. Without taking time to work it out, Tony realised instinctively that if he passed in front of it, the truck would simply have to nudge the car to send it crashing down the rocky chasm to the valley floor three hundred feet below.

Placing his truck to do this, the driver had left a small gap between the back of the pick-up and the rock which had hidden his ambush. It wasn't wide enough for Tony's car to pass clean through, but it was the less dangerous of the two options on offer.

"Get down!" Tony yelled at Thalia and George. "Cover your heads!" With his left hand, he reached over and dragged his wife down on to the bench seat beside him, while he swung the car to the right towards the gap on the inside of the corner.

The tail of the truck caught the Ford on the windscreen, directly in front of the place where Thalia's face had been an instant before.

Tony's side of the car scraped the rocks at waist height with a screech of rending steel.

The truck driver had his gear lever in first, his foot on the clutch and no brakes on as he waited to push Tony and his family down the mountainside. The impact of the large car hitting the tail of the lightweight, unloaded lorry pushed it forward. The driver's foot jerked off the clutch, adding momentum as it careered inevitably towards the edge of the road and the chasm below.

Tony brought the car to a broadside halt in a cloud of dust. He leaped out and ran round to see the truck – it seemed in slow motion – tip and disappear over the edge of the road. The sound of crunching and crashing echoed up the gully as loose rocks and shattered trees joined the tumbling truck.

Tony ran to the side and saw a trail of broken timber and sliding scree which marked the passage of the vehicle, now lost from sight among the trees on the valley floor.

George was beside him, staring in horror and relief at the trail of destruction that should have been made by their own vehicle.

"It was one of them," he gasped.

Tony turned to him. "One of who?" he asked sharply.

"One of Panos . . . my grandfather's brothers. I saw him at the house."

Tony growled bitterly. "My God, these people are fucking savages. Their brother's daughter was in the car, for God's sake!"

He turned and looked at the Ford. Its panels were torn and battered but it was still in one piece and drivable.

"Is your mother all right?" Tony asked.

"Yes. I think so. She said so. I think she's just shocked."

Tony was already on his way back to the car to see for himself. As he approached, Thalia lifted her head and turned her face to look through the misshapen gap, framed in shattered glass, that had been the passenger-door window.

Tony tried to open the door. It needed all his strength to wrench it free from a buckled front pillar. When he had opened it, he reached in and pulled his wife towards him. He lifted her out and carried her to the side of the road where he sat her on a hummock of soft mountain grass.

"Are you all right?" he asked.

Her mouth was strained tight with shock; she could only nod.

Tony felt her limbs and searched for signs of cuts or lacerations, but he found nothing. There would be bruises, of course, and the shock, but otherwise, thank God, she seemed unhurt.

"I'm sorry, my angel," he said with a growl and a tenderness he hadn't expressed in many years, "I'm sorry I made you come here."

She shook her head vigorously, still unable to speak.

"George," Tony called over his shoulder, "Find something to carry water from that stream."

George opened the undamaged boot of the car and fished out an antique earthenware pot his mother had bought the day before and took it to the small waterfall. He carried it back to Thalia and helped her to drink from it. Tony controlled his impatience as she gasped and slowly gulped the pure chilly liquid.

After a few minutes she managed to whisper, "It wasn't an accident, was it?"

Tony shook his head.

"My father?" Thalia asked with anguish.

"Your uncle. Christos, I should think."

"What's happened to him?"

"I don't know. He's in his truck at the bottom of the valley."

Thalia started to push herself up. "Tony, we must leave; get out of Cyprus now."

Tony nodded. "I think that would be best," he said calmly, to understate the horror of what had happened. He helped his wife to her feet and led her to the battered car. George climbed in the back. Tony checked that none of the wings was fouling the wheels and opened the twisted driver's door to get in. He turned the ignition key and the engine fired, unaffected by the crash. He knocked the loose pieces of glass from the edge of the windscreen housing, and carried on along the dirt road towards Paphos.

From Paphos Tony phoned the airport. There wasn't a London flight that day. He booked seats on a six o'clock plane to Athens. They abandoned the Ford and hired a taxi to take them straight to Nicosia.

At the airport the man who had rented the car to Tony was prepared to believe that it had been damaged in an accident outside Paphos. His main concern was that Tony should pay the excess insurance charge. Tony paid.

On the plane to Athens they sat in a row, George by a window and Thalia between him and Tony. For a few minutes after they had left the ground they were silent. When the plane had levelled out at its cruising height, Tony turned to Thalia.

"What a disaster!" he said in English. Then he laughed. "Bloody foreigners."

12

"Has Tony stopped seeing his mistress since you got back from Cyprus?"

Anthea Sherwood asked the question with her usual bluntness. It was a deliberate device, not to hurt her friend but to shock her into facing her husband's infidelity.

Thalia was sitting opposite Anthea on a squashy chintz sofa in her Argyll Street drawing-room. For a moment not a muscle moved in her face. She didn't want it to seem that she didn't know what Anthea was talking about, and yet she was in no doubt that Anthea wouldn't say what she had without being certain of her facts.

It made sense, of course. It explained anomalies in Tony's behaviour and in his demands on her.

"Don't tell me you didn't know about Tony and Monica Fakenham?" said Anthea, realising with surprise that Thalia did not. "I am sorry. But he's been so indiscreet for the last few years, I assumed you did. And you continental women are so much more pragmatic than the English about that sort of thing."

Thalia owned up. "No, I had no idea." She bit her lip; at least she wouldn't allow Anthea to see the tears that were trying to escape.

"Why are men such bastards?" Anthea wanted to console Thalia with the obvious fact that she wasn't alone in her predicament. "I suppose it goes back to their primitive role, when humans were still animals, and the male's primary urge was to sow his seed wherever he could."

"Are all men like that, though?" asked Thalia. "Is Edward?"

"I think I've been lucky," Anthea conceded. "Edward claims that though he wouldn't mind a bit on the side, he'd rather not have to lie to me and go through all the business of keeping it clandestine. And he knows I wouldn't stand for anything overt."

"How . . ." Thalia paused, not wanting to hear the answer to her question, "How did you know about Tony?"

"I'm afraid it's quite common knowledge. I'm amazed nobody else has told you. I suppose they thought it kinder not to. Well, as you were bound to find out sooner or later, better sooner, so that you're prepared if it comes to a head."

"You mean, if he decided to go off with her?"

Anthea gave her a businesslike nod.

"Oh, no," Thalia said, confident of this at least. "He wouldn't leave me. Whatever he gets from her, he could never get what he has from me. He may be pig-headed and arrogant, but he's fair, and he's not a fool."

"Well, I hope you're right to be so confident. Do you know Monica, by the way?"

"Not really. She's always kept her distance. Now I see why. She's been to some parties, always with that awful husband. I've met him, and I must say I can't blame her for straying. But why to Tony? I would have thought she was far too English and snobby to be interested in him."

"Tony's very attractive, Thalia. You can't be so naïve that you didn't expect other women to make a play for him. And as for Monica's snobbiness, Tony is a fascinating foreigner, and that transcends all social obstacles."

Thalia understood enough about the English to accept what Anthea was saying. "When we were flying back from Cyprus after that horrible crash . . ." Thalia shuddered at the memory, "he talked about the Cypriots as bloody foreigners. He thinks he's more English than Greek now. It's ridiculous but, after what happened in Cyprus, I think he wants to abandon his Greekness. Now, of course, he doesn't really know what he is; that's one of the reasons he works so hard. He seems to think that making a lot of money will give him an identity."

"Maybe that's one of his reasons for keeping this affair going with Monica," Anthea suggested.

Thalia shook her head. "I think mostly it's just for sex."

"Oh well," Anthea chortled, "Takes a bit of the pressure off you."

Thalia didn't answer. She asked Anthea if she would like another drink. "The men won't be here for another half an hour, so we might as well entertain ourselves."

But they had drunk only a second small, dry sherry before Tony arrived at the same time as Edward Sherwood. They were due to dine, the four of them, at Le Gavroche in Lower Sloane Street.

Over dinner Thalia had a chance to study her unfaithful husband as he and Edward debated Tony's new plans. She was sitting opposite Anthea but while she tried to follow her friend's conversation about new initiatives for the homeless, most of her attention was on her husband.

Anthea's revelations about Tony had dropped like a bombshell into her life less than an hour before, but she had already accustomed herself to the idea. Maybe Anthea was right; the continental woman's understanding of the continental male did allow pragmatism, albeit an uncomfortable and degrading state of mind. But then, Tony had not left her, as she knew he never would, and she decided there was nothing to be gained by challenging him over Monica. But she had allowed herself to become too distant from her husband's activities and interests; she realised that could lose him for her. And, despite everything that made him such a difficult man to live with, she still loved him. She watched him, confident as ever, quite unaware of the slight change in her attitude towards him. While he picked without interest at a dish of delicate veal and subtle sauce, he volubly outlined his position to Edward Sherwood.

"I've formed Theodore Investments as a holding company for the Olympus, the Vine and Pine and the Pitta and the Wolf franchise. It also handles my investment of the cash from the Oscar."

"What are you doing with that?"

"Short-term stuff, mostly: overnight money market, foreign exchange dealing, a bit of speculation in equities."

"What our friends across the Atlantic euphemistically call 'arbitrage'?"

Tony shrugged. "It's legal, and less risky than roulette. I may as well make the money work until I'm ready to start using it seriously. First I have to tidy up the mess."

"You mean Pitta and the Wolf?"

"Yes. It's been a disaster, as you must realise. It's not only people cheating me, and failing to follow my instructions for the operation of the franchise, it's all these other dirty little doner kebab stalls that have set up over the last few years. They're stinking little dumps; they serve a few slivers of half-cooked minced waste-meat in stale pitta bread and give Greek food a terrible name. Of course, they make a lot of money from drunks falling out of the pubs, so they don't see any need to change. I tried to give Pitta and the Wolf a completely different up-market image, but people still identify them with those other places. So," he shrugged philosophically, "I'll have to try to buy them myself."

"Then sell them?"

"In time. It's the only way to salvage something from the wreckage, but I won't get much for them the way they are. I'll have to change them drastically, and that means turning my back on the food of my fathers." He grinned. "Not at the Olympus or the King's Road, of course."

"But Tony, the Pitta and the Wolf restaurants are operated by franchise holders with certain rights."

"I know, I know. We made the agreements together, didn't we? Well, all of them are in breach of their agreement in one way or another. I shall offer them the chance to buy out of their contract, provided they change the name – or sell me their lease." He nodded thoughtfully. "I guess I'll have to buy around twenty of them."

"Judging by some of your franchisees, that could be tough."

"With a lawyer like you?" Tony gave a confident laugh.

"Yes," Edward said, "Even with a lawyer like me."

The two men talked on. Thalia saw the light of Tony's ambition burning in his eyes as brightly now as when she first knew him; when his biggest aim was to secure a contract to supply early potatoes to the British garrison. When their eyes met, she detected no guilt in his.

She turned back to Anthea who was asking her about George.

"How's he getting on at school?"

Thalia waggled her hand in an ambivalent gesture.

"He's clever and he knows it. The school says he has a good chance of getting into Oxford. He'd like that, he thinks that would be very smart. He could stop working and concentrate on sport and girls. You know, he's idle, but applies himself if he has a particular target."

"It would be marvellous if he did get a place at Oxford," Anthea said. She didn't need to add, especially for the son of a Cypriot immigrant.

"The problem is he's lazy," Thalia said. "As long as he finds it easy, he'll work, but when it needs effort, he won't bother."

Tony was listening to this. He interrupted. "So what's wrong with that? If he gets to the university let him enjoy himself if that's what he wants. Then he can come and work for me; he won't need a degree for that. After all, I left school at sixteen."

"We'll see," said Thalia, without articulating her doubts.

They finished dinner, and the Sherwoods, declining a lift, set off to walk back to their house in Chelsea. Tony and Thalia sank into the seats of their Bentley as it purred towards Kensington.

Tony was more relaxed and positive than he had been since the Cyprus incident. "I like seeing Edward. He's the only Englishman I know who understands me," he said.

"That's good, because I'm sure no Cypriots do," Thalia replied.

"Maybe." Tony was unconcerned. "By the way," he went on with a change of tone, "Stelios' boy, Andi is coming here tomorrow. It will be good to have a member of the family working in the restaurants."

Tony hadn't mentioned this possibility since they had come back from Cyprus two months before. By tacit agreement they had avoided any discussion of the trip. Neither they, nor George, wanted to think about any retribution that might be sought for the death of Christos Andreou. Thalia had heard nothing from her mother or brothers and she sensed that Tony had also decided to push Cyprus and his connections with it right out of his mind.

But he had been in communication, it seemed, with his nephew. Perhaps she had misjudged him. She knew that she had, as far as his attitude to George was concerned, when he went on, "It will keep George on his toes, to have Andi working for me. He's going to need some competition."

George Kyriakides was quick to perceive why his father had employed Andi. Tony, in any case, didn't trouble himself with subtlety.

"I'm going to need a reliable member of the family to run that side of the business for me as it grows," he said,

"And just in case you get too grand for a bit of hard work, I'm getting Andi started in the Olympus."

He said this after his nephew had been in England a few weeks and had already displayed practical intelligence and a handsome charm. Andi had made it quite clear he was hitching himself to Tony's star, and he was a natural in the job.

His English was good, and having managed, at the age of twenty-four, to avoid being hooked into romance and wedlock with a girl from his valley, he was single. He deployed his easy charm well and had assembled a surprising variety of female admirers.

George, six years younger, was impressed. With his father's agreement, during the long summer holidays he spent several evenings a week helping Andi at the Olympus. When the restaurant was quiet the two would sit and talk, usually with one or more of the inexhaustible flow of female foreign 'students' who seemed to find their way to the Olympus and Andi.

After Andi closed the restaurant, they would often take a few girls to one of the discothéques in the West End or a club in Chelsea. Occasionally they would take them back to the flat above the Olympus where Andi now lived and where George had been born. With Andi's blessing, George began to learn about the needs of women, and the rewards they could offer.

One evening towards the end of the holidays, George was feeling frustrated at having to go back for his final year at school. But his experiences over the past few weeks had given him a new confidence. He was sitting in the Olympus, not working that night, talking to a Polish girl called Anya with spectacular auburn hair and bouncing, unharnessed breasts.

Anya was Andi's current target; George knew, as he persuaded the girl to leave with him, that he was treading on his cousin's toes. As they went out, he felt Andi's eyes burning into the back of his head, but he carried on, and flagged down a cab to take him and Anya to a new club that he hoped Andi hadn't heard about.

But the evening was not a success. He kissed the girl as they danced, tried to insert his tongue between her lips and had it badly bitten. When they sat on a sofa with large drinks beside them his hand crept up her legs with the subtlety of a prop forward's, and was sharply smacked down again.

The girl was not the walk-over that Andi had been boasting about, which was probably, George reflected, the reason for his interest in her.

Philosophically, and with bogus good humour, he dropped her off at the hostel where she was living in Earl's Court, and went home to Argyll Street. He wasn't looking forward to seeing his cousin next evening, but decided it would be best to brazen it out and get it over with.

He turned up at the Olympus at six, an hour or so before any customers would arrive.

Andi glowered at him as he walked in.

"Hi, Andi," George said lightly and went on quickly, "I don't know how you cracked it with that Polish chick. I couldn't get anywhere with her."

Andi looked slightly mollified. "Of course not, you stupid bastard. Once they've been with me, they're not going to be too interested in you, are they?"

"Some are."

"Sure, but only after they know I don't give a shit."

"It must be that peasant charm of yours," George said in an effort to appease.

Andi's eyes blazed. "Just because you're the boss's son, don't get any big ideas. You're just as much a fucking peasant as I am. Your mother's family may be the rich people in Limassol now, but we all know where they came from, and how they did it."

George had no experience of this sort of attack. He quailed before his cousin's anger. But Andi hadn't finished.

"You think you're so smart, don't you, going to your posh school, with your rich English friends. But whatever they say, for them you'll always be a 'bubble-and-squeak' bloody upstart. I've seen how they are with you when you bring them here."

George thought Andi was wrong, but he wasn't sure. He had always struggled to be indistinguishable from his school-fellows, but that summer his very success with the girls, while a source of envy, also set him apart from them. But he wasn't going to take this from Andi.

"Look, you've been here a few months. You're lucky you had someone to give you the chance you've had. You don't know anything about how things work over here, and if you're anything like the rest of the Cypriots in London, you never will. I couldn't give a shit about Cyprus; it gave my father nothing but hassle. I've got nothing in common with those people up in the mountains. What's the point of pretending to have some feeling for them, some pride about them? You may be older than me, but you've got a lot to learn."

George banged his way out of the restaurant with Andi yelling after him. It was the end of their brief friendship, and they both knew it. But George had learned a lot from it.

He went back to St Paul's for his final, A-level year, determined to make it to Oxford. He had been to see the university the previous term, had been captivated by the architecture, and guessed at the glamour of the antiquated life-style. And he knew that being part of one of Britain's oldest institutions would raise him far beyond his current status as the son of a successful immigrant. For this, he was prepared to work. His father, who never really doubted the consistency of his genes, observed this with fond pride.

His son was only doing what he too would have done. If he had had the chance.

During George's last year at school Tony Kyriakides acquired fifteen Pitta and the Wolf premises for negligible sums and was operating them himself as tidily as he could.

But this was not his long-term aim.

Having accepted that the kebab was no real match for the hamburger, he now combined his hunches with a serious study of the alternatives. He had seen the potential and the success of the pizza chains that had sprung up and he appreciated that Italian food appealed to a broad market. The Italian trattoria, serving traditional meat and pasta dishes, was already an established part of the British restaurant scene, and he had no intention of directly challenging the pizza operators. But he thought there was still an unexploited market for pasta.

There was nothing new about spaghetti houses as such, but there were a hundred other variations in the serving of pasta which had never been offered to the English public. It could be presented in a cheap but stylish way to appeal to an increasingly sophisticated public.

The most important element in this would be the operator. Tony needed to find someone who knew pasta and had the management skills to run a chain of restaurants – an entirely different skill from running a single one.

Discreetly, he scoured the Italian restaurants of London. He was well known, but it was normal for a restaurateur to visit the opposition and Italian proprietors were not surprised to see him. Nor were they averse to rubbing in the well-documented problems of his own chain.

As it happened, operating them himself, his fifteen Pitta and the Wolf kebab houses were holding their own, and no one suspected that he had any plans to change them.

In a restaurant in the Fulham Road he spotted an

outstanding young waiter who was acting as manager of the place while his boss was away. It was a large, busy restaurant, always fashionable, with a demanding clientele.

Alfonso was in his late twenties. Tony noticed the calm efficiency with which he dealt with customers and staff, who were for the most part older than Alfonso. Tony recognised the same quiet dedication with which he himself had impressed Neo Michaelides.

The third time Tony lunched at the restaurant he gave Alfonso his card and asked him, discreetly, to ring him.

The young Italian was on the phone that afternoon.

Two months later, the first Alfonso's Pasta Bar opened in Notting Hill Gate. Tony created the rumour that he had simply sold the premises, and the next few pasta bars were launched in Manchester and Newcastle, unnoticed by the London-based competition.

They were simply and inexpensively decorated. The pasta dishes, consisting as they did mainly of flour and water, carried a huge profit margin.

Alfonso had needed little conversion to the simplicity of the concept, and was thoroughly committed to it from the day Tony first put the proposition to him. "It's so simple," he enthused after they had been open a few weeks, "We take a sack of semolina, and turn it into a sack of money."

During that first year after the Cyprus visit, Tony worked fourteen hours a day, laying the foundations for the next stage in his career. Running the restaurants was no more than a holding and consolidating operation, but it had to be done right. He was in no doubt that he deserved the success that the pasta bars were already delivering. His two original London restaurants were both performing well, and he hadn't ignored them: he made a point of visiting the Olympus and the Vine and Pine at least twice a week. But they were established, with loyal, though different clienteles, and running them was mainly a matter of maintaining standards.

Amidst this frenetic work, Tony saw no reason to abandon Monica Fakenham. As far as he knew, he had kept the affair secret from Thalia – although this sometimes surprised him. He and Monica had maintained their pattern of regular but infrequent meetings which kept their liaison fresh. The guilt Tony had briefly felt over Monica had faded. There was no question in his mind of his ever leaving or abandoning Thalia, and Monica had no wish to divorce Charles Fakenham. Tony, for his part, was sure that Thalia knew he would never leave, and he believed she felt no insecurity in their marriage.

But Monica remained an influence in his life. He wasn't aware that it was her influence which had given him the circumspection to take a long-term view of his business. The fact that he had money in the bank and no borrowings helped, and the experience of his visit to Cyprus. But it was Monica, cool, cynical and perceptive, who gave him the confidence to control his Greek impulsiveness. She also affected his appearance and manner. Though still manifestly not English, he had developed an air of internationalness that was not specifically Greek.

Since Anthea had first revealed Tony's affair to her, Thalia had maintained her decision to say nothing to him about it. But, despite her expressed interest in his business, she found it difficult to become practically involved again. Her work with the Society took up most of her time and, whereas in the early days scarcely a day passed when she didn't visit or work in one of the restaurants, now she seldom went near them. Since her heart-to-heart with Tony which led to the creation of the Pitta and the Wolf, he avoided discussion with her about the business. She didn't fight it; and she spent more time with her own friends, whom she found more congenial than most of Tony's business acquaintances.

Thalia did, though, make sure that she kept up a rapport with her fast-growing son; she knew and liked most of George's friends and encouraged him to bring them home. She was much more integrated into the English way of life than Tony and, with considerable success, she helped her son to be the same; George's schooling had done the rest. Through her charity activities, Thalia now had a wide circle of English friends. This led to regular invitations to spend days in the English countryside which she learned to know and love.

But one thing she had not done. Despite the overwhelming temptation, she never contacted her old friend from Cyprus, Mrs Cuthbertson.

Mrs Cuthbertson – she knew – had come back to England. Thalia had kept up to date with her moves and changes in circumstance since then. She scoured the gossip columns and discreetly questioned friends who had connections for news of the family. But she could not bring herself to contact them directly.

George, meanwhile, was performing as well as she could have hoped. In his final year at St Paul's he was captain of their winning cricket side, passed three good A-levels and was offered a place at Worcester College, Oxford.

In the autumn of 1972 his parents drove him up to Oxford and moved him into his first rooms at the college.

While Thalia fussed about his clothing and domestic arrangements, George showed his father what little he already knew of the city. It was the first time George could remember his father specifically seeking an opportunity for the two of them to talk.

Tony felt slightly awkward in this venerable place whose ethos was so alien to his own background, and yet, when he cast his mind back to his schooldays as an eager bookworm, he envied his son.

"Being in this place, away from home, is going to have a big effect on you," he said as they strolled up the Broad in autumn sunshine. "It could drive you away from me and your mother. I want you to promise you will never feel any shame about us."

"That's not the sort of thing one can promise; either one feels it or one doesn't," George replied. "But I don't see why I should."

"You have to think about why you've decided to come here," his father said. "Is it to learn, to grow and develop, or to waste three years of your life on childish amusements?"

"I thought, a bit of each, actually, Dad."

Tony laughed. "Get the balance right. It won't do you any harm to get a degree, and it won't do you any harm to have some fun. But don't forget, when you leave, you come and work for me. Provided you understand that, I'll give you all the financial support you need."

It was a naked bribe. George didn't let his pleasure show too strongly, but this was exactly what he had been hoping to hear.

"Of course I realise that, and I expect I'll get used to the idea," he said with a lightness that convinced his father. "I won't let you down."

At the age of nineteen George Kyriakides was a good-looking, self-possessed young man. He didn't find it hard to settle into university life, although he wasn't always comfortable with the few anachronistic, aristocratic throwbacks who were still to be found at Oxford. But he was prepared to extract the maximum enjoyment from his time there. He had chosen to read Politics, Philosophy and Economics, deliberately for the woolliness of these subjects which would allow him time to pursue his other interests.

Not the least of these were the women – in the university and in the quasi-educational establishments which the city spawned to make up for the shortage of females in the university itself.

Within a few days of arriving at Oxford, George had found himself an ally in his quest for entertainment.

Peter Protheroe was also a freshman, with rooms on the same staircase in college. The first few times they passed on the stairs or outside, they nodded, acknowledging each other warily. On the third day of term George found Peter carrying half a dozen wooden cases of expensive-looking French wine up the stairs to his room.

"Do you want a hand?" he asked.

"Yes, please. I'd like to get them up as quick as poss before some other bugger pinches them, and I can't find the scout."

The two students soon had the wine installed under a table in Protheroe's room. Peter wiped his brow. "I can't really avoid offering you some, I suppose," he said with languid indifference.

"It looks worth drinking," George said, "So I'll accept."

Peter wrenched open a case and extracted one of the bottles of '66 Haut Brion. "My father would be appalled at our drinking this at eleven in the morning, but then, he's still rather common and has to worry about that sort of thing. I'm Peter Protheroe, by the way," he added without ceremony. "And you're some kind of Greek, I take it from your name in the porter's lodge."

"I'm a Cypriot type of Greek," George said.

"You certainly don't sound like one," Peter said. "What was your name again?"

"George Kyriakides."

"Where have you come up from?"

"St Paul's. And you?"

"Winchester."

He had filled two glasses with crimson claret and gulped his appreciatively. "I must pinch some more of this next time I go home. Where do you live?"

"Kensington."

"No country place?"

"My father doesn't feel comfortable in the country."

"Nor does mine, but that doesn't stop him. He's determined to become a country squire and make people forget that his father was born in a Sheffield back-to-back. Personally, I'm rather proud of it, gives one a kind of Lawrentian mystique."

George thought Peter Protheroe looked the epitome of an upper-class Englishman. He soon realised that Peter did too, while making much of his *nouveau riche* background. It was a technique that required arrogance and confidence, but it worked, and it precluded anyone from ever using his working-class origins against him. Although George's initial and, to some extent, lasting impression of Peter was that of a supercilious twit who ought to have known better, he also recognised the practicality of Protheroe's attitude. For Peter Protheroe was also skilled at obscuring his academic ability. He had come to Worcester College with an Exhibition to read Classics but talked down his brightness in a way that served only to heighten other people's awareness of it.

Peter detected a similar tendency in George. Almost from the start, the two established an unspoken mutual appreciation. To himself, though, George recognised that where he was quite bright and quite idle, Peter was very bright and very idle.

They fell into the habit of having a drink together every day, either in college or in a pub. In most aspects of their relationship, Peter was the acknowledged superior. But George was patently more successful with women. For the first time George appreciated how the Englishman's natural aversion to making a fool of himself inhibited his behaviour with females.

George had no such reservations. He had already learned to turn an initial rejection to an advantage. He had slept with a few of the girls he had taken out with Andi, and one or two before that whom he had met at parties in London. The girls here presented, for the most part, a far greater challenge. For one thing, the competition was a lot more intense, but his foreign good looks and, more importantly, his laid-back approach gained him a reputation for worldly maturity in matters of sex, which reality did not entirely justify.

George was satisfied he would get what he wanted from the university. He attended most of his lectures and his tutor was occasionally complimentary about some of his perspectives on European politics but, with his Finals three years away he found he couldn't bring himself to worry about them and his academic work became a secondary occupation.

Unlike Peter Protheroe, George enjoyed his sport. He played rugger for his college and even held out a faint hope of being selected to play for the university. He was amused by the difference between the type of undergraduate he met on the rugger field and the sybaritic types to whom Peter was attracted, and enjoyed them both.

He also enjoyed going to the debates at the Oxford Union. He relished the proximity to the famous and significant figures who were prepared to come and speak to this privileged institution. One unlooked-for bonus was the sight of the President of the Union. At the age of twenty-two, sophisticated, cynical and supremely self-confident in the face of world-class statesmen who had been persuaded to appear, the President could present a case of outrageous controversy for the sheer enjoyment of it, while half the audience ogled the long, black-stockinged legs that she displayed beneath the scanty length of a plain black dress.

To George and Peter, Anna Montagu-Hamilton was the epitome of a desirable and challenging woman. She had long, coal-black hair and enigmatic, deep brown eyes. They imagined that her body would have looked perfectly at home in the pages of a glossy girly magazine, and all this attached to an intellect of impressive force. Usually after debates their discussion would revert to Anna with unbridled admiration. They both knew, though neither would admit it, that, apart from anything else, being in her final year, she was out of their range, and they joked with each other about how they were going to achieve their goal of getting her into bed.

But to his shame, during the year George came face to face with her only once and in ignominious circumstances.

One sunny, Saturday morning, during Anna's last week at the university, George was on his way back from a game of squash, still in his shorts and singlet. He was on his bicycle, with his head down, cutting a corner, when he ran straight into her mini coming out of Parks Road.

George saw the driver and, to his horror, felt himself redden.

"Christ, I'm sorry," he mumbled with none of his normal fluency.

She looked at him over the top of a pair of dark glasses. "Well you haven't done any damage to me, so if you're all right, that's fine."

George was hit between the eyes with a sudden dazzling smile as she put her car in gear and drove on.

He watched her go, feeling he had performed like an adenoidal adolescent. What was more, Peter Protheroe had witnessed the encounter from the other side of Broad Street.

"That wasn't up to your usual standard," Peter said as he strolled over to gloat "And I'm ashamed of you, riding about the town in a sweat-stained singlet."

George shrugged his shoulders. "Oh well, I know my limitations," he said lightly, and untruthfully. "And I spotted a horny look in her eye. I think the singlet and the rippling torso turned her on."

"Like the sparkling repartee?"

"I bet you I get there before you do," George challenged.

"You'd better make it a large bet, then, because the way the poor old pound is faring, it'll be worth bugger all by the time that woman lets you inside her underwear."

PART TWO

Anna Montagu-Hamilton

13

Anna recognised the good-looking man who, for no good reason, had run into her car as she waited to turn into the Broad from Parks Road. She remembered seeing him at Union debates but she had not, as far as she remembered, heard him speak. She had no idea what his name was, but despite his standard public school accent as he apologised – more than was necessary – she guessed it was foreign.

But as she drove away, she gave it no more thought. She was on her way to see Martin Vickers, a philosophy don whose lectures she always attended and whom she had chosen as her mentor. She had just completed her finals; he would want to know what she had thought of them. But that wasn't the only reason why she was going to see him.

She parked her silver mini outside a rambling Edwardian house on the Banbury Road. She climbed out and stretched her long, bare legs. She wore a short, yellow cotton skirt and an embroidered Indian blouse. On her feet were simple white sling-backs. She pushed open a rickety side gate and crossed a neglected wilderness of garden to the front door of the house.

The door was ajar. She pushed it open and went in without announcing herself. The only sound in the large hall was the deep ticking of a grand, long-case clock. She was struck, as she often had been, by the appeal that the untidiness of the place held for her – not the untidiness itself, but as its expression of the householder's personality.

Martin Vickers had no interest in the superficial impression he made on anyone. It would not have occurred to him that anyone might be critical of the shambolic existence he led, the lack of late twentieth-century obsessions with cleanliness and modern mechanical conveniences. A cleaning woman was known to appear at irregular intervals, but she was discouraged from excessive zeal.

The hall was carpeted with a fine old Shirvan runner. Anna noticed a hole at the edge where some small animal – perhaps registering approval of the pattern – had eaten into it.

Since he had inherited the house from his mother, Vickers had changed nothing, beyond having shelves erected for some four or five thousand books in what had once been called the morning-room, and where he now worked.

His father had been a don too, and the air of scholarliness hung thick in the house. It possessed a particularly bookish smell, blended with odours of tobacco and French coffee and comforting, faintly manorial whiffs of woodsmoke and dry sherry.

Anna stood for a moment in the gloomy hall and inhaled the familiar smells; she thought she would miss them.

"Martin?" she called, in case he had a student with him. The sound of a book falling on the floor announced that he was in. A few seconds later, he appeared.

"Ah! Medusa." He glanced at his watch. "Good God, I'd no idea it was so late. I've been struggling with the proofs of Jovial Jim Bolton's book – the influence of Greek classical thinking on the growth of Christianity – a positively senile chestnut. But much more important, my love, how have you done?"

Anna shrugged her square shoulders. "A congrat second, if I'm lucky," she grinned.

"That bad, eh? Still it's more than you deserve; you're not really First material, let's face it."

"Sure," she replied, "I've faced it."

"I wonder, perhaps, when we're marking degree papers

242

whether we shouldn't allow a little positive discrimination to creep in. After all, there are some tremendous academic disadvantages in being as rampantly desirable as you are. Where is the incentive to work, to assimilate knowledge if everything else is granted you with such woefully little effort on your part? You're as deprived as any student I've ever come across, deprived of the need to try."

He had walked up to her and reached a hand behind her head to stroke her long, black hair while he looked deep into eyes the colour of dark coffee.

Abruptly, he leaned down and, placing his other arm beneath her thighs, lifted her and carried her towards the stairs at the back of the hall.

It was early evening when they came down. Anna didn't want to go, but she was hungry now, and Martin never seemed to eat.

He took a bottle of Burgundy from a half-open cardboard case in the hall, and led her into the kitchen where he found a corkscrew and filled two large goblets.

"Are you leaving Oxford, then?" he asked, as if the past three hours had merely been an interruption of another conversation.

"Yes, of course."

"You're probably right. What now? The bar, I suppose, or publishing or politics?"

"No. Commerce."

Martin was appalled. "What on earth do you mean?"

"I'm going to be a businesswoman."

"Don't be absurd. That's not for people like you, for God's sake. You've got a mind. Why not read for another degree?"

"It is possible to use one's mind outside Academia, you know."

"Perhaps it is. I hardly know anyone from outside. But it seems a terrible waste. After all there are millions of other people to engage in commerce." He tipped his goblet for a long gulp of wine. "What sort of commerce? No," he interrupted her answer. "Don't tell me. I'd rather not know."

"I don't know why you're suggesting I'd be such a loss to the university," Anna said. "You've told me often enough that I was little more than average."

"Intellectually you are, but you have an aggressive curiosity which makes up for that. And anyway, people like you don't benefit from flattery."

She looked at him with the frustration and fascination he always evoked in her. He was such an absurd contradiction of himself. On the one hand a completely unworldly, brilliant teacher of modern philosophy, on the other a man of arresting good looks, and a schoolboyish enthusiasm for sex. These two aspects of him seemed to exist apart, in a way which only added to his attractiveness. Anna was certainly not alone in her interest in Martin Vickers, but she had held his attention longer than any other woman in Oxford.

She had known he would disapprove of her ideas for her future. For that matter, so would most of her contemporaries, but that didn't worry her. She had known he would try to shame her for such unworthy ambitions, but he couldn't. She had unbounded regard for Martin Vickers' intellectual powers but she also knew her own talents and how she intended to use them.

The remnants of sixties liberal attitudes still pervaded the university, but they left her cold. They were too passive; they relied on an idealistic view of the world that was unlikely, in her view, to persist.

Buried deep inside her was a fierce instinct for survival which showed itself in her very practical approach to everyday problems. Sometimes this surprised her – it seemed so un-English – but she was incapable of even pretending that she had time for the still-born hopes for an 'alternative' ideology so enthusiastically aspired to by most students at the time.

She had been brought up in an atmosphere of old-fashioned disdain for transitory, easily-obtained pleasures. She had been taught that, if a taste for something were easily acquired, it was not worth acquiring. Recondite pictures, inaccessible music, esoteric literature were all savoured and praised in her austere, diplomat stepfather's house. Downright enjoyment of simple pleasures was regarded as something for the uneducated and unprivileged.

Anna understood these terms of reference at home and at Oxford. She could talk that language, and talk it convincingly. Privately she did not subscribe to it, but this facility and readiness to deal two-handedly with life, she realised, could be a useful skill.

Anna found no guilt in relishing easy pleasures. Above all, she wanted to be entirely free of the crushing pressure to conform to the attitudes imposed by her stepfather and the university. Up until then, her private aims had remained unvoiced. She had deliberately chosen Martin to hear them first.

At that stage she had only a vague idea of how and where she planned to make money. She had simply decided that she was more likely to achieve intellectual and personal liberty by making some money and, more important, being her own boss. She was in no doubt that she had the intelligence, perceptiveness, personality and determination to succeed in business at least as well as in the more obvious fields that Martin assumed would attract her. She was a desirable woman, and this would oil the hinges of some doors normally difficult to open. And, unlike the bra-burners who were currently vocal on many platforms and whose shrillness she despised, she relished that advantage.

*   *   *

"My aggressive curiosity, as you call it," Anna answered Martin, "suggests to me that there are thousands of places and people in the world that I want to see and hundreds of experiences that I ought to have. And I'm not going to do it from the back of an old van or with a rucksack on my back."

Martin sighed. "You see. I told you, there are too many temptations for women with bodies like yours to allow them to keep their minds untainted."

"For 'untainted' read 'narrow'," Anna said. "I don't want to be untainted."

Martin laughed. "You don't have the choice any more."

He poured more wine into her empty glass. "By denying your intellectual integrity, you'll lose all that's valuable in you. Don't you mind?"

"I don't think so."

"You must come back and tell me some time. I think I'd be interested."

"You're not really interested in anyone, whether you're teaching them or screwing them."

He smiled, unashamed. "You're quite right, of course."

Two days later, Anna flew to join her parents in Vienna.

Typically, her stepfather didn't come to meet her at the airport. He had, though, allowed his wife, Susan, to use the official car and driver to greet her daughter.

Anna sank gratefully into the soft seats of the ageing Rolls-Royce.

"How are you, Mum?" she asked. "You don't look as serene as usual."

"James hasn't been all that happy here, I'm afraid. He feels the posting was a bit of demotion. He hopes he might still get Bonn or Moscow, but he's worried that he's too close to retirement for that."

"Does he take it out on you?"

"Good heavens, no. He doesn't really let it show at all,

but I can sense it in him. It's a terrible shame; Vienna's a very nice place to be for a while. There's such a lot to do. I hope you'll stay for a bit."

"I could do with a few weeks of doing absolutely nothing. I must have worked harder than I thought for my finals."

"And what sort of degree do you think you've got?"

"Some kind of a second."

Susan sighed. "James will be disappointed."

Anna already knew that. And if he was feeling frustrated in his current posting, she would be just the target he needed.

When Sir James had married Anna's mother, he had willingly accepted her three-year-old daughter as part of the package. Susan was so ideal as a diplomat's wife that this was not a great price to pay. She had travelled with her first husband, and had made a point of becoming familiar with local cultures and people, and, while not highly intelligent, displayed a great deal of Anglo-Saxon practicality.

Over the years Sir James had not been able to restrain his own intellectual arrogance and tendency to belittle those who did not match it. Susan had suffered, and been completely defeated by it. She ceased to take the kind of interest she had in the local peoples and places, because her husband consistently told her she was mistaken in her judgements. As time passed she retreated into herself, and devoted all her enthusiasm to her talented daughter.

As Anna grew up, Sir James recognised and appreciated that she was a more challenging woman to deal with than her mother. He developed a healthy respect for his stepdaughter's determination and academic ability.

When she won an Exhibition to Somerville, he flew straight to London to congratulate her. In return for his support he expected to be provided with a worthy and tireless opponent. Anna had been easy to stimulate and glad to play that role. But, until now, Sir James had always been secure in knowing there had been no blots or hiccups in his progress up the diplomatic ladder. Although, as Susan had said, his vanity, and therefore any damage to it, was almost invisible, Anna was as aware of it as her mother and she didn't look forward to seeing how disappointment had affected him.

He greeted her with his normal, finely judged charm, allowing just a hint of affection to show.

"You're looking splendid," he said truthfully. "I was concerned that you would be suffering from post-examination pastiness. Or did you find you were able to cruise into a first without burning too much midnight oil?"

"Lurched into a second, would be more accurate," Anna said lightly.

Sir James lifted an eyebrow, and the slight smile left his lips. "Surely not? What can you have been doing? I heard only recently that better things were expected of you. Perhaps you're merely being modest."

"I'm afraid not, Dad. But there it is. Frankly, I don't care. I've had enough of the tiny, introspective world they all live in there."

"What are you intending to do?"

"I'm not sure yet. Travel a bit; see what the real world has to offer."

"At least you haven't come back dressed in an Indian bedspread with flowers in your hair," Sir James said, attempting to soften his criticism.

"All that sort of thing's rather on the way out now, Dad," Anna laughed.

"It'll be good to have you here for a while. We can talk through all the possibilities that a Second Class degree has to offer."

Anna had known that Martin Vickers' disapproval would be pale beside her stepfather's, so she had decided that, for the sake of a few quiet weeks, she would have to be vague, if not downright dishonest about her future plans.

After the few days that it took to adjust Anna settled into the sumptuous diplomatic residence, with all the fringe benefits that accompanied it. There was a period of calm while she was expected to rest after the effort of her finals, and the results were awaited.

The good Second Class, when it was announced, evoked resigned congratulations from her stepfather, and proud, almost incredulous enthusiasm from her mother.

While an atmosphere of approval prevailed in the household, she took the opportunity to put a proposal to her parents.

Her mother was one of only two surviving descendants of a line of hardy Lowland Scots who had been entrepreneurial engineers in the second half of the nineteenth century. Her ancestors had undertaken the demanding contract to build the first railways in Sicily. Against political and geological odds that would have thwarted many, they had succeeded, and the rewards had matched the arduousness of the task. The villa her grandfather had subsequently built in Sicily, on the eastern coast between Messina and Taormina, was one of the most magnificent constructed on the island at the time.

Regrettably, following the fashion of Edwardian England, the subsequent generations of the family had turned their back on the skills and determination that had made their small fortune. They were now gentlemen, they decided, and did not have to earn a living.

The fortune, quickly amassed, dwindled almost as fast in the twenties crash and stagnant economy of the thirties. The Second World War brought Susan's family to the edge of penury. When it was over there was little left to show for their grandfather's efforts besides the magnificent Sicilian house. And the Villa Ypolitta, as it had been called by a man espousing classicism after a life of profitable industry, devoured money. It had been commandeered first by the Germans, then the British as a suitably impressive place in which to set up an HQ, but neither set of officers, while enjoying its qualities, had taken the trouble to protect or preserve it. It became clear that it was not practical for its inheritors – Susan and her sister – to live there and, having moved to England late in 1939, they decided not to return to live in Sicily. Since the early fifties the house had been regularly let, a year or so at a time, while winter gales ripped at its decaying fabric, and its letting value diminished. The house became a regular topic of depressing, inconclusive conversations.

Anna had visited the place with her mother and step-father five years before and had developed a strong rapport with the island, its people, and the Villa Ypolitta. Now Anna proposed she should go to Sicily, check on the villa's condition and the state of the furniture, as well as look at the possibilities of finally disposing of the splendid white elephant. She told them vaguely that she would look for a more permanent career in London that autumn. A few months off after a good university career seemed perfectly reasonable.

Her parents agreed that for the months of July and August, when there were only a couple of short, unsatisfactory lettings arranged, she would be safe in the house, or in the servants' wing when the house was occupied, looked after by the old couple who were still retained as hopelessly inadequate guardians of the place.

Three weeks in Vienna spent for the most part arguing, or at least disagreeing with her stepfather had stifled Anna. As she left Austria in a plane bound for Rome Anna felt a weight of oppression lift from her shoulders. She planned to stay for a few days there before taking the train to Calabria and the ferry to Messina.

For the first time in her life Anna was a free, independent woman. She had no commitments to anyone or any

250

institution. She was answerable to nobody. Her mother and stepfather hadn't tried to place any restrictions on her. Sir James made her a small allowance, and she had recently inherited a few thousand pounds from her grandmother's estate.

Emotionally too she was unfettered. It was well within her scope to subjugate the – anyway fairly controlled – infatuation she had nursed for Martin Vickers; and she had no illusions about his commitment to her. He had aroused and fulfilled her inexperienced body more than any of the three undergraduates who had tried; although she had no doubt that other men existed with the capacity to lift her to those elusive heights of ecstasy.

She arrived in Sicily thirsting for adventure

14

Crossing the ten-mile strait from Reggio, Messina came into view through a haze caused by the sun on the sea and the exhaust fumes of a city full of overworked motor-vehicles. This brownish tinge, unable to escape into the upper atmosphere through the layer of anticyclonic, sultry air which hung above it, didn't distress Anna greatly, and as the details of the place became clearer, her excitement grew.

As she walked down the passenger gangway, every smell that greeted her, every flash of sunlight on bright surfaces, every man on the harbour front, seemed to announce a new phase in her life. From the skinny boy, no more than fourteen, who hustled her to carry her bags, to the daredevil taxi-driver who hurled his threadbare Fiat south along the old coast road between the Pelorita Mountains and the sea, she sensed animal responses which gave a frisson of alarming excitement to her stilted conversations with them.

It wasn't that she had not come across the unambiguous approach of Mediterranean men, just that she was less inclined to condemn them than she would have been in her former life as a female student leader.

Recognising this, she smiled at the shimmering sea like a proselytising vegetarian about to embark on a private feast of beefsteak.

The Villa Ypolitta was approached by a drive that ran a hundred yards through unruly woodland of pine, ending in a jungle of stubby palms and hibiscus in front of the house.

From the outside the house was more run down than Anna had remembered five years before. It appeared now not many stages away from dereliction. The woodwork, unpainted in twenty-five years, was peeling, and sections of the elaborately carved veranda had fallen away.

The villa had been built along Palladio's lines and could have been commended as a faithful reproduction of the style of this much plagiarised architect. It was a brand of classicism that had appealed to her great-grandfather's sense of order and romance. And, commissioned by an engineer, it was fundamentally well-built.

The taxi-driver leaped out of the car with a flourish of gallantry to open the back door for his passenger and to heave her luggage from the boot. He showed his appreciation of Anna and the generous tip she gave him with a lingering, squeezing shake of her hand and a gaze of undisguised lust.

Feeling that she should offer something in return, Anna said in her uncolloquial Italian, "Give me your name and phone number, for when I next need a taxi to Messina."

"Signorina, for when you need a taxi *anywhere*," the handsome man declared.

At this moment one of the double front doors at the top of the crumbling stone steps creaked open and a wizened, scantily white-haired old woman appeared and displayed a set of overlarge false teeth in greeting.

"Welcome, Signorina. Your mother has told us you were coming. It is wonderful news that you are to see about the repairs."

This was less wonderful news to Anna, who had not understood that repairs were her brief. Obviously her mother had been unable to admit to Signor and Signora Testa that selling the place was the favoured option.

Anna smiled back and waved a hand at the dilapidated place with a cheerful, not entirely defeatist shrug. "It's lovely to see you again, Magdalena. I hope I can do something here."

The old woman brusquely signalled the driver to carry Anna's bags into the hall of the house. With a mild display of truculence he did this and, unable to think of an excuse to stay longer, he drove his car away with an extravagant spinning of wheels and scattering of dry earth and gravel.

Inside the fifty-foot reception hall, furnished in high Victoriana, there was less evidence of disrepair. The grand old English furniture and Scottish paintings showed no more than a respectable patina of age. The cushions of the deep sofas were only a little threadbare, and the curtains, though severely faded, still possessed an air of opulent elegance. But the paintwork was chipped and scuffed with the comings and goings of careless soldiers thirty years before.

Signora Testa took Anna on a tour of the rest of the house. A suite of three reception rooms led through double doors one into the other. They gave on to the veranda and a tangle of brightly-flowered vegetation that had once been a fine, formal garden.

As the house was between lets, the furniture was mostly under dust-sheets. Anna tweaked up the corners and was surprised to see how well-preserved it all was. The fact was that, apart from the years during the war, the house had seldom been continuously occupied, and had not suffered long periods of use or abuse. The dining-room housed a twenty-foot table and chairs of Scottish baronial proportions. The library was furnished with vast mahogany bookcases, desks and reading-tables.

"Some people from Milan were here," Magdalena said disparagingly. "They had booked for a month but, I explained to your mother, they left after a week; they didn't say why. Some American people are arriving next week. I think they will find it too old-fashioned, though."

She gave a shrug of piteous contempt for this kind of philistinism.

Anna laughed. "I'll look forward to seeing their faces when they arrive. Where do you want me to stay, when they're here?"

"We have prepared the flat above the stables. It's not very beautiful, I'm afraid, but it's clean."

"I'm sure it'll be fine," Anna said. "It's kind of you to have gone to the trouble."

"Oh, we like it when someone from the family comes. Your aunt was here three years ago, and that was the last time. I'm so glad your mother wants the house repaired now, but it will cost billions of lire," she added doubtfully.

By the time Anna had toured the whole house, all fifty rooms of it, she was enchanted. The idea of selling it seemed deeply disloyal now that she was within its solid, handsome walls and among the comfortable mustiness of its furnishings.

Magdalena led her through the kitchens and sculleries of the house, out to the back courtyard of laundries, store-rooms and boiler-house, and through an arch to the stable-yard.

Unlike the architecture of the house, the stables and coach-house were unequivocally British in flavour with a cobbled yard and English loose-boxes. The only horse that occupied them now was an old draught animal. Chickens ranged, unchecked, alongside an army of skinny cats and, presumably – though unseen – sleek rodents.

A rickety wooden staircase ran up an outside wall to the rooms which had been prepared for Anna. Light, white and full of flowers, the bedroom contained a simple wide iron bedstead, and a pine chest of drawers with a cracked triple glass on top. In the second room was a small stove, a table with two chairs and a sideboard. In one corner was a large square sink with a single tap above it. Beyond this room was a tiny bathroom with, Anna noted thankfully, two taps over the bath.

Wisteria surrounded the windows, trying, where it could, to intrude between the window frames and the walls. The sound of chirruping birds among the foliage on the outside wall was continuous, and sun streamed into the tiny apartment.

Anna turned to Signora Testa. "This is wonderful, Magdalena. I can't think of anywhere I'd rather be for the next couple of months." And she meant it.

The American tenants arrived the following week. They had booked the Villa Ypolitta for the month of August.

There were only four of them to occupy a house that could have held thirty. They were an earnest, academic family from Princeton. Howard Franklyn was a professor of European History, his wife, the university librarian. With them were their daughter, in her early thirties, apparently unattached, and a son, Bill, who was twenty-eight, an alumnus of Princeton and a junior partner in a firm of New York lawyers.

Far from expressing horror at the lack of modern facilities, as predicted by Signora Testa, the Franklyns were ecstatic about the archaicism of the villa. For the first few days they could be heard crowing with pleasure as they discovered yet another antique characteristic of the house and its offices.

Anna's first reaction was annoyance. They were much too close in their outlook to the people she had left at home and in Oxford, whom she felt she was betraying in nurturing her desire for physical adventure. The daughter, Barbara, particularly made Anna feel guilty about her frankly uncerebral urges.

But there were compensations in having people around who used the same terms of reference as she had for the last few years. It was inevitable that she would find herself spending a lot of time with the Franklyns, joining them on trips to ruins belonging to every civilisation that had established itself on the island over the past three thousand years and experimenting with food and wines in the grandest and simplest restaurants in the surrounding towns and country.

Professor Franklyn, not unexpectedly, considered his visit a working holiday. Barbara and her mother shared a particular interest in the works of Luigi Pirandello and Giovanni Verga, and they organised for themselves several literary pilgrimages, leaving the less romantic Bill to find his own entertainment. From the start he made it clear where he thought that was to be found.

He was not what Anna had in mind when all her female instincts had been aroused arriving on the island, but he was attractive enough for her not to want to discourage him. He scored points with her by discovering the tennis court and, with some help from two boys he recruited from the village down on the coast, reinstating it to a usable condition.

He was a good player who, with little subtlety, allowed himself occasionally to be beaten by her. After their games, they would sit on a bank above the court talking with no great sense of self-importance about anything that interested them, from food to Freud, Beowulf to Bauhaus – anything that presented itself to their well-schooled, well-stocked minds. Their talk was non-combative and, they knew, inconsequential; it was just an enjoyable habit which they recognised in each other.

This mental diversion contrasted with Bill's taste for physical activity. He took Anna out in a small fishing boat and impressed her with his maritime skills. At the end of the first week in the house he disappeared for a morning and returned at lunchtime with the largest motorbike he could find for hire in Messina.

Anna didn't deny the pleasure she found in riding astride

the big machine, with her long hair flowing free and her arms around Bill's waist as they wound up the side of Mount Etna or raced along the coast road in the setting sun after a day of swimming and diving in the caves beyond Taormina.

But Bill made no hint that he might be interested in any kind of physical relationship with her. This puzzled Anna, for he certainly wasn't gay, and it annoyed her slightly. She admitted to herself that he was turning out to be as good a companion as she could have wanted in these circumstances and, though her instincts were against his Ivy League manners and good looks, he had an impressive, athletic physique.

Once or twice, when she turned down his invitations for no particular reason, she was impressed by his apparent lack of pique. She was in no hurry to start organising builder's and decorator's quotes for the work that needed doing on the house, but she felt that she should use these by-days from Bill's company so that she would have something to show for them, and a genuine purpose for having denied him.

The builder who had been recommended to her by the family agents in Taormina arrived early on the morning she had arranged. Lucio Martino was in his late thirties, supremely confident of his skills, and dismissive of his new client's ideas about what needed doing.

Lucio was tall for a Sicilian, a little under six feet, and possessed, with conscious pride, classic, deeply-tanned southern Italian features, coal-black, wavy hair and moody brown eyes. Soon after he arrived he found it necessary to remove his Levi jacket to reveal a wiry brown torso clad only in a black, skimpy singlet. Anna, trying to preserve some dignity under the onslaught of his arrogant disdain for a woman's views, took care to show him everything on her own list of the building's defects.

Lucio lifted his eyebrows. He knew the house, he said, and she had barely scratched the surface.

He was, of course, more adventurous than she had been when it came to inspecting the roof. He clambered out and teetered along the ridge of the shallow gable, stopping every so often to create more work for himself by removing previously secure tiles. By the end of his tour, Anna's list had been doubled and the contempt with which Lucio treated her had not diminished.

It was, Anna thought, a virtuoso performance of Mediterranean chauvinism and she could not help herself thrilling to the challenge of taming it, of reducing the man to blubbering submission. It would be a long task, but she had time; and there was a possibility, though no certainty, that there might be some enjoyment to be had on the way.

Lucio left with a surly, non-committal shake of his crinkly hair. Thoughtfully, Anna watched him go and decided that Bill deserved a reward for his sang-froid in the face of that morning's rejection.

Professor Franklyn and his family had spent the day in Taormina, inspecting the Greek Theatre for the second time. They had lunched well and arrived back in a cheerful, garrulous mood. Bill came to find Anna in her rooms, where she was lying on her bed, reading Jack Kerouac and listening to Pink Floyd on a small record-player she had bought herself.

She looked up and smiled as the big American came in.

"Good dose of antiquity today?" she asked.

"Yeah. There are so many goddam ruins on this island, Dad's as excited as a monk in a brothel. He sort of wallows in it."

Anna liked his deep voice and Anglophile, East Coast accent.

"Would you like a drink?" she asked.

"Sure, thanks," he nodded.

"There's a bottle on the kitchen table. Could you open it and pour us both a glass?"

Bill went through to the other room and came back with two full glasses.

There were no chairs in the room. Anna propped her back up against the iron bed head, and patted the edge of the bed beside her for him to sit.

He sat; the bed squeaked. They both laughed.

"Have you been lying here all day?" Bill asked.

"Certainly not. I had a builder round to look at the place. We're having a few repairs done, at least, we're finding out how much it might cost."

"Don't do too much. It's a fantastic old place the way it is."

"I'm only talking about leaks in the roof and rotten woodwork."

Anna had already told the Franklyns the history of the house, but Bill asked, "What will you do with the place?"

"We don't know. It belongs to my mother and my aunt now, and neither of them will ever want to live here. They hardly ever come to stay. I only said I'd come and have a look at it as an excuse to live here for a bit."

"What did your builder think?"

Anna laughed. "I think he saw a very big job which he wasn't certain he'd be paid for. He was reassuringly surly, very weak on sales pitch. I don't think he liked the idea of dealing with a woman, but he's very good-looking, and probably very randy."

"He couldn't be as randy as I feel," Bill said without emphasis. "This heat, the wine." He shook his head with a smile of self-censure.

Anna reached out a hand and laid it on his thigh. She glanced at the bigger than normal bulge at the fork of his jeans. "Oh dear," she said. "You have got a problem."

He grinned.

He leaned his head towards hers and searched in her dark eyes for confirmation.

She tilted her head and gave him half a smile.

He leaned close until their lips were touching. He felt her hand slide up his thigh and gently knead the long hard lump in his jeans.

Bill was a vigorous, tender lover; Anna had the impression that his gratification depended, at least in part, on hers; and he was not disappointed. He made love to her without extravagance or exhibitionism, but with a gradual, then suddenly explosive increase of pleasure that gave her as deep a satisfaction as she had ever known, even with Martin Vickers.

Afterwards she clung happily to his solid, chunky body, idly kissing and caressing him back to firmness until he was ready to come into her again.

While they were making love, the sun lowered and the birds stepped up their evening chorus among the wall-climbing shrubs outside Anna's bedroom window.

They lay side by side, later, touching each other and listening to the birds, for the moment utterly content.

An hour or so afterwards, they went back to the house to eat dinner with Bill's parents and sister, who, if they noticed a change in the relationship between Bill and Anna, gave no sign of it.

At the end of August and the Franklyns' last week Lucio, the builder, came to see Anna for the third time.

He had followed up his original visit with another to make a more detailed inspection. Now he was to tell her what the work would cost.

The Franklyns had left early that morning on a trip to Syracuse. There was less urgency in Anna's desire for sight-seeing, and she had declined to accompany them on the long trip before she arranged for Lucio to come.

When he arrived in his brand-new, bright-red Alfa Romeo it was at once obvious that the builder had decided to change his approach. He saw Anna waiting at the top of the stairs as he drew up, and leaped out of the car, with a broad, untrustworthy smile on his face.

Anna wondered if this was merely a commercial expedient on his part, or a sudden realisation that Anna was, after all, an approachable woman. On balance, she preferred the idea that it was part of his sales technique.

She invited him to sit at a table in the hall to look at his assessment of what needed doing to prevent the house from deteriorating any further.

Lucio had prepared an impressive list. Anna's lack of technical and local vocabulary put her at some disadvantage, but she was determined to understand every detail of what he was proposing.

But the projected prices of each job were not clear. Lucio's manner became evasively vague when Anna raised the question, but he said that a practical solution would be for her to pay him a fixed sum of money each week until he had finished the job, but he was unable to commit himself on the amount of time it was all going to take.

Anna shook her head at this proposal. A look of intense hurt appeared in Lucio's eyes, at the implication that he might take advantage of her feminine lack of commercial sophistication.

"Signorina Montagu-Hamilton," he said, "I can't do what you ask. I don't know what some of these jobs will cost until I start doing them. I can't guess. After all," he pleaded, "I am a businessman, not a fortune-teller."

Anna stood up. "Can I offer you a drink, Lucio? And then we could go through it all again, and you could try to put a price to some of the work, couldn't you? I'm sure we can reach some kind of understanding, but it must be more definite than you suggest. I can't give you the job without any idea of what it will cost, can I? And you don't have to call me Signorina Montagu-Hamilton; just call me Anna."

Lucio's eyes lit up, whether at the prospect of a drink, the increased familiarity she suggested or the opportunity to extract some kind of decision from Anna that day, Anna could not tell. He leaped to his feet and asked if he could assist. Anna said no, but he followed her to the large mahogany cabinet which held the drinks, and stood behind her, admiring her bottom and bare legs as she leaned down for glasses. When she straightened herself, she felt his breath on the back of her neck. She turned to find a look of appreciative lust in his eyes and a smile of such naïve unsubtlety that she laughed.

Lucio was encouraged. Before she could take evasive action, he had his arms around her and his lips close to her ear.

"Signorina Anna, of course we can come to some kind of understanding. You are a very beautiful woman and I am a . . ." he paused, "Well, I am a man," he said simply, as if it were quite unnecessary to state his obvious manly qualities.

"I wouldn't disagree with that," Anna giggled as she wriggled herself from his arms and handed him the wine bottle to open.

After that, she managed to keep Lucio under control, holding out to him only the vaguest hint that his clearly stated ardour might at some point be reciprocated. She had also, as the quickest way of finishing the tricky discussion, agreed to let him start work on the unsatisfactory basis of paying him weekly against bills for specific tasks done, so that the job could not get too much out of hand.

He drove down the drive as if he were competing in the Targa Flora, and Anna smiled at the fantasies she had allowed herself about him. As soon as he had smiled, all the mystique of his surliness had vanished.

*   *   *

That night Bill came to see her and they made love, as they had done almost every day since the first time.

Her zeal this time surprised him.

Afterwards he said, "Hey, what happened to you today? It's only twenty-four hours since we last made love."

"D'you know, I think I'm going to miss you," she replied.

"I doubt it. Not for long, anyway," Bill said with unexpected pragmatism.

"It's been great, you being here. When I got here I had an idea I wanted a hot, sweaty scene with one of the locals. Now that I've seen more of them at close quarters I'm not so sure. But that's probably just my northern European prejudices subjugating my physical instincts."

"They usually take a lot of subjugating, and I'd have thought, looking at you, that there's a bit of Mediterranean blood in you too. Maybe your great-grandmother committed a few indiscretions."

Anna laughed. "I doubt it. Have you seen the picture of her in the hall? It would have taken more than an oily smile and a pair of randy black eyes to turn her on."

"You never know," said Bill. "What will you do here now, besides driving the locals mad with unrequited lust?"

"The builders start next week. I'll have to keep an eye on them, and I've got a few other ideas for the house."

"What are they?"

"Well, I don't think we should sell it. Frankly, I don't think we'd get a lot for it. Of course the pictures and some of the furniture are worth a bit, but there's not much feel for high Victoriana at the moment."

"No, but there will be some time. It's amazingly self-assured, it has to be to be so gross. I love it."

"Anyway," Anna said, "it goes with the house. What I've been thinking of doing is turning the place into a very individual sort of hotel. It could hold maybe fifty people and, if the mix was right, there could be a fantastic atmosphere here, don't you think?"

"I do. It's a great idea. Who would you be aiming to get here?"

"I haven't thought about it that specifically yet." Despite her determination to rid herself of academic prejudices against trade, Anna was still embarrassed to enthuse about a commercial venture.

Bill took a realistic, American view about commerce. "That's the first thing you want to identify, and then you know what to make of the place. What will their priorities be? You know – some people want bathrooms, some want antiquity. Some people want cleanliness, some want beauty."

"Well, they've got to be rich, intelligent and sophisticated," Anna admitted, "but the antiquity and beauty crowd, rather than bathrooms and cleanliness. That doesn't mean there won't be bathrooms, or the place won't be clean, but those qualities will be incidental. The first thing I'm going to do is look for a chef; the best chef in Sicily. And musicians – to play and sing Sicilian love songs – and a barman that looks like Rudolph Valentino. The best of everything." Anna was becoming unashamedly effusive. "I'll make the Villa Ypolitta the best, most exclusive hotel in Europe."

"Come on, why not the whole world?" Bill laughed. "You're beginning to sound like an American," he said, in a way that was not meant to be complimentary.

"I don't care. Do you know, since I've really started thinking about it over the last few weeks, I've become so excited about the idea. It's as if I were expecting a baby or something."

"What?" said Bill in sudden alarm.

"No, don't worry, of course I'm not," Anna laughed, "Thanks to good ol' Oestrogen."

"It's a great idea. You do it, and don't let anyone tell

you you don't have the knowledge or the experience. Just have the enthusiasm. The only thing is, do you have the money to do it?"

"I haven't really worked out what it will all cost, and I thought I'd do it bit by bit, plough back the profits as I make them."

"You'll need plenty of money." Bill shook his head. "I wish I had some to invest, but I don't."

"You could send me a few customers though, couldn't you, from among your more discerning New York clients?"

"Of course I will. You never know, I might just turn up here again as a guest."

"I'll have the best bed in the house ready for you."

"Yours?"

"Wait and see."

15

Sir James Montagu-Hamilton read his stepdaughter's letter with mixed feelings.

He had guided her academic career with the aim that she should realise her early potential in reaching a good university and achieving an acceptable degree. He had not concerned himself with her future beyond that point; it seemed unnecessary; if she could achieve those targets, she would have as wide a range of options as any intelligent woman could want.

He had assumed that she would gravitate towards one of the learned professions, while side-lining in the arts or politics. It had not occurred to him that she might chose a commercial career. But he prided himself in being a practical man and a realist. He had no objections to a young woman wanting to make money; if she was successful at it, it could save him some. Although he had reached the upper levels of his own profession and had inherited the rump of his family's diminished estates, he was not a particularly wealthy man.

In the short term, this posed another problem for him. Anna said in her letter that she estimated she would need £50,000 to convert the Villa Ypolitta into the hotel she planned. While he could probably raise the sum, the idea of becoming a commercial investor, with the risks, responsibilities and worries that involved, appalled him.

He spoke to Susan about it.

"Have you read Anna's letter?" he asked over breakfast in the Vienna Residence.

"Yes. She seems very excited about this plan of hers."

"I don't really know about this kind of thing, but it seems all pretty much pie in the sky. Obviously I can't invest fifty thousand, even if I wanted to. And your family certainly can't. How on earth did she think we could help?"

"It does sound a lot of money. Of course, Margaret and I did say we were prepared to spend a few thousand to make the place saleable, but this is something we hadn't remotely considered. And I wonder if there are that many people who would want to stay in a funny old place like Ypolitta."

"She seems to have no doubts about that, and maybe she's right, but she can't begin to do it without some capital, and there isn't any for her," Sir James said simply, with a shrug of his shoulders. "I'll write to her and suggest that she carries on getting the repairs done, and puts the place on the market, that is, provided you and Margaret are in agreement."

"Yes," said Susan, "I'm sure you're right, and Margaret will agree. I do hope Anna isn't too disappointed though."

"For goodness sake, she's only twenty-three. It won't be the last disappointment she'll have in her life. I'll suggest that we meet in London when she gets back from Sicily and we can discuss other possible careers."

Susan accepted his ruling, as she had learned to do over the previous twenty years. These days, she simply accepted the superiority of her husband's intellect and knowledge, though, in occasional private moments of mutiny, she asked herself how on earth he ever negotiated with his opposite numbers when he always thought that his was the only tenable point of view.

Sir James had not allocated time to write the letter of rejection to his stepdaughter before a second letter arrived from her.

It was brief:

Dear Dad
Since my last letter, which you should have received

a few days ago, I have been approached by someone who's very keen to invest in my plans for the hotel here. It only needs Mummy and Aunt Margaret to agree to signing a lease, for which they would receive a good rent from the company that will operate the hotel. This seems like a much better proposition than the family investing. Please let me know by return what you think, and I will send you complete details.
Love to Mummy
Anna.

Sir James gave a sigh of relief and immediately dashed off his approval, confirming that he was sure that his wife and sister-in-law would prefer this option. Obviously there would be legalities to deal with, and why didn't she arrange to meet him at the family's solicitor's in Lincoln's Inn when she could provide the details.

He despatched the letter, happy that an annoying burden had been fortuitously lifted from his shoulders.

Henry Pedersen had turned up at the Villa Ypolitta without any warning.

Anna found him one morning towards the end of September, wandering about the reception rooms of the house with an appreciative, speculative look on his face.

"*Buon giorno*," she said with a faint question mark.

He glanced at her.

"Hello. Are you Anna?" His accent was educated middle-American.

"Yes. And who are you?" She studied the small man. He was, she guessed, in his early sixties, with thick grey hair and a straight back to compensate for his shortness. His grey eyes gave the impression of understanding everything they saw.

He walked towards her with brisk, energetic strides, and held out his hand.

"I'm Henry Pedersen. I know Bill Franklyn."

The simple statement told Anna all that he had intended it should. Pedersen, she soon realised, was a man who seldom said anything superfluous or irrelevant – like how he knew Bill, what he thought of him, or what Bill's state of health and mind were.

Anna took his hand and returned his short, firm shake. "I see. Why have you come here?" she asked, unconsciously aping his brevity.

"To invest in your hotel."

She had already guessed at something like this, but his directness took Anna by surprise.

"Bill told you about my plans?" she asked unnecessarily.

"Of course," he answered. "Where shall we talk? Right here?"

They were in the library. He waved a hand at one of the great mahogany writing-tables.

"Why not?" said Anna. "Let me get my papers and some coffee."

With a single-minded intensity that precluded all distraction, Henry Pedersen spent the next three hours with Anna going into every aspect and cost of her plans. He identified dozens of problems in setting up and running an hotel – things that she hadn't even considered. He allowed for every contingency, down to a complete failure of the whole project.

He suggested forming a hotel management company which would be separate from the ownership of the property. The building, he said, should stay in Anna's mother's family's hands until the hotel had proved a success, at which point the operating company could exercise an option to purchase at a fair, current price.

At the end of this first session he summed up.

"You're going to need a quarter of a million dollars to get this thing going, with another hundred thousand to carry the operation until you reach seventy-five per cent occupancy. Provided your mother's family are agreeable to granting a lease on the building, I am prepared to provide the funds, interest-free for the first two years, and thereafter at prevailing US commercial rates."

Anna was stunned by the vigour and speed with which he had reached his decision. She didn't see how she could trust it. But she tried not to let her doubts show; she tried not to let any emotion show.

"I see," she said without emphasis. "And what would you want in return for your investment?"

"Fifty-one per cent of the operating company."

"On the face of it, that sounds generous, although it gives you total control. What's the catch?"

"No catch. I'll grant you an option to buy one per cent of the company from me, after the third year of operation. You may offer what you like for that share, but I shall have the right to buy your forty-nine shares, if I am prepared to pay you a higher unit price."

Anna took this in.

"Let me make sure I'm understanding this right. If I were to offer you £1 for the share, you would have the right to buy my forty-nine for, say £50. If I offered you £100,000, you would have the right to buy my shares for anything over £4.9 million?"

"Yeah. You've got it."

Anna appreciated the fairness and logic of the proposition. It would be up to her, as the operator of the business, to judge its real potential and market value.

"Tell me, Mr Pedersen, how have you made your offer so quickly? Surely you need to know more about the condition of this place, and the market for hotels in this part of Italy. And more about me. After all, I'm twenty-three, I have no commercial experience at all, and my highest qualification is a Second-Class degree in PPE from Oxford."

"I know all about the market. I had a full report prepared for me before I left New York. I own over a thousand private and commercial properties in six countries; I'm accustomed to looking at buildings and making a physical assessment as efficiently as possible, and I have seldom been wrong. I have just spent three and a half hours with you, and I'm satisfied that those skills you do not already possess, you will acquire quickly, and that you have a clear, receptive mind, and a decisive personality. I also think you have a compelling need for success. You are what they call in the States a born achiever."

Anna could not help demurring slightly under this barrage of approval. "You know more about me than I do, then," she said.

"Very probably. It's often the case at your age. But my business has been built on making sound judgements about young people; it's a lot cheaper to buy a sapling than a mature tree."

"So I'm a cheap sapling?"

"That's right."

Anna smiled. This man was the easiest she had ever dealt with. She had never encountered anyone who obscured their purpose less. But she was still puzzled by his approach.

"Would you tell me," she asked, "Why you should choose to invest in what will always be a relatively small hotel in a notoriously underfunded region of Italy?"

"Why I choose to makes no difference to you or the deal I'm proposing. But I'll tell you this: I've always loved Sicily; I shall probably visit two or three times a year, not at special rates though. And since I met you, I believe that you will go a lot further than a small hotel in Sicily."

He was looking into a future that Anna had not even contemplated, but what he said thrilled her strangely. Maybe, she thought, only a little reluctant to give weight to his earlier pronouncement, he was right about her. Maybe she was the compulsive achiever he suggested.

A compulsive achiever! She smiled, and wondered what Martin Vickers would think of that.

The first guests arrived at the Villa Ypolitta for Easter the following year, 1974.

They had mostly been attracted by small, discreet advertisements in top American and European magazines.

Anna had personally taken each booking. Sometimes, even for periods that were still completely void, she turned them down if they did not sound like people who would suit the ambience she aimed to create.

Superficially, the house itself looked little altered since her arrival the previous summer. It had been mightily cleaned up, and a team of gardeners had laboured outside all winter. The reception rooms for the most part were unchanged, although the dining-room now contained several smaller tables, rather than the large mahogany original. In order to provide bathrooms for every room, the capacity had been reduced from her original plans to forty-five. And, unlike the rooms on the ground floor, the bedrooms were redecorated in a traditional Italian style.

The kitchens had cost more than any other element of the conversion of the villa. Their design and installation were overseen by an inspired young Roman chef who had responded to the chance to do exactly what he wanted with what promised to be a captive, sophisticated clientele. Anna was delighted, and a little surprised despite her growing confidence, that Giovanni expressed no doubts that she could attract the kind of customers he liked to feed, and word had worked its way back to Rome that something special was going to happen at the Ypolitta.

On the day the first guests were expected, there was an air of excited nervousness around Anna and her staff of twenty at the Villa Ypolitta. It was after lunch on Friday.

Anna thought she had inspected everything ten times that morning, and everyone else had checked every detail of their particular responsibilities. Anna had recruited all the staff except Giovanni, the chef, from local towns and villages. In the few weeks and months they had been there Anna had inspired an enthusiastic loyalty among them. They were as concerned as their young boss that everything should go well. Signor and Signora Testa had been given positions of nebulous authority, in deference to their age and long service at the house. The others were all in their late teens and twenties, chosen for what Anna judged to be their capacity for work and ready smiles. Her policy was that guests should get to know the Christian names of the maids, barmen and restaurant waiters, in keeping with the informality she wanted.

When a large Mercedes crunched up the drive Anna glanced round at her team, waiting in the hall with her, and thrilled at the thought that the fantasy to which she had so audaciously given birth was about to become a reality.

She could not restrain the urge to peek through the window beside the front door.

Two local men climbed out, and opened the boot of the car, from which they each carefully lifted armfuls of flowers. Anna beckoned one of the maids to open the front doors as the men staggered up the steps. The floral mountain was deposited on a large oak table in the hall, and a note was handed to Anna by the driver.

It was in Henry Pedersen's own hand:

To Anna Hamilton and everyone at the Villa Ypolitta.
With my best wishes, and confident hopes for a great success. I'm sorry not to be with you all, but I'm sure you don't need my help. Please book me your best room for the first week in June. I expect to have been recommended to come by then.
Henry Pedersen.

Most of the staff had met Henry, and were aware that he had an interest in the place. He had turned up at very short notice a month before, and had offered quiet approval of most that he saw, and a few justifiable criticisms that Anna had been glad to act on.

The gesture of the flowers, timed as it was, touched them all, and intensified their will to succeed.

Anna was impressed, as she had been continuously since first meeting the man, by his complete dependability and indefatigable attention to detail, wherever he was and despite whatever other megadeal he might have been engaged on.

A few moments later, as two girls excitedly added Henry's flowers to those already adorning the public rooms, another car crunched up the drive.

A chauffeur opened the doors of a large Fiat, and the Ypolitta's first guests climbed out.

They were two Germans from Hamburg; he a jet-setting son of a major industrialist, she a top model. They were the fore-runners of a group of six who had booked for a few days while waiting to join a yacht in Taormina.

Anna greeted them but passed them on to her eager staff to show them to their rooms and unpack for them.

Within an hour the others in their party had arrived, and a group of four Americans.

The only other guests booked for that first night were an English fashion photographer and his journalist girlfriend, looking for locations for a *Vogue* shoot. They came late, but in time for Giovanni's first dinner.

When they arrived it turned out that the photographer knew the German model, so the English and Germans decided to eat at the same table. Soon the Americans were talking to them, and after a lavishly praised dinner the whole group sat out on the veranda drinking, talking and laughing. Anna invited them to join her in a few bottles of champagne to celebrate the first day of her hotel. At one o'clock, though not wanting to sleep, she was so excited at having created exactly what she planned, she excused herself and left Gino, her most presentable barman, to look after the guests until whatever time they wanted to go to their bedrooms.

The guests all stayed up until after three, and went to bed in happy mood. Anna thanked God that the first day had passed without disaster.

The weekend also passed without major mishap, so Anna began to relax and enjoy running the hotel. The yacht the Germans were joining arrived at Taormina, but the Italian owners were persuaded to stay a few nights at the Ypolitta before carrying on.

They had not heard about this new hotel but they telephoned friends in Turin and recommended them to come and stay there before joining the yacht two weeks later.

The Americans asked to extend their stay, and word of Giovanni's cooking spread to the guests of other hotels and villas along the coast. By the end of the first week, the restaurant was full.

That summer of 1974 in London was passed in a mood of gloom as the stock market and property crash took their toll. But the glossy magazines were not in the business of promoting gloom, and continued to research and reveal new ways to spend money on fashion, food and places to go, as if nothing had changed.

Tony Kyriakides, who had taken advantage of the recession to buy three more medium-sized hotels at bargain prices, was intrigued, and just a little jealous to read about this sensational, though small, new hotel that was reported to have opened on the Sicilian coast. It sounded as if the woman who had started it had aimed at something similar to the Oscar in ambience, but in an exotic, sub-tropical setting. He had never heard of Anna Hamilton. He guessed that she must be an old pro, perhaps one of the women who had passed through the Swiss Hotel school and found a backer. It was not until a week later that he read more details about her, and saw a photograph. He was impressed, and relieved. This was a young woman who had got lucky; a fluke of fashion. He wished her well. He took the first article and that day's gossip column home to show Thalia.

"Here's a girl who's been lucky. She's got the right ideas and it sounds as if she's got a good feel for that niche market. But she can't have much experience and I doubt she's got the toughness to survive. Either its popularity will fade, with a fickle type of customer like that, or if it does well, the other Italian groups won't let her keep it." He shrugged, and glanced over at his wife.

Thalia was reading the article for the second time.

"I hope she does well," Thalia replied, with no apparent interest as she pointedly put the papers down.

"Like I say," said Tony, "if she does, the others won't let her for long. But I hope George has the balls to get up and do that kind of thing."

"With you for a father?" Thalia replied. "How can he be motivated? When you're not undermining his confidence by telling him how useless he is, you're spoiling him by flattering him for all his unimportant social achievements at Oxford. I'd far rather he got a good degree than sat around getting drunk at those silly clubs. I think you just confuse him."

"Nonsense," Tony blustered. "He appreciates my frankness. At least he knows where he is with me. And I'm glad he's having a good time at Oxford. He may as well get it out of his system now."

"It's getting it into his system that worries me."

The next day Tony saw Monica. She too, was in a critical mood.

"I don't understand you sometimes, Tony, you're so

unheroic. Your funny little island has just been torn apart and you don't give a damn."

"It's not that bad. It's just that all the Turks live in one part and all the Greeks in another. What's so wrong with that?"

"What do you mean? Two peoples who have lived together for four hundred years ought to have sorted out their differences by now. That sort of tribalism is so uncivilised."

"I have nothing against the Turks. I've employed them from time to time. And the first girl I fell in love with was a Turk from the next village." He thought of Fatima, and the innocent emotions she had aroused in him, but quickly brushed the memory aside.

"Have you heard of someone called Anna Hamilton?" he asked Monica, without explaining his abrupt change of topic.

"You mean this woman who's opened a hotel in Sicily? Yes, I've read about her and a few friends have stayed there. Apparently it's quite sublime and she's wonderfully clever and sexy, though nobody has ever seen or heard of her in London. Actually, Charles and I are going to stay at her place for a few days in August with the Hampshires. I'll be able to tell you all about it."

Tony didn't like hearing any of this. "How can it be so wonderful? She's only a girl, twenty-four or five. There's no way she could be running something that's truly up to international standards. It will only be a matter of time before she's found out."

"Sour grapes, Tony! I haven't often heard you admitting to envy."

"I'm not admitting to anything. I just get annoyed when I hear everyone raving about somewhere that's obviously second-rate."

Monica laughed and shrugged her shoulders. "I'll make a point of meeting her and introducing you to her some time.

She sounds a bit of a star, this Anna Hamilton. I read that she was some kind of student leader at Oxford, who took over an old family house out there. It's interesting how property-owning changes people's priorities."

"Not all students are left-wing hippies," Tony said drily. "I sometimes wish my son George would rebel a bit and show some enterprise. Some of his smart English friends at Oxford are as complacent and smug as they might have been two hundred years ago."

"Maybe George's sense of enterprise has been suffocated by yours? But I shouldn't worry. If he's developing expensive tastes, he'll need to work to satisfy them, provided you don't just give him what he wants, as I suspect you will. You Greeks are such doting fathers."

Tony laughed to hide his annoyance at hearing Monica repeat what Thalia had said. "You wouldn't say that if you'd met my father. Anyway, George is doing all right. I was just saying that this Anna Hamilton may not have been a crazy left-winger just because she was something at Oxford, so perhaps Oxford won't completely destroy any sense of enterprise in my own son."

Sir James and Lady Montagu-Hamilton also read stories in the papers about Anna's hotel.

"It sounds as though she's doing rather well," Sir James said ungrudgingly. "Perhaps we ought to go down and see her." He had not got the Bonn posting, or Moscow, but unexpectedly he was given Rome, a significant improvement on Vienna. He was due to take up his new post in October. "I should have handed over to Williams by the end of August. Let's go to Sicily in September."

"Yes, I'd love to," Susan said, happy at her husband's interest in Anna's success. James had kept his promise to meet her in London to check out Henry Pedersen's agreements with his lawyers and their New York correspondents. When the deal was explained to him, he had been struck by the apparent generosity of the terms. He had not really accepted Anna's explanation that Pedersen was taking a calculated gamble on her abilities but, whatever Pedersen's reasons, he could see no way in which Anna or his wife's family could be damaged financially and, with Anna tactfully supporting the charade that it made a difference to her, he had given the project his blessing.

Sir James and Susan landed in Sicily on a blazing early autumn day. They drove up the stunning coast road from Catania to the Villa Ypolitta and stepped out of their hired car in astonishment. The gardens, after a year of continuous work, were more outrageously beautiful than they had ever been in Susan's lifetime. The spruced up villa lay among these gardens with a grand serenity. Flowers tumbled from the verandas and the window-boxes of the upper rooms. The sound of rich singing could be heard from the kitchen windows at the back of the house.

The Montagu-Hamiltons had not imagined that so much had been done to the old white elephant. To Susan, it seemed incomprehensible that her own daughter, little more than a schoolgirl, had achieved all this.

This feeling grew as she and her husband mounted the reconstructed steps and walked into the fresh coolness of the main hall. The whole place was so much lighter than she remembered. It occurred to her, without any sense of disloyalty, that it must have been the man whom she regarded as Anna's benefactor – rather than investor – who was responsible.

"Hi! Welcome to the Ypolitta," Anna called from the gallery at the top of the wide walnut staircase, and ran down the shallow treads to kiss her mother warmly.

Her stepfather accepted his kiss on the cheek gracefully: "It's wonderful to see you looking so well, Anna, not to mention the old place."

"Thanks, Dad. The Ypolitta gets lovelier every day. It's

fascinating seeing things you started a year before coming to fruition."

"Did you organise all the garden?" Susan asked, doubtfully.

"Of course I did, with a bit of help from my wonderful gardener. I found some pictures of how it was at the turn of the century, and we're aiming at reproducing that. After all, a lot of the plants are still here, though rather gigantic now. You should have seen the rhododendrons in the Scottish garden in the spring. I've never seen anything like it in Italy. Great-grandad must have spent a fortune getting them here."

"I never thought it would look so magnificent, and the house too, it's so fresh and light!"

"Wait till you see your room," Anna said, keen to show off everything to her parents.

She knew they would not have been able to conceive what had gone on here, and she wanted to show her stepfather that, although she may have disappointed him in her choice of career, at least her executive skills manifestly made up for that in restoring a place of such beauty.

After they had settled into their rooms, with Susan enthusing to her husband about everything in sight, they took a stroll around the fifteen acres that surrounded the house. They encountered guests doing the same or playing tennis or croquet. The unhurried, mildly decadent atmosphere of the place did not escape them, nor the obviously cosmopolitan nature of the other guests.

In a dell, hidden from the house, but no more than fifty yards from it, a swimming-pool was being built. A mosaic of the goddess Hippolyte was being laid on the floor, in quiet, classical colours. At one end of the pool, nestling among a stand of cypress, the Greco-Roman ruins of the temple which had supposedly given the house its name were cleaned, but picturesquely unrestored.

"Do you suppose Anna was responsible for all this?" Susan asked again.

"I don't see why not. She always had a good knowledge of the classics and she's always been brought up to appreciate the finer things."

"I know, but somehow I hadn't equated the idea of a commercial hotel to this sort of standard."

"They always say that there's a market for the very best, and that seems to be what your daughter has achieved."

"Oh, James, I do think you can give yourself some credit for what Anna has done. As you say, it was you who encouraged her to learn all that she has. I'm so relieved it all seems to be going so well. We must tell a few of our friends about it."

"I think most of our friends are probably too fuddy-duddy for this hotel, not to say too darned poor. I had a quick glance at the luncheon menu. It's not cheap."

"Do you think we ought to pay for things, while we're here? Anna said the room was on her, but I don't know about meals, and wine."

"I shall insist that we pay for our meals," Sir James said. "We can always go out for the odd picnic, or down into Taormina for some meals."

When it came to it, they were never given a bill, despite asking three times. During the week they were at the Villa Ypolitta the Montagu-Hamiltons found themselves dealing with their daughter, just twenty-five now, in the same manner they would employ with a successful man of their own age.

Susan was not unaware of this. "The only trouble with Anna's success, as far as I can see, is that it frightens off the men. It will take a very strong man to make an impression on her now."

"Or a thoroughly useless one," Sir James added.

16

Anna didn't trust Gavin Sykes.

That didn't prevent her from keeping her appointment with him at the Ambasciatori in the Via Veneto in Rome. The proposition he had put to her was plausible enough; that the crumbling Castello and its satellite hamlet were ideal for Anna's treatment; the family who owned it were desperate to sell.

Henry Pedersen had agreed in principle that if the site was right and the whole conversion could be paid for from the profits accumulated over the first three years' trading at the Ypolitta, it had his blessing. In any event, he had recently accepted Anna's £50,000 for one per cent of his holding, and Anna now ranked equal with him in control of their company. She had lost none of her respect for his judgement. But her respect for her own judgement had grown.

The Ypolitta was now firmly on the map of the world's exceptional hotels. The trade had heralded this as a major achievement for anyone, let alone a young, untrained Englishwoman. Her success was attributed to a natural understanding of her market, her skill in selection, delegation and execution, a great deal of hard work, and her own, now famous, personal charms. She had a knack and the strength of character to be warm and friendly without losing any of her sophistication – all these characteristics had contributed to her success and the good fortune to have the Ypolitta at her disposal.

Anna wore her success lightly. She worked because she enjoyed it. She was a natural cosmopolitan: she liked most of her guests. And she ran no distracting love affairs.

The first time Gavin Sykes had turned up at the Ypolitta he had been accompanied by an oddly-assorted group of four women from Monaco. German, French and Russian, they were rich, husbandless and all older than him – he was, Anna guessed, a young fifty.

They were women who were used to getting what they asked for and complaining if they did not get more. Anna was curious about Gavin's role for the room-maids, swift to assess these things, reported that he was not sleeping with any of them; nor was he paying for anything.

Three days later, a much younger and considerably more beautiful Austrian woman, Marie-Christine, arrived, to be greeted with unambiguous attention by Gavin. Within minutes, a furious row had broken out between the new arrival and a sixty-year-old German baroness, of indomitable wealth and arrogance.

"Gavin, my darling," the baroness turned to him, "I thought this girl was one of your domestic servants. What is she doing here?"

"My dear old Fritzi," Gavin Sykes stressed the 'old', "I'm a liberal man; I'm always kind to my domestics, like I take pity on retired strippers."

"You pig," the baroness screamed. "You'll never get so much as another pair of socks out of me."

Anna and her staff giggled with each other as the row raged on and off most of the day, and they were not sorry to see the four older women leave the following day, when there was some awkwardness about settling the bill for Gavin's room. But the Austrian girl appeared at the front desk to announce that she would pay.

"With what?" the baroness spat out in German.

Anna, listening to the row from the gallery, came down and intervened.

"Baroness, don't worry. Mr Sykes is a guest of the house. We'll deal with it. It's not important."

The baroness was furious at having her chief weapon neutralised. She stormed out, hurling abuse at anyone in sight, and vowed never to return.

When the car containing the quartet had drawn away, Anna asked Gavin and the Austrian girl to join her for a drink.

"By the way," she said as they drank a bottle of Krug, "You can stay one more night for free, and that's it."

"I shall buy the champagne, in that case," Gavin declared, pulling from his pocket a wad of notes that would have covered a few weeks at the Ypolitta. Anna cursed her weakness.

But this man always made her behave abnormally. As far as she could see, he was so devoid of morals as to be unreachable. He was slim, with light, possibly unnaturally-brown hair and the bland eyes of the truly wicked. Anna had never met anyone who so obviously didn't give a damn what he said and whom he offended. And he couched his insults with an articulate flair and disregard of consequences that was exciting in itself. He had been to Eton, then the House; impressively educated, but with a frivolous glibness which partially belied this. He could pluck literary and classical references from the air to suit any conversation. He appeared to know anyone of interest or doubtful reputation in Europe and he made dozens of phone calls in half a dozen languages every day.

And yet he had no shame in telling anyone about his complete impecuniousness. He reminded Anna of Evelyn Waugh's Basil Seal. He was an old-fashioned cad, and revelled in the role. And for no reason that she could justify even to herself, Anna was entranced by him.

Gavin was also a great hit with the staff. He talked to them in animated, florid Italian with an apparently instinctive understanding of Sicilian peasant mores. He flirted with the maids in a way they would not have allowed other guests to do, and told dirty stories to the barmen and waiters. He seemed to be able to strike up conversations with the most reticent of the hotel's other clients. By the time he left with Marie-Christine, after staying ten days at the hotel and paying for five, it was as if they were losing an old friend.

There was not much doubt, though no absolute certainty among the staff, that Gavin had been sleeping with Marie-Christine. But Anna knew that he had also taken more than a passing interest in herself. To her irritation, she found herself thinking about him after he had left.

In the four years since arriving at the Villa Ypolitta she hadn't attached herself to any man. There had been the month with Bill Franklyn, and another week when he had arrived at the hotel a year or so later. But he had friends with him then, and Anna was aware that he was showing her off; suddenly he seemed too naïve to be taken seriously.

Anna was surprised, a few months later, to find that her fame had seeped even into the consciousness of her old moral philosophy mentor. She received a letter from Martin Vickers, written in uncharacteristically flowery terms, with a suggestion that he might visit her in Sicily. But between his whimsical lines she saw an attempt to use his old influence to score a free holiday. She smiled to herself as she despatched a tariff and a booking form, with a scribbled note: "It would be lovely to see you if you decide to come." He did not come. And Anna was not disappointed. But she couldn't hide from herself that she was sometimes lonely.

Lucio, the builder, had broached her half-hearted defences, inevitably but briefly, shortly after the hotel had opened. While he was working on the house he had seen a lot of Anna, and had become increasingly suggestive, without actually propositioning her. After a few weeks of this Anna, more out of curiosity than anything else, had said, "What is it, Lucio? Do you want to make love to me or something."

"Do I want to?" he had throbbed in return. "I dream about it every night, Signorina Anna."

They were in one of the bedrooms, checking a malfunctioning shower.

Anna walked to the side of the bed. "Well, stop dreaming and do something about it."

The effect on Lucio was disastrous. He kissed her with a great show of passion, and began to undress her. Anna could feel his hands shaking as he unclasped her lightweight bra and grappled with her pants. By that stage, she was ready for any man, such had been the tension of the previous few months; but she wanted no more than the physical fulfilment of her healthy libido. She watched Lucio's efforts with detached impatience.

When finally he stood naked before her, his face reddened as her eyes dropped to the dangle of limp flesh between his legs.

"Anna," he pleaded with embarrassment, "You go too fast. I must do this at my speed."

Standing in front of him, magnificent in Lucio's eyes and flawless in her naked beauty, she reached a hand down to his coyly retreating cock.

"I'm sure you can do better than that," she murmured encouragingly, and felt a tweak of response as she fondled his balls.

In a minute, Lucio was ready to perform. He pushed Anna hurriedly back on to the bed and flopped on to her. Within seconds he was in her; within a few more, it was all over, and he lay on top of her, his magnificent chest heaving, spent and devoid of new initiatives.

Anna, feeling sorry for him, and sorrier for herself, pushed him off.

"I'll give you this, Lucio, you're a very good builder,"

she said, "but you've had your chance at this and you haven't got the job."

Lucio referred to the episode only once, on the day after it occurred. "What happened, it's our secret, yes?"

"It certainly is, Lucio," Anna replied.

Anna immersed herself in the task of running the Villa Ypolitta. She knew that standards had to be maintained without any effort being apparent to the clients. With the place full for nine months of the year, and sometimes half full for the other three, she had little spare time to think about her own emotional or physical needs.

But they had not atrophied. They had welled up within her, and were ready to burst forth if a suitable outlet presented itself. For her, that outlet had to be no ordinary challenge; no pig-headed Italian actor who sneered at his women to keep them interested, no bull-headed American who liked to treat a woman like a doll he had bought from Bloomingdales.

Gavin Sykes presented a much more interesting challenge, for while he could flirt and charm and be outrageously attentive, in his soul – if he had a soul – there seemed no capacity to love. If she could extract love from him, she thought, that would be a real achievement.

Besides, she admitted to herself as she lay in bed after he had left the Ypolitta that first time, she also wanted him to take her hot, ready body and use it until she collapsed exhausted.

Gavin had come back to the Ypolitta a month or so later; this time with the estranged wife of a Milanese banker. She was a Roman and, according to staff gossip, very demanding.

Anna gave Gavin no sign of her interest in him. She was impressed that he appeared able to keep up with the woman's demands, and still spend time drinking, swimming, playing backgammon and teasing whoever else was available, including Anna.

It was then that he mentioned the Castello. He did not

tell her the name of the place, but showed Anna a pile of photographs.

"They're lovely old dears, the family, but financially naïve, I'm afraid. They were persuaded to invest a great deal of money in jeans, I ask you! I made the mistake of introducing them to a friend of mine, no longer a friend now, of course, who absolutely bulldozed them into building a factory for him among the vineyards of the Veneto."

"What happened? Didn't he make any jeans?"

"Oh yes, millions, but he kept all the money and went to Mexico after a couple of years, and they haven't seen a penny. Every weaver in Europe is asking them for money, and a few banks too, so the poor darlings have got to sell. Naturally, I want to help them out. After all, I'm an honourable man, and it was my introduction."

Anna could not imagine anyone less honourable, but said: "On the face of it, it could be the sort of place we ought to be looking at."

"We?" Gavin asked sharply.

"I have a partner in this hotel."

"Do you? I didn't know that."

"There's no reason why you should."

"And who is he?"

"I didn't say my partner was a 'he'."

"Who's she, then?"

"There's no reason to tell you that. My relationship with my partner is strictly at arm's-length."

"I see."

Gavin feared he was talking to the monkey, not the organ-grinder. She did not disabuse him.

"Well, is it worth your while coming to look at this place?" He prodded the photos scattered on the table in front of them.

"I'll tell you when I've seen it."

There was a sudden husky yell across the bar. It was the

banker's wife, demanding Gavin, and looking at Anna with stiletto eyes.

Gavin ignored her. "Good. I'll fix it up then," he said as he deliberately gathered up the photos of the Castello.

Once again, Gavin Sykes left something of a gap in the daily life of the Ypolitta when his escort chivvied him into taking her back to Positano. There was no shame in his eyes as he said, "Goodbye," shrugging his shoulders. "I'll see you soon, in Rome," he added, within provocative hearing of his Roman woman.

So Anna was sitting in the lobby of the Ambasciatori reading a paper, struggling not to be impatient and ashamed to be looking forward to seeing Gavin Sykes. He was a shit, a hustler, a man who would not recognise a moral; and yet, he had bright-blue, inscrutable eyes; he made her laugh; he made her insecure, and she knew that she could never reach him.

It was a fine, clear May morning outside on the Via Veneto. Romans paraded themselves, their dogs, their wardrobes, their lovers with leisurely self-confidence. Anna saw them as she glanced out from time to time for Gavin. It pleased her to think how successfully she had understood these people; how accurately she had reflected their tastes in her hotel. How stimulating and much more challenging it would be to do it all again, here on the mainland of Italy, without the romance of the Ypolitta's isolated, island position.

Clients ambling through the hallway of the hotel eyed her with appreciation. The men raised loquacious eyebrows. They thought she was a model, or a starlet, a mere body. She smiled to herself.

She was not surprised when Gavin was just forgivably late. He walked in with oddly short strides of his long legs. The doorman gave him an effusive, familiar greeting, which Gavin returned with an affable nod. He spotted

Anna and, with a simple gesture of hands and shoulders, conveyed deep remorse for lateness due to circumstances beyond his control.

"You look lovely," he said, kissing her lightly on the cheek. "Let's not stay here. It's ferociously expensive, unless you're buying the drinks?"

"I can't see anyone else who's likely to, but I wouldn't mind going somewhere else. This place becomes a little dull after an hour or so."

"You haven't waited an hour!?"

"It feels like it."

"I'm going to take you to the best restaurant in Rome for lunch. A German cardinal's paying," he added quickly.

Outside the front door of the hotel they turned up towards the Villa Borghese. Gavin prattled as they walked, overflowing as usual with implausibly licentious gossip about famous figures he had recently encountered. He had for the past few weeks – and for no reason that he volunteered – been spending a lot of time in the company of senior Vatican officials and seemed to have gained an intimate knowledge of their vices. He spoke in a kind of Wodehousean English, spiced with arcane cockney rhyming slang, all delivered with a just perceptible stutter.

"You do talk a lot of balls," Anna slipped in between anecdotes.

"It may be *colliones* to you, my dear, but to me it is my livelihood at the moment. A knowledge of the Achilles' heels of important men can be a valuable commodity."

"Does selling this Castello to me constitute part of your livelihood?" Anna asked.

"It's the only reason I can think of for seeing you." He gave her an earnest, ambiguous smile. "Here," they had come alongside a café which sprawled its tables across the pavement, "let's stop and talk about it."

They sat and Gavin ordered coffee and cognac.

From the inside pocket of a limp linen jacket he pulled a sheaf of folded dog-eared papers. He unravelled them and flattened the top sheet.

"First, you must sign this. It merely confirms that in the event of your buying the old place I will be entitled to a two and half per cent commission from you."

"Are the poor old family so skint you don't want to take your cut from them?"

"Certainly not; they've agreed four per cent."

Anna looked down the simple document, took a pen from her bag, crossed out 'two and a half per cent' and wrote 'one and a half per cent', initialled the change, and signed the bottom of the document.

"You're a greedy boy, Gavin. Do you still want to show me the place?"

Gavin looked at her with eyes that were at once pained and haughty. "Anna, you amaze me. I should have thought you of all people appreciated that a labourer is worthy of his hire."

"Labourer!" Anna scoffed.

"You're a tough old boiler, aren't you?" Gavin said as he picked up the signed paper and put it back in his pocket. The next sheet of paper revealed the name of the property, Castello di Prosini, and its position, above Lake Como.

"The lakes," Anna said with disappointment, "Old farts' country."

"You obviously haven't been there for a while. With your sort of treatment and the reputation you've got at the Ypolitta, the rich, young Milanese will use it, the rest of Europe and the Americans will follow. It's handy for Italy, France, Switzerland, and on the way to the skiing. I admit it's a slightly different sort of trade to the Ypolitta, but catering for the same market."

"Of course I'll come and look at it."

"Great," Gavin said, "Now I can spend the rest of the day seducing you."

17

Six months later, Anna arranged to meet Gavin Sykes at the Meridiana, in the Fulham Road. Knowing his tendency to be late, she suggested to a journalist from *Harper's and Queen*, who wanted to interview her, that she should meet her at the restaurant for a drink before lunch.

Lynn, the interviewer, was a thrusting, breathless woman, ten years older than Anna. She had wanted to lunch with her subject and didn't disguise her vexation at being granted this hasty meeting.

The two women sat either side of a low table in the bar, with a bottle of champagne and a bowl of olives between them. The journalist vented her resentment of Anna's youth, beauty and success by asking her about the men in her life.

"You've been very skilful in avoiding any publicity about your love life," she remarked with unambiguous cattiness.

"Running two hotels doesn't leave much time for men," Anna replied without embarrassment.

"You have a partner in your hotels, I gather. What's your relationship with him?"

"I've never told anyone what sex my partner is, let alone my relationship with him or her."

"Why's that?"

"Because my partner wishes it."

"I saw a piece in *Dempster* linking you with Gavin Sykes."

Anna laughed. "You'll be able to do your own linking soon; he's meeting me here for lunch."

Lynn's eyes opened with interest. "I've never met him; he's not the sort of person I come across. I'm told he's basically a gold-digging old lush."

Anna laughed. "Among other things," she said, "But he introduced me to the Di Frosinis who sold me the Castello, so I let him buy me lunch occasionally."

"He's a very attractive man, isn't he?"

Anna shrugged. "If you think so."

"How generally do you find men react to you, being so young and so commercially successful?"

"Look, Lynn, I told your editor I was happy to do an interview about my hotels. You can speculate all you like about my sex life, but I'm not going to talk about it."

"But you must realise that's what women readers will find most interesting about you?"

"Tough. You can speculate, as I say, but make sure you guess right, or you'll be in trouble."

The journalist appeared to admit defeat for the moment and turned to Anna's attitude to business, her aims and methods. They had been talking for an hour when Gavin arrived in an elderly Mark II Jaguar, with rust pimples around the wheel arches and faded chrome. He parked it unceremoniously on double yellow lines in the narrow road outside the restaurant.

The Meridiana was bustling by then, full of the sort of people whose work did not occupy a lot of their time. Gavin breezed in among them. He wore, on a raw November day, a pair of white flannel trousers and a pale pink shirt, frayed at the collar, beneath a buff seersucker jacket. A scruffy, livid-hued Indian silk scarf was knotted around his neck.

The waiters greeted him warmly, almost fawned on him, for he was a man who, though he never paid his own bills, regularly brought in clients who did – very big ones.

Anna firmly brought her interview to a close, and the

journalist reluctantly left in a flurry of rainwear and over-sized bags.

"Who was that awful hackette?" Gavin asked.

"Someone to while away the time while I waited for you to turn up late."

Gavin sat where Lynn had and, without turning, called over his shoulder to the barman for a bottle of Krug.

"You're looking particularly seedy today," Anna said.

Gavin ignored this. "My God, it's a pleasure to look at a woman under forty."

"Where have you come from?"

"Monaco, I'm afraid. The only people there now are the very rich and the very dull. It's so awful when it rains there. It only really works in the sun."

Anna had not seen him for a month and was surprised, as she always was, by how much she enjoyed his well-observed cynicism, his unabashed eccentricity.

After she and Gavin had visited the Castello di Frosini – and she had bought it – they had a short, light-hearted affair.

Gavin was a good lover in a detached sort of way, with an appetite which had suited Anna. He was not in awe of her, as most men were. He wasn't in competition with her and she found that she could relax with him and let her instincts carry her. But she was aware that the identity of his sexual partner was almost irrelevant to him. Anna assumed that was how he was able to carry on relationships with women of almost any age or build and probably enjoy it, especially if there was some other dividend in the offing.

She guessed she would sleep with him again, when it suited her. And she still enjoyed his company, but had forbidden Gavin to put any more business propositions to her, after it had become something of a habit with him, so now he expected no more from her other than that she paid the bills when they met.

They went in from the bar to eat. As they were shown to their table, Gavin glanced around and acknowledged a few friends and acquaintances.

When they were sitting he said, "Now, there's an interesting old boiler, over there by the antipasti."

Anna looked across and saw a flamboyantly good-looking woman in her late thirties; Anna thought she looked intelligent, thoroughly in control of her life, and preoccupied with trivia.

"Who is she?" she asked Gavin.

"Someone I knew intimately about twenty years ago. She's married to a banker called Charles Fakenham; I was at Eton with him. He's a very pompous fart, and I can't imagine that he keeps her satisfied. I wonder who does?"

It was a tribute to their guile and caution that, over fifteen years, relatively few people realised that the affair between Tony Kyriakides and Monica Fakenham was still going on. They had become more discreet, out of Tony's regard for his wife, and Monica's fears about Charles Fakenham's jealousy.

It was this very secrecy that still kept the relationship exciting. They met once or twice a month, and they enjoyed each other's bodies with as much intensity as they had ever done. For Monica, whose sexual relations with her husband had ceased ten years before, this provided an adequate outlet for her libido. Tony, on the other hand, occasionally slept with his wife, and had a series of short affairs with some of the women who worked for him in the hotels.

Thalia was still a beautiful woman and serenely elegant. Her reputation among London's socialites had grown steadily over the years, and she still vigorously supported her housing trust as well as several other more fashionable charities. She worked hard at organising the social events and could always be relied on to persuade artists to donate works for auctions, musicians to perform and authors to speak in aid of the NSPCC or Action Research. She made few demands on Tony, and was content to live in the Argyll Street house, despite his trying to persuade her that she would prefer to live in the country.

He had even gone as far as putting in an offer on a house in the Test Valley. When he told her, Thalia reacted almost violently to the idea, and was openly angry with him for the first time in years. It was almost as if the prospect of living there terrified her. Tony shrugged it off, and wondered if his wife was perhaps not as well integrated as he had thought. After that he gave up, and accepted that she would always want to live in London.

Their only true point of communication now was George, but much of this was contentious. George had left Oxford with a Second-Class degree and a book full of grand addresses. Tony, looking at his son, sometimes could hardly believe that he had fathered this suave, self-assured young man who, to the untutored eye, appeared utterly English in everything down to the leather elbow patches on his jackets.

George had also left the university with a good grounding in the art of spending money tastefully and lavishly. People he met assumed from his name that he must be connected with one of the big ship-owning families; he did not tell them otherwise, for his father had been less in the news since he sold the Oscar. He developed a taste for flying and for polo. He was charming, uncomplicated and good-looking; he fitted easily into such international activities.

Besides Greek, at which he had worked hard since his first visit to Cyprus, he also spoke good French and Italian, and gave himself plenty of opportunity by extensive travelling.

Tony was slightly mesmerised by the glamour of his

own son, and saw no reason to stop him leading the life of a junior jet-setter. He agreed to make George a market researcher for Theodore Hotels, paid him a generous salary, and allowed him to travel on the pretext that he was looking at new markets for the time when Tony decided it was appropriate to expand his hotel chain beyond Great Britain.

At that stage, in the late 1970s, Tony Kyriakides' business was in good shape, but it was restricted by his abhorrence of borrowing which followed the Oscar débàcle. He currently owned three restaurants in London, and four small hotels, all paid for and all operating profitably, if not spectacularly.

Since selling the Oscar and, three years later, the small chain of Alfonso's Pasta Bars, he had bought, traded and sold another seven hotels, making between a quarter of a million and a million on each turn. But he had been low-key about it, approaching his purchases camouflaged by a string of holding companies and nominees. He had not attempted to re-create the Oscar. From a distance he watched all that he had achieved in his first triumph being undermined by the impersonal, commercial principles of John Sullivan and Scottish and Lakeland. Without Tony's flair, the Oscar became just another expensive London hotel.

He had seen Anouska Hempel open Blake's Hotel, aimed at the market and style that he had originally pursued at the Oscar, and realised he had lost the edge that the Oscar's previous individuality had provided. But he had now decided he was ready to expand seriously.

Since the revival of property prices after the 1974 crash, he estimated his company's worth to be something in the region of six or seven million pounds, with a good yield on capital, even after all the normal tricks of creative accounting had been produced for the Inland Revenue. He reckoned that, within a couple of years, he should be able to raise another twenty million in the stock market without yielding up more than a third of his company.

That autumn, he approached his bankers and asked them to prepare for quotation on the Unlisted Securities Market the following year.

It was this planned expansion which allowed him to pretend that George had a useful job to do. Father and son would meet, and George had learned how to play his father and did just enough work to convince Tony he took an interest in Theodore, but he flatly refused to get involved on the ground floor of hotel management. He had no plans to curtail his night life in order to get up early and oversee breakfasts in a Bayswater Road hotel.

The old Vine and Pine in the King's Road still belonged to Tony Kyriakides, but he had renamed and expanded it two years before. The mood and scope of the place was altered completely, for the original image was a product of the early 1960s. Despite a loyal clientele, it had been gaining few new younger customers. The premises next door came up for sale; Tony went to Paris to look at the big brasseries around St-Germain-des-Prés. Within weeks of his return, he had closed the Vine and Pine, incorporated the next building, and reopened it three months later as the Brasserie Athene. Since then, turnover had quadrupled, and Tony had started a second brasserie. He had not lost the enjoyment of running restaurants and he derived satisfaction at seeing himself proved right once more; but he considered it small game, something to keep him busy until he was ready to re-enter the heavyweight end of hotel-owning.

The evening after they had lunched at the Meridiana, Gavin took Anna to dinner in what had once been the Vine and Pine in the King's Road. Anna vaguely remembered the forerunner of Brasserie Athene. Now she was impressed.

"Would you believe this place belongs to a bubble?" Gavin asked.

"A bubble?"

"Bubble-and-squeak; Greek. It displays more taste and understanding of social trends than one normally associates with the average Greek kebab merchant, don't you think?"

"I have no experience of Greek caterers – or catering, come to that. I might have come to this place when it was a sort of Retsina and kebab joint, but I didn't pay much attention at the time. I was still at Oxford and it was what was said, not what you ate, that one remembered."

"I can't remember a single thing I said the whole time I was at Oxford. I don't think I was sober long enough to speak."

"You weren't up before the war, surely?" Anna said with mocking, wide eyes. "I thought all that went out with Evelyn Waugh."

"I'd forgotten what a serious little student you were. I don't think I went near the Union once; I couldn't stand the sight of all those earnest, ideology wielders."

"That's rubbish. I was in Oxford a few weeks ago, and I looked up the Union records of the time you were there, and you spoke at length, very successfully, about the dangers of creating a Jewish state in Palestine. You and Vanessa Redgrave make unlikely allies."

"Did I? I'd completely forgotten. I'm tremendously flattered that you looked me up."

"Well, don't be. It's only your utter inability to lead a real life at the age of fifty that fascinates me."

"Oh dear, you're not going to give me a scolding, are you?" he said with an excited grin.

That night Anna got drunk in a way she seldom allowed herself. After dinner they went to a club which had recently opened further up the King's Road. They stayed for an hour or so, danced a little and ignored the other people there. After that, they took a taxi to Tramp in Jermyn Street, where Anna's face, relatively unknown in London, was a source of general conjecture as she danced with Gavin, who introduced her as his niece to anyone who asked.

They went back much later to Blake's Hotel, where Anna was staying.

In the morning her head told her that Gavin Sykes was bad for her. She felt as if she had behaved like an ingenuous student. She supposed that bouts of escapism were good for her. At least she knew she sometimes craved it, and Gavin was the only person who could provide it. But although on a personal level she didn't mind what people thought of her, she was glad she had not been identified the night before. Association with Gavin could be damaging to her business reputation.

It was time to put away her pubescent urges, and control her emotional life as she had so successfully controlled her commercial life.

Gavin took it well. Not a hint of hurt or sadness showed in his eyes as she sent him packing.

"You don't lose the craving by throwing away the fags, you know," he said.

She looked at him, tried to look into him, and failed. "I don't have a craving for you, not now anyway. You're just a bad habit it's time I gave up," she said.

Although Gavin had occupied only a small part of her life, his disappearance was a watershed for her. It represented the moment when she realised that her hotels meant more to her than anything else in her life. She possessed the normal urges of a young woman, but the thrill she got from controlling her own destiny, taking on other people, usually men, and winning, was the game she had a real compulsion to go on playing.

She arrived back in Italy feeling lonlier, but stronger. The new hotel was already established and attracting more people in its first year than her most optimistic projections suggested.

She had decided to ask Giovanni, the Ypolitta chef, to open the restaurant in the Frosini, where there was a much bigger audience for his skills. He left behind in Sicily a superbly trained junior, and was now attracting custom from all over Europe.

The Frosini was three times the size of the Ypolitta and the clientele was generally older, though just as keen to spend money. People came from greater distances and stayed for shorter times; they were often there only for a weekend, or for a few days on their way between Lombardy and St Moritz. It soon became famous for the standards and the lightness of touch with which it was run.

Henry Pedersen arrived at the Frosini for his first visit after it had been open for six months. He had told Anna to make her own judgement about buying the Castello, and had backed her up unreservedly when she rang to tell him she wanted it.

"So," he said now with quiet satisfaction, "I was right. You want to be the best, now you should think about being the biggest as well. Give another year of your time to this hotel and the Ypolitta, then start looking again. We should aim to open a new hotel every year, and keep an eye open for any cheap packages – small groups with at least one good site. Then what you've got to teach yourself, and it won't be easy, is to communicate your particular talents and methods to the people you hire, so they learn to do things your way, not any other way, when you're not around."

Anna gave weight to everything Pedersen said. If he was confident she could go on to start building the kind of chain he had originally envisaged, then so was she.

"It was tougher getting this place together," she said, "because everyone I approached already knew where I was coming from. Nobody did any favours, like they did in Sicily, but I don't think we overpaid for much."

"Don't worry; you did well. You did it inside of your budget. I'm proud of you."

At this, Anna flushed like a schoolgirl in a way she would not have done with anyone else.

They carried on walking around the gargantuan stone rooms in the medieval part of the Castello where the bars and the restaurant were beginning to fill up. Most of the sixty bedrooms were in the two nineteenth-century wings of the building which extended at right angles from the original castle. A swimming-pool lay behind, with one end cut into the rocky cliffs from which a fresh spring cascaded straight into a second pool where hardier guests could swim.

The main rooms faced the lake, a hundred feet below. Anna and Henry stepped though a pair of French windows on to a terrace and walked to the edge to look down. The drive up from the road wound between lush gardens that had been the main preoccupation of the last generation of Di Frosinis to live in the castle, and the only part of the estate on which they spent any money. The summer sun was lowering on the opposite shores, turning the lake to a pool of vivid crimson. It flashed off the windows of a Ferrari crawling like a beetle up the lakeshore road towards the hamlet at the castle gates.

"Very romantic," Henry observed drily. "Don't you think?" He turned to look at Anna.

She wondered what this quite uncharacteristic remark was leading to.

She laughed. "I only see it as one of the hotel's assets, like Giovanni."

"I heard you gave your boyfriend the rush."

Anna turned and gave him a quick look of astonishment. "You're extraordinary, Henry. I don't suppose there are more than a couple of people who knew there was a boyfriend to rush, if you could ever have called Gavin that."

"He's a bum," Henry said with a shrug. "Opposites attract. Why did you get rid of him?"

"I was out with him in London a few months ago and it felt like he was my last piece of juvenile naughtiness, my final act of adolescent anarchy. It's rather sad, really, but I was glad to get it out of my system."

"There aren't many men around who could handle you," Henry said. "I'm glad you don't waste too much time looking for them. They'll find you."

Pedersen abandoned the topic of Anna's love-life as abruptly as he had broached it. He wanted to go back to Anna's office and look through the operating accounts of the two hotels for the six months since Castello di Frosini had opened.

They settled at a table, as they had done the first time he came to the Ypolitta. He studied thirty pages of summarised accounts with total concentration.

"The Ypolitta bookings are well up on last year, even though you haven't been there for a lot of the time," he remarked.

"Yes. People who have been here have wanted to try it."

"And have you had old customers from Ypolitta coming here?"

"Yes, a lot."

"Good," Henry nodded. "That's the way it should be, but you're probably finding that they expect to see you, to deal with you. It's vital that you start looking for the right deputies now, because your customers aren't going to see so much of you in future, but they'll still want a worthwhile face to relate to. May I suggest that you look for women?"

Anna smiled. He was quite right; he was right too in assuming that she had thought of men for these critical positions.

Henry Pedersen stayed for two days before setting off again with the usual cloud of mystery in which he liked to cloak his activities.

Anna watched him go. Since she first met Henry six years ago, she had spent less than ten whole days with him. Nevertheless his influence on her and the way she operated their business was profound. He telephoned every two or three weeks and expected up-to-date, accurate information. He also required Anna to post monthly trading figures to his office in New York, which had been a time-consuming but productive discipline. She had even now only a rough idea of Henry's other business activities, but she guessed he ran many of them in this way, by piling enormous concentration into the small amount of time he allotted to each of them.

Henry was one of those anonymous tycoons the public never heard about. Watching the back of his silver head as the modest car and driver he had hired headed down the drive and back to Milan, Anna wondered at the fact that she did not even know how old he was. She knew very little about his private life. She did not know if he was married or had children. His manner made it clear that these things were none of her business, and he simply ignored direct personal questions. It was odd how this kind of personal reticence created an aura of strength around him. It wasn't only the Vatican who understood the power of mystery.

18

George Kyriakides met the girl on a Sunday when he was
playing polo at Cowdray Park. Everyone else seemed to
know her and treat her with benign contempt. George
couldn't understand it. She was witty, lively and attractive
by any standards, with long, silky-brown legs. She knew all
about polo and who was who in the game. She seemed to
know most of the Argentinians by name, and they certainly
knew her.

It was fairly obvious that she had slept with some of the
players and, for all George knew, a good number of the
spectators. He attributed the general attitude of tolerant
disapproval of her to a peculiar English hypocrisy which he
had not yet learned to emulate. After drinking champagne
with her in the marquee beside the ground for half an
hour, George's view was that Liz Seymour was a more
than acceptable, effortless dead cert.

She gave him a look of slight surprise as he opened the
door of his Aston Martin for her, and he caught several
knowing, not entirely unenvious grins from some of the
other men as he drove her away from the polo ground.

He had earlier arranged to have dinner with one of
his team-mates, a property whizz-kid who lived in baronial splendour in Hampshire. But he didn't want to wait
another six hours to get into bed with this long, blonde
prize beside him.

Tony Kyriakides had taken Thalia to Paris. He was in the
habit of doing this once a year in order to let her loose
among the couturiers with limitless funds.

The house in Argyll Street was empty, therefore, and George headed back to London. Liz talked and joked about the people who had been playing and watching polo that day. She was observant, cynical and viciously funny about them. George was enthralled by this unusual forthrightness in what he judged to be a well-bred English-woman.

Around Guildford he thought that he ought to go through the motions of conventional behaviour and asked her if she would like dinner somewhere.

"Later, Georgey boy," she replied. "I'm feeling so randy, looking at all those men in tight breeches and leather knee-pads all day. Let's get back to your place and have a really good fuck first." She gave George a wide smile and wagged her tongue at him, in case he hadn't understood her.

George felt suddenly sick with excitement. His stomach churned and his cock hardened uncomfortably in his tight trousers. It was not that he had no experience – at the age of twenty-eight he could no longer count the women he had slept with – it was the bluntness of her offer that was new to him.

When they reached Argyll Street, they almost ran from the car to the house. George let them in. Stopping only to collect a bottle of cognac and two glasses, he led her up to his room on the top floor.

Four hours later Liz murmured to him, "Well? What do you think?"

"I've never had anything like it," George said truthfully. "Do you always do it like this?"

"One tries, but not many can keep up. You almost broke the record tonight, five lovely orgasms you gave me."

"I'm not finished yet," said George, "Let's go for the record."

They didn't fall asleep until the sun had been up for three hours.

When he woke, George felt the soft, sweet-smelling flesh beside him and he began to grow once more. Half asleep, she turned to him and he slid into her with long, leisurely thrusts. There was a reassuring, dream-like quality to this semi-comatose love-making, which slowly, imperceptibly became more urgent. She had her long legs wrapped around his back and was rocking gently to his rhythm. But the voice that broke into their lazy half-dream was harsh and raucous.

"What the hell are you doing, George, screwing tarts in my house?" In his anger Tony Kyriakides' Greek accent was more pronounced than normal.

George was instantly awake, and flaccid.

He rolled over, naked and uncovered on the bed. He reached for a sheet to hide himself from his father's furious gaze.

Liz, unfazed, propped herself on one elbow, and slowly unwrapped her leg from George.

"Hello? Who's this?" she asked brightly.

Tony looked at her long legs and large, broad-nippled breasts, and felt a surge of appreciation in his own groin.

She smiled at him. He tried not to show that he would have liked her too. He glanced uncertainly at his son, and left the room without speaking.

They heard him thump downstairs.

"I think he wanted to join in," Liz said.

"Maybe, but he's definitely pissed off. Don't ask me why, but he hates the idea of me bringing girls here. He's worried about what my mother would think, for God's sake."

"And it probably makes him feel guilty about his own escapades," Liz added.

"How the hell do you know he has any?" George asked, wildly wondering if she already knew his father.

"I know a randy man when I see one," said Liz, which did not dispel George's absurd doubts.

311

"You'd better get out of here. I'll drop you somewhere. If he's back, my mother's back. Do you know what Greek mothers are like?"

"'Fraid not."

"Well, I'm not about to show you. Get dressed and we'll try and go without them seeing."

"Can't we finish what we started? It won't make things worse and I was just beginning to feel tingly."

"No, not with my mother downstairs," George said firmly, and climbed off the bed to stagger through into his bathroom.

He showered, washed his hair, and stepped out feeling better able to cope. He walked back into the bedroom. Liz had gone.

He shrugged his shoulders, aware that he had handled things badly, but there was nothing he could do about that now.

He dressed and apprehensively descended the two flights of stairs to the drawing-room where he guessed his parents would be waiting.

His mother was not there. Tony looked up from the paper he was reading when George came in.

"I've told you before," he growled, "No fucking in this house, do you understand?"

"Why not?" George asked.

"Because it shows no respect and because I say so, that's why not. I've let you do what you want for too long now, and I expect some obedience in return. What have you done with the girl?" he asked in a slightly different tone.

"Nothing," George said. "I was having a shower and when I came out, she'd gone."

Tony looked relieved and relaxed back into his chair. George stayed standing.

"Look, George, I accept the fact that you're going to go to bed with women; you probably have for years, and I'm not saying that girl didn't look pretty hot." He gave a roguish smile. "And thank God your mother isn't back yet; she's taking a later flight. But you've got to learn that if I tell you not to do something, I don't want it done. Anyway, I've decided that you've been fooling around for too long. I'm going to give you a choice. Either I stop your money, we stop pretending you're doing anything useful for me, and you go out and look after yourself; or you come and work for me properly. You're twenty-eight now. It's time to start taking things seriously, understand?"

George's heart sank. He knew a time would come when this would happen, and he had dreaded it. To work, every day, with no time to have lunch with his friends, or take trips to shoot in Spain, or gamble in France, or go racing in Ireland.

"Fair enough, Dad. I understand." His father looked relieved. George went on, "I'll go out and look after myself."

Tony's face clouded and became ugly with anger. "What are you talking about? What can you do?"

"I don't know, but I'll think of something. Maybe I'll become a professional polo player. I'm good enough."

He said it with easy conviction.

It was not what Tony wanted to hear.

"Don't be crazy," Tony yelled now, "I've built up a business here, a big business that will soon grow bigger, many times, and I want you to take it over from me when you've learned how."

"Dad, I've got a degree in PPE. You can't expect me to want to learn how to chop onions and make beds."

"Your cousin Andi has learned all there is to know about his side of the business. I don't have to go near the Olympus now. There's no reason why he shouldn't learn about the rest of the business, and he is my nephew."

"Don't threaten me with Andi, Dad. And don't compare me. He didn't have any choice unless he wanted to stay in the backwoods of the Troodos. And he knows nothing about anything else; he's still a bloody peasant."

"You'd still be a bloody peasant if I hadn't got off my arse and been prepared to work. Andi knows what it is to work hard."

"He could work his bollocks off for twenty years and he still wouldn't get a degree." George shrugged his shoulders and shook his head. "Sorry, Dad. I've no intention of spending my time worrying about chambermaids or head-waiters or whether the linen's come back from the laundry, or whatever one does to run an hotel. I'd much rather take my chances playing polo."

Tony levered himself up from the deep chair and stood. He took a few paces towards his son. He wanted to grab him and shake him for his insolence and ingratitude. But when he was facing him, he dropped his hands abruptly. He glared at George. "Get out of my sight, then," he snarled, and watched, distressed, as George turned and strolled from the room and out of the front door of the house.

George found his car and climbed in. Then his stomach reminded him that he had not eaten since lunch the day before. He drove to the French Brasserie near Conran's, not his father's, and sat down to breakfast and the newspapers for a few hours. Later, when he judged Tony would not be at home, he telephoned Argyll Street. His mother answered.

"Hello, Mum. Can I come over and talk to you?"

"You've been arguing with your father, he tells me."

"Nothing serious, but I wanted to talk to you about it."

"All right, come over then," Thalia said, resigned to the fact that she was to be a buffer between these two self-willed men.

"Look, Mum," George said to her when he was sitting with Thalia in her drawing-room, "I admit that I had a girl here with me last night. Dad goes on as if you don't know the facts of life, but I wouldn't have brought anyone here if I'd thought you were going to turn up."

"I know that, George, and I know that men, especially at your age, need to have sex. If your father doesn't feel a little guilt now and again – and God knows he should – I'd be surprised, and maybe he needs to take it out on someone else sometimes."

"Guilt? Dad? That doesn't sound very likely."

"Maybe I'm being too kind, I don't know. But it's hard for men like your father to consider anyone else's feelings; they don't have time. I've seen it in lots of businessmen like him. They are obsessed with playing their game, nothing else matters, life is like one long poker game that never ends. There is nothing I could do about that."

"But didn't you realise that when you married him? You ran away with him, after all."

"Of course I didn't realise. What did I know then, a girl from Limassol?"

"You had been to London before though, hadn't you? You must have learned something then."

"Yes," Thalia nodded, "But only for a few months. It was just after the war; it was a different world then, and I had other things to think about."

"Was that with those people the Cuthbertsons that you used to know?"

"How did you know about them?" Thalia asked sharply.

"Dad's brother mentioned them to me, that time we went to the Troodos."

"Don't talk about that awful time. When I'm awake at nights, I often wonder if my father will appear again."

"He would never admit that they had anything to do with what happened over there. Why did you write and tell you that Christos had drowned out fishing? I saw him in that truck as it went over the edge. It was definitely him."

"My father did not want us to know that his brother had behaved so crudely. He's the only half-civilised member of that family, and he rules it with an iron fist. God knows what will happen when my brother Michael takes over."

"But you haven't said, was it the Cuthbertsons who you came to England with when you were eighteen?"

"Yes," she answered with an odd, bitter edge to her voice.

"Have you seen them since?"

"No."

"Why not? They must have had quite an influence on you."

"I couldn't, not after I had run away from home to become the wife of a waiter in a little Greek restaurant."

"But you're not that now."

"It's too late," Thalia said, as if she wanted to drop the subject, "I can never see them now."

"Where do they live?" George persisted.

"I don't know, and I don't want to know. It was another time in my life, and I've made a new life and I don't want to be reminded about what went on when I was young and foolish. Now I want to ask you what you've done to upset your father."

George shrugged. "He offered me two options: to work in the hotels, or to lose my income and go out and fend for myself. I told him I'd do that – become a polo professional."

"You must realise that he's desperate for you to join him."

"If I did, he wouldn't let me do anything worth doing. I can't mess around being a waiter or a sous-chef or whatever else he expects me to do to learn the business. I quite like doing the odd bit of fact-finding for him. If he wanted to make more use of me like that I'd be happy. But I'm enjoying myself at the moment. I've got a lot of friends I wouldn't be able to see if I was tied down to some hotel."

"George, you are bluffing," Thalia looked hard at him.

316

"You don't want to fend for yourself, really. I know that. You were just negotiating, weren't you?"

"I'm prepared to compromise, if he is," George admitted.

"He will be, I know. You're the only thing in his life that he's weak about, and look at you, you're one of the most spoilt boys I've ever met."

"I know. But it's not my fault; it's not me who's done the spoiling."

Thalia reached out and put a hand on his. "At least you're honest about it, and that makes you bearable. Look, I'll talk to him. There'll be a compromise. Just promise me you'll do some useful work for him and not argue with him."

"I promise. Come on, I'll take you out to lunch."

Thalia shook her head indulgently. "I don't know where you got your charm from."

In the autumn Tony Kyriakides went to Italy to look at hotels, he told his wife.

Monica Fakenham went to Florence to buy some pictures, she told her husband.

It was not a coincidence that they met at the Castello di Frosini.

"We haven't had a long weekend together for two or three years. What about Italy?" he had suggested.

But it was not all play. Tony was intrigued by what Anna Hamilton had achieved in what had been a rambling architectural hotchpotch. He had heard all about the Ypolitta, but he had not visited it – it would have seemed too much like a pilgrimage, but he could guess from the style of the Frosini what its Sicilian counterpart was like.

He asked to see the proprietor the evening he arrived, but was told that she was away for a few days.

He was impressed that this seemed in no way to have diminished the personal feeling she gave to her hotel.

"I wish you'd stop talking about this bloody woman," Monica complained when, over dinner, he pointed out to her the dozens of small touches and the fine tuning that lifted the hotel above the norm.

"I'd like to meet her, give her a job," he said.

"Why the hell should she work for you, with a few ordinary run-of-the-mill hotels in London?"

"Not for long," Tony said. "We launch our first issue on the USM next month. That should raise twenty million, and the Theodore Hotels Group is born. I aim to have half a dozen places like this within five years."

"As you know," Monica said, "I'm commercially illiterate, but surely it must take more than money and your slave-driving tactics to create a place like this."

"Sure, but don't forget, I did it once before, at the Oscar."

"I know about the Oscar. If you remember, I found it. But I don't think you could do it again. You've changed. Those ideals you had for perfection, they must have been eroded away by running your salesmen's places in Kensington."

"For God's sake, Monica, why are you so scathing about them? There are very few salesmen staying at my places. They're perfect examples of how hotels should be run. They didn't cost a lot, and they make a lot of money."

"I know you're very successful and all that, but I just don't think I want you to try and employ the hustling woman that owns this hotel. She's young, and she's too bloody good-looking. I don't mind you having it off with your wife occasionally, or with the odd receptionist from one of your doss-houses, but Anna Hamilton might be a little too much of a temptation for you."

Tony laughed. He liked it when Monica was jealous. "Nobody's going to take your place," he said, reaching a hand beneath the table and sliding it as far as he could up the inside of her warm thigh.

*   *   *

Although for the past few months he had tried hard, and searched every possible source of information, Tony could not find out anything about the ultimate ownership of the Ypolitta and the Frosini. He could not believe there were no other people involved. The woman on her own could not have achieved it all. But he could think of no other places to look. He asked his lawyers and investigation agencies, but they had all drawn blank.

He and Monica drove up to Venice and stayed a few days in the Cipriani, where they were both recognised and had to pretend they were not together. Someone must have told Charles Fakenham that she was there, because he telephoned and demanded that his wife return to London at once. Tony wanted to brazen it out.

"But we can't," Monica urged him. "It would never be the same again, you know that; wouldn't we lose a lot?"

She left, and Tony felt suddenly very alone. But he was not going to let Charles Fakenham cut short his stay. He spent the evening wandering through the quiet alleys until he went to Harry's Bar to eat with a day-old English newspaper for company.

He found the Cipriani's launch by San Marcos. It was still early, before ten, when he reached the hotel. He went to his room and tried to read but could not. He rang Thalia, who was out, then the manager of the Brasserie Athene, who cheered him by telling him they were having a record week there. Buoyed up by this news, he went back to the bar of the hotel.

As he walked in, he was startled to see Liz Seymour. For a bad moment, he thought perhaps she might be with George who was supposed to be in London. But as he passed, glancing sideways at her table, he didn't recognise the man she was with.

Liz had seen Tony only once before, for a few minutes in circumstances in which she could have been excused for not registering his face. But she said as he passed, "Hello. You're George Kyriakides' father, aren't you?"

Tony stopped and looked at her with fake puzzlement. "Have we met?" he asked.

"Yes, of course," she replied with a grin.

"Remind me where?" he asked unkindly.

"I was in bed with your son, in your house," she said.

"Of course," Tony replied. "It was your clothes that confused me."

"Can I introduce you to my husband, Tatton Seymour?"

Tony extended a hand to the husband of his son's one-time lover. When he shook the limp, damp fist that was offered in return, and looked for the first time into the man's pale blue eyes, he understood Liz's lack of reticence.

"Why don't you have a drink with us?" Liz asked.

"Why don't I?" Tony laughed, and sat down opposite her.

Later that night, when Tony had undressed, there was a tap on the door. He wrapped a towel round his waist and went to open it.   Liz Seymour did not wait to be invited; she strolled in, pulling off his towel as she brushed past him.

"Well, that was fun," she said to him brightly next morning. "Now I'd better go and have breakfast with Tatton. Though he can't touch me, he gets lonely if I'm away for too long."

Tony rolled over and looked at her. She was already dressed and her long blonde hair was wet from the shower.

He had never come across anyone quite like her, and his heart pounded with jealousy and doubt as he thought about her with his son. But he couldn't bring himself to ask the question he most wanted to. He had felt so out of control of events since he was a small boy.

"I'm going back to London this morning," he said. "I'll see you there some time?"

"Maybe," she replied with a small wave, then strode towards the door and let herself out.

19

The recession of the early 1980s, followed by the Falklands conflict, did little to hinder the growth of Theodore Hotels plc, for Tony Kyriakides, cash strong with no borrowings, was able to take advantage of the bargains that inevitably surfaced.

By 1985 he had ten hotels in his group and money in the bank. Since he floated the company he had sold only forty per cent of the equity in Theodore to the public. The share price had held up well and the company was in good shape to go for a full listing that year. From the trends in his own business he judged that the economy was on the up, and prices would soon start to rise. He wanted to have funds in place to bid for any other groups that became vulnerable before that.

He was as confident now as he had ever been, despite the early humiliation of losing the Oscar, and the horrific scene in Cyprus. His social standing was as high as he could ever have hoped for the son of a Cypriot hill-farmer. Thalia was a credit to him and, for the most part, tolerant of his moods. The only aspect of his life which worried him, and over which he had no control was George.

George had become expert in handling his father. He knew just how far he could push him and created for himself exactly the job he wanted within Theodore. He was now in his early thirties, as good-looking as ever and more skilled in using his natural charm. Though he still liked to play, his first mad rush to over-indulge in pleasures of the flesh had been tempered by a growing appreciation of more esoteric things. His early curiosity about his own Greekness, for example, had developed, to his own surprise at first, into an interest in classical architecture and culture.

His Oxford friend, Peter Protheroe, had grown out of his student dilatoriness in time to leave Oxford with a First. He had gone on to have some precocious success writing art reviews and clever, self-indulgent pieces on almost any topic for the Sunday papers and the weeklies. He and George had kept in touch, but as George grew bored with his polo and flying friends and their conversations about money and sex, he sought out his old friend and now frequently lunched and occasionally dined with him. He then suggested that Peter come with him to Sicily.

The trip was ostensibly so that George could look at the Ypolitta and report back to his father, who had become increasingly obsessed by Anna Hamilton's reported success.

George had told his father about his single early encounter with Anna at Oxford, and Tony, not entirely fairly had angrily castigated him for not making a more satisfactory connection at that stage. But now that he and Peter were setting out to stay in this famous hotel, they both admitted that the chance of seeing Anna was a far bigger attraction than the island's wealth of classical buildings.

They were impressed beyond criticism by the Ypolitta. George, as was his practice when visiting hotels for Theodore, booked in under a false name. Of course, if they met Anna, that subterfuge would have to go by the board. But they did not. The chic, businesslike Italian woman who was manager of the hotel told them Anna was in the West Indies, where she was shortly opening a new hotel. George and Peter resigned themselves to a week of sightseeing and supreme food and wine.

Back in London, George arranged to meet his father in the handsome Victorian house he had recently bought in

Harley Gardens. Tony arrived and grunted his approval of the purchase, and the way George was dealing with it. Though he wouldn't have admitted it, Tony was going to miss having his son in Argyll Street, but Thalia had persuaded him that he couldn't expect a young man in his thirties to stay at home for ever.

After his quick look around the house, he asked about the Ypolitta.

"Is it as fantastic as all these write-ups say?"

"Better, really. It's certainly the best hotel I've stayed in. I can see what she's done; she hasn't relied too much on decorators and has managed to keep the place feeling like a big family house. It's not the sort of thing we could ever do."

"Why? Why not? I did it with the Oscar."

"But a London hotel is bound to respond to a different sort of treatment than one in the Sicilian countryside. Anyway, I've made a lot of notes; I managed to talk to some of the staff without letting them know what I was doing. But frankly, it's all irrelevant to us. She's not our competition; at least, we're not hers."

"Why the hell do you have to be so negative? Why aren't you inspired to do the same?"

"That I can't tell you, Dad. I've never claimed to be a pioneering entrepreneur."

"Was she there?"

"Anna? No, I'm sorry to say. I wouldn't mind seeing her again."

"Don't you ever get mixed up with a woman like that. You wouldn't last five minutes."

"I think I might," George said thoughtfully.

"Remember, she's a competitor, and business always comes first."

George didn't bother to argue; it was hypothetical anyway.

George was now a director of Theodore Hotels plc, but

his views carried as much weight as a feather on a lump of lead. Father and son had, though, arrived at a working relationship which suited both of them. Tony used George as the soft man in negotiations, or sent him to butter up bankers when that was needed. George's function was defined nebulously as 'head of new projects'. But it was Tony who decided what those projects would be and if they should go ahead. So far Theodore had not set foot outside Britain.

The search for publicly quoted hotel companies on which to prey had not thrown up much, and Tony was becoming frustrated. As well as getting him to check out the opposition, he despatched George to look at possible targets all over Europe and America. George enjoyed himself, but he worked hard. He frequently returned from his sorties with a string of propositions, most of which his father threw out immediately for not possessing those peach sites that he coveted.

And, at a distance, Tony continued to watch with frustration and envy as Anna Hamilton's Mediterranean and Tropical Hotels went from strength to strength, breaking new ground in new or unproven destinations – Mauritius, The Maldives, the Comoros and the Grenadines.

Like George, Tony had visited several of her hotels now, but had still not met Anna. On each of his visits he was struck by things she had done that he would not have thought of. This reminded him of Monica's words a few years before, when she suggested he no longer had the flair or capacity for innovation. He realised he had fallen into the habit of setting up and running his hotels by the book, taking no chances on untried approaches.

After George's trip to Sicily, Tony and George sat down to study maps of the world, and George set off again to look at fresh possibilities from Ireland to Chile, Thailand to the Gambia. Sometimes Tony would go too, but he was beginning to realise that George was probably right;

greenfield projects in far-flung parts of the world were not an option for Theodore. He would have to be content with picking off individual, established hotels as they came on the market until a good-sized group became available. He was operating several well-established, quality hotels, but he had to admit to himself that none was as special as the Oscar had been, and the Ypolitta still was.

Mediterranean and Tropical Hotels, or Med and Trop, as they were generally known, was still a secretive, private company in 1987, owning eight famous hotels, each unique in some aspect of its siting or building. Its clientele had been the least affected by the gloomy economic conditions of the first half of the 1980s, and profits had stayed high.

After the Frosini, Pedersen had had to provide no more funding. When a new project needed cash beyond the group's liquidity Anna preferred to go to the banks, rather than to Henry. He always looked at her proposals, however, and agreed.

At thirty-five, Anna Hamilton was still remarkably young for the success she had achieved. Much of this success, she knew, was due to Henry Pedersen and his hands-on financial management. Sometimes Anna asked him if it would not be sensible to declare his interest, but he always declined: "It would make no difference to the running of the business and it would take away some of the mystique."

Anna was accustomed now to her reputation for being a kind of awesome prodigy. It was only a partial illusion and she appreciated Henry's reasons for not wanting to be overtly involved. Only sometimes she wished the image the world had of her did not keep so many people at arm's-length from her. When she really wanted to remind herself that she was just another woman she went to see her mother and stepfather.

Susan Montagu-Hamilton still treated Anna as if she

were a schoolgirl who had grown breasts a little sooner than her contemporaries. She could not assimilate the idea of her daughter being as important as the newspapers and all her friends told her.

When she saw her, she fussed about Anna's lack of weight and lack of boyfriends and worried that her hair was getting in her eyes. There were times when Anna enjoyed this uncomplicated affection, especially when lapses of identity assailed her.

After the election of Mrs Thatcher's third Tory government in 1987, Henry Pedersen suggested that it might be an appropriate time to open an hotel in England. Anna was glad of the excuse to spend more time in London. She was conscious of the great gaps in her knowledge of English culture caused by her going straight to Sicily after university.

She bought a pretty house off Cheyne Row. She filled it with solid, reassuring old English furniture and tartan fabric. The first people she invited to dine there were Sir James, now retired from the diplomatic service, and her mother.

"Oh, Anna. You've done it all beautifully," Susan gushed enthusiastically when she arrived, thinking of the worn carpets and curtains at her house in Hampshire. "It feels like a real home," she added in some surprise. "I was imagining it might feel like an hotel."

"One of the characteristics of my hotels is meant to be that they're like private houses, not hotels," Anna said. "So I'm used to doing it."

"No, it's more real than that. Anyway, it's lovely that you've decided to buy a house here."

Anna showed them round, and opened doors from her drawing-room on to a small garden that already glowed with autumn colours.

"Will you be in England quite a lot now?" her mother asked when they were sitting with drinks beside them.

"A little more. I felt that I'd rather missed out by not spending a few years here before I started on the Ypolitta."

"But you must have some other reason," Sir James said.

"Yes," Anna admitted, "We thought it would be an appropriate time to open a place here."

"In London?" her stepfather asked.

"That depends on what's available. I'll look at places outside London, if they're reasonably accessible. I prefer doing country places."

"I saw an old friend of mine at lunch in the Carlton today. He was Lord Buckingham's agent for a long time, and he was telling me that Graveden Place is coming on the market."

Anna's ears pricked up. "Graveden? On the Thames above Marlow?"

"That's it. You went to a dance there once, I seem to remember."

"I did, with the ghastly Johnny Chiltern, my first year at Oxford. God, how naïve I was then," Anna remembered.

"I can see you going off to it now," Susan said. "You looked about thirty. I was terrified."

"You needn't have been. Nothing happened, except, I think, Johnny threw up on the original tapestry of a Queen Anne chair."

"Don't you think," Sir James said, "that it might make a stunning hotel? With the kind of treatment you gave the Ypolitta?"

"Yes, of course it would, Dad. It's a bloody good idea. Can I go and see this old chum of yours about it?"

"By all means. I'll arrange it for you in the morning."

Med and Trop opened their first hotel in England six months after Anna had arrived in London. Graveden Place was a grand Regency mansion which soon became a gastronomic Mecca an hour from London on a steep bank of the Thames.

It was supremely sited and instantly lauded by Anna's fans among the travel writers. Tennis stars began to stay there for Wimbledon, Arab princes for Ascot, and, occasionally, Heads of State on private visits. Officially Med and Trop was run from Curaçao, but Anna set up a head office at Graveden, and she now spent at least one week each month in England.

Despite her enthusiasm for living more in England, she found that she no longer felt like a native. Nevertheless, she made an effort to establish herself in Chelsea, and see more of her mother and stepfather at Bishops Lowton.

She was now a regular item in British news columns, gossip and financial. Her face was well known and she only had to be seen with an unattached man for speculation about a forthcoming marriage to erupt. A rich, famous, beautiful and independent woman was not allowed to get away with being single.

The reality was that Anna enjoyed several different kinds of men, but found that they reacted to her with predictable attitudes. Some were intimidated by her; some disapproved of commercial success in a woman; others admired her for what she had achieved, and wasted no time in telling her about their own, superior achievements.

She had resisted the urge, for the past few years, to resume contact with Gavin Sykes. And he had made no effort to see her. The gratification of her libido was limited to the occasional one-off encounter with the kind of men she didn't expect to see again – seldom English and usually spoken for. Ruefully she recognised that her success had a price, but on balance she was prepared to pay it. It was too late, anyway, to back-track.

Towards the end of 1988 Anna was dining with an American actor who had become a regular at Graveden Place.

Her manageress approached her and asked if she could speak urgently with her alone. The actor accepted Anna's shrug and raised eyebrows with good grace and she went to her office.

"What is it?"

"There's a woman waiting in the library who wants to see you. Nothing I could say would put her off until later."

"Hell! I've only just started dinner. Poor old Jack will get very miffed if I leave him sitting on his own. Did this woman say what she wanted?"

"No. Just that she must see you at once."

"What sort of a woman is she?"

"American, about sixty. Very well dressed – Halston, I should think – and quietly spoken. But it does seem as though something's upset her."

"Okay. I'll deal with her. Just pop into the restaurant and tell Jack I won't be long, and does he want to hold dinner until I get back?"

The manageress nodded her short-cropped head with an efficient smile.

Anna made her way to the library, one of her favourite rooms in the hotel. She had bought all the books with the mansion and they lent an air of sedate calm in which it was impossible, comfortably, to speak in a loud voice or to make a scene. At this time of the evening her visitor was the only occupant.

"Good evening?" Anna approached the woman with a neutral smile. "I'm Anna Hamilton."

Her visitor raised herself from a deep wing chair and took a few paces towards Anna.

"Good evening, Miss Hamilton."

Her accent was American with a hint of middle Europe in it. She was a small neat, handsome woman, self-possessed and capable, Anna guessed.

Anna nodded. "Yes. I gather you wanted to see me?"

"My name is Olga Pedersen."

329

Anna could not suppress a start of astonishment and, in the few seconds before she spoke, conjectured wildly on what could have brought her to the Graveden.

"Are you Henry Pedersen's wife?"

"No. I'm Henry's widow."

Anna's knees trembled and gave way beneath her. She sank into the nearest chair. She had spoken to Henry the week before. He had given no signs to her of any ailments. He had sounded as abrupt, businesslike and strong as he always did. Somehow she had never considered Henry was mortal like other men.

"How . . .?" she muttered, "What . . . happened? God, I'm sorry."

Olga Pedersen sat down again, opposite Anna.

"I'm sorry too, to bring you the news in this way. But Henry had asked me before he died to tell you, and some others, personally, before you could hear about it any other way."

"But what happened? He wasn't ill, surely, last time I spoke to him."

"No. It was a foolish accident." Olga looked across and saw the sadness in Anna's eyes. She was making up her mind how much to tell, and she wanted very much to tell someone, besides the police and the lawyers. "Henry had only one passionate interest outside his businesses," she went on in a low, even voice. "He won't have told you. He kept gorillas." His widow shrugged at the bizarreness of such a hobby. "He had for thirty years. Some of them he has had all that time. They were his oldest friends, he always claimed. Last Saturday, he was home, and as usual, he went out to see them. There are twelve in the troupe now. He used to stay with them for an hour or two sometimes, talking to them, feeding them tit-bits, scratching them. He used to tell them anything that was troubling him. At least, I think that's what he told them."

Olga Pedersen stopped for a moment, and Anna was

looking at the saddest woman she had ever seen. But she carried on, with no faltering in her speech.

"When he had not come back in after an hour, I went out to join him. The gorillas were sitting around in small groups as they normally did. And Henry was lying in the middle of the compound, quite still. I knew at once he must be dead. But I called his doctor anyway. He had been suffocated somehow. Three of his ribs were bust. There was such a look of surprise on his face. He must have felt so betrayed."

Anna stared at her as she quietly told this extraordinary story which revealed whole aspects of Henry Pedersen's personality that she had not even guessed at.

"What did you do about the gorillas?" she asked, feeling foolish as soon as she had.

"Nothing. I didn't know which one had done it. It could have been any of the adults. He had always trusted them. He had never had any reason not to, in thirty years. When people used to say to him, 'They're wild animals,' he would just say, 'we're all wild animals.' In a way he was right. He could just as easily have been killed by a mugger, or a gunfreak."

"Mrs Pedersen, I'm so sorry, I should have offered you something. All this must have been a terrible shock to you, and coming to England too, so soon."

"I have had other shocks in my life," Olga Pedersen replied. "But I should like some coffee."

Anna nodded, and sniffed back some tears. She rang the old servants' bell by the fireplace and a waiter appeared a moment later.

She ordered coffee, and a 'Do not Disturb' sign to be hung on the door of the library.

"You shouldn't have come here on your own, so soon afterwards."

"I buried Henry yesterday. I thought travelling would be a distraction and he left very particular instructions on what should be done on his death. I knew really very little of his business – he didn't need my support in that part of his life. As you may know, his businesses were spread very widely, but he took a particular interest in your hotels. I guess that's why he asked me to tell you personally when he died. Now Henry was a very private man, and he won't want any hooha over his death. There have been no reports in the States, and I hope there won't be any; that's the way he wanted it. For the last twenty years Henry ran his business almost for its own sake. I have very beautiful homes in Maryland and in Northern California, and he kept his gorillas, but he wasn't an extravagant man. He has made ample provision for me and his apes; we have no children. He left instructions that the holdings in your business which he controlled were to be offered to you on particular terms; I have them here. Or else the business must be wound up and the monies distributed pro-rata. Either way, his share is to be made available to a trust he set up in Ruanda for the further study of primates."

Olga Pedersen pulled an envelope from the bag at her feet and handed it across to Anna. "Take a look at these, and when you have decided what you want to do, you're to instruct Mr William Franklyn of Franklyn Liebowitz in New York."

Anna didn't think of opening the envelope there and then. She hadn't fully heard the last part of Mrs Pedersen's monologue. She was trying to adjust to the fact of Henry Pedersen's abrupt removal from her life. Suddenly, without him, she felt desolate. Suddenly, she was very conscious of just how much she owed to Henry Pedersen.

"You know that I owe all that I've done to Henry. If he hadn't backed me, I'm sure no one else would have done. And he always gave the right advice. I simply couldn't have achieved what we have without him."

"Believe me, he derived as much satisfaction as you. He knew that you've been totally committed to this business

332

from the start. And he knew the disadvantages of that, especially for a woman."

"How do you mean?" Anna asked.

"Do you have any boyfriends?"

"None in particular. I don't feel I need them."

"I think that's what I meant," Olga said gently.

Anna looked up at Henry's widow, who sat still and upright, not allowing her sadness to beat her, keeping the promises she had made to her husband, and humouring him in his final wishes.

From outside the library door Anna heard some diners leaving with noisy laughter and she remembered the actor she had left in the restaurant. But she couldn't leave the tragic, brave little woman on her own.

"I know this sounds crazy," she began, and asked Mrs Pedersen if she would like to join her for dinner with the famous American.

"Sure," Mrs Pedersen nodded. "He'll make me laugh. But don't tell him what's happened. Just say I'm a little old aunt you can't get rid of."

The next day Anna watched Olga Pedersen being driven away, and marvelled at her fortitude. She herself had cried most of the night, relieved and surprised that she still could. The crying did her good, and lightened the sadness. She went back to her office and opened the envelope Olga had left.

The document had been dictated by Pedersen in his own words, though it was drafted as part of a formal will. Anna was being offered an option to buy Henry Pedersen's fifty per cent of Mediterranean and Tropical at a price that showed a generous return on his original capital investment, but was a quarter of the realistic current value of the shares. They could be paid for, subject to a few minor conditions, over a five-year period, financeable from Anna's own share of the group's profits. As she read the terms, she could almost hear Henry's curt voice and laconic phrasing. Only in the last line was the formality dropped. In his own hand, Henry had scrawled, 'Don't you dare turn me down. Good Luck.'

Bill Franklyn insisted that he should come to England to complete the formalities of Anna's purchase of Med and Trop. It wasn't necessary; Anna was quite willing to go to New York. But Bill came, without his wife.

Anna had last seen Bill five years before, when he had booked into the Frosini while travelling around Europe on his honeymoon.

Mary, his bride, was a reliable Wasp girl, decorative and, it turned out, fecund to the tune of four children. On their honeymoon she had behaved as if Bill were her property, to bid and scold as she wished, and, even then, Anna could see Bill suffering. But she didn't sympathise; he had chosen Mary. Now she found herself looking forward to seeing him.

He was, as far as Anna was aware, the only person besides Olga Pedersen and some of Med and Trop's staff who knew about Henry's interest in her hotels. He had been her original connection with Pedersen, and she had not forgotten that. She craved the chance to talk to someone about Henry and she was more than glad to see Bill.

Bill booked himself in for two nights. He arrived straight from Heathrow before dinner. It was mid-week, but the restaurant was full, with an eclectic mix of famous faces among the diners.

Anna greeted him with a warm kiss on the cheek. He was in his late thirties now, fit, handsome and wearing his success with easy charm. Anna still admired and liked him. She wondered, as they sat in the bar talking before dinner, what it would have been like if she had married him. She could have done; but he was too kind, too uncontroversial for her. Yet to judge from the way he was looking at her it was not his wife he wanted to sleep with that night.

"Don't sit there looking so horny," she said with the bluntness she had always employed with him. "I keep myself strictly for the bad guys these days."

He nodded. "And I'm strictly one of the good guys." There was only a hint of regret in his voice.

They talked of Sicily and the Ypolitta, and his parents who had been back a few times when Anna had been there. Bill had also sent a steady stream of customers to the Ypolitta, the Frosini and, as they opened, other Med and Trop hotels. He had an intimate knowledge of her activities, because Pedersen had employed him for most of their property purchases.

Anna brought their talk round to Henry Pedersen.

"Now he's gone," she said, "I really miss him. I never saw that much of him, but somehow he was always present in my life since the first moment he walked into the Ypolitta. It seems incredible, with hindsight, that he should have done what he did. I was twenty-three, and utterly inexperienced in anything commercial. I had no background in it, I was just an ex-student with no knowledge of anything practical, and yet he seemed to have complete trust in me from the start."

"He didn't rely on your judgement for everything, though, did he?" Bill said. "You must have seen the way he would give orders without letting on. He'd make you think you'd come up with any ideas he had. He worked like that with me for years. He liked working with younger people; he said they had fewer prejudices."

"It certainly gave me a ridiculous amount of confidence in those early days. I operated on a sort of auto-pilot then. I'm far less sure of what I'm doing now I'm running ten hotels."

"He's left you an incredible deal," Bill said, bringing the conversation bluntly back to the present.

"Yes. When Olga first arrived here to tell me, I was worried that he might have actually *given* his shares to me. And I could never have handled that."

"Sure. He realised that. I guess he thought that a tenfold return on his original investment represented a fair return for the risk he took. The fact that you'd still be getting his shares at something like a seventy-five per cent discount no doubt gave him even more satisfaction."

"I did think about taking the other option; selling up the business so as not to benefit by his death. But I really don't think he wanted that."

"He didn't," Bill agreed. "I've brought all the documentation with me. There's a pile of stuff to sign, and I'll need to know where you want your shares held and so forth. It shouldn't take long though, and I'm booked in for another day, so when we've got the formalities out of the way, you're going to take a day off and come to Ascot races with me, and behave like a rich, beautiful young woman should for a change."

"Not so young," Anna said.

But Anna did feel young the next day. Bill had taken her at her word, and not attempted to pursue her into bed. During the night she was sorry; in the morning she was glad; she knew that, despite its shortcomings, Bill's marriage was precious to him.

It was the second day of Royal Ascot. The sky was a crisp blue, and a fresh wind stirred up the normally humid air of the Thames Valley. The enclosures and boxes were crowded with people and faces Anna knew.

She enjoyed being escorted by a good-humoured, cosmopolitan man like Bill. She relaxed and laughed in a way that the pressures of expanding her business over the last few years didn't often allow. Her elation was spotted by the gossip writers from the tabloids who habitually drank at this well of scandalous trivia, but they could not identify the man who was providing it. No matter, shots were taken through 600-millimetre lenses, and appeared with speculative copy in the next day's papers.

Monica saw the pictures as she and her husband were being driven to Ascot the following morning.

"I'd rather like to have dinner at Graveden Place this evening," she was prompted to tell Charles, "and it might be nice to stay there afterwards, though I'm sure we wouldn't get a room now."

Charles rose, as she had known he would, to the challenge. He picked up the car-phone and dialled his secretary. After a few curt instructions he put the phone back with a nod. "There'll be a room for us," he said. "Why do you want to go there? Have you been before?" he added suspiciously.

"No," she answered truthfully, "But everyone says it's very special. A lot of people I'd like to see are going there tonight, and I rather want to meet this woman who owns it. She must be there at the moment. At least," Monica pointed at Anna's photograph, "she was yesterday, with some unknown hunk."

Monica wasted no time in seeking out the famous proprietress of Graveden Place when they arrived after the races and Charles Fakenham was impressed, very impressed by Anna. The combination of an astute woman of business and desirable object of sexual fantasy was, in his experience, almost unique.

Anna, for her part, was intrigued by Charles. She knew something about him; most people who read the financial pages did. He had a reputation as one of the sharpest take-over specialists in the world of merchant-banking, and yet his manner, while not exactly gentlemanly, was bland to the point of complete inscrutability. He was also, she thought, an attractive man in the wicked kind of way which still excited her. She remembered Gavin Sykes' remark a few years before when she and Gavin had seen Monica in the Meridiana.

"I wonder who's keeping her satisfied now?" Gavin had mused.

Seeing the two of them together, Anna now asked herself the same question about Charles.

20

John Sullivan, ex-chairman of Scottish and Lakeland Hotels, prowled through the corridors and public rooms of the Oscar. There was a scowl on his haggard, sixty-nine-year-old face.

A month ago he had been forced to give up his office there – the office he had occupied for nearly twenty years since buying the hotel from Tony Kyriakides.

He refused to admit to himself that he was to blame for his own demise. It was, he told people, the fault of the economy in general – no matter that most other hotel companies had managed to stay profitable over the past few years – and the fault of unimaginative, unrealistic institutional shareholders on his board – now his ex-board.

He could not admit that his decision to expand at any cost had caused the group's borrowings to rocket, that the quality of management in half the hotels was at best second-rate, that he had paid too much for some of them in the heat of competitive bidding.

The crash of October 1987 had seen the share price of Scottish and Lakeland – already weak with lack of profits – tumble to a point that valued some properties at eighty per cent of the price he had paid for them. He had managed to bluff his way through for another year before the patience of his biggest shareholders had run out.

The caretaker chairman, seduced from another large group, had made use of Sullivan's dismissal to settle old scores by starting an internal investigation into the expense and salary deals Sullivan had awarded himself over the years. This created a pretext for holding up payments that were due to Sullivan on curtailment of his contract as chief executive.

Suddenly the business that John Sullivan had nurtured like a child for so many years had become an ungrateful teenage daughter who had turned her back on him; and he was finding it impossible to take.

The manager of the Oscar saw him walking across the main reception hall of the hotel where several clients were booking in.

"What can I do for you?" he asked with no hint of politeness.

"Nothing."

"I'm afraid, unless you're eating here or staying here, I can't allow you to wander around."

"What the hell are you talking about? This is an hotel, isn't it, dedicated to serving its clients? I'm a client and if I want to wander around, I'll wander around."

"If you're not eating or sleeping here, you're not a client. And using my discretion as manager here, I'm declining to serve you, so please leave."

"You fucking pip-squeak!" Sullivan yelled in anguish. "I started this place, I created it and made it what it was. How dare you talk to me like that?"

The manager glanced at the guests by the reception desk who were looking at the scene with embarrassed interest. He kept his voice quiet and even.

"If you insist on yelling and swearing, I'm afraid I shall have to call the police to remove you. And it's a matter of record that this hotel was started by Tony Kyriakides, not you."

Sullivan glared at the unruffled young man and stormed out of the large glass doors into Queen's Gate to clamber into his gold Bentley Mulsanne parked directly outside.

*   *   *

Charles Fakenham never allowed his distaste for other people's personal qualities to interfere in his business dealings. Sullivan, in Fakenham's view, was a loud-mouthed lout, who deserved everything he had got for letting a thirst for glory get in the way of careful management and profits at Scottish and Lakeland. But he could also provide a lot of inside information on the beleaguered group and still owned seven per cent of the shares.

Charles drew the line at Sullivan's suggestion that they should meet for lunch. But he agreed to meet him in a private room at the Westbury, where people tended not to notice who was coming and going on a busy afternoon. He spent half an hour closeted with him before leaving with a satisfied smile.

Later, in the early evening, Charles drove down to Graveden Place.

Anna Montagu-Hamilton had arrived back that day from a long tour which had taken in most of her hotels. She was feeling pleased with herself – at least, with her hotels – and her sense of triumph was boosted by finding Graveden fully booked for several weeks. She was confident now that she should look for a second prominent site in Britain.

Charles had rung within an hour of her return, and she had agreed to see him right away. She looked forward to seeing him with mixed feelings. Since their first meeting, when Monica had brought him to Graveden after Ascot, she had seen him twice; once at lunch with his wife, and once for dinner alone.

Before that dinner, Anna had heard that Charles enjoyed an unusual and what sounded rather an unhygienic form of sex. Unembarrassed, she had asked him directly if this were true and he had confirmed his preferences. He had half-seriously suggested that she should try them. She had declined, and her initial interest in Charles as a potential outlet for her own ungratified needs had withered at once. But she did recognise, and appreciate, his capacity for dispassionate ruthlessness.

They sat at a table in a corner of the restaurant and Anna gave instructions that she was not to be disturbed.

"I hope you haven't come down just to try and convert me to your dirty habits again," she said before they had started eating.

"No, no," he said, "That's a particular taste which you either have or haven't. My wife, unfortunately, hasn't."

"How is your lovely wife?" Anna asked with only mild sarcasm.

"As long as the slimy Kyriakides is seeing to her, she stays manageable."

"Tony Kyriakides? Theodore Hotels?"

"That's the one. You know him, I imagine?"

"No, I've never met him, but I'm sure he's had a look around some of my places. Does Monica know that you know about him?"

"Good Lord, no. I wouldn't want to spoil her excitement. It's been going on for twenty years. I see no point in interfering now, at least, not until I can see the bastard off once and for all."

Anna was alarmed by the the venom Fakenham squeezed into this last statement, but tried to ignore it.

"But why do you stay married to her?"

"We get on rather well, as a matter of fact; I need a wife and I certainly don't want to marry anyone else."

"Well, if you didn't want to see me for kinky sex, what did you have in mind?"

"As far as I can ascertain, you are the sole owner of Mediterranean and Tropical Hotels, aren't you?"

There was no way he could be sure of this, or indeed have any idea of the ownership of her various companies.

"Why?" Anna asked.

"Because if you are, and you want to quadruple the size

of your group very fast and very cheaply, I can help you to do that."

"Can you?" She sounded indifferent. "I think that I'm satisfied with the size of my business as it is."

"No, you're not," Charles said. "You wouldn't be human if you were. And when you're presented with the kind of bargain I'm proposing, you couldn't possibly turn it down."

"What's in it for you?"

"I've just bought a parcel of Scottish and Lakeland, very cheap, and I want to see their value double, very fast. You could do that for me."

"I've been away for six weeks. I'm not up to date."

Charles took a sheaf of papers from the slim Gucci case he had brought into dinner with him.

"Here's their current position," he said and offered the papers to her.

"I'm not going to look at these over dinner," She shook her head. "It might encourage the punters to do the same. Tell me broadly what you had in mind."

"I had in mind Mediterranean and Tropical doing a reverse take-over of Scottish and Lakeland."

"And how do I do that? Med and Trop is a private company, unquoted anywhere, with only one asset in the UK."

"That's not a problem. Provided you can get the funds – and I can guarantee that – and enough shareholders are persuaded that they would be better off having the group run by a management with your spectacular track-record, it can be done."

"How can the shareholders be persuaded? After all, we would be bringing negligible assets to the deal."

"Graveden is by no means negligible when compared with the loss-making activities of most of the hotels in the S & L group. I'm already certain of around forty per cent anyway; I can manage another ten, believe me."

"What price are Scottish and Lakeland today?" Anna asked, unable to pretend she wasn't interested.

Fakenham smiled. "One-twenty; they were over four pounds before Black Monday."

"And what are their net assets worth?"

"Conservatively, one-fifty a share. In other words, you'd be getting the whole lot at a twenty per cent discount. If they break the company up and sell off the hotels individually or in small parcels, they'd probably fetch their market value, perhaps more if there's a bit of an auction. But no one is keen to grapple with the existing group, its debts and its rotten management."

"What about your friend, Mr Kyriakides?"

"Ah, well, I'll admit, he's the one person who'd go for it, and he could probably raise the money with a rights issue, whatever I tried to do to spike his guns. And I would be very upset if he got his hands on the Oscar at a bargain price – wouldn't you? Either way, though, there's money to be made. But look, I've trusted you by sharing my information with you. You must trust me by telling me what your position is."

"If I want to do the deal, I'll make sure you have whatever information is necessary. I can tell you that Med and Trop is not a single corporate entity; it's theoretically no more than a co-operative booking agency."

"You mean all your hotels are held by different companies?"

"More or less, and I don't want to change that. Most of them are owned by Netherlands Antilles companies. I can't see any advantage in bringing them into the UK tax net."

"That I understand, of course, but it won't present too much of a problem."

"The other thing is," Anna went on, "even if we could buy these thirty-five hotels cheap, they wouldn't all respond to my kind of treatment, or even a watered-down version of it. I could improve them but they're not all the kind of hotels I want to run."

"So, improve them, then sell the ones you don't want singly or in small parcels, as I said. You must admit, it would be nice to get your hands on the Oscar."

"As far as I'm concerned, that's the only attractive thing about the deal. I never knew the Oscar when it first opened – I was too young," she grinned, "but there's no question that Kyriakides was ahead of his time. Of course, it's become pretty humdrum with Sullivan running it, but all the good ideas are still there. I took a look a couple of months ago."

"You could transform the Oscar, and with your reputation it would come right back to the top again."

"Okay." Anna was putting an end to the conversation with a simple gesture which Charles did not try to override. "Now don't do any more of a selling job on me. I've heard all I need for the moment. I'll come back to you within two days and tell you if I'm interested, and then I'll give you the information you need."

Charles accepted this. He had not expected to be able to bulldoze Anna into agreement. Anyway, the Oscar alone was a big enough carrot for her. They carried on and finished their dinner, talking generally, without much charity, about other people's difficulties.

When they finished, Charles had a Delamain in the library before Anna came out to see him off. She gave him a thoughtful wave and watched his car sweep away across the gravel courtyard. As she walked back into the regency splendour of the main hall, she was jerked up short – like a dog on a lead – by a familiar voice greeting her. She spun round to see Gavin Sykes with his old cynical smile.

He must have been approaching sixty now, she thought, but he had scarcely changed since his first visit to the Ypolitta. She was impressed, but she was not sure she was glad to see him.

"Well, Mr Sykes," she said, "Have you been dining here?"

"Yes. It was as good as ever."

"You've been here before, then?" she asked with surprise.

"Naturally. A lot of the people I do business with expect to be taken here."

"Taken? By you?"

Gavin laughed. "In a manner of speaking."

"I'm sorry I didn't see you in the restaurant. I would have done something to impress your punters."

"I saw you," Gavin said, and Anna recognised that he attached some significance to the identity of her dinner partner.

"One has to entertain one's banker from time to time."

"I see he didn't stay for a spot of post-prandial beastliness."

"No, he didn't come for that."

"What a relief. Sadly, my little party wants to be whisked back to London. It's marvellous to see you looking so unblemished. Perhaps we might meet again?"

"Perhaps we might," Anna replied.

At that moment, a group of three Japanese men in sawn-off Savile Row suits appeared from the bar and flocked around Gavin like Lilliputians around Gulliver. He raised his eyebrows a fraction at Anna and shepherded them out of the hall.

Tony Kyriakides had kept his offices in Kensington High Street, adding adjacent suites as they became available. He kept his head office staff to the minimum, not more than thirty including himself and George.

Since Theodore Hotels had gone for a full quote on the stock exchange they had been finding it difficult to identify satisfactory acquisitions, but the group had grown steadily, until now it owned fifteen sound and profitable hotels as well as four restaurants. He had recently and with some regret sold the Olympus to his cousins, Paul and Peter Michaelides. His nephew Andi had managed the place very successfully for several years and was becoming frustrated that Tony had not, as promised, elevated him to bigger things. The Michaelides wanted to give him some of the action. Tony felt he couldn't stand in his way, and the Olympus' contribution to the group's profits were relatively insignificant.

The evening the deal was completed, he and Thalia had been to dine there. Paul, Peter and their mother, Maria Michaelides, were there, and in the light of the guttering candles which still adorned the tables, Tony watched Andi scuttling about, and it took him back through thirty-five years to the time when he had first arrived in London.

He invited George to come with them but George said he didn't want to sit around eating kebabs and guzzling Retsina.

Tony became depressed over dinner and drank too much. By the end of the evening he was overtaken by maudlin nostalgia. He wanted to leave, but forced himself to stay until the new ownership of the Olympus was satisfactorily celebrated. When, after one o'clock, he and Thalia walked out into the familiar street he felt he had finally and irrevocably severed his early roots.

Tony was well used to living in the cultural limbo-land of the immigrant, but people like Gavin Sykes brought home to him more bluntly than most that there were still aspects of Englishness he would never understand.

He had seen Sykes around over the years; heard sporadic gossip about him, and could not understand how anyone could take him seriously; and yet there were those who did, at least to the extent of being prepared to accept his introductions and take his phone calls.

Tony, who was unaware of ever having spoken to Gavin Sykes, did not take Sykes' call when his secretary buzzed him through with the information that the ageing playboy wanted to talk to him on the phone.

After a moment's thought about the other things on his mind, he barked, "Put him through to George."

George Kyriakides picked up his phone.

"Hello. George Kyriakides," he said with his customary, almost English drawl.

"Good morning, Mr Kyriakides." The voice was English, but the pronunciation of his name correctly Greek. "This is Gavin Sykes here."

George, like his father, had never met Sykes but had heard of him. Unlike his father, he did not feel instinctive contempt for a man who had long managed to lead such a high-profile, active social life on such apparently slender resources.

"Good morning," he answered in a voice that recognised Sykes' identity.

"I had wanted to speak to your father. I hope you don't mind being second choice."

George laughed. "I'm used to it."

"I wondered if I might come and see you. I have some information that will interest you."

"What about?"

"I'm only prepared to talk about it privately, and after we've established how much you're going to pay for it. Can you take that sort of decision?"

"Up to a point, but I don't think it's likely you could have any information that would be helpful to us."

"You can decide that when I've seen you."

George considered the way he could handle this – if it was worth anything – to his own best advantage. "All right," he said, "But I won't see you here, or anywhere public. You'd better come to my house this evening, around seven?"

"Fine," Sykes said with satisfaction. "Where is your house?"

George gave him the address in Harley Gardens, and put the phone down with a nod and a smile. His father would never have agreed to meet Sykes.

Gavin Sykes admired the pictures, the classical antiquities and the polo trophies which crowded George's walls and shelves. He seemed to know about most of the people with whom George had regularly played. He referred obliquely to the unpublicised liaison that had once existed between George and Tatton Seymour's wife.

There was in Sykes' manner a subtly displayed sense of his own superiority. George could not help being impressed by someone who so flagrantly ignored all normal attitudes to visible material status.

"Champagne?" he suggested.

"Provided it's not too young or too fizzy."

George went off to look for a bottle of ten-year-old Dom Pérignon, while Sykes ambled around the drawing-room, picking up valuable objects, and helping himself from a box of Monte Cristos on the mantelpiece.

When they were sitting, George asked, "So, what do you know that we don't?"

"Before I tell you, you must agree to remunerate me."

"If you have something of value to us, of course we will. But it's possible, isn't it, that you're going to tell me something we already know."

"Look," Sykes said, "if as a result of what I tell you, you decide to act on it, you must undertake to pay me £10,000."

"Undertake?"

"Just give me your word that if what I tell you is new and subsequently useful to you, you'll pay."

George shrugged. "I can't sign anything as vague as that."

"I don't want a signature. Your word is good enough for me. And, frankly, if you did tuck me up, I wouldn't come back to you another time, and I can be very indiscreet when roused."

"Okay, you have my word," George said with a shrug.

Sykes, evidently satisfied with this, leaned back in his chair and took a swig of champagne.

"I saw Anna Montagu-Hamilton last night. Do you know her?"

"No," George said, trying not to show his immediate interest. "Well not exactly. I met her at Oxford once in my first year when she'd just finished her finals. I've thought of getting in touch with her dozens of times since, but I reckoned that sooner or later our paths would cross. I suppose it's surprising they haven't already. Anyway, what about her?"

"She was having dinner at Graveden, with Charles Fakenham."

"Of Berkley Berrington?"

Sykes nodded. "The so-called Acquisitions King."

"There's no particular reason why they shouldn't know each other," George shrugged, unimpressed by the news. "And I'm pretty sure Anna Hamilton wouldn't be interested in any takeovers. I've been into it and as far as we can tell hers is a private company, and she only has one hotel here in England. What's more, her strength has always been in finding undeveloped sites. Besides, there aren't any real prospects around at the moment."

"Aren't there? Earlier yesterday, I happened to be in the Westbury, and guess who I saw coming out of a room with Charles Fakenham?"

George made a face. "I don't know. Some tart that specialises in dodgy practices?"

Gavin Sykes smirked. "No. He hadn't been having funny sex, at least I doubt it. He was followed out a moment later by John Sullivan."

"Scottish and Lakeland?" George laughed. "Everyone knows they're in trouble, but nobody's going to be interested in bidding for them. Their borrowings are colossal, they haven't made a profit in three years. There's been carnage in the board- room. I've heard it on good authority their only hope is to organise an orderly break-up. That's the only way they'll see their money back."

"And you would, I suspect, be going for the Oscar."

"That's fairly obvious, isn't it? But my father's not a sentimental man."

"I don't know about that but he'd do much better to take over the group now, with all its liabilities, then sell off the dross. If Anna Hamilton goes for it, you'll never get another chance at the Oscar."

"I don't think there's any question of Anna Hamilton going for it. It's simply not the way she operates," George said with a hint of doubt creeping into his voice.

"Listen, if it's cheap enough, and John Sullivan's got into bed with Fakenham, there's a good chance they may be able to swing a sale. There are enough institutional shareholders who'd rather see the group recover under decent management than simply flog off what they can for what they can get. And when I last looked at the share register, Sullivan had seven per cent. He's still the biggest individual holder, and Fakenham had another five of his own. By now, he's probably gathered up a few more."

"Not much, though. The price is still static."

"And undervalues the properties by ten or fifteen per cent."

"Only their book value. Prices are already slipping, and we reckon they've a long way to go. But anyway, I don't see what you think is so significant. You've seen Fakenham with Sullivan, and later you've seen him with Anna. Why should there be a connection?"

"He was definitely talking business with Anna. He was trying to shove papers at her, which understandably she wouldn't read in the restaurant at Graveden. I'm absolutely certain that she and Fakenham, with Sullivan to back him up in some way, are going to go for Scottish and Lakeland. That's thirty-five hotels, of which half are in prime positions. If you don't think there's some significance in that, your father will." He drained his glass of champagne and stood up. "You tell him. And don't forget, if he decides to do anything about it, be owes me ten grand; a mere flea-bite of a fee. But he'll have to start going for it immediately. Fakenham won't hang around."

George stood up too. He didn't share Sykes' conclusions, but he showed him to his front door, and watched him lope off down the tree-lined street as if he hadn't a serious thought in his head.

Despite his lack of belief in Sykes' assessments George decided to go and see his father right away, just in case. He telephoned his parents' house. His mother told him Tony had gone to the Oscar. George was struck by this coincidence and telephoned the hotel to tell his father he would meet him there in a quarter of an hour.

Tony had been having a drink with the young manager of the hotel who had at one time worked for him. This was not a particularly unusual thing for him to do, but George was convinced now that there was more to it than that.

His father confirmed this when they were alone together.

"As there's a good chance that Scottish and Lakeland is going to be broken up," he said with a happy grin, "this place will come on the market, so we'd better not hang around. Obviously people will assume that we'll want it, but we've got to behave as if we're not that interested. What did you want to see me about?"

"I think we'd better go somewhere else," George said.

"Okay. Come and have dinner with me at the Brasserie Athene. Have you got a car here?"

George nodded. "Yes."

Tony lowered himself with less suppleness than he would have liked into his son's Ferrari and grumbled as they zipped in and out of the traffic down to the King's Road.

"Well," he said between angry complaints about George's driving. "What did you want to tell me?"

"Actually, it's about the Oscar. I had a fellow called Gavin Sykes round to see me just now."

"Oh, yes?" Tony said flatly. "He rang to speak to me this morning. I put him on to you. What the hell did he want?"

"Money for information."

"What information could he possibly have for us?"

"I'm not sure how significant it is, but I thought I'd better tell you. He thinks that Anna Hamilton and Charles Fakenham are cooking up a plan to take over Scottish and Lakeland."

"What!" Tony Kyriakides turned and yelled at his son, as if George himself were responsible for this appalling news. "Why the hell didn't you tell me before?"

"For God's sake, Dad, I came straight round to tell you. I thought you'd want to know. I must say, finding you actually in the Oscar seemed like an omen."

Tony had turned to stare at the road in front of him, his anger no longer directed, unreasonably, at his son. "Why did this man Sykes think that's what's going on?" he muttered.

"Because yesterday he saw Fakenham and Sullivan coming out of a room in the Westbury, and then he saw Fakenham and Anna Hamilton locked into some heavy discussion at Graveden Place."

"How come he was in both places?"

"I don't know. He didn't say. I guess it was pure chance, but then, he's an opportunist; that's how people like him survive."

"Did he want something for it?"

"Of course he did; ten grand; but only if we decide to use his information."

"Then he must be confident of it."

"I did think that maybe he was trying to wind us up on

behalf of Scottish and Lakeland. Maybe they've decided to try and encourage a bid."

"That's not what I heard, and frankly, they'd do better to break it up."

"Unless there are enough shareholders who think they'd do better by being taken over and becoming profitable again."

"That'll be bloody hard, with their borrowings, and useless staff."

"Anna Hamilton could turn it round."

Tony turned and glared at him. "And we couldn't!?"

"I'm not saying that."

"Listen. We've got one of the best-run chains in the country, Anna Hamilton's got one very specialised hotel – that's what she's good at, I'm not saying she's not – but picking up thirty-five hotels all over England and Scotland, she doesn't have the experience for that."

"That's what I told Sykes. But if Fakenham gets behind her, she may go for it, just to get the Oscar."

"She may go for it," Tony growled, "But she'll have to beat me to it. That woman will only get her hands on the Oscar over my dead body."

21

"Christ, you look terrible!"

Tony Kyriakides thought for a moment that he detected compassion in Monica's eyes, but chose to take it as one of her customary criticisms.

"Well, so would you if you hadn't slept for forty-eight hours."

Tony's still dark, wavy hair was perceptibly greyer than it had been a week before. There were sooty bags beneath his black-coffee eyes. His face sagged with the weight of sleeplessness.

"Who's been keeping you up late then?"

"My mother," Tony snapped.

"Have you got a mother?"

"You know perfectly well I have. At least, I had."

"Oh." This time, Monica was unmistakably compassionate. "I'm sorry. Where did she die?"

"At home, of course, in Cyprus."

"Is that where you've been for the last few days?"

"Yes. And Thalia's not expecting me back until tomorrow, so if Charles is away, we can spend the night together for once."

"As it happens, he is. How lovely."

"First I must have a shower and a drink. Then let's go somewhere quiet for dinner, out in the country."

They were in the flat in Hans Crescent. Tony had discarded his heavy coat and scattered his clothes around the bedroom on his way to the shower. He stood naked in the cubicle, wallowing in the hot, heavy downpour.

When he came out, Monica had poured a large glass

of thick Russian vodka for him. He kissed her and sat opposite her in front of a fake log fire.

He took a gulp of the vodka and laid his head on the back of the chair with his eyes closed.

"God, I'm glad to be back," he sighed.

"Did you go to the funeral?"

"I went to it; I presided over it; I paid for it; I wasn't thanked by my brothers for it. I was abused by them because my mother left something to me." He laughed. "My God, when I think how much I've sent her, and them, over the years, it's incredible." He opened his eyes and leaned towards Monica. "Do you know what she left me? An olive tree!" He laughed again. "And my brother Stelios is *mad*. And do you know, she didn't own the land where the olive tree is, just the tree, so I have the right to pick the olives, but not the right to go on the land to pick them. Crazy, bloody Cyprus! Where else could such a ridiculous thing be possible? Anyway, it's only symbolic, and I understand the gesture she was making."

"What are they like, your brothers?" Monica asked.

Tony shrugged. "How can I tell you? There is not one thing about them that you could understand. They are simple peasants. Nicos is an honest old fellow, but Stelios is pig-ignorant and vindictive. Of course, they're all much richer than they were. Independence and Partition have worked well for them. They've pulled down their little stone houses and built horrible concrete boxes which they think are so smart. And they all have Japanese jeeps. It's sad. It was a harder place when I grew up there, but it was certainly more beautiful." He stood up, feeling refreshed after the shower and the drink, wanting to talk to her in a way he had seldom done. "I had to be on my own for a bit; I went to see places I hadn't been to for years; the prettiest place was a dead village."

"How do you mean?"

"There used to be a Turkish village next to ours, called

Vrecha. In 1974, every man woman and child in that village fled to settle above the Green Line where the UN soldiers still try to keep Greeks and Turks apart. I walked to Vrecha the day before yesterday; I wanted to get away from my family, all weeping and arguing about who would have what. This village was so peaceful, flowers growing everywhere, no noise, a few wild chickens around. One old man with his donkeys living in the empty school, using one of the schoolrooms for a stable. There's a little mosque with a tin roof and minaret, still locked up after fourteen years. There must have been fifty or sixty houses in the village – all empty. I was fascinated by the place, frozen in time like that. Most of the Greeks won't touch it but I wandered from house to house with only the birds for company. Even the richer merchants' houses were simple places, just bigger than the others with a bit more decoration.

"I went and looked at the house of a family I knew. I used to see them when I passed through the village sometimes; there was a beautiful daughter; I met her up on the hills while we were looking after the goats. Fatima, she was called. I don't suppose she was more than eleven or twelve, but my God, I thought she was lovely. I used to dream about her every night and imagine I was kissing her. Of course, I didn't know about all the other things I could have imagined." Tony smiled at the thought of his innocence. "There was nothing left in their house; just a few odd rotten shoes, old bottles and things, and a couple of bits of broken furniture. There's no way of knowing where they went to in the north. They just packed what they could and ran, lost everything, I suppose, but then, so did the Greeks who had to come south. Stupid, stupid people. Why can't people learn to live together? They do here. That's one thing I respect the English for. I might resent them for their snobbishness and sense of their own superiority, but they give any man who comes here a chance to make a living, to make a fortune, even, if he knows how and works hard."

Tony stopped and looked at Monica, who had never heard him speak like this about Cyprus or his early life. "Excuse me for talking so much. I won't bore you any more. I'll just say that, now my mother is dead, I will never, ever go back to Cyprus. I'm finished with it completely." He sliced the air with both hands, one palm across the other. "So, how have you been?"

"Who cares how I've been?"

"I care. I must; I've been coming back for your insults for long enough."

"Would you stop coming back if I stopped insulting you?"

"I don't know. Try it and we'll see."

"No, I don't think I will. Someone has to keep your feet on the ground. Let's go to Graveden for dinner," she added abruptly.

Tony looked at her with surprise. "Why there?"

Monica shrugged. "You've never been – it's time you did. Maybe Anna Hamilton will be there; don't you think it would be interesting to meet her?"

Tony laughed. "You're right. Maybe it would. But there'll be a lot of people who know us."

"What the hell? Nobody will take any notice, and I'm sick of always worrying about that."

Tony felt the adrenaline pumping through his arteries like a dose of cocaine. The depressive influence of Cyprus and his mother's death lifted as he saw confrontation beckoning.

Monica booked a table in her name and drove them in her Porsche. Forty-five minutes later they were being shown to the only empty table in the large dining-room.

Tony was feeling almost light-headed as he ordered their dinner and wine. He noticed a few people glance in their direction and show no great interest. One or two acquaintances nodded greetings, and Tony relaxed. That evening, he didn't care what speculation his presence with Monica might cause. If it ever got back to Thalia, he could think of a dozen explanations.

After they had eaten a couple of dozen oysters with a big, long-tasting Chablis, Monica rose to her feet.

"I've got to have a pee," she announced. "Try not to pick up too many young stars while I'm gone."

"I'll try," Tony grinned.

A moment after Monica had left the room, Tony, watching her go, saw a tall, striking woman, younger than Monica and somehow familiar, walk into the restaurant on her own.

To his surprise, the woman looked at him and came straight over to his table.

"Good evening, Mr Kyriakides."

Tony half rose, still trying to remember where he had seen her. He couldn't have met her – he wouldn't have forgotten such a beautiful, strong-looking woman as this.

"Good evening. How are you?"

"You don't know who I am, do you?" she said with a grin of surprise and amusement.

Tony gave an apologetic gesture. "If we have met, I don't see how I could have forgotten you. But, please, my dinner guest has gone to the ladies and I'm getting lonely. Why not join me for a moment; have a glass of Chablis?"

The woman nodded. "Thank you, I will."

Tony hadn't expected her to. He had assumed she was on her way back to her table. She raised an authoritative hand to a waiter who hurried over. "Bring another chair to this table, please, Mario."

Puzzled, Tony sat down in his chair as she occupied Monica's. Then, to his consternation, Monica reappeared, making her way back to the table. Tony, brazening it out, gallantly filled a glass with Chablis for his unexpected guest.

Monica didn't seem put out, though. She sat in the

chair that had been brought by the waiter, and gave the intruder a smile of recognition. "So you two have introduced yourselves?"

"No," the other woman said, "I know who Mr Kyriakides is, but he doesn't know me."

Monica's eyebrows rose with cynical humour. "In that case let me introduce you. Tony. This is Anna Montagu-Hamilton."

Tony was raising a glass to his lips. His hand stopped abruptly a few inches above the table. The blood that rushed to his face wasn't visible beneath his swarthy skin, nor could the women have known about the sweat that broke out beneath his light worsted suit.

How could he have been so stupid as not to realise who she was at once? Always know your enemy, he had told George a hundred times, and he hadn't recognised this enemy even when she had invited herself to sit at his table. Of course, all his instincts would have discouraged him from perceiving this woman as an enemy. So she had completely wrong-footed him and stolen the initiative. And Monica had known for sure that they would meet.

Outwardly, Tony displayed an unruffled calm. The hand raising the glass continued its journey to his mouth after a barely visible pause, and he let a slow smile spread across his face.

"Of course, I knew your face. I'm so sorry not to have been able to put a name to it – a name which I am very familiar with. Monica, I didn't know you knew Miss Hamilton."

"Anna's a client of my husband's," Monica said, then rose to her feet once again. "Look, I've seen someone I must speak to for a moment. Tell them to hold my main course, Tony." With no attempt at subtlety, she didn't wait for Tony to object to her departure and wove her way between the tables to the far side of the restaurant.

"Something tells me Monica thought we should meet," Anna said.

"It looks to me as though Monica told you we would meet." Tony looked at her blandly. "I wonder why?"

"You can do better than that, Mr Kyriakides."

"You tell me why, then," he said.

"When two parties are pursuing the same purchase, the vendor is normally the winner."

"That depends on how hard the purchasers are pursuing."

"No it doesn't, as you well know. If it were only my company who were to show an interest in Scottish and Lakeland, for example, they would have no leverage to increase my bid. The minute another party expresses an interest, they have the makings of an auction. Now, I don't doubt that you have strong reasons for wanting to buy the group, despite its problems, but so have I, at the right price. At the same time, if you were to bid against me, it only makes commercial sense for me to make you pay too much. However, if you were to leave the field clear for me to get the bargain that Scottish and Lakeland ought to be, I would feel you were owed some compensation for giving up the chance to bid."

Tony gazed at the beautiful woman opposite him, impressed by her unabashed gall, but with a churning in his guts at their coming battle.

"Miss Hamilton, the Oscar was my creation, and I'm going to get it back. But I have no intention of offering you inducements to stay out of the bidding. My company is well-funded, publicly quoted with a strong track record. Even with Monica's husband to guide you, I think you would be unable to convince those with an interest in Scottish and Lakeland even to consider a bid from the small private company you control in this country. I admire your cheek in offering me a bribe, but really it was the action of someone young, and inexperienced in this kind of sophisticated transaction."

"So, your answer to my inexperienced, unsophisticated offer is 'No'?"

Tony nodded.

"Will you please do me the favour of remembering that I made it. You'll regret you turned it down."

"I don't think so. But it was a pleasure to meet you."

"And you, Mr Kyriakides. And, by the way, I hope you will have dinner with my compliments." She rose from her chair.

Tony inclined his head. "Thank you. We will."

As he watched her go, he was seething with frustration and humiliation. She had won this first round of their fight. And she was going to be a tougher opponent, especially with the machiavellian Fakenham tending the sponge in her corner.

Monica reappeared soon after Anna had gone.

"Useful meeting?"

"You shouldn't have fixed it without telling me."

"If I'd told you, you wouldn't have come."

"I nearly made a complete fool of myself, not knowing who she was."

"For God's sake, Tony, that's your fault. I had no idea you didn't even know what she looked like."

"I've seen photos of her, of course, but I'd never met her or seen her in the flesh. But meeting her achieved nothing; I could have told you that."

"Tony, you should have listened. She wants those places, and Charles is backing her. I can't do anything about that. The only way I could risk coming here with you tonight will be to tell Charles I aimed you at Anna to try and keep the Scottish and Lakeland price down. But after this, I can do no more to help."

"Monica, I didn't ask for your help. I don't need it. I'm grateful for things you've done in the past, but I'm strong enough to carry this one through on my own terms. After all, though Anna has this place," Tony waved an appreciative hand around the room, "she has no standing in the City, no track-record. No one knows anything about the profitability of her operations in other countries. She's an unknown quantity, and I have no intention of allowing her to interfere with my plans."

"Brave words, Tony, but don't underestimate what you're up against."

Tony shook his head and glared at her. "I told George, and I'm telling you, I won't ever let that woman get her hands on the Oscar."

Two days later, Thalia went to see George in his small Victorian house. Sun and bird-song filled the drawing-room through windows which opened wide on to a small secluded garden and a light breeze fluttered the curtains, but Thalia Kyriakides faced her son with anguish in her eyes.

"I don't know why your father is behaving the way he is," she said to George. "I haven't seen him so obsessed with a deal for years. He seems absolutely desperate to win Scottish and Lakeland, whatever advice he's been given." There was an odd sadness in her eyes. "And it's all because he doesn't want Anna Hamilton to get the Oscar."

George was surprised that his mother was showing any concern. She had, despite her efforts not to, become increasingly distanced from the day-to-day problems at Theodore.

"Does it matter to you that this time his rival is a woman? I don't think there's anything personal about it. You're right that he's desperate to get his hands back on the Oscar, and he's got good commercial reasons for that, provided we don't have to pay too much for the rest of the dross in S & L. But he's influenced by the fact that the Oscar was the best thing he's ever done."

George could see that his mother wanted to tell him something, but wouldn't let herself.

"That is partly what concerns me," she said, "It's nostalgia, that's why he wants it, I know. I've seen him buy and sell dozens of restaurants and hotels, but I've never seen him so irrational about any as he is over this."

"But it's not just that, is it, Mum? For some reason you seem to be concerned that Anna Hamilton's bidding against him." George judged that she was feeling some jealousy over this famous, glamorous woman. "There's absolutely no reason why you should see this fight any differently from others Dad's been involved in. It doesn't make any difference to him that the main obstacle to his ambition happens to be a woman."

"Oh yes it does. You should understand that. You're as Greek as he is."

After his mother left, George didn't feel that he had done much to calm her doubts; and to some extent, he shared them.

Since he had told his father about Sykes' visit to his house, and his conclusions about Fakenham's meetings with Sullivan and Anna, Tony Kyriakides had thrown himself straight into preparing a bid for Scottish and Lakeland, and had talked and – as far as George could tell – thought of nothing else since. Only old Christina Kyriakides' badly timed death had distracted him, and then he refused to take George and Thalia to the funeral, on the grounds that it would make the trip longer than necessary.

But Theodore Hotels, with its shining record and substantial cash reserves, had no difficulty finding underwriters for most of the cash that would be needed for a bid. A rights issue had been announced and fully subscribed without difficulty. The stock market was firming up after the battering it had taken during the hurricanes of October 1987, and there was still money around to follow a good thing.

Two days after what he considered his humiliation on Anna Hamilton's home ground, Tony and Edward Sherwood were in the back of his Bentley on the way to a meeting with Theodore's merchant bankers.

"I don't think this is going to be too difficult," Tony said with a casualness that wasn't genuine. "I can't see Anna Hamilton and Berkley Berrington getting their act together in time to put up much of a counter-bid."

"I hope you're not being serious," Edward replied. "If Fakenham's going for it, you can be bloody certain he's got it all in place. He's bound to try something. He simply can't lose, and he knows it. That's what worries me. You're going into this deal with the opposition knowing your reasons aren't purely commercial, and they're going to play on it."

"My reasons are entirely commercial. I know exactly how much I can afford to pay, because I know the kind of performance I can get out of Scottish and Lakelands' hotels. They're running at half cock right now."

"Look, Tony, if you can't be honest with me, I don't see how my advice can be worth giving. You know that Anna Hamilton could make a great deal of the Oscar and several of the others in the group."

"Anna Hamilton!" Tony said dismissively. "She's not a serious woman. Did I tell you, she tried to bribe me to keep off? I ask you!"

"It wasn't such an idiotic idea. How much did she offer?"

"Good God, you don't think we got as far as discussing that, do you? Whatever it might have been, it wouldn't have been enough."

"Now you are being irrational."

Tony turned and glowered at his old and trusted friend. "For God's sake, Edward, you know what I mean."

"I'm afraid I do. You're determined to get the Oscar back, whatever it costs. You'd better not tell the bankers that or they might get scared."

"There's no way we'll have to pay over the odds. Look at the price this morning – 95 pence! That capitalises them at £28.5 million. They've got debts of around £25 million. We'd be getting all their hotels for £53.5 million. We've been over and over their property portfolio and, even as empty shells, their hotels are worth at least £75 million. If we bid £1.20 a share, we get to control those hotels for an outlay of £13 million in cash and twenty-four in paper. We're standing at £2.20, we'll offer two of our shares and 40 pence for every four S & Ls. The institutions will jump at that, it'll be the quickest way for them to see their money back. Med and Trop couldn't get near a package as attractive as that. We can't go wrong!"

"If you get them for £1.20," Edward added.

"There's no way Fakenham could advise Anna Hamilton to bid more. She hasn't got that kind of cash in England; she'd have to borrow, and rates could suddenly get nasty if this boom overheats."

"Tony, we don't really have any idea of her resources overseas, and she and Fakenham can probably add up too; she won't want to hang on to most of S & L's hotels. She'd be able to cash them in pretty fast – clear most of the debt. Fakenham can easily back her with time to do that."

"Who's side are you on, Edward? Don't you want your client to win? We've already had many victories together. Why are you so shy of this skirmish?"

"I wouldn't like to see you win a pyrrhic victory – not on that scale – it could finish you off, just when you're at your peak and just because you don't want anyone else to have the Oscar."

"Not *anyone* else, but there's no way I'm going to let that young woman take the Oscar from under my nose."

22

Charles Fakenham grinned with frank approval across the expanse of polished walnut that separated him from his client. What a pleasure, he thought, and how exciting it was to be doing business with a really beautiful woman.

And how exciting to be doing business that could not fail to show a profit, with the additional, spine-tingling bonus of seeing Tony Kyriakides get buried.

For Charles Fakenham was determined that Kyriakides would pay very dearly for his vanity, for the Oscar and for his twenty-five-year affair with Monica.

"Mr Kyriakides has bid pretty much what we thought," he said, "in normal circumstances, a well-judged price. Enough of the shareholders and the banks would probably go along with it, if there weren't about to be another bid on the table."

"Would they?" Anna asked. "I can't see why. They must know that Theodore would simply strip out the rubbish and concentrate on the prime sites. They could do that themselves."

"If they thought there was a management there to do it. But what they have to contend with is our old friend, a crisis of confidence – in this case in a management badly demoralised by Sullivan's recent egocentric ineptness. A stake in Theodore's track record looks a better bet. Now, we don't have a visible track record to present. No doubt everyone assumes you know what you're doing and that Graveden is making money, but because of your off-shore set-up they can't be sure. So, we offer cash for the lot, I renegotiate the debt repayments until you've

367

disposed of the dross and you bring Graveden into the group."

"Charles, I've told you, I'm not prepared to do that. And it's a little too late to start trying to persuade me now," Anna said. "I know what your supplementary reasons are for wanting to do this deal. I'd certainly like the Oscar, but only if it's cheap. I get the feeling we're in for a dull trading patch and I won't risk what I already have. If you want me in, it's going to have to be at arm's-length from Med and Trop."

Fakenham sighed, although they had had this discussion several times. He hadn't really expected to be able to change Anna's mind at the last minute, but it was worth a try; it would have provided a much more attractive package, and allowed a lower bid. He was annoyed, though, that Anna seemed to be aware of what she called his supplementary reasons for doing the deal.

"Let me assure you that my reasons, like those for any other deal I've ever done, are simply concerned with profit; that Tony Kyriakides may suffer as a result is nothing more than an enjoyable by-product. Talking of which, I've arranged for our PR people to put together what they call a negative campaign to back up our bid. Would you like to hear what they propose?"

"Is this all entirely necessary?" Anna asked with distaste.

"My dear and lovely Anna, I can't believe that you're squeamish about that sort of thing? I'm afraid it's the norm for highly visible bids of the type in which we are about to become engaged. It's all about impressing voting shareholders, and recently American presidential candidates have led voters throughout the world to expect a slanging match with a great deal of dirt being hurled about." Fakenham pressed an intercom on his desk. "Tell Bill Eaton to come in," he said to a secretary in an outer office.

A moment later a short man in his late thirties and a broad-lapelled suit strutted into the office and offered Anna a firm, cold hand.

"So," Fakenham said, "have you got your ammunition in place?"

"Certainly have," Eaton said with a curt grin and an Essex accent. "Cyprus has thrown up all sorts of shady-sounding shit. Kyriakides was a sort of minor fruit and veg merchant in his early days, but he fell out with some of the big cheeses, his wife's father among them. He ran away with his wife, did you know that? – but we won't dwell on that because it's rather romantic and he's still married to her. He was involved in an accident where one of her uncles was killed in 1974. Though no one will talk about it very specifically, there was obviously something dodgy about his being there. His mother died a few weeks ago. He went over for her funeral but she was just a poor old peasant woman – we've got some shots of her that suggest he didn't do much to look after her."

Fakenham was unimpressed. "This all sounds too historical. We need more recent misdemeanours."

"Commercially, there's not a lot. There are some people around who say he pulled a fast one on them when he wound up the Pitta and the Wolf franchises, but nothing really usable. Then," the PR man's confidence wobbled a little, "There's his personal life."

"Be very careful here," Fakenham warned.

"Sure," Eaton answered hurriedly. "There's a string of receptionists and manageresses from his hotels that he's screwed. We can produce a few tales from them, though we might have to spice them up a bit for tabloid consumption. We've got hold of a few photos, but nothing strong, and no tales of kinkiness or anything. They mostly say he was a pretty good performer."

"Well, you can sit on that," Fakenham said brusquely. "It doesn't sound as though you've got anything useful.

What the hell have you people been doing? We need him to be seen by the public as an unreliable, opportunistic dago upstart."

"I think if we hint at dodgy dealing in his early days, we might stir up some doubt – that seems our best bet," Eaton said defensively.

"You'd better get back and start digging a bloody sight harder. You've got two days to find something useful, and current." Fakenham dismissed Eaton with a wave of his hand, and the PR man left the room with less cockiness to his strut.

When he had left, Fakenham turned to Anna. "He'll find something, and if he can't he'll make it up."

"I think the whole idea stinks," Anna said. "If you haven't got anything real on him, it seems a complete waste of time, and frankly," she added, looking at Fakenham, "it could back-fire."

"Bill knows that any hint of anything to do with my wife has got to be sat on hard," Fakenham rasped.

"I don't want anything to do with all that crap. I don't want people to retaliate by grubbing around in my personal history."

"Got a bit to hide, have you, Anna?" Fakenham smirked.

"Not a patch on you, but I'm not proud of everything I've done. Anyway, that's not the point. I just dislike the idea of what ought to be a logical commerical battle ending up as a gruesome smear campaign."

"No room for student ideology in corporate take-overs. You have to use every weapon at your disposal. You must have seen it time and again. That's the way you change people's minds. Blame the people, if you like, but what we're doing is a justifiable means to an end. We both know it would be better for Scottish and Lakeland's shareholders if you ran their company, but we need everything we can get to persuade them."

"Just make sure I'm kept out of it as much as possible."

"People will need to know that you'll be heading up the new management if our bid succeeds, but I don't think anyone will have time to do much damage to us in PR terms."

"They'd better not. Right, you know my position. When are we going to launch this bid, and at what price?"

"Tomorrow, at £1.50 per share in cash. We already control twelve per cent, and I can speak directly for about five more. We should be able to convince another thirty-four per cent."

"How much of an improved offer can Kyriakides make?"

"That is the question. I fear he may go far too high. Theodore has dropped four pence since their announcement, and S & L are up six, so he's already got some leeway to make up in the cash element, just to stand still, and you can expect Theodore's price to drop further, in anticipation of the projected dilution of shares. It'll be Kyriakides who's running uphill. We will just calmly crack the whip from the sidelines."

Fakenham sounded entirely confident, and Anna felt a surge of excitement as the once vague prospect of getting the Oscar was beginning to look like a real possibility.

Anna left the offices of Berkley Berrington as animated as she had ever been about a deal. To be given the running of thirty-five disparate hotels was the kind of challenge she wanted now, and she was certain she could do it better than anyone, especially the smarmily handsome, deeply chauvinist Tony Kyriakides.

She had been prepared to risk £3 million herself, in order to secure the management of the group if Fakenham's tactics were successful. If they weren't she would certainly show a healthy profit. But she was much more interested in the Oscar. Her only concern was that Fakenham was not. She knew she hadn't learned to read him yet and though she was confident of not losing money on the deal, she didn't trust Fakenham's motives or approve of his tactics. But she was prepared to take a punt on that, too.

She drove back to her Chelsea house where her mother and stepfather were waiting to take her out to dinner.

"What have you been doing today, dear?" her mother asked, as if she had spent the day shopping, which, in a sense, she had.

"Hovering like a vulture over other people's misfortunes, blackening people's reputations, seeking ways to chisel the public – normal sort of stuff."

Her mother laughed and shook her head. Anna felt only a twinge of guilt.

Tony Kyriakides had launched his bid a week after he had met Anna Hamilton. The Theodore offer, though expected by some, had generally come as a surprise to the market. Tony had taken his bankers' advice not to attempt to build a stake first, as this would certainly have been noticed and have affected the relevant prices – Scottish and Lakeland upwards; Theodore downwards. Because of the seriousness of S & L's problems, no one had been expecting a strong bid. Theodore's was not. It was greeted with mixed reactions by Scottish and Lakeland's shareholders.

Some of the more cynical institutional holders were inclined to dismiss it, on the grounds that Kyriakides was certainly going to strip out the dead wood and keep the cream. They felt they would do better by doing that themselves, as they had been hinting since Sullivan had been jettisoned.

Others took the pragmatic view that Theodore, though relatively small, was a known and tested entity. They would do far better on a rising market by swapping their S & L shares for Theodore's.

Both camps were a lot more excited by the rival bid that was announced two days later: Anna-Hamilton of the now world-famous and highly prestigious Mediterranean and Tropical Hotels, backed by twelve per cent of S & L's shares and Charles Fakenham's Berkley Berrington Bank, was offering £1.50 per share, in cash – £45 million for the thirty-odd million issued.

It was, the analysts now said, too low, even taking into account Scottish and Lakeland's appalling assets/borrowings ratio. The shareholders of S & L agreed. And they were delighted that suddenly they had an auction on their hands, with other groups beginning to take notice. If two well-known names like Theodore and Med and Trop were prepared to do battle over such an ailing corporation, they had to look more closely at this cheap package of thirty-five hotels, including the Oscar flagship, which alone, people were now thinking, had to be worth twenty million, at a bullish estimate.

Tony Kyriakides' banker phoned him as soon as Med and Trop's bid was announced at seven thirty in the morning.

Tony, already at his desk with half a pot of thick, Greek coffee inside him, felt as if a mighty fist had been plunged deep into his solar plexus.

He went to the lavatory and sat on it, feeling sick, while his stomach churned and would not empty.

Even though in his guts he had been expecting the rival bid he had not expected it so soon, and so strong, and he didn't want to believe it when it came.

An all cash bid would certainly tempt a significant number of jaded S & L shareholders, who would rather cut their losses and run on to other things than sit around with the banks' Damoclesian sword dangling over the floundering group.

Tony knew with sickening certainty that a fight between Theodore and Med and Trop would flush out a few more players, and his hopes for a quick, clean and – above all – cheap deal were irreparably dashed.

It was not the first battle of this sort in which he had played, though it was the largest. It was his normal practice to set his limits, and work his way up to them. If someone else pushed the price beyond that, he was always ready to take a profit on shares he had bought, and walk away. This time, he had bought very few shares, and he could not countenance walking away. This time, there was a joker in the pack, the Oscar.

Charles Fakenham sat back and waited for Theodore's next move. He had set in motion the positive side to his press campaign, calling in all the favours owed to him by half a dozen Fleet Street financial writers to stress the fact that Med and Trop were offering a little over the odds, because only their expertise and prestige could transform the half-dozen major hotels in the group. They also suggested that for anyone else to bid more, especially the workaday Theodore, would be madness.

George Kyriakides, with no real stomach for this kind of fight, wondered wildly if Fakenham had done this deliberately to goad his father into raising Theodore's bid; he was certain that Anna Hamilton could not rely on Fakenham's loyalty if a quick, fat profit was on offer. And he had no idea how far his father would go.

Tony Kyriakides did not look to his son for support or justification. This didn't surprise George. But a week into the Med and Trop bid he received a telephone call which did.

It was half past eight in the morning.

"Hello, I'd like to speak to George Kyriakides, please," an arousing but unknown female voice announced.

"Speaking," he drawled with the huskiness of the day's first words.

"Anna Hamilton."

George was completely fazed; he could not answer for a moment.

"Hello," she went on, "I'm sorry to ring you at home so early."

He was struck by the freshness, the youngness of her voice. He had no clear recollection of it from his one encounter with her twenty years before, but he imagined it could hardly have changed.

George shook his head to clear his confusion and the drowsiness caused by the previous night's drinking.

He glanced across at the smug, sleeping face of a girl whose name he couldn't remember.

"Hang on," he croaked into the phone. "I need to take this on another line."

He put the handset down, and heaved himself out of bed. He grabbed a towel and wrapped it around his naked body as he left the room to go down two flights of stairs to his basement kitchen. There he took a jug of orange juice from the fridge and filled a glass which he drained. He coughed and cleared his throat before picking up an extension.

"Hi. You did say Anna Hamilton, didn't you?"

"Yes. I'm sorry to have got you out of bed."

"You didn't. I've just come in from jogging."

Anna gave a light, fluting laugh that couldn't have belonged to a hard-nosed businesswoman. George was enchanted.

"I don't suppose you expected to hear from me," Anna said.

"Well, frankly, no. It's rather like Hitler ringing Churchill while the Battle of Britain's going on."

"Or Churchill ringing Hitler, depending which way you look at it. But just think how much trouble they might have saved if they had phoned and talked to each other and sorted out a bit of common ground."

"I can't see there's much of that in our case," said George, trying to think what his father would have said.

"There could be," Anna answered. "Can I come and talk to you?"

George grunted ambiguously.

"Look," Anna said, with a harder edge to her voice, "Your father need never know. You obviously know it's the Oscar he wants, and why he wants it. If he tries to outbid us, he'll overpay, very heavily. You should know what the options are. I'll come over and see you, as long as you're confident you haven't got any reporters lurking outside."

"All right," George tried to make it sound as though he were doing her a favour. "There aren't men in macintoshes lining the street."

"Good. I'll come right over. I should be there in ten minutes."

"Fine," said George, then, remembering the girl in his bed, "Well, not right away. I've got to shower and make a couple of calls. Make it forty-five minutes."

"You mean, you've got some nymphette to dispose of," Anna laughed. George winced at his own transparency. She went on, "I'll see you in forty-five minutes."

George called a mini-cab for half an hour's time.

Back in his room, he shook the girl awake.

"Morning, angel," he said brightly. "It's ten thirty, and I've got to get ready for lunch."

The girl sat bolt upright. "Christ!" she said, "I'm supposed to be at the studio at ten."

"Better get that lovely little arse into gear then, hadn't you?"

When the girl had showered, dressed and was struggling to squeeze twenty minutes' application of make-up into five, George said, "Okay, don't panic, there's a cab on its way and it's only nine o'clock."

"You silly bastard. What d'you want to scare me like that for?"

"Because I've got things to do, and I need you out of here. That'll be your cab," he added as the doorbell

376

rang, and he glanced down into the street outside where a battered Ford was waiting, double-parked.

The mini-cab had barely reached one end of the road when a maroon, convertible Aston Martin nosed in the other end and cruised up the road while the driver looked at the numbers of the houses.

George hadn't expected her to drive herself, but he guessed it was Anna.

She had evidently spotted someone drawing out a little further up, and roared up to pounce on the space.

George, watching discreetly from behind his drawing-room curtains, felt his heart thump as she climbed out of her car, like any rich young woman without a care in the world, and walk towards his house with a long, swinging stride.

He had seen dozens of photographs of her over the last few years. But in the flesh, moving, she made a much stronger impression. She was, he thought, twice as striking as she had ever been at Oxford, though she must be in her late thirties by now. She was dressed with a fashionable simplicity that made no concessions to her role as businesswoman.

But above all the other impressions she made on George was one of total confidence. Unconsciously, and for reasons that were sexual, commercial and old-fashioned chauvinistic, he braced himself to meet her.

He waited until she had rung the bell at the front door before he went to open it and stepped out on to the front step to greet her.

"Hello," he said, cursing himself for the lameness of it.

"Hello." She stepped through the door without waiting for him to invite her. "You were right. No journalists."

George shrugged. "It isn't that kind of a story."

"Yet," added Anna.

George followed her back into the house.

"Would you like some coffee?"

"Why not? Are you going to make it?"

"Yes. This isn't an hotel," he laughed.

"We'll talk while you're doing it," Anna said, and followed him down to the kitchen.

There, George offered her a rush-seated chair at an old elm table. She sat and watched him.

She had done some research into her subject before ringing him that morning. Arrogant – she had been told – spoiled, attractive, intelligent and idle.

Certainly, she judged, he looked relaxed for someone so close to what, for the Kyriakides, must have been a nerve-wracking fight. She guessed that he was indifferent to the result of the battle for Scottish and Lakeland. His father already owned half the equity in Theodore Hotels, worth £60 million at current prices. He probably thought that the acquisition of the Oscar and a lot more hotels, by diluting their shareholding to raise the money, wouldn't make much difference to him and no difference at all to the power and influence he didn't have.

She had to convince him that it would make a great deal of difference, the wrong way.

"Have you heard that a third bid for S & L is expected today?" she asked.

George, fiddling with coffee and a cafetière, shook his head. "No, but it's been rumoured for the last few days. Who is it, THF?"

"No. CIGA."

CIGA was an Italian group which had been proliferating all over Europe for the previous two decades.

"I'd be amazed if they bid more than you have. They like a bargain."

"And they like the Oscar, like your father."

George casually gathered up some cups and put them on the table in front of Anna. "He's got a good reason to. He started it, saw it succeed like no other new hotel

378

since the war, then had to watch the place deteriorate into a run-of-the-mill commercial hotel after he sold it."

"But he seems to have concentrated on run-of-the-mill commercial hotels ever since."

"Sure," George shrugged, "but very profitably." He shoved the plunger down the cafetière and filled the cups.

Anna took a drink from hers. "Which suggests," she said slowly, "that is where his skill lies these days. Look, if he took over S & L, I'll concede that he could make a lot more of some of their existing places than I could. Frankly, I'm not that interested in them. There are only three which I really want; you know which those are. I'd like to do a deal with him on the rest of them. There's not a lot of point running each other up. That way, neither of us can win."

George sat down opposite her. Ignoring her last statement, he asked, "Why did you come to see me?"

"I should have thought that was obvious. Given a choice of two parties to talk to, it makes sense to talk to the one with whom I have more in common. Let's face it, your father does have a reputation for being difficult and as stubborn as Balaam's ass. And you may know I've already spoken to him. I don't think he was listening, though."

"He's not one of the great listeners. But what do you think we have in common?"

"You were at Oxford, about the same time as me. We may even have met there."

"We did," said George. "I ran into you on my bicycle once, when you were turning into the Parks Road in your mini, just before you went down."

Anna closed her eyes, and thought back. In an instant, she was there, the day she had slept with Martin Vickers for the last time, delighted with herself, optimistic and about to take charge of her own destiny at last.

And George had bumped into her on that day.

She opened her eyes and smiled with a brilliance that almost knocked George back.

"It's perfect, isn't it?" she said, "that I should be talking to you like this half a lifetime later."

"Yah," George returned her smile, "There is a nice irony to it."

"I'm glad I never went to business school," said Anna, "Or I would have been discouraged from trusting my instincts."

"Well, your instincts haven't served you that well, this time. Of course, I hear what you say, and I don't deny the logic of it, but in my family I'm a non-voting shareholder. My father listens to very few people, and I'm certainly not one of them. I assume the company, or at least our shares in it, will be mine the day I plant him, but until then, you may as well talk to one of the office cleaners as me." He gave her a smile of indifference and apology.

Anna nodded her head with some disappointment but little surprise. "I wouldn't have had any trouble with you, would I? You don't really care one way or the other."

"It's not a question of not caring. Like I say, there's simply no point in my holding a view; I tried for a while, but it was futile and very frustrating."

"And you're not someone who likes to be frustrated, are you?"

The tone of Anna's voice, and the look in her eye had altered; they were talking about something else now.

George felt a heat inside him that had become rarer as he grew older. Suddenly, he saw Anna stripped of the persona of businesswoman and rival, stripped of her simple blouse and leg-revealing skirt. He saw a warm-blooded woman. with simmering dark eyes like his own and soft, bountiful mouth, breasts and hips that denied her hard-headed reputation.

It was an alarming and deeply exciting sensation. He could see that she was also thinking what, in these circumstances, was unthinkable.

"No," he answered her question with a dry throat. "But I have learned to be patient."

A few hours later Anna saw Charles Fakenham.

"You were right," she said to him. "The son is a mere cipher, though to give him his due he's quite honest about it. If we were dealing with him, we'd have no trouble at all. I suppose it's beyond even your rather extreme methods to bump off Tony Kyriakides?" she laughed.

"Only because we'd probably get caught. Look, if Kyriakides is going to ramp this thing up, and I think he will, he'll take it all the way. He wants the Oscar back so badly he won't be bothered by a cool, realistic sense of value. I'm afraid you're not going to get this one, my dear, at least not yet. We'll run him up all the way, and watch him flounder for a few years."

"He may turn Scottish and Lakeland round," said Anna. "He's one of the best operators in Britain; there's no point not acknowledging that."

"He may turn them round. And possibly you could, but why go into a project with the odds stacked heavily against you from the start by paying too much? At least there's a nice profit to be made on the shares."

"For you," Anna retorted.

"And you. But I haven't forgotten that you're an essential element in this heart-warming scenario," Fakenham said. "I'm not a particularly fair man, but I am practical. If you bid him up to about £2.25 a share, then pull out, I'll organise the flotation of Med and Trop in the British market for no fees. That'll save you a few million, and put you in a better position when Kyriakides gets into trouble – as he surely will."

"First, you'll have to convince me that it's worth going public. But in the meantime," she smiled, "I'll keep bidding."

23

By the end of 1990 no one in Britain was left in any doubt that the Tory government's late 1980s boom had fizzled out and collapsed beyond imminent recovery. While the world cheered at the fall of the Berlin Wall and the dispatch of the despotic Ceausescu, the news at home had become steadily worse.

Almost every business in the country was affected as interest rates rose and spending power dropped. The first casualties, of course, were those who had geared their borrowing too high.

Tony Kyriakides hadn't wanted to borrow, but when he finally outbid Anna Hamilton for Scottish and Lakeland, the much-expanded Theodore Hotels inherited a pile of debt. Tony's plans to reduce this by selling off the lesser hotels in the group were stymied almost from the start by a sharp drop in prices. Each time he reluctantly agreed with his agents to lower his asking prices, the market demonstrated that it had fallen still further. And with each painful hike in lending base rates, Theodore's debt mountain grew, like some vast, unruly monster's back emerging from a black and turbulent sea. There was a mind-numbing inevitability to it as it topped £30 million. There seemed, this time, to be nothing that Tony could do to allay a moment of reckoning.

On Christmas night he stalked through the Oscar. The hotel was full for once but the sight depressed him. In the eighteen months since he had taken it back he had scarcely put into effect any of the changes he had so fondly planned. Money was pouring out of his lumbering group of fifty hotels much faster than it was coming in. There was simply no budget available for the improvements and updating that the Oscar and all the other hotels badly needed.

He went back to his office on the top floor of the Oscar and slumped into a chair, too ashamed to go home and tell his wife the truth or to make any pretence at Christmas merriment next day. What he wanted, in the black hours of that night, was a warm hand on his forehead and a soft unchallenging voice in his ear.

"You're a stupid, stubborn bastard with no one but yourself to blame."

Tony would not have allowed anyone but Monica to talk like this. If his wife or son, or any of the advisers who had warned him against buying Scottish and Lakeland had dared to question his judgement, they would have been met with the full force of his famous anger, because he would have known they were right, as Monica was now.

He didn't answer her.

They were in the flat behind Harrods for the first time in a month, on the last day of the year. They were sitting naked, side by side on the edge of an undisturbed bed.

"I distinctly remember," Monica went on, "after you'd first sold the Oscar to Sullivan, you told me you'd never borrow again; shareholders' funds, yes; bank borrowings, no."

"*I* didn't borrow; Sullivan had. But it was cheap money then, and the first thing I did was put half the premises on the market to clear that debt. So far I've sold three of them at their 1985 valuations." Tony shrugged, overtly hopeless for once. "I don't suppose even Charles foresaw how badly the bubble was going to burst."

"We won't let this Bubble burst, though," Monica said, allowing a hint of tenderness into her voice. She put a slim, unwrinkled arm on his shoulder. "When I think where Lawson's bloody spending spree has got us, I could murder him," she went on with feeling. "But I haven't seen his chubby smile at many financial functions recently. For God's sake, though, you knew that cheap money never stays cheap for long. The very fact of it's being so cheap – with banks desperately trying to talk every Tom, Dick and Harry into buying new houses, new cars, new Japanese video cameras to record the dreary lives of their foul children – that should have told you there was a recession coming. Charles knew it all right, when you were bidding for S & L."

"Well, why the hell didn't you tell me?"

"Because he didn't tell me, and you wouldn't have listened anyway."

Tony was goaded into finding some reserves of optimism within himself.

"This recession will be over by next spring, anyway," he said. "The bloody English have totally over-reacted as usual."

"I think we react rather less than most, as a matter of fact. Everyone knows what went wrong, and now it's a question of sitting it out. And if Saddam Hussein doesn't get out of the Emir of Kuwait's palace soon, he's going to get his wrists slapped, and the oil price will go through the roof."

"He'll get out. He's just bluffing. He must be."

"I wouldn't say that. You can't judge him by normal rational criteria."

"Since when have you been such an expert on Arab politics?"

"Since I saw the news on television for the last few months. What are you talking about? There'll be a war in the Gulf, and God knows where that'll lead."

"How the hell was I supposed to know?" Tony shouted at a universally held view that he didn't want to hear.

"Okay, okay," Monica put an arm around his waist and massaged his back. She felt him relax, as he always did when her smell filled his nostrils and her body touched his. "I know what you need," she murmured.

Troops, from disparate countries with a common interest in the free flow of oil, amassed in northern Saudi Arabia, and their battleships filled the Persian Gulf. President Bush issued his ultimatum and the world held its breath.

When the deadline passed, the rout, just a few days work for fit fighting men, was almost an anti-climax. The Western nations breathed a sigh of relief and turned their attention back to their own battered economies. The end of the war was going to bring an end to recession.

But it did not.

Tony Kyriakides watched in anguished disbelief as bookings dropped, revenue sank and his debts to banks, now desperate to reverse the effects of a decade of bad lending, burgeoned beyond his control.

Thalia saw his anguish, his bafflement at his own impotence, and wanted with all her heart to help, but she could not penetrate his surly defences. She suffered in silent dignity the knowledge that he sought his comfort elsewhere.

Charles Fakenham looked at his wife across the dinner-table. The French windows of the room were open to an acre of garden rich with trees and shrubs which muffled the noise of choking traffic in Holland Park Avenue, a few hundred yards away. The air here was filled with strident, spring bird-song as the shadows lengthened.

Fakenham knew where his wife had been that afternoon, and guessed what she had been doing. He couldn't hate her for it. In a way, she had been fair with him over the years of their marriage. She had never questioned his actions, absences or preferences, and when he had asked her, had given fine public performances as a loyal spouse.

But he did hate Kyriakides for providing what he, apparently, could not. He hated Kyriakides for his flashy good looks and charm; for being a 'good performer' with women whose names filled a fat dossier locked in his office desk.

He wondered what Monica would think if she knew that he had just bought – through his normal, arm's-length nominee in a scruffy Earl's Court office – three million shares in Theodore Hotels plc, very cheap.

"I've got the lovely Ms Montagu-Hamilton coming to see me tomorrow," he said, wondering if this might provoke his wife into offering herself that night.

Monica's reaction disappointed him. She looked more worried than jealous.

"Why?" she asked. "I thought you'd done all you were going to do with her since she floated Med and Trop."

"Of course not. A banker's like a doctor, or a shrink. Every so often, clients have to come back to them, to reassure themselves that they're in good shape."

"She'll no doubt be in excellent shape, but try to avoid handling her in public, if you don't mind."

Fakenham laughed. This was promising.

"Our meeting, *force majeure*, has to be private, so I shall manage to avoid that."

"Are you going after Kyriakides again?" she asked, disguising her trepidation.

Fakenham assumed a look of surprise. "Good Lord, no. It'll be a while before he's screaming for mercy; what's more, it'll probably be too late – for him."

Monica said nothing. She was sure he was lying, and Tony was so exposed now that they would be able to make mincemeat of him.

It was a measure of Tony Kyriakides' new lack of confidence in his own judgement that, a few days later, he confided in his son George.

"Some bastard's been buying our shares in small parcels for the last couple of months."

"Hasn't the share register shown up who it is yet?"

"Of course not. They've all been bought by separate little nominees, but I know they'll all be controlled by one person."

"Who the hell would want to buy us now?" George asked. He was sure he wouldn't.

"It could be one of several people who know the banks are getting twitchy. But I'll fight the bastards off. Bookings for January are no worse than usual. When this recession ends in the summer, we'll start consolidating."

George wanted to question this prediction but, on balance, he didn't see that it would achieve anything. Though he did see an opportunity for taking an initiative of his own.

George rang Graveden Place to enquire if Ms Montagu-Hamilton was there.

No, came the reply, but she was expected from Italy next day.

George decided to do the thing in style. In the first flush of excitement, when Theodore had surprised everyone by absorbing Scottish and Lakeland for the inflated price of £2.70 a share, he persuaded his father of the benefits of getting around their fifty hotels by helicopter. Theodore Hotels now kept one at Battersea heliport. George had held a chopper licence for five years, and used it regularly for his own entertainment, despite his father's constant grumbling.

He phoned the Graveden again and arranged for an H-marker to be left on the lawns behind the mansion and drove to Battersea.

From there, with uncharacteristic forethought, he telephoned Graveden Place once more to make certain that Anna was back.

She came to the phone herself this time.

He announced that he planned to come and see her at once.

"George! What a nice surprise. I hope you'll stay and have lunch with me?"

"I insist," George said, knowing that he didn't have to.

It was a crisp, clear spring day. The Thames sparkled below him as he followed it out to Berkshire. Flying the helicopter gave him the high it always did, and a sense of optimism which the state of his family's business did not merit. Besides, he was much more excited at the prospect of seeing Anna as a woman than as a business rival.

He conjured up pictures of her, prompted by a glowing account in a weekend colour supplement of the island resort which Med and Trop had created in the Virgin Islands. The piece had been illustrated with photographs of a beaming, bikini-clad Anna with the black barman whose personality famously dominated the resort. The feature in the supplement contrasted uncomfortably with an account in the business pages of the troubles at Theodore Hotels.

From the air, Graveden lay among its vast formal gardens with the bright morning sun lighting its pale grey stone to give the impression of a square, over-decorated wedding-cake.

George spotted the white 'H' that had been laid on a lawn between two large sequoias, and took an unnecessary couple of turns around the place before he started to descend.

He executed a good, clean landing, switched off and jumped down to walk briskly below the idly rotating blades.

He ran up a long flight of shallow stone steps to a terrace along the back of the house to find Anna emerging to greet him.

She took his hand, as if he were an old friend, and offered him a cheek to kiss. George, with a hand on her hip for an instant, squeezed it in return. He felt as if he were meeting a lover.

"Let's have a drink in my office first," Anna said and led him through two impressively tasteful public rooms to her office on the first floor which looked out across the lawn where he had landed.

"Champagne?" she asked.

"Of course," he answered.

She opened a bottle herself, and poured the lightly bubbling, amber wine into a pair of silver flutes.

"It's funny you should have rung me," Anna said, "because I was beginning to think it was time we saw each other again."

George took a good sip from his goblet. "I wish I hadn't come to talk business," he said.

"You have, though, haven't you?"

"Don't tell me that surprises you."

"No," she said. "Things haven't gone so well for you, have they, since we last met?"

"As you predicted."

"Even I couldn't predict Saddam was going to drive into Kuwait, but I had an inkling that we were heading for an economic trough. Fortunately it hasn't affected most of our resort hotels. In fact business in the West Indies is booming."

"Yes," George said with an exaggerated, tight-lipped smile, "I did read the papers last Sunday."

"Anyway," Anna went on, "Let's get the business out of the way, then we can go and have a merry lunch. Chef's on ace form at the moment."

"Okay," said George, and plunged on with as much casual firmness as he could muster. "If you're prepared to pay enough, I think my father could be persuaded to part with the Oscar."

"That bad, is it?"

"Come on Anna, let's not pussyfoot around. You know

the score. You stand a much better chance of getting it if you do a deal with us now, before other people start chasing like they did last time. And it's in a better shape than it was when we took it over. We haven't spent a lot, but the restaurant's in line to get a second Michelin star and the right sort of punters have started coming back. Michael Jackson took over the whole second floor when he was here on his tour, and since then every American star has been booking in."

"I heard your father bought that business," Anna remarked, referring to the practice of discounting so heavily to gain the publicity value that the hotel made a loss on the booking.

"Sure, but it was worth it. Every big hotel in London wishes they had done the same."

"Of course I know it's improved there, and of course I'm interested in bringing it into our group. We badly need at least one more site in the UK, but it all depends on what you mean by 'pay enough', doesn't it?"

George took a deep breath, which he tried to disguise. "Fifty million should do it," he said as easily as he could.

A smile spread across Anna's face. "Georgey," she said, "You're a nice big, sexy hunk, and I'm looking forward to getting to know you better one day. Right now, though, we're miles apart. But don't let that spoil your lunch."

She walked across and opened the tall, panelled-mahogany door of her office, and gestured him to follow her.

George laughed at his own naïvety and relaxed. Nevertheless – he justified himself to himself – his overture couldn't have done any harm; it might have opened the door to negotiations.

They didn't specifically mention the Oscar or Theodore over lunch, but George tried to probe some of the more puzzling elements of Anna's career.

"How come," he asked, "a raging bluestocking turned into one of the world's high-profile businesswomen?"

"By default, really, and partly to spite the smug assumption of everyone at the university that I would become some kind of second-rate academic, which is all I would ever have been. And the incredible faith of one old man."

"Who was that?"

Anna smiled. "I'm not going to tell you that; I'll just give you the satisfaction of knowing that I couldn't have done what I have without him." She teased George with a smile which told him that was all she would say.

It was a delicious meal, though, spiced with innuendo and flirtation that kept George throbbing inside his trousers. But he was careful not to overplay his hand. She was interested in him – that was obvious – but until his family's business was out of trouble and immune to predation by her, he couldn't let anything happen. And no doubt Anna thought the same. This very block to the development of their relationship gave a frisson to their mental foreplay. With a bottle of Petrus inside him, George finished lunch in a state of gratifying euphoria. The lack of immediate success for his business mission seemed unimportant.

George realised he had drunk too much to fly back to London. He arranged for a Battersea pilot to come down and pick up the chopper, and Anna lent him a car and driver to take him home.

He was still basking in the glow of this promise of future pleasure as the car swept down off the Hammersmith flyover, in the opposite direction to the crush of commuter traffic trying to leave London. He told the driver to take him to Argyll Street, instead of Harley Gardens. He felt that he should tell someone about the initiative he had taken. If his father wasn't there – and he hoped he wasn't – he could tell his mother.

Thalia was surprised to see George in the middle of the

afternoon but, seeing that he was slightly drunk, she did no more than raise an eyebrow.

"Where have you come from?" she asked.

"I had lunch with the proprietress of Graveden Place."

His mother, who had been fussing about, ritually preparing Greek coffee for them both, scattered a spoonful of dark grounds all over the marble surface.

"What! You've seen Anna Hamilton?"

"Yes. Why are you so horrified? I thought it might be useful."

"George, listen to me. You must not see her. It could be very bad for you. I absolutely forbid it."

Her voice almost broke in her desperation to impress him.

He laughed lightly. "Good God, what on earth's come over you? You've never been worried about any of the others I've been out with, and most of them were a bloody sight more worrying than Anna. Remember Liz Seymour? Anyway, I went to see Anna on business, that's all."

Thalia looked slightly relieved. "Your father will go mad if he knows that," she said, grateful for a sound reason for her objections. "That's what I'm worried about. Remember how he was, last time she came to see you?"

"Yes, well, it's a pity he didn't take more notice of what she said to me."

"Yes," Thalia agreed, "it is. But there is nothing that can come of your trying to deal with a woman like that. Sure, she's very beautiful and I've no doubt she's an entertaining companion, but she's also a tough and independent woman. A boy like you is no match for her."

"I'm not a boy, for God's sake!" George protested, "If Dad had let me do more in the bloody business, I would have done. God knows he hasn't made such a good thing of it lately. We must have dropped thirty million in the value of our shares since we took over Scottish and Lakeland.

It's been nothing but trouble, and I can't see that changing for a long time."

"And I don't suppose you blame yourself at all? I heard you talking with him about it at the time. You were encouraging him, almost."

"Rubbish, Mum. I knew he took no notice of my real views, so I was simply telling him what I knew he wanted to hear. As it happens, if it hadn't been for this sodding great drop in the market, I was right about the properties. Even now I've got three sales of surplus property going through which will keep the wolf from the door for a few more months. And the reason I went to talk to Anna was to see if I could get her interested in the Oscar again. If she was to buy it, at the right money, we'd be well out of trouble."

"And will she?" Thalia had already guessed that she would not.

"Eventually, if we give her the chance; maybe not for our top asking price, but not much below."

Thalia shook her head. "I don't know much what goes on in the business these days, not like when I was in the restaurants every day and saw all the comings and goings, but we aren't in a position to be too greedy in what we ask for the Oscar."

"If we can busk through this spring we'll be in good enough shape to fight off any bargain hunters, believe me."

"Me, I don't believe anyone these days, especially when they make optimistic prophecies. But I am asking you not to see Anna Hamilton again. If you promise me not to, I won't tell your father you went to see her."

This was a deal which had no appeal for George, but he tried to mollify his mother. "I wouldn't make you a promise I may not want to keep, but I promise I won't see her on anything other than business until either she's bought the Oscar, or we're out of the shit."

* * *

Anna picked up Bill Franklyn from the Connaught to drive him to the Fakenhams' house in Aubrey Walk, Holland Park.

"Thank you for coming over," she said as she nosed the Aston Martin out into Park Lane.

"It's a multiple pleasure. I love coming to London, and I love seeing you – and you're looking more beautiful than ever."

Anna wondered if he meant it. "I don't feel too beautiful, not internally anyway. That's why I wanted you to come. Fakenham's such a horrific shit, I had to have some moral support."

"What's he trying to do to you?"

"He's using me, to make money, which is fair enough, but also to put the boot into Tony Kyriakides. He's almost manic about bringing him down."

"Because he's been screwing his wife for twenty-five years?"

"Of course."

"Why do you think Monica's affair with Kyriakides has lasted so long?"

"God knows. She's a tricky bitch, and cold as hell, except when she wants something. I guess they still spark off each other. She must be forty-five now, but looks a lot less and Tony K's a very attractive man too. The odd thing is, they don't realise that Charles has known about them for years."

"Maybe they do, but subconsciously suppress it."

"Maybe. But the point is, as I say, it drives Charles Fakenham mad. Naturally he doesn't let it show too much, but there's a very nasty look in his eyes when he talks about Tony Kyriakides. That's why I had to have you here, to form an objective opinion of this deal he's proposing."

"I'm flattered."

"Never mind about being flattered; I just thought an

outsider would have a more useful view."

Monica greeted Anna and Bill with unusual nervousness. After she had shown them into a big, empty drawing-room which looked more like a room in the National Gallery, and offered them drinks and some half-hearted small talk, she left to make way for her husband.

Charles, correctly, took the American lawyer's presence as an indication of Anna's lack of trust, and was inclined to respect her for it, while barely acknowledging Bill.

"I thought it better that we should meet here first," Fakenham announced. "And I've booked a table at Cecconi's if you feel like some dinner later. I'm afraid my wife has declined to entertain here tonight. Shall we go to the library?"

Fakenham led the way to another, smaller room, lined with shelves full of books about money and racehorses. He and his guests sat on Chippendale chairs around a small Georgian mahogany table.

"The purpose of this meeting," Fakenham said with formality, "is to confirm that you wish Mediterranean and Tropical Hotels (UK) plc to make a formal bid for Theodore Hotels plc."

"We can confirm that, in principle, we do," Anna said.

"And that Berkley Berrington will act for you in this acquisition," Fakenham continued.

"Within specific guidelines," Bill Franklyn added.

Fakenham looked at him impatiently. "We must have reasonable discretion. We can't do the job if our hands are tied by the need to make constant referrals to you."

"I'm sure Anna will be readily available at any time you need her agreement to a particular course of action."

"Naturally," Anna nodded.

Fakenham's face took on a slightly pained expression, but he carried on after a moment's pause.

"We have come to the conclusion that, in the circumstances, like last time, an all cash bid would meet with the most approval, particularly as the largest single block of shareholders is the Kyriakides family. I don't think they would want Med and Trop shares, do you, Anna? Anyway, we won't give them the choice, and nor, I suspect will their bankers. We will have to come to some kind of accommodation with their bankers as far as the £30-odd million pounds of outstanding debt is concerned. I foresee no difficulty there. In the meantime I am in touch with various friendly parties who have been stake-building in Theodore and who will not be inclined to countenance any rival bids if they should arise, though I think that's unlikely."

"Why?" Bill asked.

"You may have observed that this country is in one of the worst recessions in recent history. The hotel industry has been hit as hard as any other. It is neither a good time to borrow nor to float rights issues. We know that there are few cash-strong players in the industry at the moment. Fortunately Miss Hamilton's parent company is not in that position. As I read it, we are the only plausible bidder, though I dare say one of the Indian groups might try. We don't have much to worry about from them; they would only be interested in a bargain basement deal."

"Do you have details of all your pre-bid research?" Bill asked.

"Of course. I have copies here for both of you." He picked up a pair of folders from a side table and handed them across to Anna and Bill.

"What strategy do you suggest this time?" Anna asked.

"A straightforward offer with a time limit for acceptance."

"How long?"

"Three weeks."

"That's pretty tight. It's questionable that they could

be expected to make up their minds that quick," Bill said.

"But their creditors won't take long. A significant part of Theodore's loans are personally guaranteed by Kyriakides – that was insisted on when he took over Scottish and Lakeland. If they present him with the option of accepting the bid or having the loans called, which they are entitled to do, he'll have no choice."

"What price do you advise us to go in at?" Anna asked.

"We can decide that on the day we bid. At the moment Theodore are standing at an all-time low of £1.30 and they may dip a little tomorrow. We could probably be successful at around £1.60."

Anna felt a quick rush of excitement, which she did her best to conceal, at the prospect. She would, effectively, be buying Theodore's fifty hotels at less than she had been prepared to pay for S & L's thirty-five. If she could pull off a deal like that, Henry Pedersen would have been very proud of his pupil.

"Okay," she said calmly. "But we'll tell you what our upper limit is by tomorrow afternoon."

"There's not that much rush, actually. I think we might sit and watch Kyriakides sweat for a month, or even longer, until his resistances are utterly weakened. By that time it may just be more appropriate to raise our funds with a rights issue – cheaper than using our own cash."

"We'll be advised by you on the timing. Are there any other aspects of the bid we should know about?"

"Obviously we'll back it up with some carefully placed mud-slinging."

"You mean one of your negative PR campaigns?"

Fakenham nodded. "Yes."

"No," Anna said. "I insist that we don't. I'm no more interested in your personal reasons for wanting to denigrate Tony Kyriakides now than I was last time. I'll settle for buying his hotels cheap."

"You may not be able to, if he can summon up a white knight from somewhere. Though it's unlikely, we've got to make sure that he is not seen as a remotely attractive proposition. The more smell there is lurking about his current circumstances, the better."

"Too bad. It didn't help much last time. I'm the client, Charles, and I won't allow it. I'll want that stipulated in our formal instructions to Berkley Berrington, please, Bill."

"Sure," the lawyer said, "And I agree with you."

Fakenham shrugged. "Similarly, I will want it formally recorded that I advised you to make known to the public any information about Kyriakides to which you may have been privy at the time of your bid."

"Is there any way that could create repercussions for us, Bill?"

"No, and Charles knows it."

Anna rose to her feet. "Okay, Charles. We'll let you have confirmation tomorrow. Please don't act until then. And as I guess Bill is still tired from his journey and we have a lot to do, I think we'll pass on dinner."

"As you wish," Fakenham said coldly, and rose to see them out with exaggerated politeness.

Tony Kyriakides rang seven restaurants and two clubs before he tracked down his son in a casino in Berkeley Square.

"What the hell are you doing in a place like that, you idiot?" he bellowed down the phone.

"Why the hell shouldn't I be?"

"We've got a crisis on our hands, it's no bloody secret, and what do you do? Go running down to see Anna Hamilton, then sit around all evening losing my money."

"Actually, I'm a couple of grand up," said George.

"Good. Then you can leave while you're ahead for once. Get yourself round here right away."

"Where are you?"

"In my office. I was so mad when your mother told me what you'd done I had to get out of the house."

"Okay. I'll be there in about twenty minutes."

George had learned well that, with his father, it always paid to take the line of least resistance, to take the wind of aggression out of his sails.

He gathered up the girl he was with and took her out to find his Ferrari. He dropped her at his house, inviting her to have a shower and make herself comfortable until he got back. Then he headed, with only mild trepidation, towards Kensington High Street.

In the year and a half since the Kyriakides had won Scottish and Lakeland from their two rival bidders, George's relationship with his father had deteriorated so much as to be almost worthless. He had never been close to Tony – the cultural differences made sure of that – but he still grudgingly admired his wiliness and tenacity.

Tony's irrationality over buying back the Oscar, and all its attendant baggage, had come as something of a shock to George when he realised that, at sixty, his father was losing his grip and his ability to focus clearly on the problems confronting them.

At the same time George knew perfectly well that he himself did not possess the single-mindedness or the dynamism to steer an unwieldy group of fifty disparate hotels, and while he yearned for freedom from his father's tiresome despotism, he didn't yearn for the responsibility which his demise would bring. And of course, he had for years enjoyed spending the fruits of his father's labour.

This ambivalent attitude towards his father, he realised, made him less vulnerable, and that gave him the confidence to deal with him without cringing.

His walk was almost jaunty as he entered Tony Kyriakides' office.

"Why the hell are you looking so pleased with yourself?" Tony greeted him.

"No point looking miserable, is there?"

"Maybe not in public," his father conceded, "but we're not in public. So, what did you go and see Anna Hamilton for?"

"To try and find out if she was the buyer of our shares."

"And is she?"

"I don't think so," George shrugged, "But I don't know for sure."

Tony stared at him. "For God's sake, you mean you've done all this, exposed our hand, and you haven't found anything out? You stupid fool." He shook his head in disgust.

"I suggested that she could get her hands on the Oscar, for fifty million."

"Fifty million? You're a bigger idiot than I thought. I guessed she just laughed at you."

"Not exactly. I knew I was pitching it high, but you have to start high when you're bargaining, you've always said so."

"Sure, but not at some ridiculous price; then no one takes you seriously. Anyway, I have no intention of selling the Oscar. If I ever sold any of my hotels, I'd never sell the Oscar."

"They're not really yours to sell at the moment. The banks and the shareholders have more of a say than you."

Tony's black eyes burned in a flash of fury at this questioning of his autonomy. "I built this business from nothing; me – a penniless immigrant peasant. A few others have come along for the ride, that's all, and I make all the decisions, no one else, and they know that; they trust me."

"They did, as long as you were making money for them," George said quietly. "Why the hell don't you admit that we've got problems? We're not alone, you know. The economy's in the shit with no sign of a recovery. Most of our hotels are in Britain, or depend on British tourists who have disappeared off the face of the earth. Americans are wary about travelling, if they're not skint as well. There's nothing we can do about it. I've managed to sell off a few bits and pieces, for which you've given me no credit. That might see us through for a month or two. Otherwise we're living on borrowed time. To sell the Oscar for a good price now would halve our borrowings, and we could survive. At least, that's my no doubt utterly misguided reading of the position," he added with a smile that oozed sarcasm.

His father stared at him without speaking for a moment, then, with a momentary turning away of his eyes, he said quietly but with an attempt at unarguable emphasis, "I will *never* sell the Oscar."

24

May 1991

Thalia Kyriakides crammed the minutes of the last committee meeting of the Society for the Provision of Shelter for the Homeless – SPOSH as her son liked to call it – into her bag and went to let herself out of her large, white stucco house in Argyll Street. The front door opened before she reached it and her husband walked in.

She glanced at her watch; she was late. And she looked back at Tony's face.

"What's happened, Tony?" She put down her bag and closed the door behind him.

It was four o'clock on a Friday afternoon – an unheard-of time for Tony Kyriakides to come home.

He didn't answer her and walked on through into their drawing-room where he sat down heavily in one of the deep, linen-covered sofas. He pulled a large corona from his cigar case and lit it. As he drew on the smouldering tobacco leaves he looked at Thalia who had followed him in.

She saw defeat in the dark eyes that watched her.

"Tony, tell me, what has happened, please; you must. I've hated it, watching you suffer and closing yourself off from me. I'm your wife; I don't want to blame you, or criticise you."

He nodded slowly. "We must talk," he growled, commanding her attention because he did not know how to ask for it.

"You look so tired, Tony; you've hardly slept for weeks. Is it this business?"

Tony looked at her for a moment as if she were a complete fool, then struggled to stifle a crushing retort. "Yes," he sighed, "Of course it is. Have you seen what the papers are saying this morning?" He held out a rumpled roll of newsprint, then threw it on the hall table.

"I haven't read them, Tony," Thalia said, truthfully. "You convinced me long ago that they seldom told more than half a story."

"This time, they're more right than they realise."

He stood up in the English drawing-room, which oddly reminded him, in a moment of intense self-pity, of Major and Mrs Cuthbertson's in the officers' quarters at Polemidia.

He went to the drinks table and poured himself a slug of Keo brandy.

"Do you want a drink?" he asked her gruffly.

"No, thanks."

Tony flopped back on to the sofa. He took a long swig, and leaned his head back to rest it on the back of the chair. He closed his eyes and did not speak.

Thalia sat down opposite him and waited.

Still with his eyes closed, as if that would hide the humility he felt, Tony sighed again. "If only there hadn't been this bloody war – it's hit everything, airlines, travel companies, hotels. The Americans still haven't started travelling yet – it's pathetic. And there's still no end in sight to this recession. Meanwhile I've been stuffed by the banks – *again*."

"What have they done?"

"They're telling me, if I don't accept Med and Trop's bid, they'll call in the personal guarantees I had to give on some of Scottish and Lakeland's debt when we took i over. I've got two weeks left to find it." He shrugged. "] can't do it."

Thalia did not say 'I told you so'. She didn't even want to; she wasn't entitled to.

"I wish I had kept closer to the business," she said, "Then maybe I could have helped. But you pushed me away, Tony."

Tony, with eyelids still closed, went on as if he hadn't heard her. "After I sold the Oscar in 1974 I promised myself I would never borrow like that again, and now I'm in worse shit than I was then. I'm in worse shit than Sullivan was when I bought the place back from him."

He opened his eyes and brought his head forward to look at his wife. "Fakenham!" He spat out the name, at the irony that this banker, of all bankers, should be in the front line of his attackers. "He's talked Anna Hamilton into making this bid. He thinks he's persuaded all my shareholders to desert me. But he bloody well hasn't." Tony's eyes blazed again with some of their customary fire. "He hasn't. He'll get a shock on Monday when it's thrown out."

Suddenly he was the familiar, unbeaten, unbeatable Tony Kyriakides again. Thalia couldn't bear to watch the discredited braggadocio; the arrogance which refused to face stark realities. There was no function for it now, no one left who was prepared to be convinced by it or even listen. She hated to reduce him to the beaten man he had been when he came in, but she had to.

"Tony, it's only a matter of time, and a few more pennies on the bid before they accept it."

"A lot can happen in a short time. They haven't beaten me yet. I've had an offer for ten of the Scottish hotels; I should be able to announce that next week, if the bastards don't back out." But once again his shoulders slumped with frustration and a lack of real faith in his defences.

Thalia leaned across and put her hand on his where it lay on the arm of the chair.

"Maybe it'll work out, Tony, but if it doesn't, it's not the end of the world. We started with nothing, you and I.

I gave up whatever there was for me from my family. You and George, you're all I've got or care about. You haven't been an easy man to be married to and God knows I've been hurt, but as long as I have my small family, I won't mind if you lose your business to Anna. There would be a sort of justice to it."

Tony looked at her in astonishment. "What on earth are you saying? What do you mean, 'Anna'? Why should you not care if she ruins me?"

Thalia shook her head. "I'm just telling you that business and money aren't everything. Your old mother, look at her. She lived the life of a peasant – wouldn't take any money from you, and yet she was a real woman, much more real than most of the millionaires' wives I see on my charities. Can you remember how beautiful life was, when we had nothing, when we slaved and struggled in the Olympus, and our only treat was a trip to the cinema?"

Tony grunted. He could not countenance the notion that all the work, all the ideas, all the fighting might have been for nothing. But he let Thalia lead him back, right back to their first meeting in the Municipal Gardens in Limassol; the assignations at the little coffee shops by the port; the first meal she cooked for him before the first time they made love.

This was what Thalia had wanted to do – to draw him back, to show him other perspectives to his current condition. It was all relative, she knew. Even if Tony lost the whole of Theodore, once the borrowings had been cleared they would still be worth a few million, in a fine house in London, with a charming, healthy and popular son. But it was not only as a kindness and a therapy that she wanted to travel back in their lives to times that belonged only to them. Most of all she wanted at last to bring him back to her, completely. For him to realise that only she would stand by him; that her loyalty was the bedrock of his existence. She knew she deserved that, and now she had a chance to claim her reward.

They talked, and Tony drank. As he drank, he remembered and let the early part of his life, which had seemed for twenty years or more to belong to an entirely other person, re-enter his consciousness.

They went down to the kitchen, where Thalia cooked them a simple Cypriot meal. They sat at the kitchen table. Tony opened a bottle of Retsina, and the tastes and smells of chilli and charred lamb helped their reminiscing.

It was much later, when the sun had set and the future seemed less bleak, that the telephone rang.

Thalia answered it and listened for a moment before silently handing it to her husband.

"Hello?" Tony said guardedly, his suspicions aroused by Thalia's manner.

"Tony. It's Monica."

Tony's head swam. Monica had never rung him at home since he had first met her.

Why, of all times, should she ring him here now?

He took the telephone. "What is it?" he croaked.

"I had to ring you. I'm sorry I got Thalia, but I had to. I'm staying with Charles at Bishops Lowton – the Montagu-Hamilton's, Anna's parents. She asked us for the weekend. George is staying here too."

"George?" Tony did not want to believe it.

"Your son George. I just thought you'd want to know, that's all. And . . ."

Tony slammed the phone back on to its cradle.

He stared at his wife across the table.

"I'm sorry she rang."

The significance of the apology didn't escape Thalia, but she brushed it aside.

"What's happened, Tony?" she asked in panic. "What has happened to George?"

Tony shook his head at the horror of his son's naïve

foolishness – or was it treachery? "Nothing's happened to George, except he must have gone mad. He's staying the weekend with Anna Hamilton."

Thalia turned white and her eyes started from their sockets as if the earth had quaked beneath her chair.

"My God!" she whispered. "My God," she repeated louder. "I begged him, pleaded with him not to see her after the last time."

"Why, why did you beg him?"

"Because . . . because I knew what it would do to you," she said quickly. "I know how last time, when he went to see her, how angry it made you. You must ring him, and tell him, he's got to leave, at once."

"Maybe he'll achieve something by seeing her this time. Maybe she likes him; maybe he can persuade her to change her approach." Tony could not say why he was hedging. He didn't believe what he was saying. But neither could he ring Anna Hamilton and ask her to send his son home. He could not sink to that.

But Thalia was quivering; tears trickled down her cheeks. She implored her husband to get their son back, cried that he was caught in a trap he didn't understand; if George stayed with Anna their lives would never be the same again.

It took her an hour to persuade him to pick up the telephone, and ask for Sir James Montagu-Hamilton's Hampshire phone number.

The telephone was answered by a woman, some kind of servant, Tony assumed.

"Good evening," he said, trying to squeeze some dignity into his voice. "Is there a Mr George Kyriakides staying in the house?"

"Yes, sir."

"Would you please ask him to come to the phone."

"Who shall I say is calling?" the woman asked.

"His father."

"Right you are, sir. I'll go and see if he can come. They're in the middle of their dinner at the moment."

"Thank you. It's very important."

Half a minute later, Tony heard his son's voice.

"Hello?"

"George? George? Is that you?"

"Yes, Dad. What the hell are you ringing . . ."

"Don't give me any bloody excuses." Tony's normally faint Greek accent was pronounced by his anger. "You've got to get out of that place right now, do you hear? Right now."

"Don't be ridiculous. I'm in the middle of dinner, and I've been invited to stay for the weekend. I'll be back on Sunday evening."

"George," Tony bellowed. "You don't know what you're doing. That woman is a dangerous scheming bitch. I've been fighting her for three years. You don't want to believe a thing she says. You get out of there now, or I tell you, you lose everything, every bloody thing I ever gave you. And your mother is very upset. She's right here beside me, crying her eyes out."

"I can't, Dad, d'you hear? I'm in the middle of dinner, and I came in my chopper. I've drunk too much to bring it back."

"I don't care about your bloody dinner. And if you're too pissed to drive *my* helicopter, that's your bloody problem." Tony paused, and abruptly changed his approach. "It's not just for me, it's for your mother. I know you don't want to hurt her, even if you don't care about me." Once again, the anger took over, "You just get out of that place now, or, by God, you'll regret it."

Tony slammed the phone down, took a deep breath and looked at his wife.

"He'll come back now. Don't you worry."

*   *   *

George Kyriakides gazed hazily through the lower glass panels of the helicopter's cockpit. He could see the lights of the cars which even at ten o'clock at night streamed east and west along the motorway below him. He was still slightly drunk and bitterly frustrated at not being with Anna on the night on which, he knew, he would first have slept with her.

And for the twentieth time he cursed the humiliation his father had inflicted on him.

He could have done some good, for God's sake – he told himself. Anna Hamilton and Charles Fakenham were his family's principal protagonists in their bid for Theodore and he had been under the same roof as both. It was inconceivable that he would not have had a chance and, in Anna's case, an advantage in talking to them about the deal over the weekend. His father was such a peasant, he thought business battles could only be resolved by fighting, when talking could avoid so much bloodshed.

He glanced up from the road below.

A pylon loomed like a giant alien out of the darkness in front of him. George realised abruptly that he had not allowed for the rising contours of the sandy hills of Surrey. Focusing for a second on the motorway, a little to his right now, he saw that he was barely a hundred feet from the ground. In the fraction of a second it took to react, he swore savagely at himself and his drunken complacency. But the adrenaline that flooded through his body sobered him up as no other tonic could have done.

He jerked back the stick and banked to the left to lift his machine over the 45 megawatt cables. He gasped with relief as his eyes picked out the first of them beneath him.

A second later, he tried to force a yell from his throat but it was paralysed with panic.

Two cables gleamed, like damp spider's threads, inescapable, a few yards ahead across his flight path.

*   *   *

The drivers on the motorway saw one brilliant flash followed by another. Some unexpected lightning – they thought – until, a moment later, a ball of fire burst into being and seemed to hover in the air a hundred feet above the ground, before it plunged to the gorse and scrub that covered the heathland below.

The dry bushes caught the flames and crackled into instant conflagration, fanned by a light south-westerly wind.

The blaze had spread a quarter of a mile before thirty fire-engines and a hundred firemen could bring it under control.

More firemen and police made their way towards the epicentre of the fire from the south-west. When they reached it, the helicopter was a buckled ball of scorched metal; inside it, everything combustible had been consumed.

An hour later – the hour it had taken to confirm the identity of the helicopter and its pilot – the telephone rang in the Kyriakides' house in Argyll Street.

Tony expected his son with an excuse.

"Yes?" he barked.

"Mr Anthony Kyriakides?" An unknown, official-sounding voice.

"Yes."

"This is the Surrey Police. We have some information regarding your son, Mr George Kyriakides. Two officers are on their way to your house and should be with you in a few minutes, if you would wait for them, please."

"Information? What sort of information? Has he been arrested, or what?"

"No sir. I'm afraid he was involved in a flying accident."

"What happened? For God's sake! Is he all right?"

"No sir. The officers will give you all the details."

"I don't want to know the details," Tony shouted. "Just tell me he's alive."

"I'm afraid I can't tell you that, sir."

411

Tony dropped the receiver. He ignored the crash as it hit the tiled floor. He ignored the disembodied squawk of the policeman trying to get his attention. He sat without moving a single muscle as tears welled up and filled his eyes, to trickle from both corners down his dark cheeks.

Two local police officers came from the Earl's Court Road. One was an inspector who had been thoroughly briefed on the details. The other was a WPC, thought necessary to comfort the mother of the victim.

Tony showed them into the drawing-room, where he and Thalia listened without speaking as the inspector told them as much as could be certain of what had happened.

"There were no remains, I'm afraid. But there is no doubt that it was your son. He was witnessed leaving the home of Sir James Montagu-Hamilton in Hampshire fifteen minutes before, and he had radioed to Battersea for landing permission. The controller there recognised his voice and confirmed his identity."

"You're right. There is no doubt it was him," Tony said at last. "I asked him to come back to London right away. And he usually did as I asked."

"Obviously, we have informed the people he was staying with, and an officer has gone to get a statement from the witnesses. We won't trouble you with that now, but we will have to in the morning, if you don't mind."

The WPC had busied herself making coffee and patting Thalia's hand. "Is there anything I can get for you, Mrs Kyriakides?" she asked gently. "Would you like me to stay here, or bring someone else round to be with you?"

"I have my husband," Thalia spoke for the first time since the police had arrived. "But I would like to see Anna. She is the daughter of Sir James and Lady Montagu-Hamilton, where my son was staying."

Despite his own anguish, Tony flared up. "Why should

you want to see her? If it hadn't been for her this wouldn't have happened."

Thalia ignored him. "Could you arrange that for me, please?" she asked the policewoman.

"Of course, we'll try, dear," the WPC said.

Tony was going to object again, but Thalia raised a hand. "Please, Tony. I want to see her. She was the last person to see my son."

"I'll see it's done now," said the inspector, and went out to his car to use his radio.

"Would you like me to stay with you until she arrives?" the policewoman asked.

Thalia gazed at her bleakly and shook her head.

When they were alone together Tony sat down beside his wife and put an arm around her shoulders. He stared blindly at a bronze figure of a horse which George had given him for his birthday.

"I killed him," he said quietly. "I killed him knowing that, if I was angry enough, he would come back. He always did; he hated rows."

"It was me who begged you to get him back," Thalia reminded him. "Please forgive me."

Tony didn't reply. He took his wife's hand in his and squeezed it with more warmth than he had shown for many years. "Of course it wasn't your fault. I didn't want him there either. My God," his voice cracked, "Losing a business is nothing when you lose a son."

Thalia returned the squeeze of his hand.

They sat side by side, drawing comfort from each other, needing no words, savouring the close warmth of shared tragedy.

When the door-bell rang, the policewoman went to open the front door. A moment later, she showed two women into the room where Tony and Thalia waited.

Tony glanced up at them, then looked away, as if he could not bear to see them.

It was the first time he had been in the same room as Anna since their one meeting at Graveden, three years before. And he didn't recognise Susan Montagu-Hamilton.

Thalia let go of her husband's hand, stood up and walked across to them, looking from one to the other.

Susan's eyes met hers with a tender understanding, and recognition.

"Hello, Thalia," she said. "I'm sorry it's been so very long – that it had to be this that brought us together."

Tony looked up sharply. "Do you know her?" he asked Thalia, nodding in the direction of Susan Hamilton.

"Yes, Tony, and so do you."

Tony looked at the woman again. He searched her face for familiar features, but he found none and shook his head.

"No. How would I have done?"

Anna, standing beside her mother, witnessing this reunion, was as puzzled as Tony. She recognised George in his mother, and all her instincts urged her to go to her and wrap her arms in sympathy around this woman, but looking at her again, there was something more, something else that she recognised.

But she could say nothing. She turned and looked at Susan, who smiled with gentle sadness. Turning her head again towards Tony, for the first time, she took a long hard look at the man she had been trying to ruin.

Thalia answered her husband's question. "The last time you saw Susan was when you went to look for me in the married quarters at Polemidia. She was called Mrs Cuthbertson then."

Tony's eyes gaped wide in bewildered shock. He rose slowly to his feet and took a few paces towards the three women. His mind had been jerked back across nearly forty years, to the neat, flower-filled drawing-room, the kindly,

414

understanding woman who had been Thalia's friend, who had taken her to London, while he had searched southern Cyprus for her.

He remembered the prefabricated house, the flower-filled room, the ticking clock, and the baby that had cried from another room.

The baby!

It must have been Anna! She was the right age, and Thalia had known Anna's mother all this time!

It was extraordinary, unbelievable that she should have kept this to herself, without a hint, during all the time that Anna had challenged Tony, first over Scottish and Lakeland, and now over Theodore itself.

Suddenly Thalia's inexplicable attitude to Anna Hamilton made sense, if Anna was the daughter of one of her oldest, and once most loyal friends.

But why had she said nothing?

He turned to his wife, not angrily, but puzzled and pleading. "Why didn't you ever tell me you knew who Anna's mother was?"

"It would have achieved nothing, and until now, it wasn't necessary."

"But why do you only find it necessary now that she's nearly brought my company to its knees? If I had known earlier, we could have talked, maybe."

"You didn't want George to talk to her about it, remember. Why would you have done? And whatever Anna has done to you in business would not have made it necessary to tell you about her. It was only when George started seeing her that it mattered."

Anna listened to this in astonishment. Now she could no longer hold back the horrific notion that was forming in her mind. She turned almost angrily on Thalia.

"But why did it matter so much to you that I was seeing George? George had hundreds of girlfriends, didn't he? Why should you object to me so strongly?"

"There's nothing in you I object to. It was your relationship with George that made it impossible."

Anna paled beneath her copper skin.

"W . . . What relationship?" she almost whispered.

Thalia glanced at her husband, and then at Susan, who nodded slightly.

"You and George are . . . were brother and sister," she said slowly, "Full brother and sister."

Anna gasped. Her face whitened; she turned to look for somewhere to sit. She found a large armchair and flopped into it. She gazed at each of them – first at Susan, then Thalia and, finally Tony.

Tony stood as if he had been turned to stone, his eyes fixed on Anna. Then, abruptly he turned and went to the drinks table. He poured himself a brandy. As an afterthought, he poured one for Anna and took it to her. She accepted it without a word.

Susan and Thalia watched father and daughter in silence. They could contribute nothing now.

But Thalia longed to take her daughter in her arms, and hold her for the first time since she had left her, three months old, with Major Cuthbertson's gentle wife.

Anna gulped the brandy, still staring, not able to cope with these new parents, so suddenly thrust into her life. Then she glanced at Susan, whom she had taken for granted, teased and abused for most of her adult life; and she wanted to beg her forgiveness.

Without thinking, it was to Susan that she reached out her hand. Susan took it and squeezed it.

"Mum," Anna was in no doubt about the answer to the question she was going to ask. "Is it true?"

Susan nodded.

Anna turned to Thalia and Tony. "I'm sorry, I'm going to have to talk to my mother . . . Susan, on my own. I must listen to her story first. Is there somewhere we could talk together alone?"

"Of course," Thalia said. "Tony, come with me. We'll go and make some good Greek coffee. That policewoman had no idea."

Silently, without objection, Tony followed his wife from the room and shut the door behind him.

In the kitchen Thalia made some pretence at preparing coffee. Tony slumped down on the chair he had occupied for several hours earlier in the evening, when he and Thalia had talked back through time, and the emotions of those times were fresh in his mind now as if they were memories a few days old. He gazed into Thalia's soft dark eyes for several minutes before he spoke.

"The first time you disappeared, when you went to England, you were expecting Anna?" It was not really a question. "Why, oh why didn't you tell me then? Why didn't you ever tell me? Don't you know how much I was wanting more children, after George, when you could have no more? Why have you denied me my daughter all this time?"

"Tony, I denied myself Anna. Do you think a single day of my life has passed when I haven't suffered for it? Tonight we lost our son, but perhaps we have our daughter back. Why don't you thank God for that? I couldn't tell anyone I was pregnant the first time – only the Cuthbertsons. Don't you remember how terrified I was of my father? If I had been pregnant by anyone it would have been bad enough, but to have a bastard child by the son of Theo Kyriakides; I cannot imagine what my father would have done. Then, he might have killed you. When I got pregnant the second time, I couldn't go through with giving away another child. That's why I ran away with you, but you know that, at least. Susan and Simon Cuthbertson, and the people in the hospital, were the only people who ever knew I had Anna. All the adoption was done in England before we came back. My father had been only too pleased when I told him the Cuthbertsons wanted to take me there as a companion. And my mother was far too wrapped up in her own affairs even to notice any of the signs. Can't you see? I had no choice."

Tony gazed at her. It was as if a curtain had been drawn aside to reveal a woman he had never known. For the first time in their life together, his wife had humbled him with this evidence of a strength that had allowed her to live with the agony of this secret for nearly forty years.

He stood up and crossed to her. He put his arms around her and held her tight, in the way he had when they first came to London.

With his mouth beside her ear, he whispered, "My God, Thalia, I am so sorry about George; but I must thank you too, my precious angel, I must thank you . . . for our daughter."

EPILOGUE

London June 1991

A press conference was called at the Connaught Rooms near London's Kingsway, convenient for the City and the City press. The large hall was crowded. There were not enough seats. People stood three deep along the back walls, and overflowed into the lobby.

The crowd talked animatedly to one another, speculating about this latest development in one of the most publicised, personalised takeovers in recent commercial history.

In the front row Charles and Monica Fakenham sat side by side.

"I'd say that we were both losers this time, wouldn't you, Charles?" Monica said casually.

"I've never done a deal where I've lost, and this is no exception, but what have you lost?" he gloated, wanting to hear her say it.

"Oh, about twenty-five years of my life," she answered lightly.

"At least we still have each other, though," Charles grinned unpleasantly.

"No. We haven't." Monica looked straight ahead at the platform where Tony Kyriakides had emerged from a door at the side. "I'm leaving you. Life with you, without Tony to go to, would be unendurable."

Tony walked from the door to the centre of the platform. As he reached the rostrum there, the buzz of conversation

419

in the hall faltered with surprise at his wide smile and springy step. The audience had expected to see Antonios Kyriakides broken; expected to see him admit the defeat of Theodore Hotels at the hands of Mediterranean and Tropical.

Only when the crowd was completely quiet did Tony begin to speak.

"Thank you for coming. I apologise for needing to make the announcement I'm going to make in this way, but I felt it was only fair that as many of you as possible should have the same opportunity to know what I am about to tell you."

He paused, and the gathered journalists and financial foot-soldiers held their breath.

"The boards of Theodore Hotels plc and Mediterranean and Tropical Hotels (UK) plc are pleased to announce that they have agreed to their mutual satisfaction terms for a complete merging of their equity in a group to be known as Theodore Mediterranean and Tropical Hotels, which we shall refer to as TMT."

There was a loud, collective gasp from the audience at this extraordinary development.

Tony acknowledged this with a grin.

"Holders of shares in either company will hold the same number of shares in the enlarged group."

At this, there was a smattering of uncertain applause as Tony's listeners tried to decide just how good this news was.

He went on.

"An EGM will take place formally to confirm the decisions of the two boards. Full details are in the press release which will be handed to you on your departure. I have been appointed chairman of the new group. And I would like to present to you the chief executive of TMT."

Tony looked towards the door through which he had

entered. It opened to a second, louder gasp of amazement. Tony turned back again to his audience.

"Ladies and gentlemen, may I present the chief executive of our company, whom most of you will, of course, recognise. One of the most respected young hoteliers in the world . . ."

Tony took the new chief executive's hand as she reached the rostrum.

" . . . my daughter, Anna Kyriakides."